Murder Always Gets It Right

Jeff McDaniel

ISBN: 979-8-89316-883-9 (Paperback)
ISBN: 979-8-89316-885-3 (Ebook)

Acknowledgments

When beginning any new journey, such as becoming a historical fiction writer, one needs help from others. The list is long; for everything I have ever wanted to accomplish in life, God has provided me with the right people at exactly the right time. In my early days growing up in West Virginia, it was teachers and coaches from Musselman High School (*once an Appleman, always an Appleman*). In later years, I was greatly influenced by my professors at Tennessee Tech. University and Tennessee Bible College, both in Cookeville, Tennessee.

To my daughters Amy and Faith, my son AJ, and all of my grandchildren, I love all of you.

As with any acknowledgment, there are always those who are inadvertently left out; I apologize for that.

Several individuals played pivotal roles in the creation of this novel. One such person is my brother Mike, who was the first to read *Murder Always Gets It Right*. Mike, your unwavering support and availability during the character development phase were invaluable. Our strong bond grew even closer during the intense months of writing this book.

My greatest support is my wife, Judy, whom I have loved for over fifty years. No man is luckier than me. You are my partner and my rock—you are so much more than a wife; you are my best friend.

My parents, Max and Mary Lou McDaniel, are the last two people I owe so much to. Mom and Dad, "I wish you were still with us; I miss both of you so much."

It is to all of those mentioned and unmentioned that I dedicate this book.

Murder Always Gets It Right

Chapter One

"I got nowhere else to go," bellowed an unfamiliar female voice as I reached the top step leading to my second-floor office.

"And for the last time, I'm telling you, he is not here right now!" answered the very familiar voice of my secretary, Miss Ashley O'Connell.

Picking up my pace, I reached the office door as it flung open, nearly striking me. Startled but trying to maintain a professional persona, I asked, "May I be of assistance? I am Ambrose Forde, and you are?"

"I'm Mrs. Joseph Brathwaite; call me Kate," the stranger wailed. "My daughter is missing, and I can't get anyone to listen, much less care."

"How about this: let's have a seat while you tell me everything you can about your missing child. I promise you, Mrs. Brathwaite, I will listen. Ashley, please bring us two cups of coffee and hold my calls?"

"Yes, Sir," came a sarcastic response accompanied by dagger eyes. "Cream and sugar, Mrs. Brathwaite?"

"Yes, I'd take a coffee with a little cream, no sugar, though."

"I'll bring it in as soon as it's brewed," came the response in a more civil tone.

Ashley O'Connell was a twenty-three-year-old Winchester native, an alumna of Handley High School and the State Teachers College of Harrisonburg, Virginia. The highly motivated woman has been with me since I opened the Ambrose Forde Detective Agency in Winchester, Virginia., this past January. A spirited woman who believed it was time for all women to challenge the status quo controlled by men and forced upon women. Now, please make no mistake: Ashley respected all women who came and gone before her, but it was now 1931, and women must begin to *shake off the shackles and spread their wings,*' and she intended to do just that.

Meanwhile, Mrs. Brathwaite and I entered my private office to discuss her daughter's disappearance.

"Please have a seat," I invited while extending my left hand to the chair across from my nineteenth-century oak desk. "Before we begin, I need some background information: what is your daughter's name and date of birth?"

A little misty-eyed, the desperate mother answered, "Her name is Ada Jo Brathwaite; she goes by Jo. When you find her, don't even think of calling her Ada; she hates that name. She is Jo, born on April the 8th, 1910; she's a *daddy's girl,*" as the tears intensified.

Mrs. Brathwaite was allowed time to wipe the stream flowing down her cheeks. In just seconds, I witnessed the emotional extremes of a loving mother.

Now composed, the mother continued. "Her middle name, Jo, is from her father's middle name, Joseph; I know she loves me, but she idolized her daddy."

"Where is her father?"

"Buried somewhere in France, killed in the Battle of the Meuse-Argonne Offensive, October 8th, 1918. He was part of the Twenty-Ninth Blue and Gray Division, mostly men from here, Frederick County, Clarke, Shenandoah, and a couple from Page and Fauquier. All served under Captain Conrad. My Joe was so proud to serve under such a brave man as the captain; he was a Winchester man, too. Killed in the same battle, shot in the head, I hear; don't know how my Joe got it, just told it was bad, really bad," the war widow, now openly crying, continued.

"A lot of brave men gave their lives for this country; we must always remember them and honor their sacrifices." Trying to console the grieving woman, I passed her my handkerchief. After another short moment of silence, I continued. "If my math is correct, Jo is twenty-one, right? Does she live with you?"

"Yes, she's twenty-one, and no, she ain't lived with me since last year. She got a room on South Braddock. I told her it wasn't proper for a young lady to be out on her own being so young, but she couldn't wait. She doesn't care much about country life; she wants more. She wants the life only a city can offer."

"So, what is the address of the Braddock Street house?"

"She rents a room at 304 South Braddock Street. A Christian lady named Wilma Poston owns and runs the place. Several other women also rent rooms there, all trying to make it on their own. Jo's room is small but clean. She ain't there all that much. She's got a job in Martinsburg, makin' good money," the proud mother boasted.

"Martinsburg? That's a little far away. What does she do in Martinsburg?"

"Cleans and cares for an old lady that claims she's an *FFV*; that's what she tells Jo anyway."

"Help me here. What's an FFV?"

"First Families Virginian, of course. The old lady says her roots trace back to one of the first families that settled in Jamestown in the early seventeenth century. That's a big deal around here; it gets you special treatment with some folks," the proud Virginian explained.

"That's right, Martinsburg was part of Virginia until the Civil War," I stated, remembering my American history classes.

"Nobody round here calls it that; it's the War Between the States," she barked, reminding me of two important facts: that I am not from here and that, to some, the war is not over.

In an attempt to smooth any ruffled feathers, I returned to my questions. "When was Jo last seen? Who might have been with her?"

"I don't know; I can only tell you the last time I saw her. It was Wednesday morning, May 6th, around 8:00 a.m. or so. She stayed with me the night before but wanted to get back to Winchester before the parade started. She was going to meet a couple of friends. I don't know their names; they're friends she's made since she moved to town." The tears returned.

Trying to ease the tension, I exclaimed, "That was some parade. What's it called, the Apple Blossom Festival?"

"It is called The Shenandoah Apple Blossom Festival."

I was again reminded that I was not from Northern Virginia. "I stand corrected—again. Perhaps I need to hire you to teach me the local customs and correct verbiage. You can teach me how to be a Southerner."

"Southern is something you have to be born with; it can't be taught. That's something *outsiders* don't get."

"I want to apologize if I have offended you, Mrs. Brathwaite; I meant no harm. I am an outsider, but I am sincere in my promise to you: I will work day and night to find your missing daughter."

Seconds passed as we both attempted to clear our minds and focus on the task ahead. I couldn't imagine what this mother was going through; however, I do understand the pain one suffers when a loved one has vanished. Mrs. Brathwaite was also correct when explaining the necessity of a Southern birth to understand Southern ways; only they can truly understand the depths of the culture.

The same was true with losing someone you love. The pain of death is often brutal, but it does offer closure. Pain born of a missing person has no finality; it just continues, gaining strength with each passing minute. Unfortunately, I knew both.

"Who would know the names of the friends Jo was going to meet?" Again, I directed our conversation to her missing daughter. "How did Jo get to Winchester Wednesday morning? Does she have an automobile?"

"No, she ain't got no automobile, as you call it...She caught a ride with Boots, Boots Kline. He and his wife Doris own the Route 50 Emporium, a local store about two miles from the house. Boots takes his Model T to town twice a week to buy supplies for the store:

Wednesday, the 6th, happened to be one of the days. He said he dropped her off outside the boarding house." The tears again formed in the corner of her eyes.

"Why do you believe Jo is missing? Could she have returned to Martinsburg?"

"She isn't supposed to go back to work until today, the 8th. She said she would see me Wednesday night after the parade. She said... she said... her friends... was going to bring her home," Kate answered, her voice trembling while her hands shook. "No one has seen or heard from her."

After nearly a minute of silence, Mother Brathwaite again erupted, "Oh, God, where's my baby?"

When the moment seemed appropriate, I asked, "Do you have a recent photograph of Jo, something I can have to help me?"

"Yes, I brought a picture of me and her at her cousin's wedding last year," the nervous woman said while searching through her time-worn handbag.

As I reached for the picture, Ashley entered with two cups of hot coffee and a few delightful-looking doughnuts. "I'm sorry this took so long; I went down the street to the Golden Glow and bought a dozen of TJ's best glazed," my only employee explained.

"Thank you, Miss O'Connell, that was very thoughtful," I answered in an appreciative voice while reaching for a doughnut.

"You're the one we should thank; I took the money out of the petty cash drawer, but they're worth it, best doughnuts in town," the slender, 5' 7" assistant confessed.

Mrs. Brathwaite took the cup of coffee, adding the necessary amount of cream but, staying true to her words, passing on the sugar and a doughnut. "Doc says I gotta' watch my sugars. Diabetes and all. Life gets hard when you pass forty."

"I just realized you gave me your name but nothing else about you. Do you mind starting with your full name, address, and such? Just routine."

"Katherine Doyle Brathwaite, and, like I said, call me Kate. My birthday is November 5th, never mind the year. I'm considerably older than you and proud of my Irish roots; ask the little girl who just left. I live out Route 50, about eight miles west of town, a little place called Hayfield. As for my address, I pick up my mail at the Rt. 50 Emporium that sits on the left; stop there. Somebody can give you the directions to my place," Kate informed in a much more assertive voice.

"Do you have a telephone?"

"No, can't afford one. When you need to talk to me, call the Emporium and tell the operator to let it ring. Doris is sometimes slow to answer: she's a busy woman with the store, the post office, and, of course, just being a wife."

"You gave me the address of the house on Braddock Street, owned by Mrs. Poston, but I need the name and address of Jo's employer in Martinsburg. Possibly her phone number? Also, have you been to the police, and if so, what did they say?"

Kate's face turned a shade of red I had never seen as she sprung from her chair. "The police said there was nothing they could do!" she exclaimed, matching the volume first heard in the hallway. "They told me women Jo's age often just run off for a while and that the Winchester police just do not have the time or the manpower to investigate every stray that has wandered off. Every stray, how *dare* he call my baby a stray!"

I paused again before addressing this. When the red in Kate's face faded, I carefully asked, "Would you happen to have the name of the officer you spoke with?"

More composed, Kate answered, "Johannsson, Captain Sonny Johannsson, fat guy losing his hair with all the charm of a jackass! He then handed me off to some guy named Osborne."

I quickly interrupted the irritated mother, not needing a repeat performance. In a firmer voice, I asked, "Okay, how about we do this? You give all the information you can, Jo's Martinsburg employer's name, address, phone number, and anything that may be helpful to Ashley. I ask you to please not yell at her. Starting now, she and I are on your side; we both work for you. Once you have finished, please go home and try to get some rest. I cannot imagine what these past two days have been for you. I will be in touch with you in a day, two at the most. Please, trust us: as I said, Ashley and I now work for you."

Mrs. Brathwaite, still standing but a little calmer, agreed to my request while shaking my hand. She sat by Ashley's impeccably organized desk in the outer office and began giving the requested information.

I paused by the office door before leaving, ensuring the two Irish-blooded women would be okay together. Surprisingly, each appeared to enjoy the company of the other. In less than a minute, Ashley had Mrs. Brathwaite telling a story of Jo and her dog. My assistant, while sometimes aggressive, had natural compassion to comfort those in need. Sensing all was well, I proceeded down the nineteenth-century staircase leading to my car. It had taken over four months, but the Ambrose Forde Detective Agency finally had its first case.

Chapter Two

After meeting Mrs. Brathwaite, I drove to the Winchester Police Station, hoping to speak with Captain Sonny Johannsson. Having met the veteran officer several times, we had several things in common, but on opposite ends of the spectrum concerning many others. Johannsson, like myself, was not a native Virginian. A lifetime lawman, he retired early as a homicide detective from the District of Columbia. I agreed with Mrs. Brathwaite's physical assessment of the officer: he was a massive specimen of a man, 6'5", easily 280 pounds, with little hair left on his head. Cursed or blessed, Johannsson also possessed a deep, gruff voice that echoed in an open field; saying the least, he was intimidating and knew it. Following his 1920 retirement, under a suspicious, dark cloud, Johannsson found employment with the Winchester Police Department in 1921. A decade later, he became the city's top cop: Chief of Police.

The trip from my North Loudon Street office to City Hall on Cameron was a short distance, but since the weather looked a little overcast, I drove. It was nearing noon upon arrival, and remembering Johannsson's size, I surmised he may be at lunch. Exiting my car, I saw another member of Winchester's finest, Lieutenant Wilbur Osborne, who was considerably younger and much easier to converse with.

"Lieutenant Osborne! Got a few minutes?" I shouted while waving my left arm.

"Not really, just got a call about a missing boy," answered the slender detective.

"Mind if I tag along? That's kind of the subject I would like to discuss."

"Johannsson will have my hide." Pausing a moment to rub his chin, the Lieutenant responded, "Oh, what the heck. I've already got a private room in the big guy's doghouse. Come on, but when we get there, I do all the talking. Understand?"

"Understood," I falsely proclaimed, uncrossing the first two fingers on my left hand hidden in my pocket.

After we were well on our way in the black 1928 Dodge Police Car, Lt. Osborne opened the conversation. "So, what was it you wanted to talk about? Understand that I cannot discuss official police business, including this case. I'm just letting you come because I think you may have something for me. Do you?"

Caught off guard, I asked, "What could I tell you? And what are you talking about?"

"I know you had a visit from Kate Brathwaite this morning; that's why you're here. She wants you to investigate her missing daughter because she believes the local police don't care. That about right?"

Trying to gather my preconceived thoughts, I asked, "So, what am I missing, and how did you know of Brathwaite being my client? I just left her less than an hour ago." My curiosity grew.

"Fact is, the missing girl is a person of interest; there are many unanswered questions about her. Have you been to her place on Braddock?" Osborne's interrogation continued.

"You've been to her place?" I asked with a surprised voice. "Because I haven't. I met her mother this morning and asked a few routine questions about the general stuff. What information could I possibly have? And, before we get much further, where are we going?" as we leave the city limits, instantly surrounded by the beauty of the apple blossoms.

"Heading to Gore, a family named Witten have a sixteen-year-old boy missing, been gone two days now, just up and gone."

"Gore is quite a piece out of your jurisdiction, right? Why is a Winchester detective investigating a Frederick County missing person?"

Osborne paused momentarily, then answered, "This is dangerously close to a confidential question; let's just say that the Frederick County Sheriff's Department has asked us in. That's as much as I can say right now. Why in the world did I invite you? I'm not sure. It's just that this thing is growing, and protocols are on hold—at least, for now, understand?"

The rise of the officer's voice sent a message of urgency and fear. I waited a few minutes to choose my next words, then asked, "So, the county sheriff's office and the city police, two departments that seldom, if ever, confer, are working jointly on this. Is that what I am hearing?"

"Yep, that's about the size of it; this thing is bigger than anything either department has ever seen. Truthfully, I've never seen Johannsson this scared, and God only knows the horror he saw as a D.C. homicide detective."

Neither of us said much as we continued to the Witten farm just east of Gore. A modest, two-story farmhouse appeared as we turned left and slowly proceeded on the long dirt road. Sitting just right of the house was a dilapidated barn and the car of Frederick County Sheriff Preston Neumann.

The sheriff was a lifetime Frederick County resident and a veteran of The Great War. A man in his mid-forties, Neumann wore the face of a much older man, something common with a war vet who had sustained multiple wounds on the battlefield.

As we exited the police vehicle, Lt. Osborne took the lead as I honored our agreement.

"Sheriff, a pleasure to see you again. What've we got?" asked Lt. Osborne.

"You're late! Where's the boss? I told him to come, not to send the hired help. I have nothing against you; it's just that I was expectin' him," the grizzled police officer barked.

"He's working on another lead, which may be connected, maybe not. Right now, we're chasing anything that might be part of this," Osborne answered.

Raising his massive left arm and pointing his index finger at me, nearly poking my right eye, Neumann gruffly asked, "Who's this?"

"He's a private investigator; his name is—"

"Forde, Ambrose Forde, but call me Brody," I interrupted while extending my right hand, expecting a mutual response but not receiving it.

"Private investigator? Don't you have a keyhole you should be looking through, you know, catchin' that cheatin' husband or something? I got no time for this! First, I get a city copper that's got no respect for my time by gittin' here late; probably got lost on the way or stopped for a doughnut. Then he shows up late with a guy that ain't man enough to carry a badge, that I know ain't even from around here. Some carpetbagger, I'm guessing," Neumann's daggering eyes cut through me.

"Instead of trading insults, why don't we try to focus on the missing teen, agreed?" I suggested, not falling into the sheriff's verbal trap.

"Sheriff, sir, what do you know so far, and what can we do to assist?" Osborne interjected, hoping to establish our team with Neumann as leader.

"The boy's name is Witten. Jubal Witten, sixteen years old, didn't come home from school yesterday, but that ain't that unusual. From what the father tells me, he likes to go to the Melbourne place about three miles from here and tinker on an old car with another boy named Henry. By the way, Henry has a pretty fifteen-year-old sister that Jubal's sweet on. When he didn't come home yesterday, the folks figured he was over there and just spent the night; he does that sometimes, sleeping in the barn. This morning, Jubal's father, Stoney, ran into old man Melbourne at the feed store. Melbourne said he ain't seen Jubal all week, and we know the boy ain't in school today; we checked. Nobody has seen this boy in nearly two days; he just up and vanished."

"Where are the parents now? I have a few questions. Is that all right?" I asked in a mild tone.

"They's all shooken up, but I guess it'll be okay. Just remember these folks are scared; I've known Stoney all my life, and I ain't never seen him scared. Today, he's scared, remember that," demanded the Sheriff. "I'm headin' back to town; just remember what I said, boys. You don't want to cross me," threatened the war veteran, now sheriff.

As Sheriff Neumann drove away, I walked toward the front porch while Osborne remained standing in his original spot near the barn. When I realized the lieutenant was not following, I turned and asked, "What's wrong? Aren't you coming?"

The hesitant Osborne removed his Fedora, rubbed his head, and asked, "Do you think this is necessary right now? What can they tell us that they didn't tell Neumann? It will all be in his report; I'll get a copy. Why put them through more questioning? These people have been through enough today, don't you think?"

"Three points come to mind. First, what questions did the sheriff ask? Second, what questions didn't he ask? And finally, what answers will not make it into Neumann's report?" I stressed upon the sympathetic lawman.

You're right; I know that. It's just that I've had to do several of these interviews lately, and the answers have all been the same: no one saw or heard a thing," explained Osborne.

"What are you talking about? Several of these interviews? What does that mean?"

"It's not been reported in the paper; we've kept a lid on this. There has been a rash of missing teens in the past few weeks, both male and female. There are no clues; they all have just vanished," spilled the Winchester lieutenant.

"I'm sorry, I didn't know. That's why you don't want to speak with them. If this was to remain confidential, why have you told me?"

"Because I think the leaders of this county are wrong to keep it from the general public. I was wrong in telling you. I could lose my job for breaching confidentiality. Do you understand the trouble I'm in if Chief Johannsson finds out?" confessed Osborne.

"Don't worry—the secret is safe. However, I agree with you: the public deserves to know, but they will not hear it from me, I promise," I assured my new friend as we shook hands.

A few minutes of deliberation convinced him of the necessity of conducting our own interrogation. Now in agreement, we approached the grief-stricken parents seated on the hand-crafted oak porch swing. Introductions aside, the couple agreed to speak with us.

Honoring my prior agreement, Osborne asked the first question. "Other than the Melbourne farm, is there any other place Jubal might go?"

"No, he's always been good about letting us know where he is. Other than the Melbourne's, there isn't nowhere else," answered the weatherworn mother.

"Does Jubal hunt or fish? Is it possible he might have gone somewhere secluded and gotten lost? Maybe sprained or broken an ankle and is unable to walk?" I asked, terminating my pledge of silence.

My question intensified Mrs. Witten's already swollen tear ducts. While handing his wife the red and white handkerchief from his denim bib overalls, Mr. Witten told us of Jubal's survival skills and abilities in the mountainous terrain. Mountain boys were taught early how to signal for help, but no signals were seen or heard. Another fact: Jubal would have never been able to go into the woods without his trusty dog, Sprocket.

We spent the next thirty minutes pretty much in vain. Lieutenant Osborne was right: Jubal Witten had disappeared, and nothing had been seen or heard. Before leaving the modest yet welcoming porch, Osborne asked if we might return should we find a need.

For the second time today, I witnessed tears produced by fear forming in the corners of both sets of parental eyes. Finally, Mr. Witten helplessly nodded his head in agreement. As Osborne and I turned and began walking to the patrol car, my eyes joined the majority, becoming moist as realization began to set in: two missing children in one day.

I silently questioned myself: was I strong enough to do this job?

During our drive back to Winchester, only small talk occurred, and nothing concerning the case, which I found relieving. We discussed our love for baseball, cars, the best places to eat in Winchester, and several funny stories about Osborne and his family. I was also invited to call him Will, not Wilbur; the latter was reserved for only his mother and wife when either needed to make a point.

Back at City Hall, we said our goodbyes and agreed to meet Saturday afternoon at Max's Garage around 3:00 p.m. Once behind the wheel of my 1930 Chrysler CJ-6 Royal Sedan, I returned to the office.

Stepping inside, I found Ashley hanging a massive framed photograph of Amelia Earhart. "What are you doing?" I comically inquired.

"Trying to give this place a little class!" Ashley fired back.

"I thought you were what gives this place class?"

"Can't disagree; I certainly add a measure of beauty and charm, but Amelia is just the greatest woman that has ever lived. I want to be just like her," declared my young assistant.

"Wouldn't Jesus' mother, Mary, be the greatest woman ever?" I asked, trying to get a rise.

"Well, Mary was a unique case; she had God and, of course, her son Jesus in her corner. Amelia has to take on the whole world, and on her own, I might add."

"That, I will concede, Mary was an extraordinary case, and I suppose I agree, Amelia is a remarkable woman, one deserving admiration," I said, ending the debate.

Once the Earhart photograph had been safely secured on the wall behind Ashley's desk, I related the day's events. She brought me up to speed on office activity, which wasn't much. We were interrupted by the striking of the clock announcing 5:00 p.m.

"Yoo-hoo! It's Friday, and it's payday! Other than Christmas, is there a better day than payday Friday?" quizzed Ashley.

Ignoring the question, I informed my jubilant assistant, "Your paycheck is in my left-side drawer, but first, would you like to earn a full day's pay for only three or four hours of work tomorrow morning? It involves detective work. Are you interested?"

"Absolutely! Investigation work in the field? Yes, yes, yes! It'll give me a chance to wear my new pants, just like the men wear; they even have a back pocket," Ashley announced in her Southern antebellum voice.

"Pants? I guess I never thought of women wearing pants. Sure, wear your new pants if that makes you happy," I confessed. "How about meeting here at 10:00 a.m.? We are going to Jo Brathwaite's boarding house on Braddock Street. I could use a woman's thoughts; you may see things I might miss since you are just a few years older than Miss Brathwaite. I'll bring the coffee and a couple of doughnuts."

"Remember, Golden Glow, the best doughnuts in town. See you at 10:00 a.m., don't be late," ordered My Girl Friday.

I didn't sleep well Friday night: I could not stop thinking of Jo Brathwaite and Jubal Witten. Where were they, and why were they taken? Were they hungry? The most fearful question was whether they were still alive. My inner demons took control of my deepest thoughts as I again asked myself, am I up to this? Having been a private detective for less than six months, with no experience, am I able to solve this case? Can I ease the parents' pain, especially the victims' pain?

I gazed at the clock on the nightstand to the left of my bed: 3:15 a.m. Sleep this night was coming at a premium. My demons once again filled my head. I was just a month shy of my thirtieth birthday. How did I get here? An unsurmountable weight pressed on my shoulders, a burden I could not have imagined a mere twenty-four hours ago. Demons continued adding to my load as each minute of missed sleep increased. My mind was clouded with past failures. Was I nothing more than what everyone back home believed, just a rich man's kid chasing another dream?

Chapter Three

Morning finally came, and the demons were back in their box. I gathered myself as I went through the morning ritual, then headed toward the office. Turning the corner onto North Loudoun Street, I spotted Ashley seated on the bench in front of the Shenandoah Valley National Bank, anxiously awaiting my arrival. As I pulled to the curb, she jumped from the bench, flung open the door, and jumped in before I could bring the automobile to a complete stop.

"Excited, are we?" I asked the enthusiastic blue-eyed blond as she positioned herself in the passenger seat.

"No, but it could be exciting if you let me drive. How about it? It's only a few blocks to Braddock Street?"

"Not right now. Possibly later, much later," I said, dashing Ashley's hope for the moment.

It took about ten minutes to reach the two-story green gingerbread boarding house owned by the widow, Wilma Poston. As I parked, I reminded Ashley, "Remember, I am the investigator; you are the assistant, which means assist, not lead, understand?"

"Got it, boss," she answered with her beautiful smile, giving me a left-handed salute.

We both climbed out of the car and, once on the porch of the well-preserved nineteenth-century home, were greeted by a charming elderly woman. "May I help you?" she asked.

"Yes, ma'am. My name is Ambrose Forde, and this is my assistant, Miss Ashley O'Connell. May we ask you a few questions concerning Miss Jo Brathwaite's disappearance? We have been hired by her mother, Kate Brathwaite. You are Mrs. Wilma Poston, correct?"

"Yes, I'm Wilma Poston. Are you with the police? I was told by Captain Johnson, Jackson, or something like that not to talk with anyone except the police. Are you the police?"

"That would have been Captain Johannsson, and, no, ma'am, we are not the police. We are working, sort of, with the police. I spent much of yesterday with Lieutenant Wilbur Osborne of the Winchester Police Department; you may call him for confirmation if you wish," I answered in a mild, confident voice.

"Well, I'm not sure. What exactly do you want?"

"We'd like to see Jo's room and, if you are willing, ask you several questions. Would that be okay with you?"

After a few seconds, the cautious landlord unlocked the screen door, allowing us to enter her home. Ashley and I graciously accepted seats on the hand-carved Victorian walnut sofa as Mrs. Poston informed us that her son Robert was in the backyard cutting the grass.

"Before I say anything more, I'd like to ask my son what he thinks about allowing you upstairs."

Ashley and I exchanged glances, then I replied, "I think that's a wonderful idea. Would you mind getting him, or would you like me to ask him to step inside for a moment?"

Mrs. Poston decided it would be best if she asked Robert, and after a couple of minutes, the smell of freshly cut grass overtook the pleasant air of the vintage parlor. As he approached, the broad-shouldered son extended his right hand and said, "Mom tells me you would like to ask some questions about one of her tenants who might be in trouble. Missing, as I understand. She also says you would like to see her room. Is that right?"

"Yes," I answered, then continued, "As I told your mother, you may contact—"

The six-foot, muscular son interrupted, "Yes, Mom told me about you working with the police. So, here's what will happen: First, Mom will only answer questions she is comfortable with, and you will not press her. Second, you may inspect the room with her; look as you may, but you will not damage or remove anything you may find. You will also put everything back exactly as you found it. Is that understood?"

"We agree. Neither you nor your mother will have any problems with us; we want to find Jo and ease her mother's pain," I answered, trying to help the pacing Robert understand the importance of our investigation.

"Okay, Mom, they're all yours. If you have any problems, yell. I should be finished with the yard in about an hour. I'll check with you before I leave. Mr. Forde and Miss O'Connell, it was good meeting both of you. Forde, don't forget our agreement," he said again, shaking my hand and returning to his yard work.

"You have a wonderful, protective son that dearly loves you, Mrs. Poston. I'm not sure my mother is as fortunate," I sheepishly confessed as my mind drifted. "Shall we visit Jo's room while we talk?"

"All boys need to love their mothers, including you, Mr. Forde," Mrs. Poston said, increasing my guilt.

"I love my mom, Mrs. Poston!" Ashley exhorted as my guilt continued to grow.

After we all had exhausted our love and affection for mothers, we returned to the purpose of our visit.

Now upstairs, Mrs. Poston unlocked the door, allowing entrance to Jo Brathwaite's room. At first glance, the one-bedroom apartment appeared typical and extremely clean; as Mrs. Brathwaite had mentioned, everything was in place. Looking closer, however, the room as perfect—too perfect.

"How long has Miss Brathwaite lived here?" I inquired.

"I'll have to look at the lease, but I think it's been about eight months. She is a model tenant—there is never any noise, and her rent is always paid on time. She's rarely here, though; her job keeps her away."

"What can you tell us about her job?" I asked while opening the closet door, revealing only a couple of dresses, one coat, and three pairs of dress shoes.

"Not much. She told me she works for an elderly woman; I can't remember where. I think she does okay with money; she always seems to have plenty, which is rare these days, the Depression and all."

As Mrs. Poston continued her comments, Ashley began coughing, acting as if she had something tickling her throat. Then my resourceful protégée asked, "Mrs. Poston"—*cough*—"could you"—*cough*—"could you possibly get me a glass of water?"

"Oh child, water won't help that cough; how about a hot tea with lemon?" responded the motherly Poston. "Would you also care for a tea, Mr. Forde?"

"Why yes, a hot tea would be delightful, thank you, ma'am."

As Mrs. Poston left the room and headed downstairs to the kitchen, Ashley batted her blue eyes and whispered, "We need to talk without everyone hearing."

"That was smooth; just make sure that cough returns when we hear her coming up the stairs. Okay, what have you got?" I begged my resourceful assistant.

"Did you look in that closet? I mean, really look. What did you see?" the excited sleuth asked.

"Several dresses, a coat, I think, and several pairs of shoes. Why?" I ignorantly asked.

"Where are the rest of her shoes? Where are all of her everyday clothes? I only see three slinky party dresses, which are extremely expensive, I might add, a long dress coat and three pairs of extremely high-heeled stilettos. Where in Winchester would she wear these clothes? The answer is nowhere! Where are her regular clothes?"

Ashley began telling me some things young women purchase when they first have a little money. For her, new clothes, shoes, stockings, and items that would make her feel good about herself. The style of clothes she could comfortably wear to church and work but, most importantly, in her daddy's presence. The clothes found in Jo's wardrobe would not be accepted in those circles, especially in the eyes of a father. According to my expert, the garments found have an entirely different purpose.

"I'm impressed. I only noticed what was there, not what wasn't. What else do you see?" I asked as my curiosity grew.

Ashley opened the drawers on the five-drawer chest placed against the back wall. The top drawer revealed six pairs of stylish silk stockings with garters; the second drawer held an assortment of expensive undergarments, according to Ashley. Two of the remaining drawers were empty, but in the bottom drawer were two very drab cotton dresses, one blue and the other dark green. Also nestled in the back of the drawer were a worn-out pair of inexpensive shoes.

"Look at the makeup on the vanity; it's provocative and expensive, not the kind worn by a Frederick County country girl. There's at least $50 of makeup here, and not the kind a common flapper might use. This stuff is the best of the best. Who is she, Clara Bow?"

"What are you saying? So, she likes the provocative look, so what?"

"Typical man's response. This stuff is way more than that. How can I make you understand? I have two questions: how does a woman working as a maid or something in a town over twenty miles north of here afford this? Second, no decent woman wears this, not even in 1931. This woman is living a double life and ashamed of the hidden life," Ashley stated as her voice began to rise.

"Easy, girl, lower that voice," I whispered. "Why is she ashamed?"

"Her mother told us she is a *daddy's girl*. Do you see any pictures of *Daddy*? For that matter, do you see pictures of anyone? I'm telling you there are no photographs because she is ashamed of something. Of what, I'm not sure, but I have suspicions."

I took a moment, trying not to drown in Ashley's investigative flood. With my head breaching the waters, something seemed out of place: a small blue rug under the chest of drawers we just examined. Seizing the moment to regain the lead investigator role, I moved back to the chest and, while looking at the rug, asked, "Do you notice anything awkward?"

"No, why?" Ashley asked, as her eyes focused on the rug.

"Don't you find it odd to have a rug under a chest and no rug at the side of the bed? I have a rug beside my bed so my feet are spared the cold of a morning floor. While discussing floors, I have another question: where are her dirty clothes? There is no clothes basket, no pile of clothes on the floor. My sister always had a mountain of dirty clothes in the corner of her room that the maid had to—"

"Maid? You had a maid growing up? Who are you?" the shocked assistant asked.

"Never mind that right now; I'll tell you someday when the time is right. Let's get back to clothes. There are no dirty clothes in this room. Where are Jo's dirty clothes? What do you do with your—"

Again, I was interrupted by Ashley's Southern twang. "I'm not going to tell you about my laundry, dirty or otherwise. For the record, my room is always spotless; I'm a neat person, and that's the end of that!"

"Okay, let's forget about maids and missing dirty clothes for now. What about that rug? The door is open to the room across the hall; see if the rug is under the chest."

After a quick glance, Ashley answered, "Nope, no rug under the chest, but there is one by the bed."

As my young friend returned to Jo's room, the whistling of a hot kettle pierced the hallway's silence. To satisfy my curiosity, we moved the chest of drawers off the small oval rug. As Ashley lifted the left side, the rug gave up its secret: a sealed envelope. At that moment, the creaking of the steps on the staircase sounded: Mrs. Poston was on her way back. We had only seconds to act. Ashley quickly grabbed the new-found clue and stuffed it into her back pocket while I managed to lift the chest and place it back on the rug.

We both stepped back from the chest, which was now returned to its original position, as Mrs. Poston entered with our hot tea.

On cue, Ashley coughed, then reached for her cup of relief, saying, "Thank you so much; you are a wonderful mother." Taking a sip,

Ashley continued, "*Oooh*, this is delicious," bringing a huge smile from our gracious host.

After moments of enjoying what I admit was possibly the best hot tea I had ever tasted, we returned to the comfort of the parlor. The conversation moved from hot tea back to Jo Brathwaite's mysterious disappearance.

"Can you tell me about the last time you saw Miss Brathwaite?" I asked.

Taking a deep breath, the white-haired woman began, "The last time I saw Jo was Wednesday morning, ah, May 6th, before the parade, around 11:00 a.m. She was talking with a couple of men, three, I think; I'm not exactly sure how many there were. Lots of people were walking up and down the street that day. The parade, you know. Jo and the strangers were on the sidewalk, just about where your car is parked, right by the dogwood tree."

"Did she seem nervous? How was she acting? Do you think she knew them?"

"No, don't think she was nervous or anything. She seemed okay, nothing out of the ordinary; they were talking. I don't think she was scared if that is what you're asking, but I wasn't really paying that much attention. I just wanted to make sure none of the men came onto the porch or tried to get inside my house; no strange men are allowed inside this house," she passionately exclaimed.

"Can you describe them, such as height and weight? If you saw them again, would you recognize them?" I continued as I heard the back screen door close.

"Mom, I'm finished with the yard. Do you need me to ..." Robert stopped when he saw me seated in the parlor, enjoying my tea. "You're still here, Forde? Mom, why are they still here? I thought you had a few questions and wanted to see the room. You've been here for over an hour. That's enough; your time has ended, sir!"

"Robert, please don't insult our guests; they're trying to find Jo. She has been missing for several days, and no one has seen her. Honey, I'm worried about her," his mother pleaded.

"Mom, you said time after time this woman stayed away for days, weeks even. I don't understand what makes this time different from all the other times. She's a *drifter in a skirt*, nothing more, nothing less. I don't get all the fuss?"

"If I may, Robert, do you know Miss Brathwaite? Have you ever spoken with her? Anything might help. We're not trying to be a burden on your mother or you; we are just trying to find Jo. Can you help us?" I asked, trying to de-escalate the conversation.

Pausing a moment, Robert apologized to Ashley and me, explaining that he was only looking out for his mother. Since the death of his father several years earlier, he had taken the role of protector, a promise he had made his dying father. He continued by telling us that he had spoken with Jo only once, finding her somewhat of a snob as she did not wish to converse with him in any manner, thus fostering his resentment.

Our investigation had come to an end. Ashley and I thanked both mother and son for their time and said our goodbyes. As Ashley took her last step off of the porch, she turned and, with that charming smile, asked if we might return should we have future questions. Surprisingly, it was Robert extending an invitation for a return visit, with one condition: he had to be present. Had I made the request, I was not sure the answer would have been as positive.

Not wishing the day to end and with noon just minutes away, Ashley asked if we could have lunch at the Rustic Tavern. It was an opportunity to review what we had learned, and the doughnut breakfast had expired. We spent over an hour discussing the case, bouncing ideas, but, most importantly, growing our professional relationship. As I paid the check, we heard the vintage clock on the back wall strike one o'clock.

Back in the confines of my Chrysler, I asked, "Aren't you forgetting something?"

Ashley shifted her weight to the left, removing the envelope concealed in her back pocket, and handed it to me. Ensuring no one was watching, I slowly opened it, trying not to tear the flap. To our surprise, we find an unusual key and $175 neatly tucked inside.

"Wow, can we go back and check all the other rugs in the house?" begged Ashley.

"No, we cannot. We can't keep this; this isn't a scavenger hunt. I have to turn this over to Lt. Osborne and explain how we ended up with it so we are not arrested for grand larceny. Truthfully, we stole this," I informed my novice apprentice.

"Boy, you sure know how to kill the moment. I know we can't keep it; it's just a shock to see that much money hidden under a rug. I would never keep something like this."

"I know you wouldn't. I trust you," I reassured.

Showing her confidence in me, Ashley generously offered, "When you speak to the police, if you happen to forget that I was with you when the money was discovered, well, I wouldn't be all that upset."

"Worried, are we?"

"Daddy will kill me if I get arrested. I'm a daddy's girl too, and manage to get into enough trouble without your help."

After the debate concerning our mysterious discovery, I drove Ashley to her apartment on Cecil Street.

Opening the car door and stepping onto the sidewalk, she stopped, turned, and offered a heartfelt confession. "This is one of the biggest days of my life. Thank you for treating me as an adult; I appreciate that. You're not like most men; you respect women, and you respect me. I want to show you the same respect; I know you don't like to talk about yourself, where you're from, and all the things like how you can afford to do business when you have no sign of income. Yet somehow, you always have money to pay me and all the office bills. We are working on our first case, yet you never discussed our fee with Mrs. Brathwaite. We are going to charge her, aren't we? Today, I learned you had a maid while growing up and have at least one sister you never mentioned. I'm confused, but I promise I will never pry into your personal life. Except for the part about the maid. Really, you had a maid? Lucky you!" she said laughingly and with that infectious smile while closed the door of my sedan and headed into her apartment.

Chapter Four

After leaving Ashley, I drove toward Max's Shell Station on Amherst Street, just west of town. Max, a delightful yet independent elderly man, was my most trusted friend. I first met him during my third year at George Washington University when my roommate, Randolph Hodges, brought me to Winchester for fun during the inaugural Shenandoah Apple Blossom Festival in May 1924. After purchasing gasoline at Max's Shell Station, the gruff proprietor and I became friends. He was one of the principal reasons I chose Winchester as my new home.

Carefully steering my car to the right side of the gas pumps, I spotted Max digging into what appeared to be a box of junk metal. Meanwhile, his employee, Sam, came over to my car. "Fill her up?" he asked.

"Yes, high test, please," I answered.

The lanky lad of about sixteen quickly inserted the nozzle and filled my car as I approached the open garage door.

"What are you working on, Max?"

"Hey, Sherlock!" came the usual response. "I'm not surprised you don't recognize the remains of a 1915 Indian. Thought you were an educated man?"

"Indian? Which Indian? Shawnee, or maybe Mohawk? He isn't a Cherokee, is he?" I jested, trying to get a rise out of the old man.

"You know, some people aren't as dumb as they sound, but you, well? It's an Indian motorcycle, and I'm going to give it new life," the work-worn mechanic fired back.

"I don't doubt it for a minute, my friend; if anyone can do it, you can."

"So, what do you need besides gas this sunny day?" Max asked.

I paused momentarily, caught off guard by the invitation to ask questions. While Max was my friend, he was also many people's trusted friend. How did I seek information and not overstep the invisible line of trust? Finally, I opened the exchange with a statement, not a question. "Had a visitor yesterday, Mrs. Brathwaite." I chose my words carefully to avoid violating confidentiality. "Do you know her?"

"Know her? I'm the one who sent her. Let's face it, only people going to come to you either don't know you ain't from here or, like Kate, ain't got nowhere else to go. She stopped here asking for help, and I told her you might be that man," he stated, not looking up, still sorting through the box.

"What can you tell me? I'm just starting to look into this. Any suggestions?"

"What do you know about the missing girl, other than she's disappeared? You think she's part of this missing kid thing going on? It's got every cop in the county crappin' razor blades. You think she's part of that?"

"Max, as much as I would like to, I can't answer that," I replied, respecting the line I could not cross.

"So long as you know, there are things I can't tell you. Want to, just can't. Do you understand?" cautioned Max.

"Agreed." I nodded my head in the affirmative.

Remembering I needed input into this investigation, I tried again. "Anything you can tell me about Jo, her family, friends, anything that can help me?"

"You checked out her work situation in Martinsburg? Been there yet? Kate tells me she cleans the house for an old rich woman. I ain't never heard a name, just that she's loaded," Max shared while still emptying the remains of the deceased Indian.

"I thought about driving up there tomorrow afternoon and seeing what I can find out. Is there anything else you can help me with?" I asked.

Max repeated an earlier question: "What do you know about all these missing kids, up to six or seven, I hear: think Jo is one of them?"

"I don't know, Max. She could be. I actually joined Lt. Osborne yesterday when he visited one of the families; it was one of the toughest things I've ever had to do. I must admit, it shook me. I hope I'm up to this," I confessed.

"You'd damn well better be up to this! I promised Kate you're the man who will find the answers, to find Jo. Now, pay me for your gas and get to work. Sam's filled your car. It took seven gallons, so you owe me $1.19. Pay Sam," my friend barked.

I did as I was told. I paid Sam and took my place behind the wheel.

Just as I was about to start the engine, Max appeared at my open window, calmness restored. "We on for tomorrow's game?" he asked.

"Absolutely, I'll be here right after church, and I'm going to kick your butt this week," I boasted as the old man gave me his usual glare.

"There you go again, Sherlock, dreamin' the impossible dream. I'd think you would've learned by now that I'm the best chess player in Virginia," informed Max.

"Tomorrow, my friend, tomorrow, you'll see," I joked, knowing Max was probably right.

"Hey, I forgot to tell you, Osborne called a little while ago and said he couldn't meet you at three. He said you'd understand," Max informed. After a solemn pause, he continued. "One last thing, Ambrose. Remember this: *forgive the action, forget the intent.*" Max then turned away, returning to his box of motorcycle parts.

Once on the road, my thoughts turned to Max's last words: *forgive the action, forget the intent.* What was he trying to tell me? What *action,* what *intent?* Of whom was he speaking? Having known Max these past years, one thing was certain: those words have meaning, but what?

Also, he called me Ambrose. He had never referred to me as Ambrose. He'd called me a number of things, but never Ambrose.

Saturday was melting away; it was now a few minutes past three o'clock, so I swung by the police station to see if any progress had been made on the Witten case. After parking, I made my way into the station, and, with my unfortunate luck, I literally collided with the massive Captain Johannsson while turning a corner.

"What the... It's you. What the hell are you doing here?" roared the frustrated chief.

I swallowed deeply, then responded, "I'm looking for Lt. Osborne or you if you have the time. I'm sure you know I accompanied Osborne to the Witten farm yesterday. I know you don't like me, but I'm not the enemy; I want to help. I've been through something like this before."

Surprisingly, the veteran top cop didn't immediately offer a refutation. Instead, he swiped his left hand across the top of his balding head, exhaled a nasty onion-smelling breath, and admitted, "Look, I got nothing against you personally; it's just I've known men like you. Want to be a copper, just don't want to do what it takes to be a real lawman. What could someone like you possibly have to offer? Men like you end up getting men like me killed, and I'm just too old to go through that again, understand? As far as Osborne is concerned, he ain't here right now. Now get out of my way!"

I stood fast, blocking the chief's attempt to brush by me. Several officers begin to converge, listening and waiting for the belligerent cop to rip my head off. Looking up at the infuriated officer with equal conviction, I made my stand. "Listen, first, you know nothing about me. Second, I've never gotten anyone killed nor plan to, and third, I have plenty to offer."

"What could someone like you possibly have that's worth listening to?" Johannsson countered.

"You know nothing about me or what I may have to offer. If my assistance is helpful, fine; if I fail, well, you have someone to blame. See, using your words, *I've known men like you as well*, but I'm not judging you by the poor coppers I've known. I'm taking you as you appear to me, nothing more, nothing less. Why can't you offer me the same courtesy?"

The chief's right hand formed a massive fist. Saying nothing, Johannsson's eyes burn through mine, so much so that I could feel his despise rushing through my body. Having heard of his intimidation tactics, I now had firsthand experience.

The seconds felt like hours, but in an instant, *Goliath* ended our standoff. Without warning, the giant pushed by me and returned to his corner office, slamming the door behind him. Because of Johannsson's attitude and the fear of possible arrest, I held onto the key and money found under Jo's rug. I'd surrender both to Lt. Osborne on Monday morning.

Accomplishing nothing at the police station, I went by the office and reviewed Ashley's notes of her talk with Mrs. Brathwaite. I began reading my associate's incredibly organized notes, learning several things I wasn't sure I would have asked. First, they had lost two unborn children before Jo's birth. The words, 'happiest day of our lives,' were underlined, honoring the blessed day of Jo's arrival.

Reading on, I learned Jo loved dogs, especially big dogs. She suffered from allergies, needed glasses to read, seldom fashioned long-sleeve garments, and rarely wore a coat. The missing woman was left-handed and had a clover-shaped birthmark on the bottom of her left foot, just like her father. The remaining information seemed fitting to almost any woman her age. When I had finished reading, I secured the document in the safe and called it a night.

Sunday began, as usual, with a short stack of pancakes accompanied by bacon and coffee at the George Washington Hotel dining room. Then, I was off to church, fulfilling my promise to my mother when I left home and moved south. While I try never to miss a Sunday worship service, this morning seemed to hold a greater need for me; it'd been an emotional couple of days.

After church, I kept my chess appointment with Max. Upon arrival, I found my worthy opponent comfortably seated in his high-backed office chair, with the chessboard and pieces ready to go. The radio softly played a local country station, Max's favorite music. Holding out two closed hands, one with a black pawn and the other concealing a white, I tapped his left hand. The savvy Max grinned and revealed I had selected the black pawn, which meant he went first.

The game would last at least an hour, sometimes going two or three, usually depending on the mercy of the old warhorse. Looking at Max's face today, I sensed no mercy.

When deep into a game, Max allowed little to no disruption, including idle conversation: only the faint sound of the radio was permitted while the chessboard was out. His trusty companion, a yellow and white, tiger-striped cat named Felix, was the only one allowed to disrupt his concentration.

It'd been over an hour, and, as usual, I was losing. I had my king, one rook, and several worthless pawns left, while my worthy opponent had an army poised to attack. Much like Felix playing with a helpless mouse, this was my fate.

Finally, my agony ended. "Checkmate! Any questions, son?" My weekly lesson in humility continued. "Your problem is you approach chess like a college man; I see it as a battlefield," the Spanish-American War veteran proclaimed.

"You're right, Max. Heck, you're always right." I once again conceded, shaking the hand of the victor. "You're always one step ahead of me, so answer me this: what did you mean with yesterday's proverb, *forgive the action, forget the intent*? I know you well enough to know it's important, but what does it mean? I don't understand."

Max's demeanor shifted from victor to prophet. "Problem with young people: You all want everything handed to you, a sense of entitlement, wanting everything right now. That's why you'll never get any better at chess; you gotta' study, live, and experience life, just like chess. Keep that *proverb*, as you call it, deep in your heart; in time, you'll understand."

Pondering yet another lesson from Max, we were interrupted by the screeching tires of Lt. Osborne's police car. The driver's door swung open before the cruiser came to a complete stop. Gasping for breath, the excited detective pleaded, "I gotta talk to you right now. It can't wait. You got to come with me—there's been a development!"

"Okay, sure, I'll come; let me get my hat. Max, will you watch my car until I get back?"

"No problem, go! I'll take care of things here. Go."

We jumped into the squad car and, with the siren blaring, sped through town. His eyes focused on the street; Osborne said nothing, sweating bullets as we zigzagged the streets heading east toward Route 7, the Berryville Pike. Nothing was spoken until we exited the Winchester City limits.

Osborne broke the silence once on the open two-lane highway. "Two more teens have been abducted this weekend, one from Hampshire County, that's in West Virginia—west of Gore. The other is from Nain, just outside the city. That's bad, but that's not why I grabbed you. A female body has turned up just east of Berryville, along the Shenandoah River."

"What are you trying not to say? Is it my missing girl? Is it Jo Brathwaite?"

"I don't know, but I think it might be. The dead woman fits the missing person report filed by Mrs. Brathwaite. The problem is that we are now in Clarke County. I don't have any jurisdiction, but you do. If this is Jo Brathwaite, you have been hired by the next of kin. The sheriff and the deputies won't want to deal with you, but they will at least tolerate you. For me, who knows? They may run me back to Frederick County."

The quiet little town was a blur as the Winchester police car entered and exited Berryville City limits. We continued until we saw the rapidly approaching 1500-foot-span bridge allowing safe passage across the Shenandoah River. Now, across the bridge, we made a ninety-degree right turn parallel to the aquatic landmark. Traveling a little over a mile, our journey ended as the Winchester police car joined nearly a half dozen of Virginia's finest law enforcement vehicles.

After disembarking from the safety of our car, we approached Clarke County Sheriff Deacon Walker. The veteran sheriff was the stereotypical Southern gentleman with a badge. Like so many, he was a mammoth of a man, easily six feet six inches tall, pushing three hundred pounds, with hands the size of Griswold frying skillets and just as hard. Possessing an outward appearance that scared most, he had a calming voice and a sharp mind. He was rugged when he had to be, yet he had few enemies.

"Osborne, what cha doing here, son? This ain't Winchester. What can I help you with? Who's ya' friend?" the gentleman giant asked.

"I'm proud you remember me; we've only met once, as I recall," answered Osborne. "This is Ambrose Forde, a private eye working on a missing person case in Frederick County. I asked him to join me; I thought it might be the woman he'd been looking for. Do you have a name for the deceased?"

"Naw, nothing yet, just gittin' started. The girl has really been through it; the river has really beaten her up. She's got a nasty gash on the side of her head, cuts and abrasions, you know, the typical stuff. The body is over there," the lawman pointed toward the river bank.

"Those two boys sitting in the back of Skeeter's car were fishing from a boat when they came upon her, tangled in thorns along the bank. Neither got out; they paddled back to shore and ran until they found a phone and called us."

"Do you mind if we examine the body, Sheriff?" Osborne asked. "Also, with your permission, may we question the two lads?"

"Sure, go ahead, look, ask all you want; it's a suicide if you ask me."

"Why so fast, Sheriff? How long have you and your men been here? Has this crime scene been fully investigated? Shouldn't it be secured to prevent further contamination?" I asked, much to the surprise and irritation of the local constable.

"What do you want? This ain't nothing more than a *dope fiend* gittin' exactly what—"

"Dope fiend?" I interrupted. "Have you no compassion for human life? A woman is dead, and from what I see, practically no investigation has been conducted."

Sheriff Walker, now displaying his rarely used but powerful, authoritative voice, boomed, "Osborne, you better slow your friend down, or both of you-all are gonna to spend the night *under glass*, ya follow?"

Before I could reply, Osborne interceded, "Yes, yes, we follow, sir. We mean no disrespect to you or the fine officers of the Clarke County Sheriff's Office. It's just been a rough couple of weeks for all of us. We apologize, right, Brody? I said, right, Brody?"

Using all my self-control, I complied. "Yes, Sheriff Walker, I apologize—it will not happen again."

Sheriff Walker's demeanor returned to his calming, almost hypnotic state with all tempers lowered. He then began sharing what he knew. "The body appears to be that of a twenty to twenty-five-year-old female. She's been severely beaten up by the river, especially in the face. I think she decided to end her life by jumping off the bridge just upstream—drowned while floatin' to this here landing spot where the two boys spotted the body."

While Sheriff Walker gave his brief assessment, several deputies carried the body from the edge of the river and laid her on a blanket near one of the Clarke County cars. When the Sheriff paused to load a massive chaw of Beech-Nut into his already-brown-stained mouth, I seized the moment to move toward the remains, using the time to escape the lawman's reeking breath. Osborne followed my lead, also desperate for fresh air.

I kneeled near the head of the lifeless woman, and her face was, as described by the sheriff, badly beaten, presumably by the rocks from her time in the Shenandoah. She wore a simple blue cotton dress with small white polka dots. Her shoes were missing, probably consumed by the flow of the river.

"This your first "floater" Forde?" Osborne inquired.

"Sadly, no," I answered, my mind momentarily drifting back to another time. "This is not my first."

"Me neither. We see several of these a year, you know, people just having fun, not considering the dangers; they don't respect the power of this river."

"So do you think Sheriff Walker is right, suicide?" I asked.

"I don't know, it's a possibility, I guess. Walker's a respectable police officer, extraordinary instincts, you know," Osborne added.

"Only animals have instincts, not man. Man has knowledge gained from training and experience. For instance, if this is a suicide, how did she get here? Where's her car? How did she get into the water? Did she jump off the bridge upstream and drift here? Your respected sheriff's instincts have failed to satisfy these questions," I countered.

Osborne responded, "Good questions. She could have walked, I guess. Maybe she lived around here. Right now, we don't even have a name. It could have just been an accident; she got too close to the river and fell in. I mean, who is she? If Walker is right that it is a suicide, why was life so terrible she decided to end it?"

"I'm telling you this is not a suicide. Less than one percent of women use jumping or drowning as a way to end their lives."

"Less than one percent? What are you basing your information on? How do you know this? I've never heard anything like that before. If you start throwing numbers around, you better be ready to prove them, or Johannsson, Walker, or anybody is going to have your butt in a sling. They don't want numbers; they want evidence. Where's your evidence? Where's your proof?" Osborne challenged as his eyebrows began drawing together.

"Just something I picked up in college and when... Never mind, that's not important right now. It's just I know women do not jump or use water to commit suicide; trust me on this," I pleaded, not wishing to revisit my past.

I suddenly remembered something recorded in Ashley's notes. I repositioned myself to examine the bottom of the victim's left foot: the clover-shaped birthmark was present. My legs weakened, and the fire in my stomach intensified; this was not a suicide, I was certain. God as my witness, this crime would not go unsolved—not again.

Continuing my initial study, I came upon another interesting clue. Confirming my expectation, I asked Lieutenant Osborne to examine the woman's arms. I then asked Sheriff Walker, who had followed us and was now standing over the remains, for his thoughts concerning the arms.

"So what? She's got needle marks, just like I said; she was a dope fiend," answered Sheriff Walker with tobacco juice dripping from the left corner of his mouth.

"What do you think, Lieutenant?" I asked.

Pausing a moment, Osborne nodded yes, agreeing with Sheriff Walker.

"Then, answer me this: how does a left-handed woman inject herself in her left arm?" I asked.

"How do you know she was left-handed?" Osborne inquired.

"Because I have a statement from my client, Mrs. Brathwaite, that her missing daughter had a clover-leaf birthmark on the bottom of her left foot and that she was left-handed. Gentlemen, this is Ada Jo Brathwaite, I'm certain," I proclaimed.

The mood changed; Osborne momentarily dropped his head, then looked up to the late evening clouds. Walker turned to his right, launching a disgusting spew of tobacco juice. Neither man challenged my proclamation; each stood silent, absorbed in the moment until, without warning, Walker's dominance returned.

"Skeeter, you and Feltner stay here with these two boys until the meat wagon gets here and takes this poor soul to the Winchester morgue," Walker instructed two of his deputies.

Since Clarke County was one of the smallest counties in Virginia, it did not have a hospital or a morgue. Instead, all bodies were transported to the closest in-state hospital, Winchester, which was only ten miles away. This would make my investigation somewhat easier if I played ball with Johannsson.

"Skeet, you're in charge. As soon as the body's loaded, you two get back to the station. Osborne, Forde, as far as I'm concerned, this is still a suicide, nothing more, nothing less. Your claims mean nothing to me; left-handed, right-handed, what difference does it make? She was a dope fiend; that's what my report is going to say. You boys do whatever you want once you cross the county line," said Walker in a mild yet threatening tone.

"Sheriff, before you go, may I ask a question? Why so stern? Lt. Osborne told me while riding here that you were a respectable police officer; I believed him until now. Why can't you consider this to be a murder? Why the rush to judgment?"

"Look, son, I've been doin' this longer than you've been out of diapers. I'll bet a month's pay that when Doc does the autopsy, he'll confirm it. I've seen a lot of junkies able to use either hand to inject what they need; she wouldn't be the first. Now, if we're done, I gotta get back to town," explained the wisecracking veteran sheriff as he turned and headed for his car.

With the sheriff now gone, Osborne and I spoke with the two lads still seated in the rear of Deputy Skeeter's patrol car. Shaken from the ordeal, neither offered anything we didn't already know. They had been fishing, casting their lines back toward the bank, when one of them snagged on part of a downed tree. Rowing near, they caught sight of the top portion of the torso protruding from the briars. Horrified, they quickly paddled their ten-foot wooden boat to a nearby clearing and ran several miles, just as Sheriff Walker had explained. When I had their statements, one of the deputies who had carried Jo's body from the river bank drove the boy's home.

Less than an hour before sunset, the black Model T hearse arrived, loaded Jo Brathwaite's body, and headed back to Winchester. Following their boss's orders, Skeeter and Feltner returned to Berryville. Believing the investigation incomplete, I convinced Osborne we needed to remain until darkness overtook us.

"Lieutenant, please trust me; a crime scene can talk to you if you listen. I fear the local authorities were fast to judgment. Jo Brathwaite and her mother deserve more than I witnessed. They are entitled to a thorough investigation, which is exactly what I intend to give them," I swore.

"Contrary to what you may believe, this is not my first day on the job. I've been in law enforcement for nearly fourteen years and a lieutenant detective for the past three. I'm well aware of what a crime scene can tell," the defensive officer countered.

"I meant no disrespect; please accept my apology. I never imagined my first case would be like this," I confessed.

"I get it. Believe me, I understand your frustration. So, this is your first case?"

"Yes, and now I have to find the words to tell her mother." My eyes became moist.

"I wish I could tell you it will get better; as I said, I've been doing this a while—and it never gets easy when it has a deadly ending," Osborne confided.

With the evening light dimming, we decided to split up, each taking a different area to investigate. Osborne drove to the upstream bridge while I searched the river bank. The minutes seemed like hours as I continued my infuriating search, yielding nothing of value. Several bottles, a rusty old tin box that probably proceeded the twentieth century—only the typical debris found along any river. With frustration growing, I heard the roar of Osborne's Dodge returning to the parking area.

"Did you find anything? Because I'm sorry to say, the river bank either doesn't know anything or elected to remain silent," I announced as I sheepishly recalled my earlier communication claim.

"Actually, yes, I found this," the proud Winchester Lieutenant revealed his find.

"Is that a..."

"Yes, it is; it's a piece of Jo's dress. I remember explicitly that it was blue with small white dots, just like this."

"Impressive work, detective. Anything else?" I asked as my heart rate increased.

"Not really. Lots of people travel over that bridge, and it's hard to tell what might be a clue and what's just normal traffic. It's too dark to do much more. What say we head back to town, carefully as Walker advised?" Osborne asked.

Starting toward Winchester, I reminded Osborne that my car was at Max's. I also remembered the key and money Ashley and I found in Jo's apartment. Should I tell Osborne of our discovery now or later? Either way, he would be upset with me for withholding evidence. I decided to take the latter option.

"Is there any possibility you and I can meet at my office tomorrow, say around 10:00 a.m.? I want to review what we know and where we go from here," I asked.

"I think that's possible. Actually, we do not have a positive ID; it is just your claim. We need more than that. Identification may also determine if this is a murder or a suicide, you agree?" suggested the veteran officer.

Seeing this as an opportunity to ease the predicament of my Braddock Street find, I accepted Osborne's hypothesis. Actually, if I was wrong about the identification and Jo was still alive, I was not obligated to disclose my findings.

Chapter Five

After Osborne and I finally returned to Max's garage, we parted ways; Osborne was anxious to hug his wife and two boys, while I needed a couple of minutes with my friend. Max had hot coffee on the stove in the back room of the garage, anticipating my need for his advice. I informed him of our afternoon in Clarke County and my unofficial identification.

After a few minutes of staring at our mugs, the old man lifted his head and broke the silence. "You think you're right? I mean, could you be wrong? You never met Jo, only have an old photograph to go by, so how positive can a birthmark be?"

"I'm willing to accept that I am wrong; in truth, I want to be wrong, but that same birthmark, in the same spot, on two different women? What are the odds of that?" I surmised.

"Unless Joe Brathwaite violated his wedding vows, which ain't likely—and I'm willing to bet he never strayed. Their love was as strong as mine and..." Max's voice choked up as he remembered his deceased wife, Mary. The couple had met in the fall of 1896 while Max was working for the Gulf, Colorado, and Santa Fe Railway near Mary's hometown, Temple, Texas. He had gone west for the promise of adventure and to seek his fortune. Instead, he settled for a job driving railroad spikes twelve hours a day at thirty-five cents an hour.

Sixteen grueling months would pass, but when a position in the machine shop became available, Max seized the opportunity, serving as an apprentice while nearly doubling his salary.

With the pay increase, Max and Mary decided to marry, but before wedding bells could chime, the USS Maine exploded in Havana Harbor, Cuba, dragging the United States into the Spanish-American War. Not forgetting his main reason for coming to Texas, to seek adventure, Max volunteered to serve under the flamboyant future president, Theodore Roosevelt, and the Rough Riders.

Wedding plans were halted with Mary's surprising blessing, although she made Max promise that he would return safe and sound when victory had been achieved. Much of the blessing originated from Mary's father, who had served under Confederate General John Bell Hood as a major in the Texas Brigade during the War Between the States. While he feared for his future son-in-law's life, he understood Max's desire to find adventure while serving his country.

After winning the war, Max honored his pledge, returned to Texas, and made Mary his wife. However, while away, the railroad had replaced the war veteran's shop position, offering him his original job: driving spikes. Refusing the railroad's less-than-gracious offer, Max, with his new bride in hand, returned to Virginia and opened a garage and filling station. The couple worked hard to build a prosperous life together until cancer claimed Mary's life in 1926.

Composed, Max continued, "Joe and Kate had a good life until the war. I guess I was one of the lucky ones, you know, I made it back. It's been hard for Kate since he died, trying to keep the farm going, raising Jo with not much help, being alone and all. Now, this."

"Max, how am I going to tell her? How do you ask a mother to come and identify her dead child?"

Slowly standing, Max advised, "Why don't you bring Kate to town and tell her in your office? Not the police station, your office. If you tell her in her home, Jo's home, she will always remember getting the news there, in that room, that very spot. Understand? She already lives with one ghost; don't add another one."

Several hours passed before I finally decided to end this horrible night. Max offered the spare cot in his backroom apartment, but I graciously declined, knowing sleep would come slowly as the clock chimes, announcing 1:00 a.m.

Heading home, I realize the emptiness of night; the streets of Winchester have not been 'rolled up' as many may claim, but they are deserted. Each building seemed at rest, awaiting sunrise when the city would awaken, vibrant and full of life... something Jo Brathwaite would never again experience.

Now safely in my hotel, I retired to the comfort of my bed, ending this most difficult day. Exhaustion overtook insomnia, but my scattered sleep was anything but restful. My demons worked overtime; I both dreaded and wished for the morning sun to rise. Why was this happening again? Dear God, why must another mother carry the burden of a lost child? What was I going to tell Mrs. Brathwaite? How would Ashley react? The questions continued until exhaustion finally won the agonizing battle for supremacy.

The welcome sight of the morning sun crept through my curtain. How soothing the warm May sun caressed my face, inviting the arrival of the new day. Suddenly, my demons reminded me of the day's unpleasant agenda: I needed to contact Kate Brathwaite.

I quickly showered and shaved, preparing myself physically and mentally for the task ahead. Passing through the lobby of my hotel, I grabbed a coffee and a Danish, then proceeded to my car.

When I entered the office, I found Ashley at her desk, fighting back tears of sorrow; she already knew of Sunday's discovery.

"How did you find out?" I asked, handing my teary-eyed associate a handkerchief.

"Lt. Osborne is waiting in your office. He informed me about yesterday's news. Why didn't you call me? I'm not a child; I can take it. Don't start treating me like a child."

"I know you can handle this; it was just so late when we got back to town. One of us needed a restful night of sleep; I was certain it wouldn't be me. I'm going to need you today; I'm counting on you. Are we okay? Can I count on you?"

The redness dimmed as the sparkle returned to her blue eyes. She walked to my private office door and announced, "Lt. Osborne, Mr. Forde has arrived. Would either of you care for a hot coffee and a doughnut?"

"They're from the Golden Glow, the best doughnuts in town, I'm told," I grinned in my young assistant's direction. "Ah, Miss O'Connell, would you join us, please? That okay with you, Lieutenant?"

"Fine, I guess. I've never worked with a woman before, but these are changing times, after all. It's 1931," Osborne divulged.

"I create a more modern atmosphere when I assist," Ashley bragged. "You guys down at the station should try it. Hire some women; then you'll finally get some work done."

While the exchange continued, I took the role of retrieving the coffee and doughnuts. I demonstrated my skills in pouring hot coffee, earning applause from Ashley. Then, we settled in for the task before us.

"Has the police department contacted Mrs. Brathwaite? What is the protocol for something like this?" I asked.

"Johannsson has given me the case, so it's my call as to how we move forward. He wants this settled quickly, and he agrees with Walker; it's a suicide, not a murder. They say she was a dope fiend who just got tired of life, shot up, jumped off the Route 7 bridge, and drowned," explained the reluctant Winchester detective, eyes drooping to the floor.

"Why doesn't anyone want to investigate this? I'm telling you it's a murder, not a suicide; my fists clenched with rage.

"And I'm telling you there are things you don't know about this woman. Remember when we first began this investigation? I said she was a person of interest. Have you forgotten that?" reminded Osborne.

Sheepishly, I dropped my head for a moment; I had forgotten. "So, tell me now, what interest does the Winchester police have in this woman?"

"Jo Brathwaite was, or is, a high-priced call girl working in Martinsburg, West Virginia, a place called The Ivory Tower, on Queen Street. It's an upscale joint; fine cuisine, music, atmosphere, and if you can afford it, classy ladies to meet all your needs," revealed Osborne.

I sat stunned, not knowing what to say; this helped explain some of the unanswered questions concerning clothing and money discovered at the Braddock Street apartment.

After sipping his coffee, Osborne changed the conversation. "We need to focus on today; we need Mrs. Brathwaite to identify the body to see if this is indeed her missing daughter. Doc wants to do the autopsy this afternoon so we can close this book."

Realizing nothing would change until the autopsy had been completed, I yielded to Osborne's request. "Suppose we drive to Hayfield and ask Mrs. Brathwaite to meet with us here, in my office. We can gently disclose what we know, not what we suspect. I want Ashley to accompany us; we may need a woman's compassion. I suggest we keep the Martinsburg story confidential for now. Is that okay with everyone?"

Ashley and Osborne both nodded in agreement. We finished our coffees and then proceeded to the Brathwaite farm, taking my Chrysler. There was little to no talk as we headed west, finally reaching the Route 50 Emporium Kate had mentioned during our first meeting.

Once there, we entered the quaint little establishment where one could purchase anything from gasoline and a fried bologna sandwich to *Grandma's Cure-all Elixir*, a product guaranteed to ease the shingles rash and remove the stain of axle grease from your dungarees. Ashley felt the need to purchase two bottles.

After getting what we actually stopped for, directions to the Brathwaite farm, we continued our journey by turning left onto a winding dirt road off Route 50, just past the Emporium. Traveling a little over a mile, just past the Pentecostal Church, we again turned left down a steep, rut-filled driveway, finally reaching the old two-story Brathwaite home.

Upon arrival, I noticed a late-model Cadillac sedan parked just left of the front porch, safely protected from the morning sun. Pausing a moment, we eventually exit the car, instantly greeted by a confrontational barking hound restricting access to the porch. As the canine's ear-piercing warning continued, the front door opened, bringing Kate and a well-dressed man with his right arm around her waist.

"Can we help you?" bellowed the stranger as he removed his arm from the woman and placed it inside the left side of his jacket.

"It's okay, Flavius. This is the man I was telling you about. This is Mr. Forde, the only man trying to help me. Homer, stop all that racket and get back to the barn. It's okay, folks; he won't bite. Come on in. Do you all care for some hot coffee? Have you had breakfast? I'm glad to fix some flapjacks and sausage," invited Kate.

"Thank you, no, we've had breakfast and our morning coffee. Would it be all right to sit on the porch for a moment? We need to talk," I carefully requested.

"You've found Jo! Where is she? Is she okay?" Kate asked.

"No, ma'am, we haven't found Jo yet. Would it be possible for you to come to my office later today? We've got several things we want to discuss with you," I asked, remembering Max's earlier advice.

"Where are my manners? Mr. Forde, this is Flavius Brathwaite; he's Joe's youngest brother. Actually, he's about all the family that Jo and I have left since Milton, Joe's oldest brother, died in '22. Flavius came in last night to offer me help," Kate, with tears slipping from the corners of her eyes, changed the direction of the conversation.

We shook hands as introductions were formally conducted. Mr. Brathwaite, a sharply dressed middle-aged man with a firm handshake, now asked, "What exactly do you need, Mr. Forde? What is in Winchester that cannot be discussed here?"

My throat tightened, searching for the right words.

Unexpectedly, Osborne stepped in. "Mrs. Brathwaite, I don't know if you remember me; we met at the police station a little over a week ago. I'm Lieutenant Wilbur Osborne. I'm working with Mr. Forde and his assistant, Miss Ashley, on your daughter's disappearance, and we could use your help. Can we all meet in Mr. Forde's office, say, at 1:00 p.m. today? We have several leads we need to follow up on and could use some guidance from you. Would you be available today, ma'am?"

"I'll drive you to town if you need to, Kate; it's the least I can do," Flavius offered.

"Well, I guess today would be all right. Lord, have mercy! I'd better get ready; my hair's a mess. One o'clock will be fine." Kate said her goodbyes and then entered her home.

Flavius escorted us back to the car, and then, once we were seated about to leave, he asked, "Where is this going? What are you not telling us, Mr. Forde?"

Taking a moment, I answered, "Mr. Brathwaite, this is a discussion I do not want to have here. May I ask what your relationship with Mrs. Brathwaite is besides being her brother-in-law?"

"Besides Jo and a couple of nieces, I'm the only family she has. Kate's a strong woman, stronger than most, but she grows weaker each hour. Since my brother's death, she has been a rock, but now, with Jo missing, that rock is beginning to crumble. I'm here to pick up the pieces, to hold them together until she is strong again. Now, what do you know that I need to know before we get to Winchester?"

Silence seized the moment, and then Lt. Osborne confessed, "The Clarke County Sheriff alerted us that a body was recovered from the Shenandoah River yesterday. We don't know who it is, but the description is similar to Jo's. Since Clarke County does not have a hospital or a coroner's office, the remains were brought to Winchester. An autopsy will be performed later today, so we would like a little more information that might help determine if this is your niece."

Again, silence dominated until, finally, Flavius spoke, "I do not want Kate to know any of this until we have an answer, agreed? As Jo's uncle, her favorite uncle, I might add, I can help. If you're right that this is Jo, I want to shield Kate from a vision she will never forget. Agreed?"

"Let's see how our meeting goes at one, then we will have a better idea of exactly what we have. Mr. Brathwaite, thank you for your help this morning. We'll see you in a little while," I said as I started the engine.

While dodging ruts in the country road leading us back to Route 50, from the back seat, Ashley spoke up, "So *exactly* why did I come? I never said a word, never asked a single question. What was my contribution this morning?"

"Moral support, my dear, moral support. Without you, there would have been three men and Kate. As strong as she is, she would have been overwhelmed. You helped balance the scales," Osborne answered.

"You're right; two strong women easily equal three men, even four men," my forward-thinking assistant countered.

"Welcome to my world, Wilbur. Welcome to my world!"

Our drive back to town was surprisingly pleasant. The conversation was light and centered much on Amelia Earhart and the growing power of today's women. The distractive nature of the drive was most inviting and much needed. Back in town, I treated my two companions to a hearty lunch at, where else, the Golden Glow, Ashley's favorite diner. The conversation remained light until we were interrupted by a city patrolman.

"Where have you been, Osborne? Johannsson has had us looking everywhere for you. Another kid is missing; this one is from town. She went missing yesterday afternoon or last night; nobody's sure exactly when. She just never came home last night."

"Who is it? Got a name?" Osborne frantically asked.

"Girl's name is Robin, you know, like the bird, Robin Davenport. Her daddy's a copper here in town," the now frantic officer exclaimed.

"Officer Cletus Davenport? His daughter? Chief Johannsson will turn this town upside down. This just became personal," blurted Lieutenant Osborne.

"You're going to have to handle the one o'clock meeting, Forde; I've got to get to the office. Whoever is doing this just signed their death wish!"

Chapter Six

The news halted our lunch, so Ashley and I returned to the office to prepare for our difficult afternoon. We compared notes, deciding what to discuss and how the message would be delivered. While I didn't begin to understand the depth of Kate's sorrow, I recalled my similar feelings several years ago, sitting where she was about to sit, listening to an investigator like myself and several of New York City's finest. Like that haunting night, there would be no easy way today.

One o'clock finally arrived, along with Mrs. Brathwaite and Flavius. I didn't know who first proclaimed that *the eyes were windows to the soul*, but no other words could describe this moment. Kate had not seen her only child in nearly a week; anxiety and fear swirled storms in her eyes—storms we were about to intensify.

"Please, come in. Shall we sit at the conference table?" I pointed to the open door of the back office. "Lt. Osborne will be unable to join us this afternoon; he has been called away. He sends his apologies. Miss O'Connell, please join us and bring your notepad."

Once we were all seated, Ashley gave a brief review of what we knew, which, at this moment, was not much. When she finished, I carefully began asking Kate more about Jo, trying not to escalate the mounting pressure; unfortunately, I failed. Just two questions into the meeting, Kate exploded.

"Stop all of this! You either know something or suspect something. Don't insult me with your petty questions. What's happened?"

Pausing a second, I looked the grieving mother in the eyes, took a deep breath, and said, "A female body was found in Clarke County late yesterday evening. I think it might be Jo."

Flavius embraced his sister-in-law as she unloaded the held-back flood of tears. Several minutes passed, and then, as quickly as her emotions erupted, an eerie calmness appeared. Regaining control, Kate asked, "So, what now? What do you need? You asked me here for something, so what do you need?"

Before I could answer, Flavius intervened, "I think they probably need a little information about Jo; obviously, they don't know who the poor girl in Clarke County is. If they did, we wouldn't be here. Kate, honey, they didn't say it was Jo, just that it *might* be her."

"Mr. Brathwaite is correct; right now, we don't know. May we continue—"

"I want to see the body. I gotta know if she is my baby!"

"I don't think that's advisable, Kate. How about we continue talking, and let me see if it is indeed Jo?" I pleaded, trying to spare the bewildered mother.

After much deliberation and surprisingly strong support from Flavius, Kate reluctantly agreed. Ashley and I gained significant descriptive information and stories only a loving mother could provide. Kate's face glowed as one story led to another, filling much of the two hours we spent together. It was interesting learning how close the family circle was before Joseph's untimely death in France. Since then, Flavius had proudly assumed the role of surrogate father to Jo and chief supporter to his brother's widow.

While enjoying the family stories, they also produced facts that might help determine the status of our missing person investigation. Did the two Clarke County boys discover the body of Ada Jo Brathwaite?

Besides the left foot birthmark, we learned that Jo had an appendectomy several years ago, leaving a five-inch scar on the lower right side of her abdomen. Her blood type was A-positive, and she had her top left-side wisdom tooth extracted just last year. With this information, along with Ashley's first meeting notes, we should be able to determine if the body in the morgue was Jo.

Our time ended when I received a call from the morgue requesting my presence. Without drawing attention, I attempted to bring the meeting to a close.

Again, Mrs. Brathwaite intervened. "If the woman in the morgue is my Jo, what happens then?"

"Since the body was found in Clarke County, not Frederick, it's their case. The local authorities are not likely to get involved since they do not have jurisdiction. I, however, work for you and am not limited by county lines. I promise not to stop until justice is served," I pledged.

"First things first, Forde, you get to the morgue and get a positive identification on the girl. Kate, why don't we let this man do his job?" Flavius stood and walked toward the door.

Kate joined Flavius, but not before giving me a strong hug while softly whispering in my left ear, "If this is my baby, find the man responsible and make him pay."

The grieving couple, now gone, allowed Ashley and me a few minutes to confer. I needed to get to the morgue but desired this to be a solo act. As expected, Ashley refused to be left behind. My unaware assistant was about to experience her first autopsy.

While driving to the morgue, I tried to prepare Ashley. She heard, but she does did listen; then, neither did I before my first experience. I prayed the demons did not haunt her as they frequently did me; no one should experience that. No one.

A young assistant greeted us as we entered the walls of the deceased, the basement of the Winchester Memorial Hospital: The Tomb. It was sanitary, as morgues went, but it did not escape the pungent odors associated with death. The smell reminiscent of rotten eggs and spoiled cabbage produced by hydrogen sulfide and methanethiol, mixed in with the overpowering smell of feces, destroyed any hope of fresh oxygen's survival. I didn't know how much a coroner earned, but it was not enough.

Ashley was doing better than expected; I, however, felt the need to relieve my troubled stomach. We are introduced to Doctor James Stenner, a native of Winchester and a third-generation physician. The University of Virginia School of Medicine graduate originally served as one of the hospital's three general practitioners but now spent most of his time running the morgue. He was considered one of the top pathologists in the state.

Fighting to compress the raging war in my unsettled stomach, I began the conversation. "Doctor, what can you tell us about this poor soul? Can you determine her time of death? How long was she in the water?"

"I ascertain the cause of death to be drowning. I agree with both Chief Johannsson and Sheriff Walker; this is a suicide. Time of death is difficult to determine because of the water, temperature changes, and all, but if I were to guess, I'd say she has been dead for about forty-eight hours based on rigor mortis. As for the time in the water, considering the location of the bridge, speed of the water, and distance traveled, I'd say she was only in the water for about twelve to fourteen hours. Regardless of the timeline, she has water in her lungs, which proves she was alive when she entered the river."

"So, you're saying the body rested along the water line for thirty-six hours, or, in other words, a day and a half. Don't you find it strange that, with all the people that fish the Shenandoah, especially this time of year, no one saw her until Sunday evening?" I asked.

"Yeah, that's what I'm saying. It's not that unusual. People only see what they're looking for; on the river, people are looking for fish, watching their bobbins. They are more focused on what is in the water than what is along the bank. Keep in mind that the Virginia bluebells bloom along the river in spring, along with lots of wildflowers, twinleaf, and Dutchman's Breeches; literally, dozens of variations of flowers and weeds grow all along that river. Sheriff Walker told me it took nearly an hour to get the body out of the brush and up the bank. The only reason the two boys found her in the first place was that one of them hooked their fishing line in the brush near the remains. Heck, had that not happened, she might still be out there."

"I suppose that could have happened; I've never fished the Shenandoah, but I understand it can sometimes be treacherous. As for Sheriff Walker's statement, he barely looked at the body. Lieutenant Osborne and I were there when the body was retrieved from the riverbank; no one except Osborne and I examined the body."

"I wasn't aware of that, though it doesn't change anything. I stand by my conclusions with conviction; this was a suicide," said Dr. Stenner, standing firm.

Not convinced with the doctor's diagnosis, I changed my approach, making identifying the body the focal point of this meeting. "Did you notice anything unusual, anything, no matter how insignificant? Are there any scars, possibly dental work, that could help with the identification?"

"Well, to begin with, she was only wearing a cotton dress, no undergarments, and her left wrist is broken, which probably happened when she jumped in the river. Long drop, you know. She has a deep gash over her right eye that could have been caused by hitting her head on the iron bridge as she jumped. The needle marks on her left arm support the lawmen's diagnosis; she was a drug addict."

"What about dental work, medical scars, something that might be documented validating her identity?" I questioned.

The doctor retrieved his clipboard, turned several pages, and then answered, "She had her appendix removed, nasty scar, and she is missing a top wisdom tooth. I didn't see anything else, Mr. Forde; your questions indicate you know something you are not telling. So, tell me, what do you know that I don't? Who is she?"

"Yes, we know her!" interjected Ashley as tears streamed down her cheeks. "I'm sorry, Brody, I'm sorry. I don't want this to be Jo. Please, don't let it end like this."

"As my partner said, this is Ada Jo Brathwaite from Hayfield. We're certain. Can you tell us her blood type? That should confirm it."

I slowly placed my arm around Ashley as she regained her composure.

Dr. Stenner, stunned, returned to his notes and confirmed that the deceased had type A-positive blood, the same as Jo Brathwaite.

"Dr. Stenner, you mentioned she wasn't wearing any undergarments. Do you believe she was sexually assaulted?" my interrogation continued.

"Hard to tell, being in the river and all. Her body really took a beating. I do find it very strange not having undergarments, no panties, no brassiere. I wouldn't want to speculate," the veteran physician replied.

We stood silent, remorsefully viewing the remains, when I noticed something unusual. "Doctor, may I touch the victim?"

"Sure, what do ya see?"

I lifted Jo's left hand and pointed to what appeared to be a splinter just beneath the palm's skin. "Doctor, would you remove this?"

Stenner complied, removing what was now confirmed to be a dark piece of wood measuring nearly a quarter of an inch long. He handed the small particle to me, and then I asked, "What do you make of this, Doctor?"

"It's a splinter, a splinter she could have gotten anywhere, probably from a tree in the river or along the bank. This doesn't change anything. I'm closing this case; the Death Certificate will read Suicide, Death by Drowning."

For a moment, time stopped; my heart wept for the family of Jo Brathwaite. They deserved more; they deserved justice, and I was determined for justice to prevail. The emotions within me ran rampant, lashing out in all directions, desperately wanting to hit something. No, not just hit; I wanted to destroy it.

For a moment, my mind drifted to a simpler time. In school, we are taught of American equality, that we are all equal before the law. Yet the painful reality exposes the fallacy. Outside of the building of the United States Supreme Court, a statue of Lady Justice stands, holding a set of scales while a blindfold covers her eyes, a symbol of equality for all. Inside, the highest court sets precedents for all subordinate courts, which should not be influenced by an endless list of criteria: race, gender, religion, and, in this case, an invisible status built on social ranking. If this family were a member of a higher social echelon, perhaps the case would garner greater attention, but in the real world, the Brathwaite family is little more than country white trash. The eyes of Miss Liberty are not covered in the name of equality; the blindfold shields her from seeing the truth.

"Did you hear me, Mr. Forde?"

"Ah, no, doctor, I'm sorry. I'm just a little overwhelmed, thinking to myself, I guess. What were you saying?"

"I asked, would you like to continue this discussion outside where we can all get some fresh air? You and your assistant are beginning to appear a little green."

Agreeing with the doctor's diagnosis, we all returned to the elevator that first delivered us to this basement tomb of death. Once outside, Ashley and I took as many deep gulps of air as possible for about a minute, hoping to remove any stains on our lungs with our pronounced exhales.

"Lieutenant Osborne called me earlier and authorized you to get a copy of my final report, working for the family and all. He said you were okay. Now Johannsson had different words concerning you; don't cross him, mister, he's a mean one. You best stay clear of him," advised Dr. Stenner.

"Are you certain this is a suicide? What is the rush to close this? Why are you agreeing with the chief and the sheriff from another county?" I pleaded.

Firing up a Chesterfield, the doctor answered, "Look, son, you're not from here." Taking a huge draw from his cigarette, then slowly exhaling, he qualified his response. "There's an old saying around here: 'to get along, you go along.' I've been here all my life, been through plenty of chiefs, each tougher and meaner than the last. These men run this town; you cross them, you pay the price, understand?"

Deciding not to push the issue, I again redirected, "When may I have your final report? Also, so that I understand, you're not going to send the body to the State Medical Examiner in Richmond. Is that correct?"

"Yes, that is correct. I see no need to send this poor soul anywhere. Once I get her cleaned up a little and we have the next of kin confirm your statements, this case will be closed, and the body will be released to the family," explained Dr. Stenner.

Fighting back my rising anger, I requested, "May I ask a favor? Will you allow my assistant to photograph the body before you do anything else? Also, could you send blood and urine samples to the Head of Pathology, Doctor Terrance McGregor, at Boston General Hospital, Boston, Massachusetts? Please attach a note with my name, Ambrose Forde, and my address and phone number. Can you do this for me? I would greatly appreciate it, as would the Brathwaite family."

"That's asking a lot, my friend, more than a favor. I guess the photographs will be all right. I understand that's quite the rage up north. That's where you're from, right? A *Yankee* from New York?" probed the doctor.

"I assure you, sir, I am definitely not a Yankee, and I hate New York. It is true, I'm not from here, but don't link me with anyone or anything from that Godforsaken city!"

My emphatic proclamation drew the attention of both the stunned doctor and Ashley. She, now gaining strength back in her legs after our morgue experience, displayed that curious grin when learning something of my past. Before I continued with Doctor Stenner, I sent her to the car to retrieve my Kodak and two rolls of film.

"So, how about the samples? Will you send them to Boston? I need to know what is in her system, what kind of drugs, that sort of thing. I'm just curious. And, while on the subject, could you give me a small sample of each as well?"

"I'm not sure I should do it, but... what the heck?" he said with a pensive puff of his Chesterfield. "Yeah, I'll send them as you requested, and I have your information; Osborne gave it to me." He hesitated, twitching the cigarette in his fingers, then continued, "As for giving you samples, that is highly irregular, but I don't suppose it matters now; after all, she is deceased, and this is now a closed case."

"Thank you, Doctor, you've been extremely helpful. One more thing: does the mother have to identify the remains? Could the girl's uncle do it? This mother has been through enough. Will that be acceptable?" I requested.

"Just have him stop by as soon as possible. Once that has been completed, I will arrange for the body to be transported to the Jones Funeral Home; they do first-class work, so they'll fix her up so well you'll think she is just sleeping."

After Stenner finished his smoke, we all returned to the morgue, with Ashley anxious to serve as the photographer. She filled the two rolls of film as the veteran doctor positioned the body. When the final picture had been taken, I again thanked Dr. Stenner for all his help.

Back in the car, Ashely and I quickly wound down all the windows, inviting fresh air as a welcome passenger. The offensive aroma was following us.

"You know we're going have to boil these clothes. This smell is never going to leave!" my faithful assistant claimed in a convincing voice.

"Physically, the smell will vanish; mentally, it will linger a long time, maybe forever. I shouldn't have allowed you to come; for that, I'm sorry. Please forgive me," I pleaded.

"Shame on you. You have nothing to feel sorry for, and I want all of this, even the unpleasantness. I want to be an investigator, Winchester's first female private investigator."

"You'll make it, and you will be a credit to the profession; you already are," I bragged of my protégé.

Back at the office, I was surprised to find Lieutenant Osborne waiting outside. He displayed an exhaustion I'd never seen in the dedicated detective, especially since I had just been with him several hours earlier. A slight tremble interrupted his normal speech while his shoulders looked to be carrying the weight of the world. His earlier assessment was correct; Johannsson was turning the town upside down, bringing bewilderment to the police department.

"I'm sorry, Will, it took longer at the morgue than expected. You look beat; I pray you haven't been waiting long," I said, acknowledging the stress on my new friend's face.

"I just got here a few minutes ago; it was delightful to sit in peace, if only for a few moments. Is there anything new in your case? Oh, did you know you are missing the period on your door?" noted the observant Lieutenant.

"I have told him multiple times that the painter forgot to put the period behind the "O" of Ambrose O Forde. It looks dumb without the period, but who listens to a woman?" Ashley exclaimed, making her position known.

Distracting from the name on the office door, I suggested, "Let's go inside and just sit for a bit; my news can wait. Ashley, could you—"

"Make some coffee and get a couple of doughnuts? Or, better yet, take a shower and put on some clean clothes?" she said, remembering the stench we both acquired in the Tomb.

"I tell you what: You head home, get your shower and change of clothes, then come on back. I'll make the coffee. When you return, I have another job for you if you're up for another new experience."

"Sounds great! I apologize, Mr. Osborne, for how we smell. The morgue, you know," explained Ashley.

"Actually, Miss O'Connell, I hadn't noticed it. When you've been to the Tomb as many times as I have, you don't notice it," confessed Lt. Osborne.

"That's certainly uncomforting; you're telling me I'm going to get used to this?" Ashley asked in a horrified tone.

After a few much-needed chuckles at Ashley's expense, the young woman headed home, leaving Osborne and me behind to figure out the coffee pot process. Once I mastered the brewing, I brought my friend up to speed on both the Brathwaite meeting and the trip to the morgue. He, in return, explained the urgency Johannsson had placed on every lawman in Northern Virginia, demanding an arrest related to the kidnapping spree—now!

Seated, our conversation continued. "What do you believe is the motive behind the murder of Jo Brathwaite? I mean, what could she have done to warrant being killed?" I asked.

"Brody, I respect you, and I believe you are sincere, but there just isn't enough evidence supporting a murder case. You're proving this with your question: why would anyone want to kill a dirt farmer's daughter?" answered Osborne, defending the position of the authorities.

A little over an hour had passed with Osborne clinging to the suicide theory while I stood determined to prove it was a murder, an extremely violent murder. If I fail to sway the reasonable Lieutenant, I will never persuade the belligerent Johannsson. Pondering my next move, Ashley returned, sharply dressed, accessorized with a lady's Fedora-style hat and just a hint of Chanel No. 5. Even the married eyes of Osborne were drawn to the beauty of this young woman.

"Excuse me, Miss, may I be of some help to you?" I jokingly asked.

"It's me, boss. I just needed to feel good after today's lesson of life, as my dad would call it. Seeing Jo, I realized that I am alive, that life is precious, and that we must enjoy each day the Lord gives us. I hurt for the Brathwaite family, I do, but I need to feel alive right now."

Ashley's speech touched us. My protégé had become my teacher. The beauty of this young woman was only topped by the love in her heart; she was truly one of a kind.

Thoughts returned to our case and the need to collaborate. The time had come for me to share the findings in Jo's Braddock Street room. I also need Lt. Osborne's assistance to access the police's clues. I sent Ashley, now refocused on the moment, to retrieve Jo's money and the unusual key from the safe. Upon her return, I nodded toward the officer, silently instructing her to place the envelope in his outstretched hand.

Confused, Osborne asked, "What's this?"

"I've been holding these for several days, unsure what to do with them. We found them in Jo's room, Mrs. Poston's boarding house on Braddock."

When the contents were exposed, amazement quickly turned to frustration and anger. "I thought we were friends, that we shared a trust. Does that only apply when it's in your favor? How long have you been holding this?" retorted Osborne.

"Less than a week; frankly, I didn't know what to do with it. When Jo was a missing person, I had no legal responsibility to turn it over to the authorities. But, now that she is deceased, still in the morgue, I feel you need to know," I said, defending my actions.

"You had a legal responsibility the moment it was discovered," insisted Osborne.

"Actually, no, I am not legally responsible for turning over findings in this situation, as the police were not actively searching for Ada Jo Brathwaite. The items in question were found in Miss Brathwaite's room, a room I was given full permission to search by the landlord, Mrs. Wilma Poston, witnessed by her son Robert. I was hired by her mother, who gave me the full authority to conduct any searches the Ambrose Forde Detective Agency, licensed by the State of Virginia, deemed necessary."

"You sound like a lawyer. Don't pretend to know more about the laws in Virginia than I do; I carry a badge," cited the veteran Winchester detective.

"My friend, I am a lawyer, Class of 1927, George Washington University, School of Law, Summa Cum Laude," I announced to the room.

A dead silence engulfed the office, no one knowing what to say. Finally, my confused assistant softly uttered, "You're... you're a lawyer?"

"Yes, I passed the Virginia State Bar shortly after my graduation. I became a lawyer to satisfy my father by working in the family business. Then life changed, and my ambitions changed."

We spent the next few minutes trying to decide how to proceed; it was amazing how moods changed when a lawyer appeared. We agreed to set aside my confession and work together, not only on Jo's death case but also on the missing children mystery.

"So, do you have any more surprises, *Mr. Lawyer*?" Osborne asked with humor.

"No, no more surprises. I have a few questions. I hope when you hear them, you might change your mind on the cause of death. For instance, Jo has several needle marks on her left arm. How is that possible with her being left-handed? Shouldn't the marks be on her right arm?" I asked, still challenging the suicide theory.

"She could have been ambidextrous or like a left-handed friend of mine who wasn't allowed to use his left hand in school. My buddy can write with either hand and can shoot a gun both lefty and righty; it's possible," offered Osborne.

"Okay, I'll give you that for a minute, but how about this: how many female jumpers have you ever had? In my studies at George Washington University, we were taught that less than one percent of women in this country commit suicide by jumping or drowning. In your scenario, she did both. Don't you find that incredibly odd?"

"I don't know; you're quoting statistics. How about some physical evidence? Give me something concrete I can go to Chief Johannsson with," begged Osborne.

After a pause, Ashley asked, "Why was she not wearing undergarments? I assure you, if I, a woman about the age of Jo, were going to commit suicide, I'd be wearing all of my undies."

"Okay, okay, both of you have made compelling points—the missing undergarments, I guess, are physical evidence, but I need more if I am going to go up against the chief. Give me more," implored the lieutenant.

"I'm asking you to help us to get more; start by agreeing that this could be a murder. Can you do that?" I pleaded.

"Agreed, it could be a murder. Can you do likewise by agreeing that it could be a suicide?" answered Osborne, offering a compromise.

I slowly nodded yes, accepting the concession. With that behind us, we turned our attention to the missing teens, where the Davenport girl brought the total to twelve: six boys and six girls. The abduction of the first eleven left nothing but questions; however, the Davenport kidnapping was different.

"We have two witnesses in the Davenport case... Not the best ones, mind you, but right now, we'll take anything. A couple of *boozehounds* sleeping in the woods over by Handley School saw two men grab the girl walking down toward Stuart Street. She tried to run, but the men overtook her near the woods. The driver of the car drove up near the school, stopped, opened the back door of the sedan, and the other two threw her in. They then drove back toward town. The whole episode took less than a minute, according to the witnesses," informed Osborne.

"Did you say Stuart Street? Lt. Osborne, that's only a few blocks from where I live," announced a concerned Ashley, eyes widening with the news.

"How does this help? Did they get a license number? Did they know any of the men?" I asked.

"Well, no, not exactly, nothing substantial; nothing we can use right now. Neither knew them, but one of the drunks said he thought he had seen the driver before. He didn't get the license number, but he swears the tag on the car was black with gold numbers, and the first and last numbers were sevens," explained Osborne.

"You sure he didn't get confused? Yellow numbers on black, black numbers on gold plates? Was he drunk when you talked with him?" I continued.

"He seemed sure, especially on the numbers. He said it was odd to see sevens on both ends like that. Said he used to shoot craps when he was in the Great War... That sevens always catch his eyes," delineated Osborne.

"Will, my friend, that's thin. No other leads?" I surmised while scratching my chin.

"Brother, that's all we got—whoever is behind this is a pro. This is the first real mistake they've made, letting someone see them," Osborne surmised, then added, "They actually made two mistakes:

the first, being seen. Second, this time, they grabbed the daughter of a police officer."

The evening had now turned to night, and the need for sleep began to overtake Ashley, so she decided to head home before it got any later. Fearing for her safety, I called her a cab. Ten minutes later, Lieutenant Osborne and I were alone. The clock struck 9:30 p.m., yet we continued scrutinizing the cases.

"Do you think Jo's death could be connected to the kidnappings?" I asked while reaching for a second cup of coffee.

"I don't see how; all of the kids taken are teenagers; Miss Brathwaite was twenty-one. I guess she could be linked, but how and why? If she was murdered, as you insist, what's the motive?" countered Osborne while fighting back a deep yawn.

"People are killed for three reasons: they won't do something, they won't say something, or... they see something they weren't supposed to see. I know Jo was murdered, even if I can't prove it—yet. My guess is she saw something she wasn't supposed to see, and she couldn't be allowed to live. Sooner or later, Will, you're going to agree with me; she was murdered."

Our discussion went back and forth; first, the kidnappings, then Jo's cause of death. Finally, at the stroke of midnight, we both agreed to end our debate.

Before leaving, Osborne made a surprising decision. "I don't claim to know the law as well as you, being a lawyer and all, but since Chief Johannsson has officially closed the Brathwaite case, I want you to hold onto the money and that key for now. If you're right, not saying you are, and this is a murder, that evidence could prove to be valuable."

We said our goodbyes in a silent but firm handshake, agreeing to continue working together to find the truth. After locking up, I headed to my top-story room, but I was not alone. My demons were waiting for me.

Chapter Seven

A few hours of sleep energized me, so I began my day developing the film from the morgue. I studied photography while a student at GW University, and since moving to Winchester, had built a well-equipped darkroom in my apartment. Several hours passed, but as the clock reached 8:30 a.m., all the pictures were finished, and I was off to the office.

"Good morning, my dear. Any calls?" I asked as I passed the photos to Ashley.

"What are... How did you get these so fast? It took the drugstore at least two weeks to develop my pictures, and then most of them come out fuzzy."

"Well, be proud of yourself; all but three came out perfect—you did well," I said, praising my devoted assistant.

"But how did you get these so fast? Who do you know?" she quizzed.

"I processed them this morning in my darkroom," I explained.

"Wait! You... you have a darkroom? Where do you live that you can have a darkroom? Are you kidding me?" the puzzled Ashley asked.

"Can we just move on? Prepare yourself; I know you were at the morgue, but death pictures can be upsetting. I want you to examine and study them closely; use a magnifying glass," I advised.

"What exactly am I looking for? I took the pictures, and I saw her body. What am I missing?" questioned my faithful assistant.

"That's what you're searching for, anything that we may have missed, no matter how small or insignificant it may seem. We have little to go on at this point in the investigation. We need Jo to talk to us from the grave."

"That's kinda creepy, Boss. After the day we had yesterday, I was hoping for a little less drama," confessed Ashley.

"It's all part of the job. I will need you here most of the day, so take your time; it's important. Now, before you get too far into your morning, can you call Lieutenant Osborne and ask if he can stop by this morning."

"Where are you going?" Ashley asked as I grabbed my hat and headed toward the door.

"I'm going by Max's. I need gas and want to ask him a few questions. If you reach Osborne and he wants to talk before I return, tell him to call the garage or stop by. Tell him I need to talk about the two witnesses of the Davenport abduction. I shouldn't be gone more than an hour. Do you need anything while I'm out?"

"I'm good for now. I would appreciate lunch later. I'm just saying," Ashley confided while batting her baby-blue eyes.

"Anything in particular?"

"Surprise me, but if you go by the Golden Glow, a slice of pecan pie would really hit the spot. It's Amelia's favorite, mine too," Ashley said, confusing me for a moment.

"Amelia? Oh, yes, the greatest woman in the world. How could I forget that."

"Don't worry, you'll never forget her—I'll see to that. Just remember: pecan pie."

"I'll remember. Also, call Mrs. Poston and ask if it's okay for me to stop by this morning. If you don't reach her or she says no, call me at Max's; if I don't hear anything, I assume everything is fine." I gave my faithful assistant a thumb-up as I walked out the door.

My pocket watch alerted me it was nearing ten o'clock, and Ashley's last words reminded me that I had skipped breakfast. Suddenly, I was suffering from 'hunger by suggestion'; I must thank her when I returned.

Pulling into Max's, I spied my old friend violently, throwing what appeared to be part of the 1915 Indian across the driveway. Do not let it be said that Max wasted time being patient.

"Hey, did you drop this?" I sarcastically asked while picking up the remains of the front fork.

"Don't bring that back in this garage! The damn thing is broken in three places; it can't be fixed. Where am I going to find one that fits this model?" barked Max.

"Can't you just weld it? I mean, I see you welding something almost every time I stop by. Can't you make one?" I innocently asked.

"Hey, Sherlock, do I tell you how to run your business? I can't weld it because it needs to be perfectly balanced on both sides; it's too far gone to fix. I'll figure something out."

"Answering your question, yes, you do tell me how to run my business. Often, I might add—but that's all part of your Southern charm," I replied, trying to get even more of a rise out of him.

"What do you need now that you've got my blood pressure up?"

"Hey, your pressure was up before I arrived; don't blame me. Truthfully, I need gas, and I need you to 'tell me how to run my business.' What I'm saying is...I need a little advice."

"Sam, get out here! I got a paying customer. Fill his car, check the tire pressures, and check the oil—*College boy* probably doesn't know how."

With that, the bantering ended and we went into Max's office, where I got a soda and a scoop of boiled peanuts. The suntanned proprietor wiped the grease from his hands and joined me with a soda and a handful of my peanuts. As quickly as Max's temper could be triggered, it dissipated equally.

"So, where are you on this case? How's Kate doing?" Max asked.

"Got more questions than answers... Seems the more we learn, the less we know," I confessed., followed by a sip of my ice-cold Coke.

"Could you be digging in the wrong places? Ever think of that? I like Osborne, a stand-up guy, but he's still a copper working for Johannsson, who I don't trust. You need to lead your investigation, not follow theirs. You're a private eye, independent; don't let the local constabulary yank your chain. You yank theirs," advised the older man.

I pondered for a moment: Was Max right? Was Johannsson manipulating me through Osborne? Was paranoia now my master? My mind swirled—I needed to focus.

"Hey, Sherlock, I'm talking to you! Osborne just pulled in; remember what I said: lead, don't follow. You work for Kate Brathwaite, not the Winchester police."

I paid Max, then drifted slowly toward Osborne's car.

"Forde, I'm heading to the Poston house. Do you want to join? Johannsson still says this is a suicide, but it is my day off, and my wife took the boys to visit her mother. I thought I would see if your claim has any credence."

Now I was really confused. He asked if I wanted to join him, opening the door that Jo's death could be a murder. Since I hadn't heard from Ashley, the timing couldn't be better for my return visit.

"How about this: leave your car here and ride with me. We can pool our questions on the ride over," I suggested.

"That sounds good. Mr. Patton, is it okay if I leave my car here? I'll pull it around the side so it's not in the way?" Osborne asked.

Max nodded in agreement, and we were soon on our way to Mrs. Poston's boarding house. We decided to use the old police tactic of good cop, bad cop; even though I was not a police officer, I would play the role of the good cop. As we approached our destination, I spied a familiar face on the porch.

"Hello, Robert." I waved my hand while closing the car door. "The yard looks fantastic."

"Mr. Forde, your partner this morning is not nearly as attractive as the little blonde you had here the first time. I would much rather invite her in than the two of you. So, what brings you back? I heard the police found the Brathwaite woman's body in the Shenandoah River.

Suicide, I hear? Wait a minute, is that you, Osborne? I thought I told you that you're not welcome here. Mom doesn't like you!" yelled the guarded son.

"Yes, Mr. Poston, it's me. I'm sorry I upset your mother. I apologize, but I have a job to do. Is your mother home? I will apologize to her directly," promised the somewhat embarrassed police officer.

"Yes, Lieutenant, I'm here, and I forgive you." The screened door opened, revealing the attractive, elderly woman. "What can we do for you two gentlemen this fine morning?"

"We need to visit Jo's room again, and yes, a body was found in Clarke County that we believe might be Jo Brathwaite. We are still investigating but should have a positive identification later today. May we see her room again?" I asked.

"See what? The room has been cleaned out. Her brother came by yesterday and took everything," chimed Robert.

"Her brother? Jo is or was an only child; she has no brother. What was his name? Did he produce any identification?" I questioned.

"He said he was her older brother and had a picture of the two of them. He told me he was Joe Jr. and that their mother had sent him to gather all of his sister's possessions, everything," explained the confused landlord.

Osborne and I quietly stared at one another. Then I asked, "May we see the room anyway? He may have left something. Also, can you tell me more about this brother?"

"Well, he was friendly, had a soft voice, you know, the kind of voice one could listen to all day. Very well dressed and the softest hands you ever touched. He has a neat haircut; this man has no problem charming the ladies," the woman confessed in a swooning tone.

"Have you ever seen him before?" asked Osborne.

"No, no, I don't think so...Son, have ever seen him before?" Mother Poston asked.

Robert shook his head no when Mrs. Poston unexpectedly blurted, "Wait a minute! Yes, I think I have seen him before. Forgive an old woman; my mind isn't what it used to be. Yes, I have seen him before—he was one of the men that Jo was speaking to on Wednesday, the 6th, the day of the Apple Blossom Parade. He was the tall one. Yes, I'm sure he was the taller man of the three. You agree with me, son?"

"I don't remember, Mom; I didn't pay that much attention to three strangers you saw on the street. You guys sure are wasting a lot of time on a tramp that wouldn't give a good man the time of day," complained Robert as his face twisted in disgust.

Overwhelmed and shocked by the past minutes, I gathered my composure. "That's great, Mrs. Poston; there is nothing wrong with your mind. Now, can you help us? Do you remember anything else? Something he may have said? What type of "soft voice" did he have? Did he have a Southern accent? Any distinguishing features?" I asked, overwhelming our host.

"Slow down, Forde. You've asked half a dozen questions not allowing Mom to answer the first one. Only answer the ones you want, Mom; he's not the boss here," reminded the protective son.

"I apologize, Mrs. Poston. Robert is correct; I never gave you a chance to respond. Just tell us what you remember, please?" I countered, trying to suppress my anxiety.

"Well, his hair was dark brown. No, black, like yours, Mr. Forde. He was just a little taller than you, not much, a couple of inches. He had a huge ring on his right hand, and he didn't have a wedding ring, which surprised me, a handsome man like that...still single. If I were thirty years younger, well..."

While astonished by the senior woman's flirtatious claim, I demonstrated my listening skills. Focusing on the description of the stranger's ring, I pushed up my right sleeve, revealing my college class ring.

"Was his ring something like this?" I questioned.

"Yes, just like that, except his was a little smaller and didn't have a stone like yours... just gold and black. It was an eye-catcher, though, but I like your ring much better. Is that a diamond, Mr. Forde?"

Before I could respond, Osborne asked, "Anything else, Mrs. Poston? You're doing great. Do you remember anything else that could help us?"

"I think that's enough for now—you two said something about seeing her room again. How about getting upstairs and letting my mother rest?"

Sensing the tension in Robert's voice and learning his resentment toward Osborne, I began the trek up the vintage staircase. Osborne followed my lead, and in a matter of seconds, we were in the middle of an expertly cleaned room. The stranger had succeeded; nothing was left in Jo's room. Absolutely nothing. Not only was the room bare, but it had also been completely sanitized, with no marks or fingerprints to be found. Even the lightbulb had been replaced. The mystery man was a professional.

We returned to the porch, finding only Robert, as Mrs. Poston had retired to her sitting room, seeking rest from our visit. Robert was the first to speak.

"So, I'm guessing this is the last we will see of you two. Although, you're welcome to send that lovely blonde assistant anytime, Forde. As for you, gentlemen, any further calls or visits go through me, not my mother. You've worn out your welcome, understand? Now, good day." The disgruntled son went back inside, slamming the door behind him.

In my car, Osborne asked, "So, what next?"

"Why does Robert hate you so much? What happened?" I asked while starting the engine.

"I made the mistake of coming here without his knowledge—he is extremely protective of his mother. I just made a mistake that he will not forgive," an embarrassed Osborne confessed.

Heading toward Max's garage, I asked, "Do you think he is hiding something? I mean, he offered nothing in describing the stranger impersonating Jo's brother. So protective, yet he can't recall anything? I find that hard to believe. Also, he has little sympathy regarding Jo's life. Do you think there was something between Jo and Robert?"

"Could be. She was an attractive woman, and Robert loves beautiful women. Think of all the comments he's made concerning Ashley. No secret about what he thinks of her. You think he made advances toward Jo and was shut down?" countered Osborne.

"I don't know; it seems he knows more than he's willing to tell. Hey, since you seem to have free time today, what say we journey to Martinsburg to check out some things? You game?"

"Why not? I mean, nothing else to do, wife and the boys gone for the day. Remember, my badge means nothing in West Virginia; you gotta lead the questions," Osborne said as he agreed to my request.

"Great! I need to swing by the office for a minute, and then we'll be on our way."

Chapter Eight

O sborne and I returned to the office to find out if Ashley had made any progress examining the morgue photos. To my surprise, I saw not one but two new oscillating fans running full speed with the office door open and both front windows open.

"Little warm, are we? It looks as if Santa made an unscheduled visit. Where did you get the fans?" I asked while my cheeks were beginning to hurt from smiling.

My resourceful assistant answered with conviction, "Yes, Santa visited today. He said working in this hot, humid office was unwise for anyone, especially me. He advised me to go to Solenberger's Hardware on Loudon St. and buy a fan. Mr. Hugh told me that two fans would circulate the air more efficiently, giving the office a cooler feel. You know what? He was right. He also suggested setting a block of ice in front of the fans, cooling the air even more. I didn't get any ice, but it would be a nice touch."

"I'm sorry the hot air is causing you to sweat; you and Santa did well, though it is hot," I answered, still wanting to burst into laughter.

"I don't sweat, I perspire. Modestly, I might add. Men sweat, ladies perspire. How you guys can wear those suit jackets in this heat is beyond me—Lt. Osborne, you look miserable. Oh, Boss, you must stop by Solenberger's and pay for the fans. I told Mr. Hugh you were good for it; here's the invoice."

After defending her purchase, Ashley shared three discoveries uncovered by her attention to detail. The three of us sat at the conference table, with Ashley strategically positioned at the head, photos in hand. "The first thing I noticed was a kinda burn mark on her right wrist, but nothing on the left, only the right. I think she was tied to something, like a dog."

Looking closely, Osborne agreed and added, "I've seen this type of mark before; it's from being handcuffed. If I were to guess, to something denying freedom but still allowing slight movement."

The second and third photos were even more disturbing. One showed two bruises at the nape of the neck, like a strong man had grabbed her from behind, choking her, leaving two distinct thumb marks. The final picture clearly showed a bruise on her right cheek, probably caused by a hard, back-handed slap from a man wearing a prominent ring.

Astonished by Ashley's work, I offered praise. "I can't begin to tell you how proud I am right now—you did an incredible job. Now, with that said, what have we learned of Jo's final hours? What placed this woman in this torturous situation?"

"Brody, you and Miss Ashley have convinced me that this is a murder investigation, a very violent murder. I'm going to change my report; it may cost me my job, but I can't ignore the facts: she was murdered," relented Lt. Osborne.

"When are we going to have an official identification? When is the State of Virginia going to confirm Jo's identity?" asked Ashley.

Pausing a moment, Osborne answered, "Hopefully later today. Flavius Brathwaite called me late yesterday and said he would bring Mrs. Brathwaite to Jones', not the morgue. Dr. Stenner suggested the funeral home as a more comfortable environment for the family. She will be cleaned up and wearing a robe; anything to make this easier for the mother."

"Nothing can make this easy, but anywhere is better than that hospital basement. What changed Mr. Brathwaite's mind? I thought he was going to shield Kate?" I inquired.

"You know Kate, she's determined to do this, nothing changing that Irish mind. I guess she needs to do this. Closure?" Osborne concluded.

"Boss, I just remembered something. Where's my lunch? Did you get my pecan pie?"

"I'm sorry, with everything else this morning, I forgot all about food. How about this? Let's close the office for the day, and the three of us head to Martinsburg to meet Jo Brathwaite's employer; lunch is on me. Is that okay with everyone?" I asked, attempting to deflect my forgetting Ashley's dietary needs.

"Absolutely! Just as long as I get fed soon. Hey, can I drive?"

"Ah, no, my dear. I think I'll drive this trip," I answered, to the relief of Lt. Osborne.

Ashley closed the office while Will and I reviewed the facts as we knew them. The change of pace would benefit each of us, and we would finally meet Jo's mysterious employer. I was also anxious to meet my first FFV.

During the drive, we continued to scrutinize what we knew, speculate on what we didn't, and hypothesize what we might find in the Mountain State. The journey resembled more of a pilgrimage than a drive due to poor road conditions. Finally, after nearly two hours, we arrived at what was believed to be Jo's employer, just south of Martinsburg, in the tiny community of Pikeside. Unfortunately, instead of finding a house belonging to an FFV, we were forced to settle for a burned-out barn and the remains of a dilapidated house. The mysterious life of Ada Jo Brathwaite grows.

"So, what now? Who was Jo Brathwaite?" Osborne asked, wearing a concerned face.

"Will, early in this investigation, you mentioned Jo Brathwaite was a person of interest. What did that mean?" I pondered, fearing the answer.

"I have a confession; it is true I don't have anything to do today, but I do have an ulterior motive. Jo was believed to be linked to a place called the Ivory Tower."

"What's the Ivory Tower?" a puzzled Ashley quizzed.

"It's a sophisticated nightclub with atmosphere... *All the amenities,*" informed Osborne as he cautiously chose his words.

"Hey, I like sophistication. Let's go!" begged my novice employee. She then questioned, "What are amenities?"

Will and I sheepishly stared at one another, neither wanting to answer. Finally, I broke the silence. "Let's just say the *amenities* are beyond imagination—hard to put into words."

"Are you talking about sex? When will you boys realize I'm a woman, not a little girl? I went to college, and while I probably lack some of your life experiences, I'm familiar with the speakeasy, nightclubs, and the places men like to frequent. Don't you think a single woman likes having a good time? Why is it okay for you guys, but if a woman does the same thing, she's a tramp?" my analytical assistant probed.

Ashley instantly changed the tone of the conversation, making several excellent points; we do live by a double standard. *Forgive the action; forget the intent.* Regardless of what we find concerning Jo's decisions, I would neither judge nor condemn. Neither would I judge Ashley.

We finally arrived at 109 North Queen Street, and after parking the car, we entered the prestigious establishment. Inside, we were greeted by an attractive hostess who escorted us past a long oak bar on the right side. The main dining room was in the back, with a bandstand and dance floor. Also situated in the room was an elegant spiral mahogany staircase on the right and a large, white padded door to the left. The swank motif screamed wealth; for a brief moment, I was back in Boston.

We were early for the supper crowd, yet nearly a third of the white-pressed linen-covered tables were filled. Now seated near the stage, with menus in hand, our provocatively dressed hostess asked, "You are new here, first time? May I start you off with a cold drink?"

"Three Coca-Colas would be delightful. Is that okay with everyone?" I asked.

Since we would not be back in Winchester until late, I suggested we have an early supper, giving us a reason to linger and watch as people come and go. The clientele exhibited extreme wealth; most men wore form-fitting suit jackets with gently sloped shoulders and tailored trousers with cuffs that creased in the front for a stronger silhouette. The room was filled with women fashioning gowns designed by Paris' Elsa Schiaparelli and Coco Chanel. Collectively, enough diamonds and precious gems were present to open a jewelry store—and it was only a late Tuesday afternoon.

Our sodas were placed carefully on the table as we studied the menu.

The mood shifted as Ashley leaned in and whispered, "Boss, there are no prices on my menu. What does that mean?"

"It means, Miss Ashley, if you have to ask the prices, you can't afford to eat here. Trust me, I have the same sinking feeling," confessed Osborne, using a low, nervous voice while his hands displayed a mild tremble.

"Please, both of you. I invited you here as my guests. This meal is on me; call it a business expense. We are here on business, aren't we?" I reminded my apprehensive companions.

"Brody, I can't accept your charity. I'll have my Coke and enjoy the atmosphere," offered Osborne, a bit overwhelmed by the grandeur.

"Nonsense, you're both my guests; relax and enjoy yourselves," I insisted.

My friends accepted my offer while we entertained ourselves in pleasant conversation. Several minutes later, our waitress returned. "Excuse me, may I take your orders?"

"We've never been here. What would you suggest?" I asked.

"The steaks are always delicious, but I personally love the lobster. Whatever you choose, we assure your satisfaction or the meal is on us. So, what would satisfy your bodily needs: steak, lobster, or how about a combination of each, a little surf and turf?" the seductive waitress suggested.

"I like the sound of that, Boss, surf and turf for me. How about you, Lt. Osborne?"

The Winchester detective was hesitant, still not comfortable with the unknown prices. We made eye contact, and then I slowly nodded, assuring everything was alright. Finally, my friend answered. "A steak, well done, and a baked potato, please."

I ordered the same as Ashley; it had been a while since I'd had lobster. I also requested salads and a second round of Cokes for everyone. During our meal, the enjoyment of the moment took a severe turn.

"Well, folks, how's the meal? Is everything satisfactory? May I get you anything?" asked our enticing server, returning to our table.

Before I could speak, Osborne intervened with an astonishing question. "Why, yes, would you happen to have anything a little stronger than Coca-Cola?" He quirked an eyebrow. "It's been a terribly hot, tiring day; I could use something with a little kick. Got anything to help with that?"

"Sir, I have no idea what you mean. We are a respectable establishment; we have nothing of which you ask," she sharply replied.

"I just thought, a place like this, surely you have something better to offer than Coke. Are you certain you don't have something?" Osborne persisted.

The woman never wavered nor answered my intrusive guest. Unseen by our eyes, she had signaled a robust, sharply dressed man to join the conservation.

Leaning in so as not to draw attention and using a low voice, he firmly asked, "Is there a problem here? Is there something I can help you with?"

"This one asked if we had 'anything stronger than Coke.' I assured him we did not, but I don't think he believes me," explained the trembling hostess.

"I just asked a simple question; I didn't mean to cause any trouble. Miss, I'm sorry if I offended you or this wonderful restaurant," retreated Osborne as his embarrassment surfaced.

"Mister, you reek *copper*. I know you're not local; I'm guessing Hagerstown, possibly Winchester. You come in here wearing that cheap, worn-out suit with frayed cuffs and shoe leather as thin as yesterday's newspaper, asking a question like that. Do you think we are that stupid?" the 6'5" mammoth queried.

"My friend meant no harm. He's just going through a rough time, the Depression and all. I just wanted him to have a delectable meal and to forget his troubles for a while, that's all," I intervened, attempting to defuse the situation.

"I don't know your story; you definitely don't look like you should be associated with this bum. I mean, what's that, a Brooks Brothers you're wearing? Sharp, upscale, and your shoes, Italian? I don't know who or what you are, but you're not a copper like this poor soul," the giant continued, forming a fist just inches from Osborne's face.

"No, sir, I'm not a police officer. We just wondered where to get a drink; we meant no harm. May we forget all this and return to our succulent meal?"

The bouncer's temperament calmed, especially after I placed a $50 bill in the palm of his hand as we shook. The frightening man smiled and suggested we return to our meals as they were getting cold. Surprisingly, he invited us to visit again but to come after 7:00 p.m. to enjoy all the Ivory Tower had to offer. I was unsure if he wanted us or the generous windfall he just received; nevertheless, we avoided a confrontation that wouldn't have ended well for us.

The food was excellent, one of the finest steaks I had ever eaten. The lobster was above average, but I'd had better. Ashley reveled in the moment while Will began looking at his watch, wondering what his wife might say if she knew where he was.

After Ashley devoured her desert, we decided it was time to head back to Winchester. Our time in the Ivory Tower yielded no clues—not on the surface, anyway. I paid the check and slipped another $50 bill to the server. The generosity did not escape the ever-present eyes of my assistant. Safely back in the car, Ashley began the interrogation.

"Boss, are you out of your mind? You spent over a hundred dollars; it takes me almost two months to make that much. Can I have a raise?" asked Ashley

"You make $50 a month? I don't make that much, and I'm a police lieutenant."

"What can I say? I'm an essential part of the Forde Detective Agency. Seriously, Boss, why did you spend that much?"

"First, Will, I'm not sure what you were thinking—what were you thinking? I just wanted to get out of there alive and to be remembered. When I go back, and, eventually, I'll go back, they will have forgotten the episode, but no one ever forgets money. What's the old saying, money talks, and—"

"Poopy walks," Ashley interjected. "That's what my Daddy says. But, seriously, Boss, can I have a raise?"

The remainder of the drive was anticlimactic; Ashley fell asleep, and even Osborne fought the battle with the Sandman. I focused on the road, keeping all safe until the lights of Winchester came into sight. After dropping Will off, I drove Ashley home, informing her not to come to work until noon tomorrow; she had surely earned a morning off.

I headed home, pulled my car into the garage, then headed up to my fourth-floor room. It had been a busy day but not as productive as I might have hoped. After a hot bath, I settled in my wingback chair with my feet on the ottoman and a cold Coca-Cola in hand: Osborne, this one was for you.

Now came the thinking part of my evening. Who was Jo Brathwaite, and what did she see that led to her death? What was behind that padded door? Gambling, the brothel? We saw nothing suggesting improprieties, but it was our first visit. How do you earn your way behind the padded door or up the spiraled staircase? As time passed, my sight began to dim. Finally, a much-needed night of sleep, the demon's rest.

It was Wednesday morning, and it'd been nearly a week, and we were no closer to the truth. I grabbed a quick breakfast and headed to the office. Reaching the top step, I suddenly remembered giving Ashley the morning off; I must make the coffee.

After conquering the battle with the percolator, the ringing of the phone interrupted the silence.

Lifting the receiver, I heard a familiar voice. "Mr. Forde, this is Kate Brathwaite. I need to speak with you this afternoon. May I come in around one o'clock? Flavius said he could bring me. Is that okay?"

"Absolutely, one o'clock will be fine. Would you like Lt. Osborne to be here? I will gladly give him a call."

"It's up to you; I just need to talk. We'll be there by one… thank you, Mr. Forde."

I immediately called Osborne to let him know about the afternoon meeting. Unfortunately, Osborne would not be able to attend; Chief Johannsson ordered him to close the case on Ada Jo Brathwaite. Officially, her cause of death was suicide. Hearing the news, I reached out to one of the families of a missing teen. Since I met the Witten family last week, I'd offer my assistance *pro bono*.

I spent the rest of the morning catching up on paperwork, organizing what we knew, and strategizing the remainder of the week. Just before noon, Ashley burst through the door, full of energy and anxious to get to work.

"What do you think? Do you like it?" beaming with excitement, then spinning around with both arms extended.

"Like what?" I replied, knowing I was about to get both barrels.

"My hair, I had my hair cut, painted my nails, and bought new shoes. Really, I don't know why I try," my disappointed associate confessed.

"I noticed; I just enjoy needling you."

After a brief exchange on the ignorance of men, a short talk of which I again lost, we focused on the day ahead. I told her about our afternoon meeting and my thoughts on helping the Witten family. However, I was caught off guard by Ashley's request.

"With everything going on in the Brathwaite case, how about I take the lead on the Witten situation?" suggested my overly eager employee.

Pausing a moment, I finally answered, "Ashley, you are more than capable; it's that, well, it could be dangerous. We are talking about people that are kidnapping young adults, teenagers, male teens, young men old enough to put up a fight, yet they are missing, possibly dead."

"You think I don't know that? The difference is the missing teenagers didn't see it coming; they were snatched from their everyday lives. I will be alert to everything around me; I'll carry my gun."

"You have a gun?" I asked in a stunned voice, my jaw dropping.

"Of course, I have a gun, a Colt .38, hammerless, so it doesn't catch on my clothes when I pull it out. My Daddy bought it for me when I left for college. He taught me how to handle it, clean it, and especially fire it. He even had a holster designed just for me; I carry it without anyone being the wiser. I'm carrying it right now. Do you want to see it?"

Before I could muster an answer, the independent woman reached inside her blouse and produced a short-barrel, nickel-plated revolver. Needless to say, she had my attention.

"I'll tell you what: You and I will go to the Witten farm after our meeting. I will involve you throughout the process, but I have to maintain the role of lead investigator. Fair enough?"

"Fair enough; all I ask is for a chance to do more. I want to learn all I can," pleaded the zealous woman.

The rest of the morning was fairly routine. Ashley prepared for our Brathwaite meeting while I walked down to Solenberger's Hardware to pay for the fans purchased yesterday; it also gave me an opportunity to meet some of the locals who had built Winchester. This was a fascinating town; I loved Winchester.

Back at the office, the clock was a few minutes shy of our appointed meeting time when I heard Flavius comment about the door missing the 'period' in my name. He continued by asking how Kate could trust someone who would allow such a mistake.

Once Flavius had finished his amusement at my expense, both entered and took seats in the conference room. Kate informed us that she had seen the body and confirmed Jo's identity. She also offered a startling revelation.

"They gave us Jo's dress, you know, the one she was wearing when they found her. This isn't Jo's dress! She has never had a dress like this," Kate said as she removed the garment from a bag.

"What do you mean, it's not Jo's dress? Could you be mistaken? Could she have purchased it in Martinsburg, or she kept it in her room on Braddock Street?" I questioned.

"Nope, she never had a dress like this; it isn't hers," insisted the mother as her face reddened and eyes gathered tears.

Flavius placed his arm around his sister-in-law, then explained, "I think what Kate is trying to say is that Jo hated polka dots; she hated them as a kid. She would have never worn something like this."

"Could she have borrowed it, possibly from a friend?" asked Ashley as she passed a tissue to the grieving mother.

"No, I don't think so, *little lady*; this is not Jo's dress," returned Flavius in a demeaning tone while his forehead wrinkled.

The remainder of the meeting was of little value; besides the dress, we had no new leads. I did not offer my asking for the blood samples or my having sent a sample to Dr. McGregor in Boston.

Kate informed us the funeral would be Friday morning, 11:00 a.m., at the Mt. Olive Church in Hayfield and asked if we could attend. Both Ashley and I ensured our presence.

Before we concluded, I asked Kate if we could keep the disturbing garment. I did not know what value it held, but at this point, we had far more questions than answers. Perhaps this dress had a silent voice willing to give up its secrets. Our meeting ended just after two, so Ashley and I grabbed a late lunch and headed for Gore to offer our services to the Witten family.

Chapter Nine

"Boy, this is a rough road," assessed Ashley as we stopped in front of the Witten home. "Why would anyone come this far out in the *boonies* to kidnap someone?"

Ashley made a startling point, one neither Osborne nor I could claim. How were the targets chosen? What was the common denominator, and what exactly was a *boonie*?

We waited a moment while Mrs. Witten chased the dogs away from my car, allowing safe passage to the porch. Once there, we were joined by Stoney Witten, Jubal's father.

"What can we do for you two? Hey, I remember you. You were here last week with that fellow who didn't say much."

"Yes, sir, I was here last week. I don't know if you remember, but my name is Forde, Ambrose Forde. Please call me Brody. This is Miss Ashley O'Connell, my assistant. Have you heard anything concerning Jubal? Any progress in finding him?"

"No sir, Mr. Brody, not a word. We ain't heard from nobody since the day he came up missing. Not a single word," answered the grief-stricken mother.

The moment was interrupted when Mr. Witten jumped up and shouted, "Git back in the barn, you *mangy mutt*! Dog ain't been right since..."

Mrs. Witten, eyes now shedding tears, interrupted, "That's Jubal's dog, Mr. Brody; he doesn't understand why Jubal ain't here. The worst thing is the dog won't eat; we're all on edge right now."

"Well, ma'am, that's the reason we are here; with your permission, we would like to help. We want to join the hunt for Jubal—we are willing to work *pro bono*, no charge."

"We don't want no charity. We got a little money. It's just that what can you do that the sheriff ain't ah doing? You think you're smarter than the sheriff?" challenged Mr. Witten.

"No, sir, we don't think we are smarter than the County Sheriff, and we are not offering charity. It means, possibly, we can help each other. I'm new here in Frederick County, trying to start a detective business. I have experience in missing-person cases. I'm not promising anything except that we'll give you the best we have."

"Ain't going to cost us nothing? I say yes, Stoney, I want my boy back!"

The couple, led by Mom, agreed to hire us. We stepped into the kitchen and were given pertinent information and several photographs of Jubal. We were also given the names of Jubal's closest friends and permission to speak with anyone we felt could help.

Remembering Ashley's request, I informed them, "Ashley will be assisting me on this case. This means, at times, you may be speaking with her; talking with her is the same as talking with me. You are getting both of us and anyone else we believe can help find your son. Is that okay?" I asked.

"What do you think, Mother? Can we trust this *little girl* with a man's job?"

"You trust me to do a man's work. She looks up to it, and she ain't no little girl, Stoney. Yeah, she'll be fine; help your boss find our boy, Miss Ashley."

Ashley's face gleamed as the mother spoke confidently and redirected her husband. She assured the couple of her commitment to the case and asked, "What would the chances of borrowing Jubal's dog tomorrow be? I have an idea. What's the dog's name?"

"Sprocket, his name is Sprocket. Jubal loves anything mechanical, so that's how the dog got his name. What do ya want with that old dog? He can't do nothin' except eat and sleep," told Mrs. Witten.

"I don't want to get any hopes up; I just would like to borrow Sprocket tomorrow morning, if that's okay with you all," Ashley requested.

"Fine with us; you can even give him a bath while you have him if you like," joked Stoney.

The day drifted into the evening as we said our goodbyes and headed back to the city. My young protégé handled herself well, presenting in a most professional manner. I never understood the fight women must make to be accepted in 1931 and to be treated with equality in a male-dominated world. Ashley was a fighter; I admired her confidence and courage. She reminded me of my sister, Lucy.

Just a couple of miles from town, Ashley confessed, "Brody, I want to thank you. You are a man of your word. I won't let you, or the firm, down, I promise."

"I have a question: what are you thinking about the dog? What am I missing?"

"*Yankee city boy*, you're kidding. You don't know? That *mangy mutt*, as he was called, is a bloodhound missing his beloved owner; that's why he won't eat. We haven't had any rain since Jubal went missing. I want to use the dog along the road where Jubal went missing. We might find something. I think it's worth a try."

"You continue to amaze me. Obviously, I never thought of the dog. It's been close to a week. Can that dog really find Jubal's scent?"

"Just depends on the canine. I admit it's a stretch, but right now, we've got nothing. I think it's worth trying. Sprocket is hurting; he misses his master, his friend, and the person that feeds him. I want to get on it first thing in the morning, okay?"

"Okay, we'll meet at the Golden Glow for breakfast, then head for Gore. Does nine o'clock work for you... er, boss?" I asked.

"Works for me. Can you drop me off at my house? I need to plan our steps for tomorrow."

"Yes, ma'am... You're the boss." I followed my instructions by delivering Ashley to her front door, then decided to return to the office to call Osborne. To my surprise, Osborne and another man I'd never met were waiting outside my door.

"Must be nice to come and go as you like. Mr. Ambrose Forde, this is Detective Jason Billings. He and I have been assigned to packing shed murder. I thought you two should meet," offered Lieutenant Osborne.

"Packing shed murder, when did this happen? Do you have a name or any suspects? Come in; fill me in as much as you can," I pleaded.

While entering the office, I heard Billings make the familiar comment about the missing 'period' in my middle initial. "I know a guy that can fix that," he offered.

"I'll let you know. Now, what about this new murder? Why are you including me? I thought Johannsson hated me, yet here you are. What's changed?" I skeptically asked.

"Well, you know I'm off the Brathwaite case. As far as the Winchester police are concerned, it's closed. Johannsson has paired us up on this one; it is definitely a murder. Why am I talking to you? I think there is a link to the Ivory Tower, and we have no jurisdiction across the state line, but you can operate in West Virginia, and they liked you," confided Osborne.

"Does your boss know you are here, speaking to me?" I grilled.

"Yes, he does. He despises you, but in a crazy way, he trusts you more than the Martinsburg police. To Johannsson, you're a necessary evil. You can easily cross the state line; we can't," Osborne confessed.

"So, how does this work? What's expected of me, of Ashley?" I added, not forgetting my earlier promises.

"We share information as much as we can. But in the end, the Winchester police call the shots, understand?" Billings chimed.

My first impression of our new working relationship was full of red flags. Johannsson resented Osborne and my relationship; he didn't trust his Lieutenant, so he planted someone among us he does trust,

Billings, to report everything back to him. I didn't like it, but at least I could continue to work with Will, a man I trust.

"Ah, yes, I think I understand. So, what can you tell me about the murder? Why do you believe it may be connected to the Tower?" I asked as I gained control of the interrogation.

"A local man named Rolf Schlesinger was found sitting in an old Model T Ford truck inside a packing shed, motor running. He died of carbon dioxide poisoning," explained Billings.

"Suicide? Your boss is quick to call a death suicide," I sarcastically asked.

"Only if he tied his own hands to the steering wheel, his feet also bound, and the shed door locked from the outside," Osborne offered.

"Yeah, hard to call this a suicide. How is he connected to the Ivory Tower?" my questions continued.

"Hidden in his billfold was a Martinsburg phone number, which we called. A woman with a sweet voice answered and said, 'Ivory Tower, may I help you?' Within seconds, we could hear a man cursing, and then the call was immediately ended. When we tried to call again, we were told by the Martinsburg switchboard supervisor the number was no longer in service and that we had made a mistake," explained Billings.

"I admit, that's suspicious, but there's not enough to connect the dead man to the Tower; we need more, much more," I replied, prodding for more information.

"This is where you come in; we need you to become a regular patron of the Ivory Tower, to earn their trust, to see what is behind that padded door," Osborne concluded.

"That's asking a lot, but I suppose it might help me with the Brathwaite murder. I know the Winchester police have given up on the case, but we haven't. By the way, Jo's funeral is Friday," I informed.

"So, you're in?" Billings asked in an inquisitive tone.

"He's in!" answered Osborne before I could speak.

"Yeah, we're in, but with conditions. First, I'm in the loop all the way; neither of you will have secrets. Second, I need access to the packing shed, the body, and any locations necessary to do my job. And finally, my assistant, Ashley, is part of the team; she is to be given all the respect any man would receive. And, for the record, none of these terms are negotiable. Understand?"

Both men nodded in agreement, and handshakes were exchanged—the bond had been established.

The remaining time was used to decide how to proceed. We decided to meet tomorrow afternoon to examine the packing shed and plan another visit to the morgue. In less than a week, the Ambrose Forde Detective Agency had gone from no cases to three of the biggest cases this city had ever seen.

Thursday morning arrived, and I actually had enjoyed a restful night of sleep. I was so exhausted even my demons could not intrude on my solitude.

After going through the morning rituals, I decided to run by the office before meeting Ashley. As I approached my office door, the sound of typing echoed from within. Was that typing? I gently opened the door to find an attractive brunette seated at Ashley's desk, diligently concentrating on her task so much that she didn't see me.

"May I ask who you are and what you are doing?" I said, startling the young intruder.

"I'm... I'm Emily, Ashley's little sister. She hired me last night to replace her as your secretary," answered the surprised new employee.

"She hired you last night? What exactly did she tell you?" I stumbled for words.

"Ashley said that since you and she would be working on one of your toughest cases, you would need a capable secretary to take calls and keep the office running smoothly. I recently graduated tops in my class from the State Teachers College at Harrisonburg, much higher than Ashley, which should be no surprise. She's three years older than me, but I'm at least ten years smarter than her," she proclaimed with a grin much like her sister's.

"Well, I am Ambrose Forde; please call me Brody, and welcome to the firm. Ashley is right; we will both be out of the office quite a bit in the coming weeks, and your presence is greatly needed. Is there anything you need, anything that can make this an enjoyable working environment?"

"No, I'm okay for now. Here is the folder Ashley said you would need, and she told me to remind you not to be late for breakfast. She's a real stickler for being on time."

"Seems you have everything covered; carry on with your work, and don't forget, you get an hour for lunch. One of us will call you a little later to see if there are any messages."

I left the office slightly overwhelmed but satisfied with my new secretary. I guessed this was partly my fault; after all, I did refer to Ashley as "*the boss*." In the future, I must be more careful when speaking figuratively.

I entered the Golden Glow and saw what must now be my new assistant detective seated in a corner booth, enjoying what I hoped was her first cup of coffee. "So, what's new?"

"Well, I did something very positive to build the agency and ensure the Ambrose Forde Detective Agency is the best firm in town. I hired a secretary to help with the office while I assist you with the Witten investigation. After all, someone has to be at the office while we are both in the field fighting crime," reasoned Ashley.

"Yes, I just met Miss Emily, and I agree, we do need additional help. In the future, could you include me in the interview process," I responded in an upbeat tone.

"Did she tell you she was my baby sister? Now, Brody, give her a chance. She's not as smart as me and probably not as attractive, but boy, can she type fast, with hardly any mistakes."

"She will do fine; I'm pleased with Emily becoming part of the team."

After a hearty breakfast, we headed to Gore to pick up Sprocket, Jubal Witten's pet bloodhound. While riding, our conversation centered on using Sprocket's talent.

"I know nothing of hound dogs. How exactly will this work?" I asked.

"First, we get a piece of clothing last worn by Jubal. Then comes the tricky part: where to begin our search. Let's walk along the road leading away from the school and heading toward the Witten home since he was last seen leaving school."

"This isn't going to be easy, is it?" I surmised.

"No, it's not, but right now, it's all we have. By the way, stop at the Emporium; we need to get something before we pick up Sprocket," directed Ashley.

"Not more of Grandma's Elixir? You surely haven't used both bottles of that stuff?" I jokingly questioned.

"No, I'm not out of Elixir, and for the record, that stuff really works, my Daddy swears by it. No, we need to pick up some bacon."

"Bacon, you just ate at least a half-pound of sausage for breakfast; you can't possibly be hungry," I inquired, wondering how she could eat so much and maintain her slender figure.

"Just wait, you'll see."

My curiosity grew.

We finally arrived at the Witten farm after a short stop at the Emporium. Hard as it was with their son missing, the farm work must go on. Both mother and father labored in the field, tending to a team of stubborn mules. When they saw our car approaching, Mrs. Witten abandoned her chores to greet us.

"Began to think you'd forgotten us; the day is nearly half gone. Why is it pert-near 10:30?" exclaimed the bewildered mother.

Forgetting a farmer's day begins well before sunrise, I apologized, "I'm sorry, Mrs. Witten. We had several things to take care of, but we're here now; we need Sprocket for a few hours. We promise to take care of him."

"He's a-layin' over there by the barn; he don't hardly move since Jubal's been gone," Mrs. Witten confessed.

"Mrs. Witten, can we please have several pieces of your son's clothing, perhaps a shirt and a pair of his dirty socks? Anything that has Jubal's scent on it," Ashley asked.

"You sure you want his dirty socks? They really stink," admitted the mother.

"Yes, Ma'am, I'm sure; the worse they smell, the better," advised Ashley.

After a few minutes, Mrs. Witten, fighting back the tears, presented Ashley with the needed items. She grabbed Sprocket by his long ears, gently stroking them with her fingers, and begged, "You, old mangy critter, help these people find Jubal." She erupted into a river of tears, then returned to her husband and the mules.

Back in the car, the aroma of a country farm dog made its presence known.

"Boy, that dog smells almost as bad as the morgue. I'm not sure this was such a great idea," confessed my assistant.

"Come on, Ashley. You told me you never had a bad idea. It'll all be worth it if we can find just one clue. How about we crank the windshield out and let some fresh air in?" I suggested.

"How about we just break the windshield out and let a lot of fresh air in? Seriously, this dog stinks!" she fired back while hanging her head out the right-side window, her hair whipping and tangling in the wind.

After a fifteen-minute drive that seemed like an hour, we reached the small country schoolhouse. Once out of the car, Ashley gave Sprocket a sniff of one of Jubal's dirty socks. Instantly, with a leash, I wisely attached to the old dog, the once listless canine pulled me toward the road.

"He senses something, not sure what, but suddenly, this dog is alive," exclaimed Ashley.

"I can hardly hold onto him. This dog is a beast!" I shouted.

"Hang on to him, Brody; I'll get the car and follow you—don't lose him."

The exuberant hound began a series of zigzags up the hill, then down to a gully parallel to the road. Several times, he stopped, deciding which path to follow. This animal's strength was amazing. The only question was what he was following: the scent of his missing owner, a rabbit, or some other wild animal abundant in Virginia?

We continued about a mile, and suddenly, Sprocket stopped and circled several times, beginning a constant bark that pierced my ears. He continued his noisy barrage until Ashley, now out of the car, approached.

"Ashley, get up here! Sprocket has found something over to your right. He's going crazy; I'm afraid to take even one hand off the leash. What is over there?"

While I fought to hold on to the leash, Ashley moved up the thorn-covered hill to retrieve the source of Sprocket's excitement.

"Be careful, Ashley, don't get cut up by the thorns, and watch out for snakes."

"You just hold on to the dog; I know how to handle thorns and snakes. If I can reach in a little more, I got it. Brody, it's a shoe—a really stinky shoe!"

"Do you think it belongs to Jubal? This is my first experience with a bloodhound," I asked as the dog continued to pull hard on the leash.

"I don't know, but if it is Jubal's, he needs to wash his feet more often," she stated, holding a well-worn, low-cut boot high in her left hand while her head turned hard to the right, avoiding the aroma.

The strain on the leash intensified, so I finally succumbed to Sprocket's demand. He pulled me down the bank toward the dirt road. With no warning, he took me into a dense thicket, holding a piece of blue and white fabric. The material was consistent with the description of Jubal's shirt.

While picking the cloth from the clutches of nature, I heard a familiar voice, "Where are you? I was coming to show you this shoe, and then I heard Sprocket barking and the loudest thrashing sound ever. Where are you?" Ashley yelled.

"We're over here! Wait, let me come to you; the thorns are terrible here," I pleaded to no avail.

After a few minutes, the over-exuberant country girl waded through the briar patch with the shoe, as well as a barrage of thorns and scratches covering both arms.

"Are you okay? You're bleeding everywhere: hands, arms, even your face. Let's get back to the car; I have a few medical supplies I always carry," I pleaded.

After a few minutes of treatment, we assessed our findings. Amazingly, the dog ceased his barking and took a rest beside the rear door of my sedan, looking at the two of us as if to say, I've done my part; now, find my master.

I cleaned Ashley's battle wounds, several of which were somewhat deep. She pushed me aside as I learned the purpose of the bacon.

"Here you go, Sprocket, good boy, good, good, boy!" She rewarded the impressive bloodhound with a pat on the head first and then a strip of perfectly cooked pork. Once again, my assistant became my teacher.

After our *hero of the day* finished the last piece of bacon, he returned to napping by the car while Ashley and I began a more exhaustive search of the area. We found no more retrievable evidence but realized something else: a tremendous struggle or fight had occurred here. Not only was the ground cover disturbed, but it became evident the entire area was trying to tell us something. Rocks were overturned, low-hanging limbs from several trees were either broken or splintered, and soft moss exposed what appeared to be boot marks. No question, a major fight had taken place here.

Ashley took multiple pictures of what we both believed was a crime scene. No additional clues were discovered, but all in all, this was a productive morning. Sprocket was delivered safely home to a grateful family who praised him for his contribution. We carefully showed both pieces of evidence, trying but failing not to add to the couple's burden. After a moment of deafening silence, the mother spoke.

"Yes, both pieces belong to Jubal. Where did you find them?"

"Along the road, about a mile from the school," I answered.

"Why did this happen? Who would take our boy?" asked the disheartened father.

"I don't know, Mr. Witten, but I promise we will do everything possible to find Jubal; I give you both my word."

The four of us continued the difficult conversation until I stressed the need for Ashley and me to return to Winchester. Turning my car around, I saw the loving parents hugging the once-called *Mangy Mutt*, now a proud member of the Witten family.

Chapter Ten

The drive back to town was a quiet one after a satisfying morning on the one hand, but a much more disturbing one on the other. We knew where the kidnapping took place, but the who and why questions lingered.

Now back in town, we headed upstairs to our office, finding Emily had rearranged Ashley's desk, to the displeasure of the former tenant.

"What have you done? I had everything carefully organized; now it's a mess!"

"I made things a little less cluttered, more efficient, if you know what I mean."

"Ladies, before this escalates, let's do this. Emily, call Swimley's Furniture Store on Piccadilly Street and order a new desk for you, two comfortable chairs, one for each of you, and anything else either of you might need or want. Now, ladies, don't take advantage of my generosity, but treat yourselves to whatever makes your jobs easier. And, remember, you are sisters, not rivals, okay?"

"Didn't I tell you he's the best?" bragged Ashley.

"Now, with that settled, I'm going to leave the two of you to arrange this office to work for the three of us. Ashley, I will also need you to call Dr. Stenner at the morgue to see if he sent Jo's blood sample to Boston General and when you can stop by and pick up my sample. Emily, I need you to call Lt. Osborne at the police station and tell him I am on my way to pick him up. Both of you play well together while I'm gone."

Leaving the two women, I headed to the police station to find Osborne and Billings waiting for me, seated on the bench in front of the courthouse. Pulling up, I also spied Chief Johannsson standing by his car. When he saw me, he drifted over, sternly staring down his two officers. "Forde, I'm giving you a lot of rope; make sure you don't hang these two out to dry with it. Let's make this clear: I don't like you, and I sure as hell don't trust you, but I don't have much of a choice. Are we clear?" barked the overbearing god of the local police. "Just remember, I know more about you than the rest of these fools."

Not trusting my verbal skills, I nodded my head in agreement. What had I said or done that warranted this kind of hatred? Did he just call two of his men fools? While I hadn't told everything about my past, I had nothing to hide.

With Billings and Osborne in my car, we began our short ride to a small agricultural area just northwest of town called Nain. There were few residents, but miles and miles of apple orchards dominated the terrain. The sheriff's department held jurisdiction in Nain but, with recent events, had again invited the Winchester police into the investigation. I found Nain to be pleasantly tranquil, that was, until we arrived at our destination.

"Brody, turn left just past Cutter's Welding Shop. It's a rough dirt road, so take your time; I don't want you to damage the undercarriage of this fine automobile," sarcastically advised Detective Billings.

"It's probably best to park here; we'll walk up to the old garage over there," Osborne said, pointing to his left.

I pulled my Chrysler in the direction my friend suggested, though getting completely off the *wilderness trail* was nearly impossible. Now stopped, we began our trek to the crime scene.

We spent half an hour hiking the five-hundred-yard path mistakenly called a road, an arduous entry using over-grown thickets, downed trees, and whatever else needed to preserve its past. The single-car structure stood near the remains of a once proud home, consumed by fire decades ago.

With the key in hand, Osborne unlocked the wooden death chamber, exposing everything but the body that had been taken to the morgue. All else seemed undisturbed.

"How many people had been in here, and who found the body?" I inquired.

"I don't exactly know, five or six people, ole' man Nester Perkins found the body; he said he comes back here to pick blackberries from time to time and noticed a padlock on the door, which was odd since there was nothing inside worth stealing. He heard a motor running and walked over to investigate. It was then he smelled the exhaust fumes and, since he couldn't open the locked door, decided to get to the nearest phone at Nain's Market and call Sheriff Neumann," answered Billings.

"Will, you said nothing has been disturbed. How do you know that? If five or six people have walked through this small shed, evidence has been altered. The question is, how much?" I proclaimed.

"Well, first, the truck is still here, and Neumann had one of his deputies, a new man, Tripplett, Grover Tripplett, take a whole roll of pictures. Before they left, Neumann placed this padlock on the door himself and gave me one of the keys. Brody, I was here for all of yesterday's investigation and preserved the scene as best I could," defended Osborne.

"I apologize, my friend; I meant no disrespect to you or any of the officers. You men were successfully solving crimes long before I arrived; it's just that I've seen firsthand what can happen when a crime scene becomes contaminated, accidentally, or for other purposes," I apologetically replied.

With that behind us, I began my investigation. According to Osborne, the victim's hands were bound to the steering wheel of the old Ford while his legs were tied together just above the ankles. His head had been secured across the forehead using an unusual knot pattern, keeping his neck in an upright position, not allowing it to drop to his chest, thus adding to the torture.

"I sure hope Deputy Tripplett got pictures of all that. Remind me to call the sheriff as soon as we finish here; I can develop the film tonight and make copies for both departments," I explained to the surprised Detective Jason Billings.

"Seriously, you can do that?" Billings probed. "You have access to a darkroom?"

"Later Billings, later—you have no idea the extent of this man's abilities," revealed Osborne to his new partner.

We spent the next few minutes looking but not touching anything inside the shed.

The weight of the silence was finally lifted when Osborne asked, "What is that on the running board?" pointing to the passenger side of the worn-out *Tin Lizzy*.

"Looks like flour, is that flour?" asked Billings, extending his right hand toward the truck.

"Stop! Don't touch it!" I screamed while reaching inside my jacket pocket and retrieving a small brush and a chemist tube. "Let's carefully secure it in this to get a closer look later."

"Osborne, who is this guy? Secure it so we can get a closer look at what? It's flour, plain old flour. They have tons of it in town; I think Acme has it on sale this week. We'll swing by and get ya all you want," flouted the sarcastic Billings.

"I'm going to overlook your satire for now. Remember our agreement: we need each other. I refuse to waste time explaining myself. Now, kindly step aside so I can collect whatever is on that running board," I said, using a firmer voice.

After finishing our investigation outside the truck, Osborne turned his attention to the inside walls of the shed while Billings, still a little steamed, searched outside. I focused on the truck's interior, finding only one thing of interest: a white feather on the right-side floorboard. Again, I went inside my jacket pocket, retrieved tweezers, and used them to collect my discovery.

"What do you make of this, Will?" I asked.

"Ah, looks like a chicken feather. What does it look like to you?" Osborne answered with a question.

"I know it's a feather, but what is it doing inside this truck? How did it get inside this old truck? I don't see any other feathers, certainly no other white ones." My probing questions mounted.

"Brody, look, you've proven to me that you are extremely intelligent. Heck, you're a lawyer, for God's sake, but sometimes a chicken feather is just a chicken feather. What do you think it is?" conceded Osborne.

"You're probably right, but other than this, this truck is clean—not even a fingerprint. Are you finding anything?" I asked, directing the attention to Osborne's investigation.

"No, nothing. I'm going outside to see if Billings needs help. Are you about finished?" the veteran Winchester Lieutenant asked.

"Yeah, let's close this up and get to the morgue," I suggested as we left the confines of the death chamber.

We secured the shed and began searching for Detective Billings. We found him sitting with his back against a tree, still fuming from our earlier debate.

"All finished?" I asked, wondering where round two would take us.

"I circled the building twice and found nothing but a hornet's nest in a tree behind the south corner. I did, however, notice something over there." He pointed toward the entrance road. "Correct me if I'm wrong, but aren't those cigarette butts? I didn't pick them up knowing how sensitive you are about touching things," sneered Billings.

With the detective proudly taking the lead, Osborne and I followed to examine his findings. Once there, it became obvious someone stood guard over the torturous shed. I handed my tweezers and a fresh tube to Billings, extending professional courtesy.

"Looks like four, no five butts. Do I put them all in the same tube?" asked Billings.

"Sure, if you can get them all in without damage," I answered. "Any chance we can find the brand?"

"They're *Lucky's*," Osborne announced.

"How can you tell? I'm picking them up, and I can't tell what they are," Billings asked.

"I see an empty Lucky's box on that thorn bush," Osborne bragged with a grin.

We continued our investigation of the area but found nothing of value. We fought the brambles back to the car, where both officers agreed that I should hold all evidence in my safe until tomorrow, Friday, May 15th, 1931.

I dropped both officers back at city hall and then visited Sheriff Neumann to offer my services by developing the crime scene film.

Approaching the county sheriff's open door, a deep scratchy roar bounced off the walls. "What do ya' want, boy?"

"I'm not sure you remember me, I'm—"

"You're Forde, yeah, I remember you. You're that *pissant* that's making promises all over the county. Johannsson's stuck with you; I'm not. So, what do ya want?"

I stood silent, collecting my thoughts, allowing my temperature to drop before escalating this meeting, which was exactly what Neumann wanted. "I understand one of your deputies photographed the crime scene in Nain yesterday. I want to offer my services by developing the film for you at no cost to the sheriff's department. I mean, why pay if you can get them developed for free, right?" I reasoned, using my best logical voice.

Still seated at his huge oak desk, Neumann responded, "You got a darkroom? Who the hell has his own darkroom? The only darkroom in town is at Peoples Drug Store, and they only develop two days a week. You live at the Washington Hotel, don't you? How do you fit all that equipment in your room?" the probing sheriff asked.

"I actually have several rooms on the fourth floor; I use one room as a darkroom. It really doesn't take that much space; it just has to be perfectly dark. I'm a qualified darkroom technician," I said, conveying my abilities.

"Technician? You think mighty high of yourself, don't you... *Mr. Technician.* Tell you what, I'm going to let you develop these." He reached into his desk drawer and tossed me the film. "Make a set for Johannsson, two sets for me, and I already know you're only offering so you can make a set for yourself. I want Johannsson and my sets done by 9:00 a.m. tomorrow, understand, *boy*?"

I paused again, not allowing my temper to drop but to 'draw my line in the dirt' with this arrogant bully with a badge.

After four or five seconds, I countered, "Look, I appreciate your sacrifice in serving our country in the last war. I respect you as a sheriff and the difficult task you have, but I have taken my last insult from you. I am not a boy; I'm a man! I've taken my last insult. Do you understand me?"

Silence filled the room, then, without warning, the behemoth of a man stood and stepped from behind his desk, extending his massive right hand in the name of respect. "Look, son, I've got nothing against you. I don't know you, but you gotta understand: you ain't from here. People like you come and go all the time; the rest of us, we gotta live here. It ain't personal; it's just life in a Southern town," he said, echoing words I'd heard before.

Not knowing what to say, I again stood silent. Neumann's evaluation made sense. My first thought was Kate Brathwaite's statement on our first day: '*Southern is something you have to be born with; it can't be taught.*'

After the War Between the States, the South was victimized for decades; some of it they brought on themselves, but not all of it. Virginia contained more Civil War battlefields than any state in the country. From her coastal shores to the Blue Ridge Mountains, the bulk of the war was fought on Virginian soil. The City of Winchester changed hands seventy-two times during the conflict. A few broken bodies of that horrific nightmare still lived in Winchester, still trying to pick up the pieces of shattered lives. Sheriff Neumann validated Kate's lesson; '*you can't teach Southern.*'

After shaking the sheriff's hand, I changed the subject. "Sheriff, you mentioned earlier 'that Johannsson was stuck with me,' what exactly did you mean by that, if I may ask?"

"The mayor is all over his ass, these disappearances and all. See, I don't work for or answer to the city; I answer to the state. Now, I gotta get along with all the city folk, but I don't fall into their chain of command; they got no power over me. And, I've lived here all my life; that's something neither Johannsson nor the mayor can say. Bottom line, ain't nobody in this county I answer to, nobody."

"Well, Sheriff, we have one thing in common: I don't answer to the mayor, Chief Johannsson, or even you, sir. I respect you and your office's pressures, so, moving forward, can we forego verbal hostilities?" I asked.

"Sure, why not? So, you really got a darkroom? Have my photos here by nine in the morning; shut the door on your way out."

Not wishing to push the issue, I followed my instructions, making sure I respectfully shut the door. While no closing words of encouragement were given, he firmly shook my hand; I guessed that was worth something.

I stopped by the office to find the O'Connell sisters working together, closely examining the mysterious polka-dot dress.

"So, what have you two sleuths uncovered? Has the dress told you anything?" I inquired.

"Told us anything? Clothes can't talk. Is he serious, Ash?"

"You'll get used to it, sis. He's like that, and yes, he is serious," Ashley jokingly responded.

"To answer your question, and it's a stretch, I think the *dress has spoken*. What do you make of this? Could this be blood?" Ashley asked, pointing to a light stain on the shoulder.

"I don't know; it's hard to tell. The dress was in the river for nearly a day. Let's try something; Emily, go into the bathroom and bring the hydrogen peroxide and an eye dropper," I said, sensing a teaching moment for my two inquisitive employees. In a matter of seconds, the newest team member returned, handing me both items. I slowly placed three drops of the peroxide on the stained area. "Now we wait approximately three minutes to see what happens," I instructed.

"What are we looking for, boss?" Ashley asked with a puzzled look.

"We are looking for tiny bubbles that should surface if this is indeed blood," I said, explaining the chemistry lesson.

"How would he know this, Ash? This is creepy," Emily said, as her nose cringed.

"It's not creepy; it's science, I think? You'll get used to it. I did," Ashley assured.

"You're not helping, and, for the record, Ashley, you've always been a little weird yourself," countered the younger O'Connell sister.

"Ladies, you do realize I'm standing right here, and, for the record, Ashley is not weird. A little quirky, but not weird," I said, prying my opinion into the conversation.

"Thank you, Boss. I think. I don't see any bubbles; that's bad, right? So, no bubbles. What's that tell us?" Bewilderment overtook Ashley.

"That this is nothing more than a stain. It could be blood; who knows? The test was something I saw a few years ago when I was... never mind." I abruptly stopped my words.

"When you were..."

"So, what else have you found about this dress?" I asked, interrupting my curious assistant.

A moment passed before Ashley offered, "Well, we believe Mrs. Brathwaite wholeheartedly; this is not Jo's dress. This dress size is too large for Jo, and it has been handmade, you know, like something a grandmother would make for you."

"Educate me. Your assumption is based on what?" I asked.

"This is an older dress, probably passed down, like from an older sister or cousin. It shows signs of fading from age and has been altered several times, as if it was made to fit a progression of girls," Ashley surmised.

"I can relate to that; I've inherited many clothes from Ashley," intervened Emily.

"Don't complain; you got some really stylish stuff. I have exceptional taste in clothing and shoes; don't forget the shoes," Ashley said as she established her skills in the world of fashion.

"Ladies, focus, please. Can we stay on track? You said 'handmade,' based on what?" I said, as my sewing ignorance surfaced.

"When you look at a factory-sewn garment, there are no gaps between the stitches. Also, the edges are *surged*. On a handmade dress, the edges of the fabric are raw," explained Ashley.

"What does *raw* mean?" I inquired, overwhelmed by this conversation.

"The edges of the fabric will unravel over time; this is definitely an older handmade dress," concluded Emily.

"Wow, a double team. So, I'm guessing you both have sewing experience?" My curiosity grew.

"He's a *city boy*, Emily. What else can you say? He's smart in many areas but lacking in so many more. Yes, we both have extensive sewing experience; it's one of the requirements to land a suitable husband. That and cooking—it's a southern thing, you wouldn't understand."

As I soaked in my newfound knowledge of the seamstress world, I was again reminded that *Southern is born, not taught.*

"Okay, this is not Jo's dress, so how does this help us move forward?" I asked, enjoying this moment.

"First, since this does not belong to Jo, who does it belong to, and why is this the last thing Jo wore? How did she end up with it?" Ashley delicately asked, fighting back her tears.

"Excellent questions. Unfortunately, there are there are no answers tonight, but we will find them; we owe it to Jo and her family," I declared, ending the discussion.

Following a moment of reflection, we called it a night. Because of the late hour, I drove both women home. Ashley had her own place, while Emily lived with her parents.

After the short drive, I reached my apartment; at the door were my demons, anxiously waiting for my arrival. I got ready for bed, praying for a restful night of sleep, but my mind kept returning to my personal abyss. The room was dark and my eyes were closed, yet I saw the demons laughing and dancing, fanning the flames, celebrating my failures. My thoughts turned to the words of Shakespeare, through his creation Hamlet: "*For there is nothing either good or bad, but thinking makes it so.*" Was the bard suggesting the demons were my fault? Did I encourage their visits because I *didn't* want to forget? Dear God, hold my hand; I feared this night.

Chapter Eleven

E xhaustion finally brought sleep sometime after 3:00 a.m. It was now time to welcome the glorious sunrise, my comforting friend. The demons were gone, so for the moment, life was tolerable. Then I thought of Kate Brathwaite and wondered what demons haunted her. First, her beloved Joe was buried in an unmarked grave in France. Now, her only child was brutally murdered, and she was left with only unanswered questions. Suddenly, life didn't offer as much as it did seconds ago.

Keeping my word, I stopped by Sheriff Neumann's office, giving him the two copies I had promised before 9:00 a.m. Fortunately for me, he was on the phone dealing with a missing car near Brucetown, just north of the city.

As for Johannsson, he was in the middle of berating two young members of his department. Seeing me, he plucked the envelope containing the finished product of my efforts while not pausing his rant. I hoped in a future generation, someone would write a manual on creating a more productive work environment. I could always dream.

I reached the office to find Ashely and Emily waiting for me with hot coffee and a dozen of Golden Glow's finest.

"I thought you might appreciate a hot doughnut before we head out," exclaimed Ashley.

"TJ outdid himself this morning. These are still hot; they're the best doughnuts in town, right, Ashley?" I answered, reaching for the delightful breakfast treat.

"You know it, boss. Nothing but the best, I always say," chimed my pastry expert.

We took a little time to plan our day, committing most of it to the Brathwaite family. I wanted Ashley to find a measure of closure for this part of our ordeal. I needed her to move beyond today, clearing her mind, allowing us to find those responsible and bring them to justice. She must not be allowed to welcome demons into her young world.

"Emily, I need you to do an important job today; I want you to discreetly photograph the people attending the funeral. You must remain in the background, getting as many in each shot as possible. I can't begin to express how important this task is or how difficult it will be. People will not be receptive to being photographed during this vulnerable time. Are you up to it?"

"I can do it, Mr. Forde."

"What's this, Mr. Forde stuff? My name is Brody," I reminded her of our first meeting.

"My sister is a stickler for protocol. I told her your name was Brody, but does she listen?" Ashely said.

"Mr. Forde told me what to call him, but I remember what Daddy taught us: always respect our elders and people in authority," explained Emily.

"Well, you may call me Brody. So, which am I, elder or authority?" I asked, wondering if she sees me as an older man.

A few seconds of silence passed, then both women laughed, neither offering an answer. We enjoyed the pastries, finished our coffee, then headed out the door; this would be a challenging day.

Silence dominated the twelve-mile ride from town to the little church in Hayfield. Nestled in a most picturesque setting, finding a more tranquil place would be hard-pressed. If only we were here for a more pleasant purpose.

The service was a simple graveside event, which I learned was somewhat of a custom. The single-room eighteenth-century church, though loaded with charm, lacked the capability of holding the anticipated large gathering. Unfortunately for Mrs. Brathwaite, attendance was low; less than twenty. My heart was heavy for Kate; she deserved better.

An advantage of the small crowd was that one could easily remember those present. Two faces, however, seemed out of place. The first was an attractive woman shedding tears so heavy that her makeup streamed down her beautiful face. The second was Robert Poston, who also fought back tears and stood back from the group. The unknown woman could probably be explained, but Poston's presence was a surprise.

After the preacher finished his final prayer, Flavius invited everyone to the Brathwaite home for what he called '*a bite to eat and the sweetest tea you'll ever taste.*' The ladies and I agreed; we couldn't miss the *sweetest tea.*

Arriving at the Brathwaite home, we found no dog. "Where's Homer?" I asked while stepping out of my Chrysler.

"He's in the barn, sleeping; heck, he might be dead with that old dog. Who can tell?" replied Flavius in a humorous tone. "I hope you all are hungry. We have way more food than people."

Stepping onto the porch, we were greeted by the grieving mother, who thanked the three of us for honoring her daughter. After a huge hug, Kate introduced us to a pleasant old man seated near the far-right corner of the porch.

"Homer, I want you to meet Mr. Forde; he's the one I've been telling you about. He's going to find out who did this to my baby," Kate introduced us.

"I thought Homer was the dog. Are you named after the dog?" Ashley asked.

"Yes, Miss. When I was born, my dear momma took one look at me and said, he's got the face of a mutt; I'm going to name him after the dog," the quick-witted stranger with a deep, scratchy voice answered.

"Don't let this ole fool tease you, child. Homer was Jo's dog; she got him when she was about twelve or thirteen and named him after this nutcase. He was my Jo's closest friend," Kate informed while fighting back the tears.

Now standing, Homer embraced Kate, giving her a light kiss on her cheek. We learned Homer was Joe's best friend, having grown up together in the tiny village of Gore. Joe was a year older than his friend, but they formed a tight bond so strong that when the United States entered The Great War in 1917, both rushed to the recruiting office, answering the nation's call to fight the dreaded Huns.

After Ashley's awkward moment passed, we all were drawn inside by the enticing lure of country cooking. The kitchen was a step back in time: a vintage wood stove, a hand pump over the kitchen sink, and a window displaying the beauty of North Mountain. This room could easily find its way to the cover of the *Saturday Evening Post*; Norman Rockwell should be so lucky.

"Forde! You listening?"

"I'm sorry, Flavius, what were you saying?" I was drawn back to the present.

"I asked if you would like another slice of ham. It was home-raised, just like everything on this table, and it was all Kate's hard work," Flavius bragged of his sister-in-law.

"Now you stop that, Flavius. All I do is plant the seed and pull a few weeds; the Lord does all the work," Kate modestly explained.

"I have to say, Kate, this is one of the finest meals I have ever eaten; thank you so much for your hospitality. And Flavius, you are so right, sir. This is the best sweet tea I have ever tasted," I conceded while reaching for another hot roll to accompany my third slice of ham.

After finishing our desserts, the ladies, including Ashley and Emily, remained in the dining room while the men returned to the porch, a few to grab a smoke and, for the rest, the opportunity to enjoy the pleasantness of a soft afternoon breeze.

Conservations ranged from Kate and the farm to the Depression, politics, and how much money Babe Ruth was making to hit a baseball. Finally, the women joined our filibuster.

"Have y'all fixed everything that's wrong with the world? We could hear most of it through the screen door. So, y'all don't like President Hoover. Tell you the truth, I ain't got too much good to say about him myself," Kate proclaimed while taking a seat near Homer.

"Kate, I have to ask, how do you accomplish everything, your beautiful home, this farm, livestock, crops? How do you do it all?" I asked, still trying to understand the ways of country life.

"Mr. Forde, you learn early if you don't do it, it just ain't going to get done. I do have help; a couple of boys up the road help with farmwork in exchange for huntin' rights on my property. I hire workers during the plantin' season and again in the fall when it's time to harvest and butcher. Homer helps when he's able. Usually, no money changes hands; I trade food for work," the practical widow explained.

"You're an amazing woman, Mrs. Brathwaite," I exclaimed.

Another hour passed when the three of us decided it was time to return to Winchester. We said our goodbyes, leaving the mourning mother. The conversation was light for most of the ride, although Ashley asked why cleaning up after a meal was not divided equally, with the men pitching in. Unfortunately for me, Emily uncharacteristically agreed with her sister. Help me—I was outnumbered and sinking fast.

Before dropping the ladies off, I asked Ashley if she would be willing to meet on Saturday morning to go over the events of the last couple of days. Hearing this, Emily quickly informed me she had nothing to do on Saturday and would welcome the opportunity to learn. We agreed to meet at the office at 10:00 a.m. and that I would be buying lunch afterward. As Emily exited my car, she handed me the roll of film from the memorial service. Not ready to be home alone, I decided to visit Max and feed the Chrysler. I also hoped to learn more about Joseph Brathwaite and some of his friends. Pulling up to the pumps, the sound of metal hitting the back wall of my friend's shop echoed through the place.

"Sounds like your Indian is trying to leave the reservation."

"Just what I need, somethin' else that don't work. What do ya want, Sherlock?" returned the old man.

"I need a fill-up, and can you check the oil and water? We've been through a lot this week," I moaned.

"We've all been through a lot this week. If a little gas and water can solve your unpleasant week, ask yourself, was it really that bad?"

Max was right; my week hadn't been that difficult. I just left a mother who buried her only child. On top of that, few people offered any sign of comfort or support. Why did so few people attend Jo's memorial service? And worse of all, we had no solid leads into her murder.

Suddenly, a shout came from the gas pumps. "Pull your car closer; the hose can't reach that far. I gotta ask, who takes care of you when I'm not around? Honestly, how damn dumb are you?" my friend sarcastically asked.

"That's why I come to see you as often as I can; no one can take your place, Max. And you're right; sometimes I am just plain dumb, like right now," I agreed, not understanding the hostility.

"Now that we agree on that, what's wrong? I hear your Brathwaite case is a mess, and Johannsson's put a spy in your office," the interrogation continued.

"How could you possibly know all that? Do you have a spy in my office?" I asked, wondering how Max always knew my actions.

"When you pump gas for a living, you hear things—lots of things. Things like me sending a dear friend's widow to you to find who killed her only kid, and right now, you got nothing, absolutely nothing. Son, you disappoint me!" as the aggressive tone grew.

"I don't need a reminder. I know it's going slow, extremely slow, but I am doing all I know how to do. What do you want from me? What do you know that I don't know?" I tried to deflect.

"It ain't about what I know or don't know; it's about what you know and can prove. Ain't it about high time you stop feeling sorry for yourself? You're the college man—what did they teach you? Was all that schooling just for show? I mean, why did you go in the first place?" Max asked, pushing me to my breaking point.

"I went because my father ordered me to go!"

"Again, poor you! Have you ever noticed everything in your life is someone else's fault? Your father provided you with a top-shelf education; my father threw me out of the house when I was fourteen years old—fourteen years old! I was all alone to find my way in the world, and I did just that. If you're looking for sympathy, the Baptist church is just down the street. You want to know what I think: it's time you get up off your ass and become a man!"

The words cut through me, deep into my heart. Had I alienated the only honest friend I'd ever had? Memories rushed through my mind. I'd heard these words before; they were why I now call Winchester my home. But was this city really my home? Was it just an imaginary refuge, a place I believed I could hide from the past? I'd never been this low or felt this alone—not even that night in New York when—my thoughts stopped. Where do I go from here?

Seconds seemed like hours. Torturous hours. I silently paid Max for my gas and got behind the wheel. Before I started the engine, Max slowly strolled toward my car, calculating each step.

Fearing the worst, I cranked the window down and respectfully asked, "Chess Sunday?"

"Board will be ready at one. Don't be late, Sherlock." My mentor patted my left arm, resting on the door.

No words had ever meant more—though angry and disappointed in me, I still had my friend. He hadn't abandoned me; he'd supported me by teaching me to find my own answers.

Now home, Max's words swirled within. *Time to get up and be a man?* Again, what was I missing? My whole life has revolved around that question. I am always missing something, but what and why? Was I that ignorant, that naïve? What was wrong with me? Did I relish the role of victim? If so, shame on me. Ada Jo Brathwaite was a victim; why, I did not know. But this I did know: Kate Brathwaite was also a victim. An innocent victim who did nothing wrong. Max was right; it was time for me to do my job.

Chapter Twelve

The evening turned to night, prompting me to develop the funeral film. Emily had done a wonderful job capturing photographs of all attending, pulling it off without offending anyone. She was proving to be everything her sister said she would be, only it was a toss-up as to which of the O'Connell sisters held the greatest beauty.

The demons took the night off, allowing me a short but peaceful sleep. After a hearty breakfast, I arrived at the office and found my two associates and Lieutenant Osborne.

"Will, I didn't expect to see you here. What's up?"

"We need to talk; I mean, really talk. There's been a development, a horrible development."

"Another kidnapping?" I asked.

"Yeah, but that isn't all; there's also been another murder. We need to talk, now, alone!"

"You know my terms. Ashley and now Emily sit in on all meetings if I feel they need to know. Guess what? They need to know," reminding the Lieutenant of our agreement.

"Miss Ashley, yeah, I agreed to, but who is Emily? You never said anything about expanding this group. Everything mentioned is confidential; no one can know what we discuss," the frantic officer insisted while wiping perspiration from his forehead.

"Understood. Emily is part of my team, and since you came to me, remember our arrangement, I call the shots. You can trust her. I do. Agreed?"

"Agreed. Can we sit down? This may take a while. By the way, Billings is not here for a reason. In other words, this meeting never happened, understood?" as Osborne's irrationality continued to soar.

I nodded as we moved to the conference room. I was taken aback; Osborne was dangerously circumventing Johannsson's orders by meeting us without Detective Billings. This decision could cost him his job.

We were all seated with hot coffee while Emily sipped her hot chocolate. Before speaking, the nervous Osborne attended to the perspiration dripping from his forehead, still holding the expression of a desperate man.

"Will, what's wrong? Please tell us what has happened. Are you okay?"

My concern grew when Osborne loosened his gray necktie and then removed it completely. His face exhibited a bluish tint, a result of a missed morning shave while his hair begged for a comb. Further investigation brought my eyes to the wrinkled suit—My friend had slept in his clothes. What had happened to Will since we last met?

"Yesterday was the longest day of my life. Where were you? You just vanished. The office was closed, and no one knew where you were," criticized the lawman.

"We attended Jo Brathwaite's funeral. Remember what I told you the other day? Then, afterward, we went to the homeplace and had an incredible meal. Later, after dropping the ladies off, I went by Max's for gas and an unexpected lesson on life," I explained of my Friday movements.

"I never thought of Max. What a fool I am. A horrible day, horrible!" Osborne's rambling escalated.

"Please, my friend, tell me. What happened?" My heart rate increased, heightening my anxiety.

Slowly, the terrified police Lieutenant began. A huge gulp of coffee, another sweat wiping, a pause, and then the painful words surfaced. "The day started with my weekly butt chewing from Johannsson on how I'm not doing my job. That's not so bad; I'm used to it, but in the middle of it, a call came in reporting another missing teen, a nineteen-year-old Lester Pruitt. Brody, I knew this boy. He used to help me with spring chores around the yard; he went to my church—Brody, they killed him!" Osborne's eyes could no longer hold the river of tears fighting to escape. The dedicated peace officer tried but failed to contain the raw emotions many lawmen experienced in the line of duty.

A few seconds passed as Ashley stepped behind the grieving man and placed her left hand on his trembling right shoulder, bending ever so slightly, trying to console our friend. Minutes passed, then Will began to relate the tragic story.

"Lester was walking along Route 522, just outside of town, when a black four-door sedan, believed to be a late-model Buick, with, you ready for this, a pair of 2s and 7s on the black plate with gold numbers. Brody, it's a West Virginia car."

"Just like the two hobos claimed near Handley School, but no one at the police station gave them much mind because of their living conditions. Sorry, I interrupted, Will. Please, continue."

"Well, as Lester was walking, the car sped by, then all at once skidded in front of him, blocking his way. Two men jumped out, grabbed Lester, and tried to force him into the back of the car. This time, though, the assailants made two mistakes: first, they tried to grab a boy who carried a knife and knew how to use it, and secondly, they let someone see them." Will stopped momentarily, took another large gulp of coffee, and again wiped away the sweat and tears meeting in the corner of his eyes.

"Who saw him, Lieutenant Osborne?" asked Ashley.

"Claude and Opal Foley; they came upon the scene just as one of the men pulled a pistol and shot... He... he murdered Lester in cold blood. Oh God, why wasn't I there?"

"Will, please don't do this to yourself. This is not your fault... Don't blame yourself for this," I pleaded, remembering similar words directed at me not so long ago.

Silence filled the room as Will tried desperately to gather himself. Looking at my two associates, I spied a steady stream of tears marring the once-perfect makeup applied just hours earlier. Death will come to all eventually. Sad but expected. We mourned the passing of loved ones but found closure over time. Murder, however, was quite different. Not a natural passing, it was a cruel breach of God's plan. Did the act of murder ever find true closure?

Slightly more composed, Will continued the horrifying story. "Claude told me Lester swung his knife, catching one of the brutes in his left arm; that was when the other pulled a revolver and shot the boy in the chest. Both men jumped back in the sedan and sped away, leaving Lester gasping for air in a pool of his own blood. He was pronounced dead at the scene. Brody, he never... never had a chance."

"We're so sorry, Will. Is there anything we can do for you?" I asked.

"Just help me catch the bastards! You help me find them; I'll take care of the rest!" Osborne vowed.

"We'll all help you with this, I promise, we will find them, but you hear this, my friend: we are not going to take the law into our own hands, right? No matter how much we hurt, we are sworn to uphold the law, right?" I reminded the veteran police lieutenant.

"What law are you talking about? We've got over a dozen teenagers missing, no clues, no idea who is behind it or what is happening. Counting Lester, we have four murders, and other than a partial license plate number, no idea of who or why these people are dead."

"Four murders? How do you get four?" I questioned.

"The Brathwaite girl, yeah, I agree, she was murdered. The man in the shed, Lester, and, you don't know this, but we got another body that has been brutally sliced to death. Brody, I mean butchered. He was found yesterday just south of the Middletown Train Depot. The train engineer coming into the station spotted him lying in a ditch about two hundred yards from the tracks," Osborne added to the harrowing day.

As the emotionally charged conversation climaxed, Emily fought back tears.

"All this talk is terrifying, hard to believe, my dear," I said, handing her my handkerchief.

"It's—it's not only the talk... I just realized I... I know, er, knew Lester; we were in school together. He was a couple of grades behind me, but I knew him. He was a really sweet..."

The young woman stopped, allowing a momentary reprieve for her eyes. How hard all this must be for Emily, Osborne, and all lifetime residents. Merely two weeks ago, the most difficult things this little community had to deal with were apple prices, when he or she would finally tie the knot, or the location of somebody's moonshine. Peace and tranquility brought me here; now, an invisible evil resided, again punishing the innocent by delivering cruel, premature death. Was this my fault? Was I the means of transport for this Angel of Death?

"I'm okay; I just needed a minute to let all this soak in," Emily confessed as her sister gives her a supportive hug.

"So, Lieutenant Osborne, where do we go from here?" I asked, politely trying to harness the emotional *elephant in the room.*

"I don't know, Johannsson, Neumann... every lawman in Northern Virginia is off the track, especially Johannsson. Off the record, Johannsson's taken the locks off the guns; said to kill on sight, not to worry, that he'd take care of anything we do, that in the eyes of the law, he would make it right."

"Dear God, Johannsson is declaring war!" I exclaimed.

"Brody, the Chief wasn't the one who started this, but he's darn certain he'll be the one who ends it. And for the record, I agree with him; these people are animals. You know what you do to a rabid animal? You put it down!" shouted Osborne.

Realizing that my original planned meeting had been replaced, I suggested we adjourn for now and offered lunch for all at the Rustic Tavern. Osborne declined the invitation, deciding to return home to be with his family, a decision I was pleased he made considering what we have been through the past two hours. The remaining three of us needed to be away from the office, and the Rustic Tavern would be our solitude.

While at the tavern, we forewent work for the remainder of the weekend to appreciate life and be thankful for all God had given us. We paused, remembering those who had lost their lives, and offered a prayer for the missing teens. After a modest meal, we said our goodbyes and headed home.

Once safely in my hotel room, I decided to call my parents; it'd been a long time since I had heard my mother's voice. Regardless of age, nothing equaled the words a loving mother could provide. I gave the Winchester switchboard operator the Boston number as time stopped; it'd been so long. Suddenly, the oh-so-familiar slurred words rang in my ear, '*Hello, hello, who is this?*' With an aching heart, I ended the call. Hard as it was, I just wasn't ready.

Surprisingly, my demons remained docile; perhaps they feared the thought of my mother. Never to know the reason, their absence was cherished. With twelve uninterrupted hours of sleep and an inspiring Sunday morning worship service, I was ready to battle Max on the chessboard.

"'Bout time, Sherlock. Where ya been?" the chess aficionado asked.

"Where have I been? We always play at one; I'm ten minutes early." I was not late.

"By the time you get a bottle of pop and some boiled nuts, you'll be late—always are," Max answered, once again proving his point.

An hour of play passed, and I was holding on. Max was tapping his face with his left index finger; do I have him worried? I had just taken his last bishop, one of his favorite pieces. Conversation was rarely allowed while on the battlefield, so I was surprised when Max broke tradition by asking a question.

"Heard about the Pruitt boy, a real shame, good kid, good family. I know his folks; I work on their Oldsmobile from time to time. I also heard Johannsson wants to suspend Osborne but ain't going to.

What's Osborne done? Besides being friends with you, Osborne's a square guy."

"Why does the chief hate me so much? Other than being a private eye, we hardly know each other."

"He's afraid of you; you're smart and educated, and most of the time, you've got a clue of what is what. Although you do have your stupid moments." Both compliments and insults from my worthy opponent.

"Are you kidding? He's not afraid of me, and I doubt the man is afraid of anything... Surely not somebody like me."

"A barking dog doesn't bite. It's those quiet ones; they're the ones you need to keep your eyes on. You're not a barking dog, so you must have some bite. Just how much bite, he doesn't know, nobody knows. That's what folks are a-feared of. Son, *you ain't from here*, and that scares most folks."

Another hour passed, and, as usual, Max snatched victory from defeat in an unprecedented move of sacrificing his queen, luring me into the inevitable checkmate. And he called me the smart one.

"How's the Indian? Have you made any progress?" I asked, diverting the conversation.

"I'm missing more parts than I have. Do you think Sam is hiding them? No, he ain't that bright. Did I tell you what he did this week?"

"No, I don't think so. What happened?" I cautiously answered and asked.

"He was pullin' Spinner Jackson's ole Flivver in the garage, let his foot slide off the clutch, ran over the Indian's rear wheel, ended up drivin' Spinner's car into my workbench. Busted the grill and a headlight, not to mention part of my bench. He smashed up the Indian wheel so bad there ain't no way I can fix it. That boy is something else. What, I'm not sure."

"I'm certain he didn't mean to do it; accidents happen to all of us," I said, trying but failing to defend the youth.

"Look, just look at this mess." He pointed to motorcycle parts spread across the floor at the back of the small garage.

"Max, you're a top-shelf mechanic, but you will never salvage this motorcycle. It's too far gone; let the old *warrior* die with dignity."

"Alright, college boy, I'll make you a bet. I'll bet you $10 that I will bring this ole' Indian back to life before you solve the Brathwaite murder. Deal?" He extended his right hand.

"Deal. You may whip me at chess, but this is a sure thing. I'm going to enjoy spending your money, my friend."

"Just don't spend it before you earn it, and you sure ain't going to earn it."

We spent the rest of the afternoon listening to a little music, engaging in typical man's talk, and just enjoying the camaraderie of two lonely souls. As the sun descended, my brief break from life was ending. I leave Max's reenergized; despite everything else, this had been an exceptional day.

Monday morning: a fresh new week, a rejuvenated attitude.

Max opened my eyes; he had a way of doing that. His words, though sometimes painful, always carried the truth. It was indeed time for me to get up off my, er, butt and start doing my job. Today was the day.

Chapter Thirteen

E ntering the office, both of the O'Connell sisters waited for me in the conference room. The blackboard had been washed clean with new chalk carefully placed in the tray. Hot coffee awaited, and, as usual, a dozen fresh doughnuts adorned the center of the mahogany conference table. The girl's enthusiasm equaled mine, so it was time to get to work.

"Ladies, it has been a rough couple of weeks; I think it is time we begin to—"

"Yeah, yeah, that all sounds great. Good for you. Now, let's stop all this and get down to business. Emily and I have been thinking, why was Robert so upset? Heck, why was he even there? Boss, we think he's hiding something, and how about that—"

"Excellent questions. It sounds as if we're all on the same page, and I agree that it's time to get to work. Let's begin by focusing on the graveside. What about Robert? Why do you think he was there? Ashley, you first."

"Well, I think he was in love with her, and she rejected him. That could be why he said those nasty things about her. Remember, he called her a 'drifter in a skirt'? I got it in my notes."

"He also called her 'a tramp that wouldn't give a good man the time of day' when Osborne and I made our visit to the Poston house.

I agree with you; I think he made advances toward her and was rejected—probably sternly rejected. What do you think, Emily?"

"Both of you make good sense. But why would he be crying? Guys, he was really fighting back the tears. Why? Do you think he may be the killer?"

"I think he did it. He's called me twice asking for a date; he was polite but didn't take no for an answer the first time. I think he got the message the second time, though. He hasn't called since and never even looked at me at the funeral; let's face it, I'm *eye candy* when I'm all decked out," Ashley claimed while standing, turning like a model on a runway stage.

"Eye candy, really, Ash? You know what Daddy says about bragging."

"The only things more adorable than me are kittens and puppies, and I'm gaining on them. As for Daddy, he says it's not bragging if you can do it. Face it, I'm the bee's knees," countered Ashley, taking another twirl.

"Ladies, can we? Now, back to Robert Poston. Ashley, I need you to promise me you'll be extra careful; we don't know this guy. I guess he should be considered a suspect; rejection of love can definitely be a motive. But what about opportunity? Jo's murder was well-planned. Do either of you think he could have not only planned this but carried it out?"

"I never met him, so I don't have an opinion. I've typed all the notes in the file, but nothing makes him seem more than a protective son and someone who is just lonely. He could be the sensitive type," offered Emily.

"My biggest question is, why was he there in the first place? I mean, if he was planning to attend, why didn't he bring his mother? Mrs. Poston had a relationship with Jo. Why didn't she attend? For now, let's put his name on the board as a suspect. Now, what about the mysterious woman standing all alone in the back of the crowd? Who is she? Why was she there?"

"I can't tell you why she was there, but her dress was a Charles James design. Also, her makeup and her jewelry were nothing but the best. It's hard to find this kind of stuff in Winchester, more like New York. Boss, this is the best of the best," Ashley informed.

"Like the dresses and makeup we saw in Jo's apartment?" My thoughts returned to our first visit to the Poston home.

"Uh, yeah, just like it. What're you thinking, Boss?"

"I may know why she was there; she just became an important link to our investigation. We must find out who she is and her connection to Ada Jo Brathwaite." My curiosity rose.

"What's a Charles James design?" Emily asked in a puzzling tone.

"Charles James is a European dress designer, very high-end; his dresses are all the rage right now—luxurious fabrics and extremely expensive," I quickly responded.

"Boss, how do you know this?" a confused Ashley asked.

"I read a lot."

The three of us went back and forth on motives and possible suspects, but in reality, we came up with very little. Whoever was behind all of this was a master at covering their tracks. The sound of the clock chimed ten, so I needed to see Osborne about the Middletown murder that occurred last Friday.

I gave them both their assignments for the day. First, Emily was to finish typing the weekend notes and apply her organizational skills, beginning with the day Mrs. Brathwaite became our client. Ashley was to study the photos from Friday's memorial service; we must learn the names of everyone attending, especially the mystery lady.

I left for the police station while both women diligently worked.

Walking down the corridor of the police station, Chief Sonny Johannsson's threats echoed off the walls.

"I've had enough excuses; I want results! You damn sure ain't gonna find them kids in here. Now, get out there and find them. I want somebody in the *hoosegow* by nightfall, understand?"

Filing out of the tyrant's office were Billings, Osborne, and several officers I did not know, each missing large chunks of their butts. Seeing me, Osborne nodded ever-so-slightly to follow him outside as Billings dropped in behind me, heading for the same door.

Safely out of the station, I sympathetically asked, "What in the world is wrong with that man?"

"You know what they say: it rolls downhill. The mayor is all over him. I don't think the chief has slept in a week, and it's beginning to show," defended Detective Billings.

"Jason's right; the mayor is threatening all of us. All jobs are on the line," Lt. Osborne said, joining the defense.

"That may be Will, but threats are not the way to solve anything. What say we take a ride to Middletown and see the crime scene? Any takers?" I asked.

"I gotta' lead that I need to follow. Why don't you take Forde out there, Osborne? I'll meet up with both of you around one. How does that work for everybody?" asked Billings.

We agreed to meet at one o'clock in my office since neither detective was eager to endure another round with their boss. During the drive, Osborne revealed a secret that would definitely cost him his position on the force.

"Brody, what I am about to tell you must stay between us, understand?"

"Absolutely, what have you got?"

"Well, I was called out here, unofficially, by a friend of mine in the sheriff's department. I won't reveal his name; it could cost him his job since he wasn't following protocol," Osborne explained.

"I thought the Sheriff's Department and the Winchester City Police were working together?"

"We are on the missing teens. This is a murder, not a missing person's case; we're not connected on this one," explained Osborne.

"I understand. So, why am I here?"

"Because this is such an unusual killing, one of the reasons my friend with the county called me; I would like your opinion," confessed the lieutenant.

"Does anyone with the Winchester police know you were out here?" I asked, concerned with the depth of the hole my friend was asking me to step into.

"Billings knows, and I would have to think the chief knows," came the expected answer. "And, there's one other thing—I brought my camera and took a complete roll of film." The depth of the hole grew.

"How does Billings know?"

"Like me, he has friends in the sheriff's department. He arrived about half an hour after I was there. He doesn't know of the photos I took of the crime scene," added the nervous Osborne.

We agreed to keep the photos between us—for now anyway. In reality, there was only one way Osborne was keeping his job: we had to be the ones to break this case. Any other scenario left Osborne looking for employment during this depression. I couldn't allow that to happen to my friend.

We arrived at the Middletown Train Depot, an impressive structure running parallel to the tracks accented with a loading dock and large water tank. The resting spot for the deceased was approximately two hundred yards from the depot. It was hard to notice at ground level but was easily seen by the engineer elevated within the confines of the locomotive cab. As I stepped over the railroad tracks, I was drawn to the wooden ties holding the rails.

"Will, wait a moment. I've seen wood like this before."

"Yeah, they're called railroad ties; you can find them all over this county. So what?"

I knelt, removed my knife from my left pants pocket, and cut a small piece from one of the ties.

"Careful, my friend, I'm an officer of the law. That can be considered destruction of public property. I may be forced to arrest you." Osborne chuckled. "Seriously, what are you doing?"

"I need a piece of this wood to compare to a splinter taken from Jo Brathwaite's hand. If they match, it may tell us something of where Jo might have been in her last hours of life."

I secured my sample in one of the specimen tubes I always carried when investigating a crime scene. Could this be a break in Jo's murder case?

Once we reached what appeared to be nothing more than a deep ditch, a glaring fact emerged: the murder did not happen here. Osborne went through the possible chain of events when I interrupted.

"You do realize the body has been moved; he was not killed here."

"The sheriff's boys disagree; remember, this is their jurisdiction, not the city's."

"Well, it's obvious they're wrong. What physical evidence are they using to prove their fallacy?" I quizzed.

"I don't know; I'm just telling you what the county's report says. They were called to the scene around noon on Friday and concluded it happened here. That's all I know; I had no say in the matter as I was an unofficial participant," Osborne made clear.

"I sense Neumann's hand guiding this. But why the rush? There is absolutely no way he was killed here; the evidence doesn't support it," I emphatically proclaimed.

"Educate me. What are you basing your hypothesis on?"

"To begin with, why would the man be here in the first place? There is nothing here. Second, how could anyone sneak up on him? The victim was a large man, yet there was no sign of a struggle on the ground. I mean, there are no fresh rocks that have been overturned, not one. This ground has not been disturbed for years."

"Good points, of which I have no answers. I doubt the county deputies have any answers, either. Brody, I guess you're right, but, as I said, this is Neumann's jurisdiction, and he has the final say."

We concluded there was nothing this location could tell us; we would have to wait for the resourceful lieutenant's film to shed some light. I invited Will back to my office as it was too early for him to return to the police station; his butt hadn't begun to heal after the severe chewing it had received earlier.

"Forde, you really have to fix your door; that missing 'dot' drives me crazy," Osborne, once again, complained.

"You'll get used to it. I have. Ladies, we have company," I bellowed while entering the office."

"Boss, boss, boss! Guess what we found? We know Miss Mystery's car and license number; that was at the funeral. Emily got a detailed photograph of her leaving and the full license number; it's a West Virginia car. I told you my sister was smart," bragged Ashley.

We had a group hug to celebrate the discovery—finally, something to feel good about. I praised both members of my team.

"See, Lieutenant Osborne, if the Winchester Police Department would hire a couple of resourceful women like Emily and me, you all would solve some crimes."

"Maybe we should hire you, Ashley."

"No way you will ever hire me; I have a position with the Forde Detective Agency. We're the best; it doesn't get any better than that," boasted Ashley.

"I suppose not. In many ways, I envy you, my dear," confessed Osborne.

We all looked at the picture that would possibly lead us to the woman in question. Osborne recorded the pertinent information with the intent of gaining a positive identification, and it was at this moment Detective Billings walked in.

"What's going on? Why all the noise? I heard you all the way downstairs," Billings made known.

"Ah, today is Emily's birthday, and Brody just said he was taking all of us out for dinner this evening to celebrate," Ashley answered, accenting her words with that southern drawl.

While Ashley's quick thinking distracted the inquisitive Billings, Emily skillfully collected the pictures she had taken at Jo's funeral, hiding their secrets in a folder. I suppose a delicious meal was in order, even if it wasn't actually Emily's birthday.

The four of us had suppressed our news, but Billings freely volunteered his. The festive mood took a sharp decline when we learned that yet another teen had been taken.

"A seventeen-year-old girl from Stephens City didn't return home last night after her date. Her beau has had the screws tightened on him; he's clean, story checked out. Starting tonight, the mayor is placing the City of Winchester on a curfew beginning at dusk. No one under the age of twenty-five will be allowed on the streets; this includes your staff, Forde."

"I'm not under twenty-five, I can—"

"No, Ashley, absolutely not. I will personally drive each of you to and from your homes until the kidnappings have stopped and the guilty are in custody. There will be no exceptions, right ladies? And, for the record, you are only twenty-four, as I recollect."

"Right, Boss. We get it, thanks. Also, for the record, a gentleman never speaks of a woman's age."

Ashley's proclamation brought a few chuckles before Billings advised Osborne to return to the station to get his curfew schedule for the remainder of the week. Apparently, all city police officers will be working their regular day shifts, and in addition, each will cover four hours of night patrol. Anyone violating the curfew will be jailed for the remainder of the night and fined $3, with the financial penalty doubling for each offense. Make no mistakes; the mayor was scared and desperate. He has imposed his version of martial law.

Little time passed before Billings and Osborne returned to the police station (God help them). As for the three of us, we celebrated Emily's *new birthday*. The unanimous choice was the Rustic Tavern. Once seated at our usual table, I shared my idea on the wooden splitter in Jo's hand. Finally, I praised Ashley for her quick thinking; Emily informed me that Ashley had the ability to talk her way out of any situation, and if a little lie is needed, oh well.

"I never lie! I *nudge* the truth along with just a *hint* of embellishment," explained the older sister.

"A nudge of this, a hint of that. You're not baking a cake, Ashley. What would Daddy say if he knew what you did today?"

"Huh? Who do you think taught me?"

The adventures today warranted an early dismissal. We'd all been working diligently and could use a little break, but also, I really wanted to develop the film Osborne gave me, and my curiosity always wins out.

Chapter Fourteen

I welcomed the two glorious hours in my makeshift photography heaven; the smell of the developer chemical took me back to the innocent days of college. Finally, the prints were dry and ready for inspection. Of the sixteen pictures taken, only two were blurry. Great job, Lieutenant Osborne.

I had an egg and bacon sandwich sent up while I pored over Will's work, and after several hours of nonstop gazing, one photo, shot from a distance, exhibited a disturbing image. The deceased appeared to be aiming a rifle while peering from a foxhole. A closer frame revealed that the would-be rifle was actually a tree branch carefully placed in the dead man's arms, thus giving the impression of a *doughboy*.

Several other pictures show a white feather peeking out of the victim's shirt pocket identical to the one found in the truck at the Nain shed. The skilled detective also captured four disturbing images of the slash and stab wounds, so whoever had committed this egregious act of violence knew exactly what they were doing. The killer was no amateur. Suddenly, my egg and bacon prompted an unwelcome return.

The study continued until midnight when I decided to give sleep a chance. To my surprise and pleasure, my demons also chose to rest this night.

Keeping my promise, I picked up each lady, delivering them safely to the office. On the door was a note from Lt. Osborne asking if I could meet him at the morgue at nine this morning. To my surprise, Ashley volunteered to accompany me, but I insisted she remain at the office to study last night's photos. I told her of the gruesome content of the photographs, but she assured me she could handle it. I did not offer my thoughts, as I wanted to get an unbiased opinion, and one thing you could count on was that Ashley would have an opinion.

A blurry-eyed Osborne was waiting for me as I pulled my Chrysler into the morgue parking lot. I had stopped to pick up two hot coffees but decided to skip the doughnuts for obvious reasons. I commended him for his photography skills and apprized him of my thoughts. Remaining silent, he shrugged his shoulders, gulped down the remainder of his coffee, and headed for the elevator to deliver us to the Tomb. Instantly, the disgusting odor attacked our fragile sense of smell.

Dr. Stenner, wearing the usual lab coat and scrubs, gestured toward the body on the table. "Good morning, gentlemen; I assume you're here for an update on our newest John Doe. Well, he's been through it, and Forde, this one is definitely a murder. The assassin is a professional; this man knows what he is doing. First, a rapid thrust into the upper left abdomen followed by a fast, ninety-degree twist. He then grabbed his victim by the hair, holding the head firmly back, then, with one fast swipe, cut the throat, nearly causing decapitation. Like I said, this man is a professional."

"Are there any unusual signs on the body, something that might help us identify this poor soul?" Osborne inquired.

"Sorry, no, he has been picked clean. No billfold or tattoos, no birthmarks, nothing. He measures 6'3" and weighs 212 pounds. The only thing unusual is his soft hands; this guy was unfamiliar with hard labor. He also came in wearing an expensive pair of leather shoes—I mean fine leather and, like his hands, soft. He had no jewelry, but he had been wearing a huge ring on his right hand; you can see the impression the ring left on his finger."

"Something like this, doctor?" I raised my right hand, exposing my college class ring.

"Yeah, just like that," came the coroner's reply.

"Is this the work of a hitman?" asked Osborne.

"I've been here all my life, Lieutenant, just like you. I've never seen anything like this. To answer your question, I don't know," confessed the good doctor.

"Well, as I'm often reminded, I'm not from here, but I have seen something like this. I know the man responsible for this is a professional killer, but not like you may think. Gentlemen, Frederick County has a serial killer on the loose," I explained, as my voice trembled.

Time stalled as our hearts fell into despair. Serial killers were meticulous planners with the ability to blend into society. Because of this, they could stay one step ahead of the authorities. They found pleasure in taunting law enforcement, leaving a message. Maybe a white feather? To them, it was a game; to society, it was a nightmare.

"Doctor, as before, may I take several pictures of the body?"

"Sure, Mr. Forde, whatever I can do to help apprehend this menace. The same goes for you, Will; whatever I can do, ask," volunteered the physician.

While taking the pictures, my eyes were drawn to the wound on the neck.

"Doctor Stenner, may I ask your opinion concerning this area?" I pointed to the far-right side of the severed neck.

"Why, Mr. Forde, you should have become a pathologist. Yes, I see what you are questioning. The knife has a jagged edge on the blade. I should have noticed that. Boys, I'm getting old; the eyes are failing me."

"Also, can we conclude the assailant was left-handed because the exit appears on the left side, suggesting the cutting pattern is right to left?" I continued.

"Again, yes, the cutting is right to left, suggesting the killer held the weapon in his left hand," Dr. Stenner concurred.

"Mr. Forde, may I call you Ambrose? Your attention to detail is to be commended. I am embarrassed at my failure to see the obvious. I sincerely apologize to both of you. Can this be our little secret?" the doctor asked with a chuckle.

"Doctor, yes, please call me Brody. There is no need to apologize; you have been swamped. The lighting here is not the best, and I see no one assisting you. What secret? These findings are in your report, not mine."

The photo session, now over, offered freedom, allowing the three of us to venture outside to enjoy the fresh scent of spring. Being true to his habits, the veteran doctor fired up a Chesterfield. Does the smoke kill that awful taste trapped in your throat? Nevertheless, Doc finished his cigarette and bid us farewell.

Osborne headed home for a shower and a change of clothes, saying he would meet me later this afternoon. I followed his lead, heading to my apartment on a similar mission. Soap, hot water, and a fresh set of clothes freed me of foul outward reminders of the morning. I was, however, considering a cigarette; perhaps Dr. Stenner was on to something. All that aside, I was now back at the office.

"Ashley, could you get the splinter we took from Jo Brathwaite's hand? I want to compare it to the sample I retrieved yesterday in Middletown."

"You think she was in Middletown, Boss?"

"No, but if they are a match, it would prove she was near a railroad. Railroad ties around here are treated with a mixture of zinc chloride and creosote on the crossties, you know, to protect them from the winter elements."

We carefully examined the two pieces of wood, and they were a match. While this confirmed my hypothesis, it brought more questions.

"How does this help us, Boss?"

"For now, not much, but suppose she was running away from someone and tripped on a set of tracks; that could explain the gash on her forehead and how the splinter came to be," I hypothesized.

"It makes sense, but where? And who was she running from, and why?" my blonde assistant asked.

"Ashley, we have got to find the woman at the funeral; I believe she can answer some of these questions."

With all my excitement about the matching splinters, I failed to notice the new cork bulletin board mounted next to the blackboard. The photos were strategically arranged from the morgue, all crime scenes, and Jo's funeral. I stood amazed, studying the addition, and summoned both O'Connell girls into the conference room.

"So, whose idea was this?"

"It's kind of both of us, boss. Emily said the picture file was overflowing. I just thought this would help our investigation. What do you think?"

Before I could speak, Emily added, "Mr. Forde, the photo file was beginning to bulge, and really, what value are pictures if they are not in sight? This board will save time and help us see things from different angles."

"Actually, ladies, I think it is an excellent idea. I'm a bit ashamed I didn't think of it. Super work, both of you. Now, we have got to keep this door closed at all times. We cannot have just anyone seeing this board. Whenever we use this room as a conference room, we'll need to place a cover of some kind, like a large bed sheet, over it, okay?"

"Okay, I'll take care of it. And, boss, you need to drop by Solenberger's; I told them you'd be by today to take care of the bill, and there is a delivery and installation charge of three dollars."

The remainder of the day was quiet until Lt. Osborne rushed up the steps. He swung open the door so hard it banged into the wall. He stood in my doorway, out of breath, struggling with his words.

"I... I've got great news... great news... Two of the missing teens have been found. They're alive!"

"That is wonderful news! Where are they? What can they tell us?"

"Oh, it's not that great... I mean, it's great; it's just that they were never kidnapped. They eloped. They are somewhere in Georgia;

I don't know exactly where—just that they're safe. That's all that matters."

Stunned but also overjoyed by the news, we all joined in the celebration; hugs, handshakes, and tears dominated the moment. In the short time I had known Lt. Wilbur Osborne, I couldn't recall seeing him this happy. His job so often ended in sadness and often death. A lawman had to grasp this precious moment, holding the feeling as long as he could, because evil demons waited. After the second round of hugs, the exuberant officer sat in the conference room ready to relate the joyous events.

"Well, it seems that Bobby Catlett's oldest boy, Bing, ran off with Rafe Bowman's girl, Velma. Apparently, they have been seeing each other, unknown to Rafe, since she was only sixteen years old—actually, she's had her seventeenth birthday since she's been gone. They got hitched somewhere between here and Georgia."

"Well, other than her father, and I'm sure he's glad she's safe, this has to be a load off of everyone's mind," I deduced.

"I'm sure ole' Rafe is happy she's alive, but he's made it clear if he catches any sight of that boy, he'll kill him...Velma's his only daughter" interjected Osborne.

"Really, would he do something like that? I mean, sooner or later, they'll come home, won't they?" I pondered.

"Sure, Rafe isn't likely to actually kill him; he'll just put some salt and light bird shot in his backside," Osborne said, clearing the air.

I wasn't sure if Osborne was kidding, but the important thing was that this lowered the number of teens missing from thirteen to eleven. My thought process was interrupted when Will noticed the new addition attached to the wall.

"Hey, that's impressive, very organized. You do extraordinary work, Forde."

"Forde? This is obviously the work of a woman. Excuse me, Emily, two women," stressed Ashley.

"Anything else new? What angles are Johannsson and Neumann working on?" I asked.

"Neumann's not talking; that's just how he operates. He doesn't trust anyone, so don't take it personally. He's been the sheriff for a long time—set in his ways,"

"What about your boss? What's Johannsson saying?"

"I don't know. Johannsson has been poring over maps, trying to find a pattern, but nothing stands out. He's trying to find a common denominator with the teens. See, the chief thinks everything that has happened in the past month is connected: the teens, the wave of murders, including your Brathwaite girl. Yeah, he's now convinced she is connected. The problem, how?"

"You mean Johannsson has changed his mind on Jo Brathwaite's death, that it is murder?" I asked in amazement.

"Yeah, he's convinced, but he isn't going to say that to you. He's a proud man and hard to understand," explained the loyal officer.

For the first time, I was beginning to see a different side of Chief Johannsson. I still didn't trust him; in the end, he might even be involved in all of this. Much like me, he wasn't from here, and he had a mysterious past. Regardless of my personal feelings, Johannsson was a seasoned cop; I just had to decide if he was an honest cop or not.

The day ended positively; even Rafe Bowman had to feel better knowing his daughter was alive. It was a much-needed day for Lt. Wilbur Osborne, me, and my group; I mean, Will never mentioned the 'dot' missing in my name, so things must be looking up.

Chapter Fifteen

Wednesday morning was a beautiful day. The sun had been hard at work for nearly two hours, yet I remained in the comfort of my soft bed. The demons had remained idle for a third night, and I failed to understand what motivated them, but I was grateful for each hour of mental peace they allowed. I had a delightful breakfast and then needed to pick up the girls. I enjoyed a relaxing driving, and Winchester was such a beautiful town. If only we could remove the lingering cloud of grief, everything would be perfect.

I dropped the girls off at the office and headed to Max's garage; I had a few questions and needed my mid-week life lecture. Pulling up to the gas pumps, my mentor was holding court at someone else's expense.

"Cecil, you need a new set of tires. I'm to the point where I'm puttin' patches on patches. Heck, if you look close enough at the *shoes* on that ole tin lizzie of yours, you can see the air through the rubber begging to get out. Let me sell you a like-new used tire with a good tube for $2.50. You ain't gonna get a better deal," offered the generous Max.

"Naw, just fix mine, it'll be just fine," Cecil countered.

"Fine! I'll fix it for $4," barked the old mechanic.

"Max, you're an old chiseler! Four dollars, and don't even think of asking, '*How dumb I am.*' All right, sell me that old dry-rotted thing you got hidden in the back, probably stolen," Cecil surrendered as he pulled several coins from his worn-out dungaree pocket.

"Uh, Max," in a whispered voice, "kin, I pay you four bits today; settle up with ya a little later?"

"Yeah, a half dollar works, that's fine. Hey, bring me a half-bushel of beans and some taters when they come in, and we'll call it even. Will that work for ya?" bargained Max.

The two men shook hands, an agreement as binding as any contract. Max told the prideful man he could pick up his car shortly after 1:30 p.m. this afternoon. As rough as his language and as direct his opinions could be, the generosity in the old man's heart was a hundred times greater. The residents of Winchester had no better friend than Max Patton.

"What you need, Sherlock?"

"That was a very generous thing you did, my friend," I said in admiration.

"Well, don't tell anybody; I've got a reputation to keep. So, what do you need, gas maybe? I could use an actual paying customer; the electric bill comes first of the month."

"Sure, I always need to feed my chariot. Fill her up. While Sam is taking care of my car, can I ask you a couple of questions? They're about a couple of people I've met recently."

"Depends on what you ask; keep in mind, I've known these people around here a lot longer than I've known you. I'll tell you what I can, but people around here trust me; when a man loses trust, he ain't never gonna get it back. So, Sherlock, who'd you meet that's bothering you?"

"Not really bothering so much; I just would like to know more about them. For instance, I met an older man named Homer, a good friend of Joseph Brathwaite, I've been told."

"That's a sad story. Homer, I mean. Good man, very good man, and Joe's best friend. I mean, they were close. After the Germans sank the Lusitania back in '15, over a hundred Americans died on that ship, and lots of people wanted us in the fight. Then that Zimmermann Note stuff we read about in early 1917—you know, that the Germans were going to pay Mexico to invade America—well, President Wilson said we had to fight back. So, Joe, Homer, and a bunch more from here, well, they went and enlisted in the Army together. Personally, I never believed all that bull about Mexico invading; I think it was all made up to get us into the war. Back to Homer, he introduced Kate and Joe. Heck, Homer was the best man at their wedding. What's your problem with Homer?" Max asked while he pulled a used tire from the parts room.

"I didn't say there was a problem; I just said I met him last Friday, actually, after the funeral back at the Brathwaite farm. He looks awfully old to have fought in the Great War; I mean, he must be at least sixty."

"Son, war ages a man, some more than others. Homer is only forty-three. Hell, he's only a year younger than Joe would have been had he come home; they went to school together."

"The man I met has to be older than that. Are you sure we're talking about the same man?" I questioned.

"There ain't but one Homer Hunt. See, there's something you don't know about Homer—he was killed in France, right alongside Joe; it's just that his body hasn't laid down yet," Max surmised.

"What are you trying not to say? I'm not following you," I asked.

"Homer was gassed... Mustard gas, the worst kind. His body still moves, but his lungs are all but gone... some kind of cancer, I heard. He should have died years ago; living on borrowed time, he is, if you can call it that. Just living on borrowed time," Max answered while lowering his head.

"I'm sorry I asked. He deserves better," my head now hanging low.

"None of us deserve better. Life is what you make of it—some good, some bad. We don't get to choose what we get; we choose how we use what we get, that's all," exclaimed the old prophet.

"Hey, before I go, can I trade you a can of corn for my gas?" I asked, trying my hand bartering on the bill.

"Only if it's liquid corn in a jar. Now, get out of here; I've got a tire to mount," snapped the old man.

We spent so much time discussing Homer Hunt I decided not to ask about anyone else. I didn't wish to push my luck.

Back at the office, I was greeted by an overly excited assistant. The morning mail had arrived, and in it was a sealed envelope from Boston General Hospital. The results of Jo Brathwaite's blood and urine samples were here.

"Ashley, step into the conference room. Emily, you remain in the outer office; no one except Lt. Osborne is allowed beyond your desk today, understand?"

"Yes, Sir," she said, giving me the same left-handed salute Ashley had displayed several weeks ago. I have got to meet their father.

Ashley and I moved to the conference room's privacy. Hesitating, I opened the sealed parcel and examined the test results. My fear was confirmed. When finished, I passed the documents to my anxious assistant.

"Is this right? Jo was nearly three months pregnant? Is that what this says?"

"Yes, that is exactly what it says, and an unwanted pregnancy is both a motive for suicide and murder," I explained.

"But, how can they tell she was pregnant by just looking at her blood? I've never heard of anything like that."

"Actually, pregnancy is not detected in the blood; it is in the urine. Several years ago in Berlin, two German scientists, Aschheim and Zondek, developed a process of injecting the urine of a pregnant woman into the body of a mature female rat. Once injected, the rodent would go into heat, which could be ascertained by dissecting the animal. It's called the A-Z Test, a little complicated but reliable," I explained.

"A little complicated? That's your biggest concern? Boss, that's the most disgusting thing I have ever heard. I mean, injecting a rat, then cutting it open, yukky! And you're worried it may be too complicated."

"It is kinda sickening, but when you really think about it...just imagine cutting open a—"

"Okay, okay. You can stop now...You've made your point. Yukky is what it is!"

"You didn't read it all, did you? Jo had a large trace of heroin in her system when she died," bringing remorse to both of our hearts.

"But, remember, she couldn't have injected herself in her left arm; she was left-handed, right?" defended Ashley while handing the unpleasant document back to me.

"You're absolutely right, Ashley. She was drugged to distract the police, and, for the most part, it worked," joining Ashley's defense of Jo.

After our biology lesson, Ashley shared the test results with her sister while I called Lt. Osborne, asking if he could stop by later today. I did not go into details over the phone, fearing who might be listening. He agreed, hoping to be here before 5:00 p.m.

The remainder of the day was spent reviewing. It had been nearly two weeks since Kate Brathwaite entered my office. In a mere twelve days, so much had happened. The number of missing teens now stood at eleven, and two of the four murders that we knew were of a violent, torturous nature, yet only a couple of feathers loosely linked them. Why was Jo Brathwaite murdered? Was the Ivory Tower part of all this? If so, how? The only things we knew for certain about the Tower were they had expensive food, and they did not violate the Volstead Act, at least not to strangers.

The phone ringing interrupted the uncommon silence of the office. Lt. Osborne informed me he and Billings were running down a lead and would not be available until tomorrow morning. I was unsure where he was calling from, so I decided not to disclose the latest on the Brathwaite case. We agreed to meet tomorrow, at 9:00 a.m., at my office. With that, he ended the conversation.

While hanging up the phone, I instructed the ladies to close up what they were working on; it was time to call it a day. Once everything was secured, we all headed to my car for our journeys home.

I was not ready to face an early evening with my demons, so I decided to make a second visit to the Ivory Tower. Going alone might be a risk, but it was the only way I could learn of the escort process Jo

Brathwaite was a part of. My greatest fear was that no one knew where I was headed.

The drive was pleasant—actually, beautiful. Apple trees and hayfields dominated the terrain, with an occasional farm every few miles. I passed a Musselman's Apple Processing Plant in the small village of Inwood, West Virginia, that I failed to notice on my first trip. I envied those fortunate enough to have been born and raised in such an impeccable environment.

Safely parked, I paid the cover charge, allowing entrance to the Ivory Tower. However, the evening crowd was already seated, forcing me to pay an additional fee for a private table. The band was playing a near-perfect rendition of Cab Calloway's *Minnie the Moocher*, and this time, it was obvious that alcohol was being served. Remembering my initial visit, why was I allowed admittance?

Now seated, a young waitress wearing a white, tight-fitting blouse and a short black skirt approached my small, two-seat table. "May I bring you something from the bar? You look like a 'Whiskey Highball' man," the midnight black-haired hostess asked in a sultry voice.

"Um, I'm not sure—I'm unfamiliar with that drink. What's in it?"

"Oh, you don't want to know that; it would ruin the surprise and the sensation of the drink. You will love it, I promise," she said in a low, enticing voice.

"Sure, I'll try anything once," I said, trying but failing to hide my ignorance.

"Here is a menu while I get your drink. The lobster tonight is excellent," advised the intriguing beauty before she turned away and headed to the bar.

Pausing a moment, I scanned the room, which was the same room I had been in just days ago. Filled to near capacity, with a live orchestra playing, the Ivory Tower held an atmosphere of sophistication. The patrons offered no evidence of the country's financial downturn. Within the walls of the Ivory Tower, there was no Depression.

My hostess brought my Whiskey Highball and took my dinner order—I decided to try the lobster again, as had been suggested. The band brought nearly everyone to the dance floor with *Need a Little Sugar in My Bowl*. I sat amazed at a club of this proportion in a small town like Martinsburg. I was so preoccupied I failed to notice I was no longer alone.

"Excuse me, is this seat taken?" asked a slender, well-endowed beauty in a slinky black party dress, matching nylons, and stiletto heels. She carefully slid the empty chair back and joined me before I could answer.

"I believe the seat was waiting for you, Miss?" I answered and asked.

"I'm Jade, and you are?"

"Ah, I'm Johannsson, Michael Johannsson," I said, not wanting to use my real name and having a little fun at the chief's expense.

"So, Michael, what brings you to the Ivory Tower?" my temptress continued.

"I heard a man can find a good time here; I'm just looking for one." Was she buying any of this?

"I'm thirsty; buy me a drink?"

"What would you like?"

Before I could signal my hostess, she stood by me with my succulently prepared meal. "I hope this meets with your approval, sir. Something for the lady?"

"I'll have my usual," came the answer before I could speak.

"So, you're a regular?" I inquired.

"You could say that, I guess. I'm a close friend of the owners," my new friend responded.

In minutes, Jade was sipping on her sangria and enjoying the music while softly batting her light green eyes. In the meantime, I was possibly enjoying the most delicious one-pounder I had ever tasted. Having grown up in Massachusetts, especially Boston, I had a sensitive palate concerning seafood; no apologies were necessary when describing this meal. For the moment, I was back at the Union Oyster House in Boston.

"I asked, how is your meal? You seem to be paying more attention to it than me," Jade softly uttered while looking down and then back up from under her lashes.

"I'm sorry. My mind drifted for a moment. What were you saying?" I returned to the present.

"I asked if you would like to find someplace where we could be more comfortable. Perhaps you want to go upstairs; I have a private sitting room."

My heart rate increased. How far should I take this? Have my demons taken human form? I must see where the mahogany spiraled staircase leads. What answers were hidden on the second floor? I came here looking for answers; I had to see this through.

"I think that could be very enjoyable. I'm finished eating. Let me pay my bill, and yes, I'd love to spend some time with you." Words I had never imagined poured out of my mouth.

My check was paid, and the dance floor moved in full swing to the latest Duke Ellington sound. Jade and I climbed the cylinder staircase to the second floor. The corridor was dimly lit and seemingly went on forever. There were a series of doors on the right, approximately ten feet apart, while only two were on the left, maybe forty feet apart. Faint sounds of the orchestra could be heard, while a soft vibrating beat gave the walls life.

Jade, ever so gently, took my right hand and guided me to the third door on the right. We entered, finding a very poshly decorated room dominated by a large bed holding four deluxe pillows and high-end lush linens. To the right side of the bed was a lavish bathroom with a ball-and-claw soaking tub for two. An intoxicating aroma of light Jasmine filled the air; I stood silent as my eyes closed. In seconds, my mind and body were under Jade's spell. She leaned toward me and pressed her warm, soft lips to mine. It had been a long time since I last felt the passion of a woman. But the moment was about to end as I stepped back, severing our contact.

"What's wrong? I thought that was what you wanted. Are you a copper?" Jade questioned as the moment quickly vanished.

"No, I'm not a cop; I'm just a man who's been alone for a long time," I admitted.

"Well, this is not a charity, you know what I'm saying?" Jade fired back while reaching for a cigarette on the stand by the bed.

"Yes, I understand. Don't worry, you'll be paid—that much, I promise. Since I am paying, how much for a few minutes of your time?" I asked, fearing she might call someone to have me removed.

"$25 gets you an hour. How you spend it is up to you," Jade informed.

"Deal! Now, tell me, what is behind the two doors across the hallway?"

"That's no secret; gambling—all kinds of gambling. Why do you ask? I can get you in if you have enough cash," Jade offered.

"Alright, how about that large padded door across the dance floor? What's behind it?"

"I can't answer. I don't know—honest, I don't know. I think it is where they keep the booze, you know, if the law raids us," she continued.

"Why hasn't the Ivory Tower been raided? I can't believe the police don't know what's happening here," I continued my interrogation as I lit her cigarette, which was now in a sleek holder to prevent tobacco stains on her well-manicured hands.

"Why should the police care? Every copper in the county is on the payroll," divulged Jade.

We spent most of the hour talking, yet nothing relevant surfaced. I feared bringing Jo Brathwaite's name into the conversation. I paid her fee and added an additional $10 for her silence. Before I left, Jade gave me a passionate goodbye kiss, begging me to ask specifically for her the next time I was in town.

When I returned to the dining room, the party was still in full swing. I tried to get near the padded door, only to be 'redirected' by two very large men. Realizing my effort was futile, I decided to end my night at the Ivory Tower.

As I walked past the bar, I noticed a familiar face; the bartender was the large man who had threatened Osborne on our first visit. I walked up to him and said, "I enjoyed the Whiskey Highball, but if you substitute regular mineral water with Apollinaris from Germany, you will find it more effervescent, you know, bubblier—it makes the Whiskey Highball livelier. Try it. I think you will find that I am right," I said as I headed for the exit.

The drive back to Winchester allowed time for reflection. I gained knowledge, but did I learn anything beneficial? The women working at the Tower had a sensual, pleasing allure that men found hard to resist, myself included. Jade held a power over me, a power I didn't want to stop. I took a small sip of my drink, allowing me to maintain judgment. Had I finished it, my ability to think rationally would have been compromised. I learned one thing tonight: I enjoyed Jade's company.

Thursday began by oversleeping, so I was forced to alter my routine. There was no time for breakfast, which was never good; how anyone could start a day without a hearty breakfast was beyond me. I darted outside, not realizing a tremendous storm had moved up the Shenandoah Valley and belted Winchester with all it had. Of course, not knowing this, I did not have my umbrella... In seconds, I was soaked.

I drove through the pouring rain until I finally reached the office. I climbed the stairs to where I found the door swung open. I forgot to pick up the girls. Expecting the worst, I removed my .38 Smith & Wesson revolver and slowly moved toward the door when I heard someone going through a file cabinet. My heart pumped as if I were running a marathon as sweat mixed with my rain-soaked head. Creeping ever so carefully so as not to be seen, I entered, pointing my weapon at the intruder.

"Boss, you forgot us. Hey, please point that thing somewhere else; it might go off, and you will have lost your best detective, me!"

"Ashley, how did you get here?"

"We're both here; Lt. Osborne and Emily have gone to pick up some doughnuts. I've made a pot of coffee. Where have you been? It's nearly ten o'clock."

"Again, how did you and Emily get here? I distinctly ordered both of you not to come here alone."

"We didn't come alone, as you put it, and don't treat us like children. We took a cab; we thought about walking, but it was raining too hard. It cost forty cents, and I gave the driver a nickel tip. Don't worry about paying me back; I took it out of petty cash. All in all, it cost—"

"Let me guess, forty-five cents, right?"

"No one likes a smarty pants. So, what happened to you? Hey, you're all wet. Why are you all wet? Why are you late? You're never late. Did you have a late night or too much party? Did you have a date? What's her name? Is she a looker?"

"I overslept, that's it, all of it. I simply overslept. Did you really ask me why I was so wet? Where did Osborne and Emily go for doughnuts?"

"Did you really just ask where they went for doughnuts? Where do you think they went? Golden Glow, of course."

"Call them, tell Emily to bring me, for that matter everyone, a hot breakfast, pancakes, eggs, whatever, and bacon and ham, country ham, enough for everyone."

"Got it, boss. No problem."

Fortunately, the call to the Golden Glow caught Emily while still in the restaurant, and my order was filled. They typically didn't cater but were able to make an allowance since the O'Connell family were regular customers. Thirty minutes later, my breakfast was before me; the unsettling morning had stabilized. All was well.

Now it was time to get back to business.

I updated Osborne on the blood and urine results, including the pregnancy. I also shared my concerns about the mysterious woman at the funeral and Robert Poston. Ashley needed to interrupt, letting everyone know of my grand entrance. I reminded her that she didn't always have to tell everything she knew; this would have been one of those things that could have stayed between us.

I also told the Winchester lieutenant of my Ivory Tower adventure. Well, most of it. I chose to keep several portions to myself. When I finished, Lt. Osborne began his frightening presentation.

"Late yesterday, we got a call from a man with the Federal Bureau of Narcotics in Baltimore. Brody, you better sit down. The man in the morgue is Luca Marchetti, the son of Emiliano *the Burner* Marchetti. Brody, what have we gotten into? Do you understand who his daddy is?"

The depth of despair racing through my mind couldn't be measured. Luca Marchetti was murdered here in Frederick County in such a violent manner that the coming retribution would be unimaginable. Emiliano Marchetti was a *man of respect* in the ranks of the Cosa Nostra crime family, a high-ranking officer with tremendous power and unlimited resources. Whoever was responsible for Luca Marchetti's death hadn't long to live.

"I understand, and yes, I am aware of his father. What has Johannsson said of all of this?"

"Well, to begin with, he used to work with the man coming tomorrow, a guy named Colgate, Byron J. Colgate. Johannsson said if I get a reason or even a chance, shoot him, he'll take care of the paperwork."

"So, Johannsson doesn't like him... Does your boss like anyone? You're not supposed to shoot me if you get the opportunity, are you?"

"You really want me to answer?"

I momentarily stopped our conversation, first giving Osborne a moment to gather himself. Secondly, I wanted to allow my startled team an opportunity to voice their thoughts and opinions. While the mob had no beef with us, they did not hesitate to take action against anyone who got in their way; innocence would not be a factor.

"What are your thoughts, ladies? I want to hear what each of you thinks of all this?"

"Gosh, I don't know, Mr. Forde? This sounds like it could be dangerous, but crossing the street can be dangerous if you don't look both ways. I'm okay," Emily said.

"Ashley, your thoughts?"

"Boss, I want to be the first female investigator in Winchester; I can't get there if I get scared at every turn in the road. I'm okay, too."

"I have no problem if either or both of you would like to take a paid vacation until all this is over. I cannot emphasize this enough: these are ruthless men, both the Cosa Nostra family and the Feds. Sometimes, it's hard to tell the difference. If you want to take time off, you will still have your jobs when you return."

"Boss, we're not going anywhere, but a vacation when this is all over, well..."

"It's a deal. We three will tread very carefully, and Emily, let all of us be sure to 'look both ways' before we cross the streets, starting right now."

Osborne decided he had already spent too much time with us and took his leave. Since the rain had no intention of stopping, we focused on reviewing what we knew, what we thought we knew, and what we must learn. As the day ended, we agreed that the storm outside was nothing compared to the storm about to descend upon this little country town.

Chapter Sixteen

F riday, May 22nd, there was no rain, so at least I was off to a better start than yesterday. The drive across town was pleasant; streets were wet with mud everywhere, but the warmth of the spring sun would quickly restore order. I made my rounds, first picking up my staff, then, oh yeah, the doughnuts. I couldn't forget the doughnuts.

Once upstairs, we were surprised to see two guests waiting: Lt. Osborne and his sidekick, Detective Billings. Ashley unlocked the door, and the two officers headed straight to the conference room. The morning was about to take a turn for the worse.

"Gentlemen, I must say, I'm a little surprised to see the both of you so early. What can I do for you this fine Friday?" I asked.

"What are those pictures? How did you get those? Why, some of them are from Middletown, aren't they? How did you get these pictures? You weren't there; how'd you get them?" Billings demanded an explanation.

"I took them, Jason. And, before you go running to Johannsson, he doesn't know. So, there, you got me. I kept evidence from Chief Johannsson," confessed Lt. Osborne with arms down by his side and both palms opened.

A tense silence filled the room. How would Johannsson react when he learned the truth? This is the moment Billings had been waiting for; with Osborne out of the way, he would move up in the department.

Without warning, Billings stood and approached the evidence board.

"Is Marchetti holding a rifle? From this angle, it looks like he's firing a rifle. Did either of you notice that?"

"Why, no, Jason, may I call you Jason? I don't think I noticed that. How about you, Will?"

"Uh, no, I never noticed it either. You have a keen eye, Detective Billings. I'm glad you're here. Sometimes, all you need is a fresh set of eyes."

"Boss, you saw—"

"Ashley, thank goodness you just stepped in. Could you *please* bring Detective Billings and Lt. Osborne some coffee? You probably want sugar with your coffee, don't you, Jason? Will, I know you want sugar. Allow me to assist you with all the coffee, Ashley."

Confused but following my lead, Ashley retreated to the outer office. I assisted my protégé and, with a soft whisper in her left ear, informed her of our delicate situation and to play along. Once she understood, we returned to the conference room with coffee in hand.

"Brody, Detective Billings noticed something in the funeral pictures; he recognizes a woman standing in the back of the crowd. She must be important to you; you have the words 'Mystery Woman' attached to the picture," offered Osborne.

"Do you recognize her, Detective Billings?" I asked.

"You know, it's funny. I do, and I don't. She was in the station maybe a year ago, but I didn't handle the case. I'm not even sure she was charged. I think she may have been there bailing someone out of jail. I don't remember."

"Is there any way you could find out? I mean, would there be documentation of her being there?" I questioned.

"Do you know how many people come and go through our station in a day, a week, or every year? I'm not even positive it's her; I think it might be her. You can see the license number on the car she was driving; go through West Virginia's motor vehicle records. Surely, they can tell you something. You didn't take these pictures, did you, Will?"

"No, he didn't take these. My secretary, Miss Emily, took them."

"She does nice work. Osborne, we ought to hire her to take pictures for us. So, have you contacted West Virginia?"

"I've been working on it. So far, nothing. I told them I was with the Winchester police, and this was a possible lead in a murder investigation; it has been two days, and I am still waiting," explained the Lieutenant.

Not wanting to upset the unexpected camaraderie, I needed to satisfy my curiosity: why were they here so early? With federal agents about to ascend, I would have expected all hands would be on deck at the station. Yet two of the five Winchester detectives were here with me, a less-than-accepted private investigator; there had to be something I didn't know.

"Gentlemen, I hate to disrupt our productive session, but what brought you here this early Friday morning?" I asked, pressing the issue.

"Well, Johannsson has made it impeccably clear; he has no intention of working with Special Agent Byron J. Colegate. He's dumping the Feds on us and you," confessed Osborne.

"Me, Johannsson wants me?" I asked, shocked by the news.

"That's what he said. He said they have no jurisdiction in an unsolved, local murder," added Billings.

"Colegate wants to meet with us tomorrow morning at 9:00 a.m. here at your office. He apparently has the same feelings about working with the chief," Osborne informed.

"Johannsson is correct. Murder is a state crime, not a federal crime. If the victim's last name weren't Marchetti, they wouldn't be here. Oh, wait a minute, that son-of-a... He's using me as a shield. Johannsson's picking his poison; he hates me but found someone he hates even more. You gotta love your boss—he's a real piece of work!" I exclaimed.

"Yeah, and he's thrown us in as a bonus. Forde, I'm going to admit it: I don't trust you yet, but I'm willing to give it a try. Will, the pictures will remain our secret for now. But know this: if either of you go behind my back, I'll feed both of you to the wolves. Understand?" threatened Detective Jason Billings.

"Trust only works if it is a two-way street, agreed? May I ask what it is about me that you don't like? What have I done not to be trusted?" I asked, hoping for a reasonable reply.

"You play things close to the vest. You're educated and, by the looks of things, rich. Most folks are barely getting by, but not you. Why would a rich man come here and open a two-bit detective business? It just doesn't add up. The best thing you have going for you is that Max Patton trusts you. He doesn't hardly trust anybody, yet he trusts you. Why?" Billings questioned.

The detective's assessment of me was fine; I'd earn his trust, and hopefully, he would earn mine. It was true, I guessed; I did hold my cards close to my vest, something my father taught me at an early age. Regarding Max's trust in me, I would wear that as a badge of honor. If I can only earn the trust of one man in this town, let it be Max Patton.

The meeting came to a close, and we decided to meet each morning, when possible, to share information and to plan our steps. They agreed to call me later today when Agent Colegate got into town, thinking he might want to meet with all of us involved in the Marchetti case. Since Chief Johannsson blessed this union, it would be a shame to let it waste. The tyrant hadn't realized it yet, but he just gave me carte blanche access to the Winchester Police Department. Christmas had come early, and I didn't get the chief a thing.

When my staff heard of the bilateral agreement, they were less than enthusiastic, especially Ashley. Her concerns were that with the addition of the two men, she might be pushed back into a servient role reserved for women. In a short time, she had risen in the ranks, and she cherished it.

Her smile returned when I said her status had not changed; if anything, it would go higher. Osborne and Billings were temporarily on loan to us. I reminded her she was a full-time employee, and she answered only to me.

The afternoon turned into night, yet the two detectives did not call. I decided to drive the two ladies home as the clock chimed 6:00 p.m. Ashley agreed to work Saturday; however, when I learned that Emily had planned to spend time with her mother, I insisted she keep her date. A lesson I had learned the hard way was that family came first.

Upon entering the doors of the George Washington Hotel, the desk clerk handed me an urgent message from Lieutenant Osborne. A shooting had occurred on 129 N. Loudon Street in front of the Colonial Theatre and he requested my presence.

Not waiting for the elevator, I sprinted up the staircase to retrieve my Kodak and two fresh rolls of film. In less than five minutes, I was speeding toward Loudon Street.

Main Street was a mess: police and rescue personnel, not to mention dozens of bystanders, were everywhere. Someone needed to do a study as to why the most Christian-hearted people felt the need to gaze at something this gruesome.

Working through the mob, I found Osborne and Billings hovering over the deceased.

"Brody, you're not going to believe this one: a sniper from the outside third-floor balcony of the theatre fired a single shot, killing this poor soul while he was talking to another man, and nobody saw a thing."

"When did it happen?" I asked.

"Just after 6:30 p.m., on a Friday, no less, when everybody is in town doing their shopping," assessed Billings.

"Anybody been up on the balcony? Has the building been secured?" I asked.

"Yeah, I've been on the balcony, and I've posted four beat cops to stand guard. The theatre had only been open a short while, so there weren't many people inside—twenty or so and just a few employees. We have most of their statements, which don't tell us much," Billings informed.

"How did the shooter get into position? There doesn't appear to be an outside entrance to any of the balconies; he had to come from inside the theatre," I surmised.

"Actually, the theatre is part of the old hotel. It has easy access to the outside balconies; with the lights down low for the show, it would be easy to get up there. Right now, there aren't any witnesses," confessed Osborne.

"None, or just none that are willing to talk?" Sensing a figurative dead end, I decided to switch the interrogation. "Who's the victim?" I asked as I took a picture of the theatre.

"Name is Giorgio Cappelletti, Pratt Street, Baltimore. He had $22 in his billfold, a little change in his pocket, and a car key. And, one other thing, look at this. Have you ever seen a key like this?" asked Billings.

My eyes nearly jumped from their sockets; this key looked identical to the one Ashley and I found under the rug at the Poston house.

Osborne took the unusual key, carefully studied it, and then handed it to me. "I've seen something like this, but I just can't remember where," pondered Osborne.

"Don't you remember? The night when you became angry with me for withholding evidence? It was when I informed you that I was a lawyer, remember?" I said, trying to jog Osborne's memory.

"You found a key like this one, didn't you? By the way, I'm still a little upset with you. Do you think there is a connection?" Osborne questioned.

"I don't know, but if there isn't, it's an unbelievable coincidence," I suggested.

"What about the car key? Is there any chance we can find it tonight? Wait a minute, what did you say? He's a lawyer? Osborne, is he a gumshoe and a mouthpiece?" Detective Billings said.

"Yes, he is both a private investigator and a lawyer," Osborne confirmed of my portfolio.

"Enough about me. As for finding the car tonight, not in this crowd and certainly not in the dark. What say we come by here at sunrise, before everyone comes to town?"

"Oh, I almost forgot. Guess what I found in his shirt pocket? A white feather. Didn't you all find a feather in the old truck, you know, out at Nain?" Billings questioned while removing a white feather from his pocket.

"We did, and a similar feather was found on Marchetti's body. What does all this mean? Jason, Brody, what are we missing?" Osborne asked, trying to make sense of the growing number of feathers.

"I have a better question: how does a sniper kill a man from a three-story building and get down carrying a rifle? Then, without being seen, stick a feather into the victim's pocket?"

"Carrying a weapon isn't that uncommon around here. Maybe he just bought it or took it to be repaired or pawned. It isn't that unusual," Billings rationalized.

"Doesn't that ever worry either of you? I mean, a man walks down the street with a rifle, loaded or unloaded, who knows, and no one pays any attention. Isn't that just a little frightening?" I asked, trying to understand the local customs.

"Brody, this is the South. Nearly everybody carries a weapon of some sort. A lot of people around here don't know the war is over," responded Osborne.

"The war in Europe?" I asked.

"No! They know we whipped the Hun. They mean the real war, the War of Northern Aggression, what *you people* call the Civil War," Billings quipped.

"*You people*? What does that mean: you people?" I fired back.

"Brody, you're my friend, a good friend, but hard as you may try, face it, you're not from here. It's hard to explain; it's just how it is," Osborne surmised.

At first, my friend's assessment hurt; then, I remembered the treatment a Southern friend experienced when visiting us in Boston. Every word he spoke carried the prolongation of the most heavily stressed syllables, followed by the weakening of the less stressed ones. While the individual was actually conversing with a faster tempo, the illusion was a slower speech pattern. This pattern gave the listener an impression of ignorance. When one is a stranger or possesses different qualities or ideas, acceptance will always be a challenge, a challenge I must accept. I had no other choice if I ever hoped to be accepted.

With the hurtful words behind me, I used my newfound luxury of being an extension of the local constabulary. I spent the next thirty minutes photographing the deceased, the theatre, adjacent buildings, and several structures across the street. I also captured as many onlookers as possible, some cursing me for my audacity. Not being from here was now a blessing; no one in the crowd knew me or my name.

When I ran out of film I returned to Osborne and Billings, who were now speaking with two patrolmen. The body had been transported to the morgue, so the crowd had thinned.

"Why didn't anyone look up when they heard the shot?" I asked as I continued to assess the scene.

"On an ordinary Friday, why would anyone think to look up? Face it, Forde, it could have easily been a car backfire. Heck, I doubt most even gave it a thought," Billings concluded.

"Why wasn't he seen inside the theatre? I mean, a guy carries a loaded rifle into a place like this; surely someone noticed. You said they had just opened the doors around 5:45 p.m., with the first feature starting at 6:00 p.m. Sharp, and no one noticed?" I countered.

"Only six people were here then: Hob Peters, the manager; the ticket girl; Julie Anne, Hob's oldest girl. He's got five, you know."

"No, Detective Billings, I was unaware of Hob's fertility prowess. Who else was there?" I redirected.

"His what? Prowess? Oh yeah, the projection guy Spence McElroy and Tink Hunt were here; he's one of the concession people. The other two were the ushers; both were busy and didn't notice anyone who didn't belong," continued Billings.

"Tink Hunt, why should I know that name? Who is he?" I asked, trying to remember where I heard that name.

"He's just a young man lucky enough to have a job. It's hard for a single man to find work these days, you know. He's a good kid;

he works to support his momma, dad dead and all," informed Lt. Osborne. "What's wrong, Brody? What're you thinking?" Osborne turned his questions toward me.

"Is he related to Homer Hunt?" remembering the name of Hunt.

"I don't know, Brody. What difference would that make?" asked Osborne.

"None, I guess, just curious," I concluded.

With nothing more to learn, we called it a night. Lt. Osborne and I agreed to meet in front of the theatre tomorrow morning at 6:00 a.m. The rising sun would enable us to expand our investigation, hoping the slightest sliver of evidence would expose itself. While I hated to wait, darkness served as a blanket, concealing secrets held by the back streets. My curiosity would have to wait.

Now home, a late-night snack, followed by a hot bath, permitted sleep to come uncommonly easy, but the solitude would not last. I had slept only a few hours before the demons arrived. Foolish, thinking the misery had ended. Everything was swirling, almost nauseating from the dizziness that had overtaken me. Nonexistent blood dripped from my finger, and, feeling the need to vomit, I sat up and turned on the lamp. The demons retreated as they feared the light as much as I feared the darkness. My pillowcase was wet from perspiration, so much so that I needed to replace it. An hour passed before I slumbered off; the torment had temporarily ceased, for this night anyway.

Chapter Seventeen

The night was now behind me; I actually felt good, all considered. I was anxious to meet Osborne in the hope of finding Giorgio Cappelletti's car. I was seated on a public bench near the theatre when I saw Lt. Osborne approaching.

"Good morning, Lieutenant, ready to begin our hunt?" I asked with enthusiasm.

Osborne first removed his hat, rubbed his uncombed hair, and then offered, "Are you always this happy in the morning? I'm off to a rough start. Gladys, my wife—you've met her—she *greeted* me at the door last night with a broken piece of glass in her left hand and a baseball in the right. Our youngest boy, Lucas, was playing in the front yard, where he isn't supposed to, and, well, you get the rest."

Finding humor, my instinct was to laugh; it was enjoyable to hear a regular life story and catch a glimpse of the other side of Lieutenant Wilbur Osborne. Socrates said, *"Our lives are but specks of dust falling through the fingers of time."* In a short time, I had grown fond of Will Osborne. Yesterday, he referred to me as a good friend, and I felt the same way; he is my good friend.

"So, do you need to be home this morning to fix a window?" I asked, suppressing my chuckles.

"No, I'll get to it. The sad thing this morning is we're out of coffee; I had to drink a glass of milk. Brody, it's not the same—I hate milk!"

The strain not to burst into an eruption of laughter was insurmountable. Hard as it was, we needed to end this moment—something I really didn't want to do. "I'll make a deal; let's find the car, and then I will buy you lunch and all the coffee you can drink. Deal?"

"Deal! Let's get to work. I brought the key found on the deceased, Cappelletti, right? Anyway, I say we start walking toward Boscawen Street, then onto Braddock."

We followed Osborne's plan: Boscawen, over to Braddock, testing the key in the doors and/or switches of the few cars we encountered. We surmised Cappelletti, not being from Winchester, would have parked fairly close to his meeting spot. That logic had us circling back toward the theatre and down Indian Alley. In the alley sat one car: a late model black Buick with West Virginia license plate number 722-817. The key was a perfect fit; we had our car.

"Brody, this is the car! Cappelletti is our first link to the kidnappings. You stay here; I'm going to a call box to get a tow truck to come and pick it up. Guard that car with your life!" Minutes later, Osborne returned and informed me a truck would be here shortly. We decided not to investigate the automobile until it had been secured in the police impound yard.

Little conversation transpired during our wait; Osborne sat on a crate while I impatiently paced. We had each searched the area around the car but found nothing of value. Finally, at 8:45 a.m., the truck arrived.

"Will, can you give strict orders that no one, I mean no one, is to touch this car? Also, we must postpone our meeting with the federal men this morning; this has to take precedence."

"I can do that. How about this afternoon, say, three o'clock, at your office? I will let Johannsson know."

Osborne rode with the driver while I picked up Ashley. I related the events of the previous night and this morning. She was disappointed not to be 'present when all the good stuff was happening,' but she was eager to get to work this morning.

We journeyed to the office to retrieve my forensic tool bag. Proper examination is critical; we only have one chance to do this correctly. We had to be perfect in our quest for the truth. With everything in hand, we drove to the county impound yard.

Pulling into the lot, I was surprised to see a crowd. Chief Johannsson, several patrolmen, Osborne, Billings, and three unexpected men from Baltimore were in attendance. As my assistant and I approached, Agent Colegate established authority.

"So, *this heap* is more important than the United States Federal government?"

"Am I to guess you are Agent Colegate? And, to answer your question, yes, *this heap*, as you call it, is more important right now. We believe it is connected to multiple kidnappings and several murders."

"Just so we get off on the right foot, Forde, that's your name, right? Nothing in this one-horse town is more important than the United States government. You understand? Nothing! Is this how you run your town, Johannsson? You let this *pinhead* do your work for you?"

"Nobody runs my town, not even you, you, horse's ass! Why are you here anyway? You ain't got a dog in this hunt. Why are you and your boyfriends here?"

The larger of the two Baltimore agents approached the irate chief.

"You'd better settle your boy, Colegate, because I'm about to give him a sincere lesson on manhood; then he's going to lock up," Johannsson bellowed while forming a massive fist with his right hand.

I found myself rooting for the chief; my world had certainly turned upside down in the past twenty-four hours. Osborne, however, positioned himself between the chief and the federal agent as I tried to decide if Will was that brave or that stupid. Because he was my friend, bravery prevailed. Whatever the reason, the tension subsided when the federal combatant stepped back but Johannsson never moved. Love him or hate him, you had to admire the chief's conviction.

With testosterone in decline, the conversation took a more civil tone. Agent Colegate agreed to meet at 1:00 p.m. this afternoon while Johannsson left for a late breakfast, asking Billings to join him in a manner one doesn't refuse. This gave the three of us a little less than four hours to complete our much-awaited task.

Osborne summoned the department's fingerprint expert, who examined the vehicle inside and out, retrieving numerous prints; Osborne inspected the outside bumper to bumper, top to bottom; I gathered samples on the inside; and Ashley took the pictures using two rolls of film. With the four of us working together, the automobile received a thorough physical.

Time flew by as we were all deep into our work. Several times, I noticed other officers watching, wanting to join the investigation; even Johannsson stopped by for a minute after returning from a long meal. Conversation was limited as we all concentrated on our work. Finally, the mission was complete.

"Wow, we've been at it for three hours. Boss, are you getting hungry? I need food. Can we go to the Golden Glow for lunch? I'm starved," Ashley pleaded.

"Sure, we've done all we can do. Outstanding work, all of you. How about all four of us head to the Glow, my treat?" I invited.

"Sounds great to me! Roger, you want to join us? You've been hard at it. How many fingerprints did you find?" Osborne asked.

"A bunch, although many of them are from the same person. No, it's Saturday; I need to be getting home, the wife and all. Thanks for the invite; another time, perhaps? By the way, Mr. Forde, it's been good working with you," offered the fingerprint expert, Roger Brinkley.

"Thank you, Roger; it's been a pleasure working with you as well," I said, returning the compliment.

We decided to ride together since all would be in the 1:00 p.m. meeting. Surprisingly, there was little talk regarding our last three hours of labor. I was about to discover I was not the only one lacking a full night of sleep; the signs of fatigue extruded from all our faces.

"Boy, that was hard work. I never thought taking pictures could wear a person out. Boss, can we buy a camera without a button that pushes that hard? My finger needs a rest," complained my blonde assistant.

"Would an extra $2 help any?" I offered.

"Why, yes, my finger is feeling better already. You're a miracle worker, Boss."

"Will, you know what they say? If money can fix it, it's not a problem. That proved it."

"I don't think that will work with my boss. I have to live with it, whatever it is," the weary Osborne explained.

"Your boss is not a pleasant man; he's not like my boss. I think your boss is mean or just mad all the time. Does he ever smile?" Ashley probed.

"Chief Johannsson has a difficult job and lots of responsibility. For insistence, he's responsible for your safety, Ashley, and yours too, Brody. Chief Johannsson has the weight of the city on his shoulders; I think he is just tired," Osborne said in defense of Chief Sonny Johannsson.

Will's words rang true; the weight of providing protection for that many people must be enormous. For the second time today, I admired the tyrant. Had Goliath suddenly become Hercules?

After a much-needed break, we readied ourselves for the Baltimore invasion. Upon return, Billings sat outside my office building, patiently waiting, enjoying the last draw from his Old Gold cigarette.

"Thought you got lost. Find anything good in the car?" Billings asked.

"Actually, yes, we did. We'll go over that once we get the fingerprint results and I have a chance to develop the film," I answered.

"Where did you disappear to? You didn't come back with the chief. I thought you might help us go over the car. It was a lot of work, but, as Brody said, we found some things that should help," added Osborne.

"It's nearly 1:00 p.m. Where are the federal boys? I've been sitting here for nearly twenty minutes. I guess they don't teach punctuality in G-man school," Billings criticized.

We headed upstairs, and, to our surprise, my office door was open and all three agents were sitting behind our desk chairs.

"Well, Forde, we thought perhaps you wouldn't show. Impressive office, very impressive; it's almost as large as my corner office in Baltimore," Special Agent Byron Colegate boasted.

"How dare you? What gives you the right to break into a private citizen's office? Get out of those chairs—now! Detectives, I want them arrested, breaking and entering!" I ordered at the top of my voice.

"You can't arrest us; we're federal agents on a case. We're untouchable!" Colegate fired back.

"We'll see about that. Now, get away from the desks!" I shouted.

The agents slowly complied, but not before shoving items around, causing several to hit the floor. As the standoff continued, I regained my composure and picked up my telephone, delivering a number to the local operator that the trespassing agents knew all too well; the number was that of the Director of the Bureau of Investigation in Washington, D.C. The arrogant smirks were instantly replaced with pale, chilled expressions of despair.

The aggressive posturing that began when the agents had stood was withdrawn as they slowly edged toward the door. Osborne and Billings, however, blocked their escape.

My call went through; I was now speaking to the director, explaining the agents' actions in detail. In less than a minute, I was asked to hand the receiver to the agent in charge, Agent Colegate.

"Yes, Sir... Ah, yes, Sir... I understand, Sir. No, Sir, it will never happen again. Yes, he's here; he wants to talk to you, Mr. Forde." Colegate sheepishly handed me the phone.

"Yes, Mr. Director, yes, I think everything will be okay now. That's good to hear, Sir. How is your mother? That's great; please send her my best. Yes, Sir, I'll pass that on to Father next time we speak. Again, thank you and take care, my friend. Goodbye."

"What just happened? You know the Director of the Bureau of Investigation in Washington?" a puzzled Billings asked.

"Yes, Jason, he's an old family friend. His father, Dickerson, and my father were close friends; that was until Dicky passed away in 1921. They met at the Washington Golf Club years ago, and our families have

bonded over time. Edgar is five years older than me; I sometimes looked
at him as the older brother I never had. He's why I attended George
Washington University instead of Harvard, my father's alma mater."

"Wow, that's my boss! Now, how about you boys pick up our stuff?
You'd better hope nothing is broken; you wouldn't want us to call your
boss again, would you?" a vindictive Ashely ordered.

"Now, boys, before you three leave, how about emptying all your
pockets, removing all jackets, and pulling out your shirttails?" Lt.
Osborne injected his authority.

"Nice touch, Osborne, but they need to remove their shoes and
socks and pull up their pants legs as well. We wouldn't want anything
to walk out of here accidentally, would we?" added Billings.

Their paleness quickly transformed into a deep red. No words
were spoken as all complied, except for Ashley's suggestion to
check their underwear. Suspecting an alternate motive, I declined
her recommendation. Fortunately, the search fostered no hidden
documents or photographs.

The redemption, while pleasing, would no doubt bring future
consequences. A man like Colgate would never forget this humiliating
event; while we did not initiate this indiscretion, we most assuredly
escalated it. We hadn't seen or heard the last of this.

The agents quietly gathered themselves and left the building. As he
was about to exit the door, the smaller, older agent looked back and
slowly tipped his hat while displaying the slightest smile. Perhaps the
number of our new adversaries had just been reduced by one.

"That'll be the last we see of them, good riddance!" gloated Billings.

"I'm sorry, Jason, but this has just begun. Colegate will make it his
personal mission to get even with us. Everyone, and I mean everyone,
keep your eyes open. We just made a powerful enemy; make no mistake
about that," I cautioned.

"Brody's right; Colegate is a dangerous man, and don't
underestimate the brute that went face to face with the chief; his name
is Bosworth, I believe. What do you make of the tip-of-the-hat guy?
What was that all about?" Osborne inquired.

"I don't know; strange, very strange. Like I said, keep your eyes wide open; trust no one," I repeated my warning.

The intrusion had wasted valuable time so we decided to meet early Monday morning to review the findings surrendered by the West Virginia car. Realizing little could be accomplished this afternoon, I drove Ashley home and followed suit; I couldn't wait to get into my darkroom.

Chapter Eighteen

S unday morning came in its usual manner; the demons had visited my sleep but didn't stay long, I had developed all the film, attended the morning worship services, and began my journey to Max's.

As I approached, I saw something new, something that caused me to stop and stare in amazement: Max had a new, one-of-a-kind mailbox. I recognized parts of the monstrosity but was not exactly sure what I was seeing. A closer examination revealed the remains of a vintage motorcycle—a 1915 Indian motorcycle, to be exact.

The gas tank had been cut and fitted with a hinge, creating the box portion, while the kickstand had been turned upside down and fitted with a welded red flag. The once broken front fork also displayed signs of welding, and it now held the gas-tank-turned-mailbox portion. The frame served as the post, securing everything in place. The surviving rear wheel had been made into an 'open/closed' sign that could be turned as needed, alerting the public. To say the least, this was a marvelous example of inventive thinking.

"What is that?" I asked.

"It looks like $10 to me. I told you I would revive that old Indian before you solved your case. So, where's my sawbuck?" the master fabricator questioned with his right hand open and extended.

"Max, that's not a motorcycle. I'm not exactly sure what it is, but it's definitely not an Indian motorcycle," hopelessly trying to save my $10.00.

"See, that's what's wrong with all you young people. Full of education but blind as a bat. You can't see the trees from the forest. See, at birth, somebody told that ole Indian he was a bike, but that wasn't true. All along, he was a mailbox pretending to be a bike. Then, one day, he found himself out of work, just like lots of people these days, down in the dumps, where I found him. I just did what they say in the newspaper: '*I increased the labor force by taking someone, er, something willing and able to work, retraining it, and giving it gainful employment. Pretty good, don't you think?*'"

"Max, I'm speechless. I can't argue with your logic, I guess. They sure could use someone like you in Washington these days," I surmised.

"It wouldn't do no good. They're all too busy staring at those trees; the easy answer is right in front of them, but they can't see it. The country needs jobs, right? Why don't they just make jobs? Build some roads; hell, we need all kinds of roads around here, so why not just print more money and pay some out-of-work men to build them? So, Sherlock, where's my money?"

Once again, I conceded to my mentor. Max was on to something, though. Why not just create jobs? I studied under one of the world's most knowledgeable economists at GW University, and he said, '*The best way to end depression was force inflation.*' Over time, inflation would subside, returning a stable economy. My friend, with only three years of schooling, understands that, yet in D.C., *they just don't get it*, as Max would say.

I gave the victor his $10 bounty as his face beamed, again besting me. You would think by now I would understand: this was the smartest man I have ever known.

The remainder of the day went as usual; I was trounced in not one but two battles. The first was interrupted when Felix jumped onto the board, sending pawns, rooks, and the like in all directions. Had anyone else committed this act, their fate would have suffered the consequences, but this was Max's sidekick, the ever-growing male cat that could do no wrong. I was shocked to see the nearly twenty-pound feline jump that high.

The rest of my evening was anticlimactic. With all the film developed and the morning meeting planned, I was free to enjoy a fine meal in the hotel dining room. Once upstairs, I got to bed earlier than usual, and I was sound asleep before the demons could muster an attack; I should try this method moving forward.

Monday was moving rapidly. Breakfast, my protective carpool assignment, and everything else were completed before the arrival of my partners from city hall. Just after 9:15 a.m., Osborne and Billings stepped into the conference room carrying the results of the fingerprinting of the West Virginia car. For once, nothing terrible had happened over the weekend.

"So, what do we know concerning fingerprints? Who's touched this car?" I inquired.

"To start, quite a few people. It appears no one thought of this car falling into our hands. Two of the murder victims, the man in the shed in Nain, Rolf Schlesinger, and the guy at the theatre, Gio Cappelletti. Jo Brathwaite's fingerprints were on the right back door window frame. She was definitely in this car," informed Osborne.

A solemn pause overtook the room, an unannounced moment of silence as it were, remembering a life that ended too soon. We all mourned, yet none in the room had ever met this young woman. The moment passed, and now we were back to solving this crime.

"Anyone else? How about Luca? Any evidence placing him in the car?" I questioned.

"No, as best we can tell, he never came into contact with it. How does Luca Marchetti figure into all this? What brings a member of the Cosa Nostra family to this area in the first place?" wondered Billings.

"For that matter, why are the Feds here? They couldn't care less that Marchetti was dead. What is their motive? They certainly are not here to help us; they proved that Saturday," Osborne offered.

"Johannsson did tell me this: Colgate still wants to meet with us on neutral ground, someplace quiet but public," chuckled Billings.

"Well, I want to think about that before we commit. One thing is certain: they are not welcome in my office. Never again. Let's get back to the evidence from the West Virginia Buick. We removed two used syringes; both need to be given to Dr. Stenner to check for blood types. Will, can you drop them off?" I asked.

"Sure, I'll do that as soon as I leave here. Back to the car, I noticed a small trace of blood on the right back fender; I'll also try to get a sample of that to Doc Stenner," volunteered Osborne.

"Anything on the car or the plates?" my interrogation continued.

"Nothing on the plates. They were reported stolen three months ago off a car in Fairmont, West Virginia, so there is nothing there. As for the car, we're trying to run that down; somebody has to own it," Billings declared.

"I found three burlap bags in the trunk; I figure they covered the teenager's heads once they grabbed them. Surprisingly, there were no weapons. What really concerned me most was this crude, hand-drawn map of Cross Junction. We may have just foiled another kidnapping," I suggested.

The ringing of my phone interrupted our session. After answering, Emily brought a message from Chief Johannsson for Detective Billings. He was to report to Sheriff Neumann immediately; there were no other instructions. Just meet with the sheriff.

Reluctantly, Billings followed the order and left.

"What do you think that was all about? We're working fairly well together, but there is something about Detective Jason Billings I'm just not sure of. I know that the two of you have worked together for a number of years, but, Will, I cannot shake this feeling."

"He's a good copper, but just like everybody, he fears losing his position. This Depression scares everybody. These are hard times; jobs are scarce," reminded Osborne.

"Boss, can I ask a question? What about all these white feathers? Makes no sense, and how did a man get shot from the third story of the theatre and get a feather in his pocket?" intervened Ashley.

"Excellent question, for which I have no answer. Now, let me ask a question: What connects the three dead men, except for their very violent deaths? What are we missing? There has to be a correlation, so what is it? Ashley, get a piece of chalk; let's look at the three collectively, not individually. After all, the feathers link them, but how?" I instructed.

"Brody, do you still believe this is the work of a serial killer? You were convinced a couple of days ago. Do you still feel that strong?" Osborne recalled my earlier hypothesis.

"I don't know... Nothing fits. Let's examine what we do know. The first guy was a local man, Rolf Schlesinger. He was firmly secured with his head back, using a military knot to secure the rope; a very slow, painful, torturous death by carbon dioxide poisoning," I explained.

"So, he was gassed. The second, Marchetti, had his throat slashed with a very large knife," surmised Osborne.

"Wait a minute, Will, he was first stabbed with the same large knife, then his neck was slashed. What if that knife was a bayonet? You know, the kind used in war," I suggested, trying to visualize each murder.

"Yeah, the stab wound was a thrust, then a ninety-degree twist, just like a soldier would use a bayonet attached to the end of his rifle. The head was held back, and then, with one swift slash, it was over. Brody, the third man, ah, Gio Cappelletti, was killed with one shot, a highly proficient shooter, a marksman," Osborne zealously declared.

"Boss, are you guys saying that the killer is a veteran? But why? Why would a veteran be doing this?" questioned Ashley, with her left hand rubbing her chin.

"How about a war buddy of Joseph Brathwaite? How about a man who served with him? A man that was his best man at his wedding?" I asked as I attempted to rationalize what was being said.

"Boss, are you accusing that old guy named after the dog, Homer?"

"The old guy named after the dog? Miss Ashley, who are you talking about?" the puzzled lieutenant asked.

"We met him after Jo Brathwaite's funeral," in an effort to bring Osborne up to speed. "But, do either of you believe Homer Hunt is physically capable? Could he have tied a man the size of Schlesinger in a truck, cut the throat of a member of the Cosa Nostra family, or shoot a man with that kind of accuracy, then run down three flights of stairs?" Opening my questions to the room.

"Boss, maybe he couldn't, but I believe Robert Poston could. Maybe he did it for Homer?" said Ashley as she refilled her coffee mug.

"That's really reaching, my dear, but why would Poston get involved in a triple homicide? What's his motive? We have no evidence the two men even knew one another," Osborne asked and answered.

"It may be a reach, but I don't trust Robert Poston. He's a liar; he may not be a killer, but he's not telling everything he knows," Ashley said as her voice rose a decibel.

"But why, Ashley? Just as Lt. Osborne said, there's no evidence proving they knew each other. Several days ago, you thought Poston killed Jo; now you think he killed three men. Why, what is the connection to the three victims?" my questions continued.

"Brody, if I may, we have fingerprints placing Schlesinger and Cappelletti in the Buick. Miss Ashley is on to something; what, I'm not sure, but at least two of these men are connected. I agree with our lady sleuth; Poston knows something he's not telling, but, for now, we have nothing directly connecting him," Osborne offered.

"We're making progress; it's just that we seem to be going in a circle. We have to branch out. I know three people who might shed some light on all this: Kate Brathwaite, Flavius Brathwaite, and Max."

"Why not Homer Hunt? Seems to me he ought to be interrogated," deduced Osborne.

"You're right, Will, he should, but not now. I have my reasons," I said, deflecting Osborne's suggestion.

The final minutes are spent planning what questions should be asked and which of us were most suited to present them. Not surprisingly, I drew all three straws. Kate and Flavius didn't trust the law, as Kate still held a grudge based on her first encounter while reporting Jo as a missing person. This, plus my personal relationship with Max, eliminated Osborne. Ashley wanted to speak with Kate, but I felt she wasn't quite ready to go toe to toe with a woman of Mrs. Brathwaite's inner strength. As delicate as I tried to convey my reasoning, I disappointed my eager but young assistant. Understanding was one thing, but acceptance was another.

"Ashley, I'm going to Max's. How about you call the Emporium to see if they can message Kate to call us? Tell them I will gladly pay them for their trouble. When she calls, ask if we can come by for a short visit, both of us. Is that okay with you? Please do not let her know why; just when would be convenient. I would like it to be later today. How's that sound?"

The sparkle returned to her eyes, and she again gave me that left-handed salute as I grabbed my hat and headed out the door.

Turning into the station, I couldn't help but stare at the old Indian, waiting to receive the afternoon mail at my expense. You have got to love the old man's creativity.

"I see my $10 is working well. I had planned to buy a new hat with your money, but, as usual, you found a way to beat me," I laughingly said.

"I don't beat you. You always lose. See, you have lots of knowledge, just not very much wisdom. You're not old enough to understand the difference," the prophet exclaimed.

"Don't they both go hand-in-hand?" I asked, showing my ignorance yet again.

"That's what I'm trying to teach you. See, knowledge is what you learn; wisdom is how you use it. Knowledge comes early to some, like you. Hell, you're one of the smartest men I've ever known; you just haven't lived long enough to have much wisdom—the wisdom that comes with age. Be patient; you'll get there someday."

"Will I ever be as wise as you, Max?"

"You're dreamin' now, son. So why are you here on a Monday, nagging me when I have work to do?"

"Max, I need some help in the Brathwaite case. May I ask you several questions? It's important."

My expression could not hide my desperation. Instantly, Max yelled for Sam, giving him instructions for the next hour, including that the two of us were not to be interrupted unless it was life-threatening or someone with money. We then moved to Max's backroom apartment. When the old man slid the bolt lock, I knew I had his full attention. "So, what's up? Whatcha need?" he asked while sitting in his favorite chair.

I breached the honor of confidentiality because I saw no other way to gain what I desperately needed. To get, you had to give. The door was locked, and we whispered. I trusted my friend.

"You told me about Homer, but I need to know more. I need to know Joe Brathwaite's other friends, especially the men he went to war with."

"Whew, that's a tall order. Well, he was close with Vernon Lawson out in Gainesboro. Duke Cooper goes by Coop; he lives over in Warren County, so they were pretty tight. Then, let me think... Oh yeah, Bagent, Marty Bagent, they were close too."

"Let's start with Duke Cooper. What can you tell me about him?"

"I met him a couple of times, but I don't really know him other than he saved Homer's life in France. Nice man, never talks about the war; most don't, you know. I don't know much else about him, just that Homer, Joe, and Cooper were close."

"Okay, how about Marty Bagent?"

"Him I know better; great guy. He comes in here about every Friday to get gas. Works at the flour mill just south of town. He's a family man with a good wife, three boys, big coffee drinker. He empties my pot every time he stops by."

"He works at a flour mill?" I asked, remembering the flour on the truck running board in the Nain shed.

"Yeah, he works like a bunch of other lucky men in the flour mill. It's one of the few places still running, Depression and all."

"What else can you tell me about Mr. Bagent? Do you think he could kill a man?"

"Remember what I just said about wisdom? The man fought in a war, what do you think? He's killed men. What you're asking is, could he murder a man? I'd have to say no, I don't think he's a murderer. He's a man with a family; no, I just don't see him killing anybody."

The thing about Max's learning lessons was that I walked directly into their path, never seeing them coming. How stupid I must look. Max was right: I needed to expand my wisdom.

"Vernon Lawson, what about him?" I asked.

"Lawson is a strange one; he don't say much. Comes to town every month or so. Like most vets, he brought the war home in his head, know what I mean?" Max informed.

"Where does he live? Any family?" my questions continued.

"He lives out near Gainesboro, out in the woods. His wife left him not long after he came home. She took the little girl and just left. Things got worse from there; he began to drink, I mean, really drink. He drifted from job to job till there weren't any. Lost the house, what was left of it anyway, then just wandered into the hills," explained Max as he wiped the grease from his callused hands.

"If he's that bad off, how and why does he come to town?" trying to make sense of this story.

"He's bad off, but he's still got some friends; they give him a ride, then take him back. As for the why, he hunts ginseng, and when he gets enough, he comes to town and sells it. Once, a couple of men tried to rob him; Vern pulled a huge knife and cut one. Not bad, just enough to discourage the want-to-be thief," Max said as he tossed the grease rag into a bucket.

"So... Vernon Lawson has a large knife and a temper. Could he kill, er, murder someone?" my curiosity rising.

"Yeah, I guess so. When a man's lost everything, what's left to lose? Some claim they've heard him talking to an imaginary person like they're standing beside him. I never seen nothin' like that, though."

"Anyone else you can think of? Anyone at all?" unable to hold back my questions.

"No, I can't think of anybody. If I do, I'll write it down and call you," promised Max.

Our time had come to an end. Finally, a few names to add to the board; worthy or not, we now had a few leads. I thanked Max for the very difficult hour I just put him through. Tough as he is, Max tried to see the good in people; sessions like this reminded us of the depths a man could fall fighting to survive.

Chapter Nineteen

B efore returning to the office, I bought lunch for the girls at a small diner near Max's. Strangely, it was a covered wagon with a cooking grill in the back. Quaint, with a limited menu, but the food smelled great. I purchased three specials and then headed to the office. Passing through the door, Ashley, smelling lunch, rushed me and grabbed the basket.

"You've been to Momma's. I'd know that smell anywhere!"

"How'd you know that? You knew it was from Momma's just by the smell?"

"You darn right I can. You just got the best-pulled pork ever. The recipe's been in her family since before the war. Her granddaddy was a slave, you know. Boss, you have no idea how good this will be. Did you get sweet tea? Please tell me you got her sweet tea; if you didn't, you're going back," my blonde assistant threatened.

Fortunately, I purchased the daily special, which I later learned is the only thing you can get at Momma's. As soon as the food left the protective basket, which I promised to return, it was devoured. Ashley was spot on; this was the best pulled-pork I had ever tasted. In addition, the meal included a hearty portion of fried potatoes with a secret seasoning and, oh yes, the delicious sweet tea.

When asked about the secret seasoning, Emily responded, "It's a secret; that's why no one can know."

Those two ladies were definitely sisters; I have got to meet their parents.

With the food gone—and I mean all gone—we related our morning activities. Ashley had set a time of 3:00 p.m. today to meet Kate. Flavius, however, was out of town on business. The names gathered from Max were added to the board; the problem was making sense of this human jigsaw puzzle.

The drive to the Brathwaite farm took longer than usual; it seemed like every farmer found the need to pull their wagons from one field to another. As we passed one, two more took their place. Finally, after an hour, we heard the deep-throated shrieking bark of Homer announcing our arrival.

"Homer, stop all that racket! Mr. Forde, would you just run over that noisy mutt? Honestly, he eats more than he's worth, but Jo loved him," the grieving mother confessed while fighting back the tears.

"You'd miss him. He's the best alarm system I have ever heard," I said, offering support for Homer.

"You're right, of course, he's bout all the family I have left." She still fought tears.

"Kate, the reason for this call is we could use a little help; help we believe you can provide."

"Well, how about I get you some sweet tea or coffee, whichever suits your needs? We can sit here on the porch; there's a nice breeze a-blowin' right now."

Ashley and I sat on the oak swing, waiting for another round of good ole Southern sweet tea. I could get coffee anywhere, but two servings of Virginia sweet tea on the same day—who could pass that up? In minutes, we are all settled in, savoring the taste of the sweet nectar.

"Kate, I would like to know some of Joe's friends, especially the ones he went to war with. Can you help us?"

"You can't possibly think any of Joe's friends had anything to do with my baby's death. They are his friends; heck, some of them he knew all his life. No, sir, if you're thinkin' they got anything to with this, you're wrong."

"Ma'am, we're not accusing anyone; we just think they might want to help. That's all we're asking. We need some help, please. Can you help us help you?" I asked, redirecting the point of our visit.

The nightmare continued for Kate, increasing each day this murder went unsolved. Tears gathered, then streamed over both cheeks of the self-reliant woman.

Without warning, her mood changed. Bolting from her rocker, Kate, with that thundering voice heard our first day, shouted, 'I'll be right back; don't move!' True to her words, she returned carrying an old box filled with pictures and letters from the war. "Don't know what's in here anymore, but here is all I got. Take these. Maybe the answer is here. Mr. Forde, this is all I got left—please take care of it. Please, will you?" pleaded Kate.

"I give my word; I will return all of this as soon as I can, exactly as you entrust it to me, I promise." With my hat in hand, I nodded, sealing my oath.

The emotion of the moment had now passed, and we focused on Joe's friends.

"Now, about Joe's friends, let me think. The first one that comes to mind is Homer, but you have already met him. Poor Homer, he's been through it, I tell you."

"Can you tell me a little more about Homer? Does he have any family, for instance?" I asked.

"Ain't got much family left. His wife and son died back in '18, Spanish flu, you know. The man is nearly killed in France only to come home to a dying wife and son. Life ain't fair," expressed the grieving widow and mother.

"You said he was nearly killed in France. Do you know what happened?" my interest grew.

"Well, as I know it, they were all *going over the top* when Homer caught a bullet in his left leg. He fell in no-man's-land, you know, between the trenches. He was lying there when a fellow named Coop, I think, ran out in the gunfire, threw Homer over his shoulder, and carried him back. They were both gassed, but Homer got the worst of it. Since you saw him the other day, well, he's back in the hospital. It's bad this time; they don't think he's gonna make it," Kate explained as her voice trembled.

"I'm very sorry to hear that, Mrs. Brathwaite. I really like him; he's funny," said Ashley, now fighting tears.

"Kate, what about family? Does Homer have any family?" as my questions continued.

"He's got a nephew, I think? Don't know his name. He's Homer's brother's boy. What is his name? It's a funny name, Tiny, Tank, something like that."

"How about Tink?" I interjected.

"That's it. His real name is Theobald, after his granddaddy on his momma's side. His real name never took hold, so they started calling him Tink since he was always tinkering with something," Kate explained.

"How about anyone else? Who would be Joe's next, closest war buddy?" as I tried to make sense of this.

"Well, there's Marty Bagent; they were friends before the war, like Homer. Marty is a dreamer, always looking for the easy way to make a buck. He ain't got much of an education, but he's really smart. After he came home, he used to come by to talk, you know, we were both a-mourning Joe."

"You wouldn't happen to have an address for Mr. Bagent? Like I said, we're not accusing anyone; we need help figuring out what happened," I delicately asked.

"I'll have to look for it unless it might be in that box. You look at that, if you don't find it, call me, I'll see what I can do. Oh, I just remembered Foster Cobb. And what's his name? I can see his face, oh, Feltner, Jebediah Feltner. Joe and him were close friends. Jeb was born here but moved near Berryville years ago. Joe and Jeb grew up together."

We met a deputy named Feltner, who was too young to have fought in the war. There was a belief that all Southerners were, in a rather crude way, related. I had always negated such claims, but as this case progressed, I was beginning to give the idea a measure of accuracy. First, the Hunts, now possibly, the Feltner's.

"Would Jebediah Feltner happen to have any children? Maybe in their early twenties?"

"Oh, yeah, Jeb's got a whole house full of kids, six boys and four girls, I believe. Yeah, some of them would be in their twenties by now," exclaimed Kate.

"Ashley, remind me to call Sheriff Walker in Clarke County tomorrow. So, Kate, you mentioned another man, Foster Cobb. What can you tell me about him?"

"He's from nearby, just short of the West Virginia line, in High View. Brody, you be careful with this one; he's just plumb crazy. Some say that, as a boy, he got too close to the working end of a mule and got kicked in the head. If that's true, the whole family got too close; they'd all be nuts if you asked me. Ask anybody; that clan is crazy."

"What does he, for that matter his family, do that warrants this reputation?" as I tried to rationalize Cobb's family dynamics.

"I don't know what *warrants* is, but if you're asking about them being crazy, I can answer that in two words: *hill people*, they're all *hill people*," came Kate's explanation.

"I'm lost; other than location, what, or who, are hill people?" I asked while mentally preparing for this answer.

"Hill people live by a code and thousands of rituals, like spitting on a newborn baby to bring it good luck, and if you see a white horse, you will have good luck. Who in their right mind would spit on a baby? If a white horse could bring me luck, I'd get one even if I had to steal it," Kate confessed.

"Yeah, I'd have to agree, that is somewhat strange. Tell me more about Mr. Cobb. Where does he work? Is he married?"

"He drifts from job to job, I hear, and no, as far as I know, no woman is stupid enough to get hitched to a nut like him. I'm tellin' you, Mr. Forde, he's crazy."

Another hour passes, mostly hearing stories of Kate's beloved Joe and how he befriended many who were neglected because they were different, like Foster Cobb. Joseph Brathwaite had been a fair man, willing to accept an individual on merit, not reputation. He was not a fool; he recognized those who possessed shortcomings that could harm him or his family, shunning them. He didn't prejudge a man but had an uncanny ability to look into a man's eyes, listen to their words, and measure the goodness within the heart. It was a pity this life was taken so young; the world needs more men like Joe Brathwaite.

We said our goodbyes, and as my Chrysler backed toward the barn, Kate came running, waving her hands in the air.

"I just thought of another name: Gunner, Gunner Tate. He's a guy Joe met during the war. He was from Loudon County. I think he made it home, but I'm not sure. Joe wrote about him a lot; you should find him in some of those letters in that box. I'm almost certain he made it back. If you talk to Jeb, he'd know. They were close, I think."

"Thank you, Kate, we'll check it out. God bless you, ma'am."

Chapter Twenty

The drive back to town was much faster since all the wagons had completed their journeys. Once in the office, we were surprised to have two visitors, Lt. Osborne and Federal Agent Harold Spivey.

"Gentlemen, have I forgotten a meeting? I'm a bit shocked to see you again, Agent Spivey. What can I do for you?" I cautiously inquired.

"First, Mr. Forde, I hold no hard feelings toward you or your staff. You were well within your right to toss and order us out. We had no legal or moral authority to violate your private office. Please accept my apology. Can we begin again?"

"I see no reason we cannot start over. However, I wonder if your boss knows you are here."

"Yes, Agent Colegate is aware; believe me, he's sometimes, well, often, pompous and overbearing, but make no mistake, he's a top lawman. He, like all of us, including the two of you, is under an unsurmountable amount of pressure."

"Lots of pressure is no excuse for bad manners, and, for the record, there are four of us, including Emily," interjected Ashley.

"No, Miss Ashley, it isn't. There is never an excuse for rudeness. I apologize to you and your sister. Please forgive me," the federal agent offered in a convincing tone.

"Okay, all apologies accepted. So, why are you here, Agent Spivey, and why did you tip your hat as you left Saturday?" I asked, recounting the strange act.

"We need to talk. May we step into your office and discuss how we can help each other?"

My mind raced. Was I hearing this correctly? A subordinate agent wanted to help us? Could this man be trusted? Were we being set up? With red flags waving in my mind, I extended the hand of invitation toward the conference room.

"To begin with, please stop calling me Agent Spivey and call me Hal. I'm an older agent and have been around longer than the other two. I'm not the top agent because I didn't attend an Ivy League school or someplace like George Washington University. I'm a Midwestern boy, a graduate of the University of Illinois, more of an agricultural school, you know."

"That's all fine, but why are the Feds here? We know Marchetti's father is a *wise guy*, but what has that got to do with the killing of Luca?" I asked.

"Do you have any idea of the war that is headed your way? Emiliano, *the Burner* Marchetti, has clipped so many people, even he doesn't know the exact count. You asked, 'Why are we here?' To save you and this town."

"We don't need your help. My chief has forgotten more about police work than your department knows. Believe me, Chief Johannsson can protect this town."

"Yes, Chief Sonny Johannsson. You don't even know who or what he is, do you? But this visit is not about your beloved boss. Have any of you ever heard of the *white slave trade*?"

The thought had crossed my mind several times, but to hear the words spoken sent chills down my spine. The White Slave Trade began centuries ago. A process of kidnapping innocent youths and then shipping them to foreign lands for two primary purposes: slave labor and prostitution. Marchetti's presence was becoming clear: the Cosa Nostra family operated a white slave operation in Winchester.

"Yes, I've heard of it, and I'm certain Lt. Osborne also has. Please, go on," I insisted.

"Officially, we are the Federal Bureau of Narcotics. The FBN, as it is commonly called. We are a relatively new department of the Bureau of Investigation, created to fight the ever-growing illegal drug trade. We believe the Cosa Nostra family is trading teenagers for drugs and has opened shop in Winchester," disclosed the agent.

"So, correct me if I am wrong, you believe the local kidnappings are part of this slave trade, but why did you need to break into my office? What were you thinking you would find? I'm working on the murder of a local woman; I'm indirectly working on the kidnappings. What do you think I have that would be worth stealing?" I asked, my temperature rising.

"We hoped you might have something, anything, that could be used in our investigation. We are somewhat intrigued by some of your techniques; yes, Mr. Forde, we know who you are and where you're from. We planned on looking at, not taking, your notes and photographs. Unfortunately, as we were entering, Billings took a seat on the outside bench. We were afraid to proceed and could not leave without being seen, so we just waited. That's when you came in, and we all know the rest."

"There is more to tell, isn't there, Agent Spivey? Yes, I referred to you as Agent. Until I hear more, I won't continue this waste of time. Federal agents don't break in, hoping to find something. You had a plan. What was your plan? What is the connection that you are so carefully holding back?" I demanded.

"You don't know my area of expertise? I'm a ballistics expert. The bullet taken from the Pruitt boy matched not one but two other victims. If you don't trust me, call Dr. Stenner; he'll confirm it. While you were playing chess, Mr. Forde, I made the comparison in the morgue."

"You said two other victims; who?" asked Osborne.

"The first was a teenage boy, seventeen years old, in Chambersburg; much like the Pruitt kid, he fought back and forfeited his life for his effort. Last week, the same gun ended the life of a decorated federal agent working undercover in Pennsylvania. Our last contact with him was just over a week ago. He told his handler he was close, extremely close. That's all we know."

"I'm sorry for your department's loss. Can you tell us more about what your agent was working on? Tell us more about the kidnappings in Pennsylvania. How many have there been?" Osborne quizzed.

"To date, there have been seven, exactly the same modus operandi you have seen here. Random teens just vanished with no clues until now. You have the car," confessed Agent Spivey.

"Was the same car used in Keystone State? Have you looked at the Buick?" inquired Osborne.

"No, Lt. Osborne, not yet. There seems to be a pissing contest between my boss and yours. I would appreciate anything you can do to get me near that car," Spivey requested.

"Do you have the fingerprints of the young man murdered in Pennsylvania? That would confirm your suspicions; it would literally tie the kidnappings together. Hal, could you give Lt. Osborne and me a moment alone? We need to talk about you behind your back, just for a minute. Ashley, I want you to be included in this," I informed.

"I'll say this about you, Forde, you're honest. No, I don't mind; I'll step out and keep your secretary company. Emily, right? Let me know when you're finished."

The agent seemed somewhat amused by my words; I desperately needed to hear what the others were thinking. In a short time, most of my earlier red flags had been removed, but not all.

"Wow, Boss, that was blunt!"

"I agree with you, Miss Ashley. Brody, you're the real McCoy. I thought he was going to apologize for being here. So, what are you thinking? Do you trust what he says?" asked Osborne.

"Ashley, you first, what do you think of Agent Spivey? Can we trust him?" I asked.

"I don't know, Boss, he did break into our office."

"Will, you're next, what's on your mind?"

"Why all the cloak and dagger? They're federal agents. Why not just make a formal request? Local authorities have to surrender evidence when requested," confirmed Osborne.

"What do you think Billings would say had he been here?" I questioned.

"He thinks like Johannsson; he might have shot him had he been here," Osborne chuckled.

I paused, sorting the words of my colleagues. Both made excellent points, but I respected the agent's candor. When one neutrally assessed what we knew, what did we actually have? We had two choices: working independently, which has produced little, or moving forward collectively. Assuming Spivey was right that this was a white slave trade operation, it's bigger than all of us.

"Before we invite him back in, let me ask you this: what do we actually know that he doesn't? This is about solving crime, not who is right or wrong. If he's right about the slave trade, and I am certain he is, the clock is ticking on the lives of nearly twenty teenagers. We've got to bring the feds in, agreed?" I surmised.

With uncertainty, Osborne and Ashley nodded their approval. I slowly walked to the door, giving either time to veto the decision. No motions or sounds occurred as I opened the door, signaling Agent Spivey's return.

"We have agreed the FBN needs to be included in our investigations. Notice I said investigations, plural. See, Agent Spivey, you and the Winchester police have one case working: missing persons. I have both a murder of a local woman and have been brought in to assist the local authorities on the kidnappings. Make no mistake, Jo Brathwaite's murder is my first priority. I, however, believe both may be connected. Do you understand my predicament?"

"Yes, Mr. Forde, I appreciate your situation. I know nothing of your Jo Brathwaite, but I will offer whatever I can; I give my word," promised Agent Spivey.

"Before we finalize this, I have several non-negotiable terms. First, I want to meet with Agent Colegate, just the two of us. Can you make that happen?"

"I'll try. I strongly suggest a public place, he's a dangerous man, Mr. Forde. What are your other terms?"

"That there will be no more break-ins, understand?" I stressed.

"Understood, that it?" Spivey countered.

"No, one more thing: both of my ladies will be given the respect male agents would receive. Any disrespect, in any manner, towards either of my employees, I'll shoot you myself!"

As the evening ended, hands were shaken, and even a few light smiles were exchanged. Everyone headed out, ending a long, tiring day.

Chapter Twenty-One

The piercing ring of the telephone interrupted my sleep. My eyes, struggling to open, looked toward my trusty Big Ben, telling me it was 5:30 a.m. Who could be calling me at this hour? Before the receiver reached my ear, the booming, imperious voice echoed off my bedroom walls.

"Ford, you there?"

"Ah, yes, Special Agent Colegate. How might I help you this bright and extremely early morning?" I questioned.

"Agent Spivey said you needed to meet with me. How about in your hotel dining room in ten minutes?" ordered the belligerent Colegate.

"They don't open for breakfast until 6:00 a.m.; it's only 5:30 a.m. How about we make it 6:00?" I informed.

"Actually, I *persuaded* them to open... *now*. I'm sitting at your table, enjoying a fine cup of coffee. I must say, I'm impressed you have a private table in a swank place like this; you must be a really big man. I'll see you in ten minutes!"

This morning had gotten off to a less-than-prodigious start. Deciding not to rush my routine, I took a hot shower, shaved, and dressed. The clock was at 5:55 as I walked out the door, heading for the elevator; let the games begin."

"Good morning, Agent Colegate. Are you enjoying the coffee? It is a delectable blend, only served here. Candace, could you please bring me my usual?" I politely requested.

"You're late! When I say ten minutes, I mean—"

"Stop, stop right there! I don't work for you. This all stops now, understand? And you owe everyone in this dining room an apology that will be given as a generously large tip, understand?" I demanded.

"Okay, big tip, that's fine. Now, what is so important that you demand a meeting with me? I'm here; start talking," sarcastically replied Colegate.

"Let's begin with this question: how would you have reacted had we broken into your office and violated your desks? Answer me, sir. How would you have responded?" I directly asked.

"Fair enough. So, what do you want? Why am I sitting here with *somebody* like you?"

Hearing those words, I asked myself the same question: why was I here? This guy had no intention of working with us or with anyone. He wrapped himself in the fictitious cloak of federal superiority, the fallacy that all power rested in the national government. While it may be true that the federal government was higher in the pecking order, the Constitution of these United States established multiple levels of government, each ordained with specific responsibilities and the power to enforce them. This want-to-be dictator was about to learn the principles of democracy.

"May I ask you another question? As an employee of the federal government paid with taxpayers' dollars, don't you, at least indirectly, work for all of us, including me?" I questioned.

The smug face retreated, the dominating eyes dropped, and the threatening voice remained silent. My stone may have struck the giant, staggering him momentarily, but he did not fall to the ground. Had I hit a nerve, softening the beast, or had I just tossed gasoline onto a raging fire? The answer came quickly and in the anticipated manner: he ignored it.

"So, what do you want to discuss? Breaking and entering? There will be no more breaking into your office; fair enough? The two young ladies who work for you will be treated with respect. We will share what I decide you need to know, and if you have an argument with that, understand this: there are things I cannot talk with any of you about. It's got nothing to do with your 'pecking order.' I am bound by law not to discuss it unless my boss allows it, and you're welcome to call whomever you wish; that isn't going to change," Colegate explained.

"Understood. So, what can you share? We are at a crossroads, unsure which direction to take our investigation. As I told Agent Spivey, my primary focus has to be on the brutal murder of Ada Jo Brathwaite. Much as I hate to say it, the missing teens are secondary on my agenda," I said, defining my priorities.

"I understand, but you could do much more if you concentrated your energy on the missing kids. That girl is going to be just as dead tomorrow, next week, or even next year. These missing teens are running out of time; some have been gone nearly a..."

Colegate stopped as the waitress approached our table with breakfast. I have my usual country ham, scrambled eggs, toast, and their delicious blend coffee. My eyes widened when I saw a double order of nearly everything on the menu placed before the robust agent: country ham, sausage, four pancakes with an equal number of eggs, sunny-side up—for starters. He instructed Candace to hold the remainder of his meal until he had finished the first serving: he hated to eat a cold breakfast. If Colegate had been as engaged in his work as he was in consuming food, this case should have been solved last week.

With maple syrup dripping from the corner of his mouth, Colegate returned to his assessment. "Like I was saying... some of these... kids have been missing for nearly a month. They may have already been traded or... may be dead. Who knows?"

"Any idea who exactly is behind the scheme? Is it the Cosa Nostra?" I questioned.

"Who else could it be? Do you think it was a coincidence Luca Marchetti was killed in this hick town?" Colegate asked, continuing to cram food into his mouth.

"Yeah, but why would he be here in the first place? Don't the top people generally stay clear? Why would he get his hands dirty?" I asked, still confused.

"We believe the kids are being held here, near the railroad. When they get enough warm bodies, they are loaded into a boxcar and shipped to Baltimore. The problem is, where are they while waiting for shipment?" Colegate informed.

"But how does that relate to the Pennsylvania teens? According to Agent Spivey, the Buick we have in impound has been used in both states. There is no rail system connecting Winchester and Chambersburg. I'm sorry, Agent Colegate. Unless there is something you can't disclose, this doesn't add up."

"When can we have a look at the Buick? That idiot Johannsson has it locked up; we can't get near it," complained the agent.

"You mean to tell me a federal agent can't get a court order forcing Johannsson to release the car?"

"You don't know Sonny Johannsson. He's got friends or, for a loss of better words, chicken-hearted contacts holding political power. How do you think he landed in Winchester as the police chief? Johannsson plays by his own rules; in time, you'll see," professed the agent.

"I'll try to get you access to the car, but I also want to be there. How about 3:00 p.m. this afternoon?" I asked.

"Fine, that'll work just right. We got a secret weapon to use on the car—it should be ready by then. I'll send Bosworth and Spivey to your office at 2:30 p.m.; you can take them with you. It will give you boys a little time to get chummy. I think Bosworth would enjoy spending quality time with all of you," Colegate sarcastically commented.

Our breakfast meeting had come to an end, so I took my morning ride, picked up the ladies, and then headed to the office. In a matter of minutes, Lt. Osborne joined us in the conference room, anxious for the details of my sunrise counsel of war.

I brought everyone up to speed, omitting many of the dramatic moments. I was surprised to see Osborne without his shadow, Detective Billings. When asked, Will informed us that the department could no longer sacrifice the time of two detectives on one lead. It's somewhat amusing thinking of this office as a lead. I supposed we would find out in time.

"Will, my friend, we must allow Agents Spivey and Bosworth access to the Buick. Can you make that happen?"

"Sure, Johannsson and Billings will be away most of the day. The chief never ordered us to keep them away, only not to tell them anything he doesn't first approve. He never said a word about the car," explained Osborne.

"Boss, I once heard it's easier to ask for forgiveness than permission," proclaimed Ashley.

"It's that attitude that troubles our daddy. She's always been that way, Mr. Forde," said Emily.

"Who do you think told me that, sis? Yeah, it was Daddy," the older O'Connell sister explained.

"Actually, Ashley, our grandpa told us that, not Daddy," corrected Emily.

"Okay, sisters, return to your corners. I have assignments for each of you. Emily, I need you to call the Clarke County Sheriff's office, use that alluring voice God gave you, and request Deputy Feltner to contact me at his convenience. Make sure he knows it is part of an ongoing investigation. Do not surrender any information; just ask him to call."

"I will do that, Sir. I can follow orders, unlike someone else we know. I don't have to seek forgiveness later," answered Emily.

"Okay, fine. Ashley, I need you to go through Kate's box. Separate the photos, carefully read each letter, note, or whatever, and assemble them in some order. Pay careful attention to addresses, numbers, and anything that seems remotely relevant. Ashley, this may be the key to our investigation," I carefully instructed.

"You can count on me, Boss. I won't let you down."

"Emily, when you finish with Feltner, help your sister go through the box—and both of you remember, you are sisters with vital jobs. Okay?"

My heart eased as both girls gave identical left-handed salutes, confirming adherence.

I then turned my attention to Lt. Osborne. "Will, what are your plans this morning?"

"Well, I just wanted to hear about your face-to-face with Colegate. I've got a few loose ends to tie up, but most of my day will center on the feds and the Buick. What do you need?"

"Can you call the Loudon County Sheriff's Office and find the whereabouts of Gunner Tate? He was Joseph Brathwaite's war buddy; we must speak with him."

"I can do that. I know Sheriff Jackson well; he's a good and dedicated lawman. If Tate is in Loudon County, Jackson will find him."

"If everything sounds good, I'll meet all of you here around 2:00 p.m.," I said.

"Just so we know, should we need you, where are you heading, Boss?" asked Ashley.

"First, I'm going by the hospital to check on Homer Hunt; Kate says he's dying. I thought he might welcome a visitor. This man is fighting death because he fought for our country. I believe he deserves a little of my time today."

"I agree with you. Do you mind if I join you?" requested Osborne.

"Not at all, Will, I'd enjoy the company. Ladies, I'll check in around noon. Call the Glow, have them deliver lunch, and pay them out of petty cash."

"We always do, Boss. Thanks."

Overlooking Ashley's latest confession, Will and I arrived at the hospital; fortunately, we were not going to the basement. We signed the visitor register and headed to the second floor, room 206.

We slowly entered the room to find two extremely ill men. Only a few ago, this highly spirited man joked with Ashley about being named after the dog. Now, Homer Hunt lay before me, barely alive, gasping as if each breath may be his last. We stood as if his body had already given up his spirit when a shout came from the other bed.

"Hunt, you got company! He's awake; we talked a minute ago. Homer, people here to see you," the unknown patient bellowed.

"Ah, Mr. Forde, where's the... the sweet-looking little blond? I... I want to see... see angels, not ole... hound dogs like... like you two."

"How about I bring her around or get her to come by very soon? Would that be okay with you, sir?" I asked.

"Yep... that... works. I'm glad... glad you're... here... we need... need to talk."

"Why don't you just try to rest and get your strength back? Then we can talk all you want," I answered.

"No... it can't... can't wait. Who's this... this goober?"

"I'm Lieutenant Wilbur Osborne, Winchester police, Sir. I just wanted to thank you for your service to our country."

As the veteran tried to speak again, he turned to spit an excessive amount of blood into a coffee mug on the tray to the left of his bed. Upon inspection, the mug was nearly full. "After... you hear... what... what I'm gonna' tell... tell you... you gonna... gonna change... your mind. Forde... I, I want to con... confess... I killed some... some... some bad people." Before another word could be uttered, he added to the blood mug, then began what seemed like an eternal, choking cough. Gathering what little strength remained, he continued his story.

"Who did you kill, Mr. Hunt? Can you give me any names?" asked the startled lawman.

"Don't know... know names... just killed... killed all... all of em."

"All of who? Who did you kill? Please tell us, who did you kill?" pleaded the Lieutenant.

"Will, he's out of his mind... delirious, as it be," I said, defending the dying man.

"Brody, this man just confessed murder to an officer of the law. I cannot ignore his confession, not to you or anyone."

While Osborne and I were conducting our debate, Homer drifted to sleep. His breathing continued to be erratic, and he was still tightly grasping life. The visit had ended, so we returned to my car.

"Brody, he confessed to murder. Why else would he have mentioned it? He wants his conscience free to meet his maker."

"What did he actually say? 'He had killed men; he never said who or when. I'm telling you, his body may be in Virginia, but his mind was on the battlefields of Europe."

"So, you would have me pretend I never heard of this? Is that what you want?" as Osborne directed his interrogation to me.

"I didn't say that; I'm just asking you to consider other facts. We have five unsolved murders, right? We know he didn't kill Lester Pruitt or Jo Brathwaite, agreed? Now, let's be objective: how could that old man have subdued Rolf Schlesinger and tied him to the steering wheel of a truck?" I challenged.

Osborne, holding his position, repeated, "Regardless of his physical condition, I heard Homer Hunt confess to murder. How do I ignore what I heard?"

"How about a highly connected member of the Cosa Nostra family? Kill him, then move him to a ditch? What are his chances of killing a man from the third-story of a theatre, running down three flights of stairs, and not being seen? Will, he was confessing the war, that's all," I continued, maintaining my defense of Hunt's innocence.

"So, Brody, what am I supposed to do?"

"Do what you were going to do before we visited the hospital—in my mind, nothing has changed," I said, concluding my point.

Now back at the office, Will climbed out of the car and abruptly turned back, placing his hands firmly on the front passenger side door. Pausing, he took deep breaths and looked me firmly in the eyes. "I know you're trying to help; I appreciate that. For now, I'm going to agree with you. For now. Mr. Forde, you're a solid detective, but so am I. I was on the force walking the streets of Winchester, gaining wisdom while you were still in school getting smart. It's with that wisdom I'm telling you this: that dying old man knows something. I hope we learn it before it's too late. Talk to you later, Brody."

His words pierced my heart: Osborne had my attention. Who was I to give him advice on detective work? I was working on my first two cases; Osborne had closed dozens if not hundreds. I had forgotten why I was invited to join this investigation. Chief Johannsson didn't want to be tied to the feds, especially Agent Colgate. I wasn't part of this case because of my investigative skills; I was here because I was no threat to either side, local or federal.

Chapter Twenty-Two

B ack at the office, I checked on the girls. On my way up the stairs, I passed a young man coming down with a large empty basket. Continuing to the open door, the wonderful aroma of roast beef and freshly baked bread enticed my sudden desire to eat.

"Getting an early start on lunch, are we?" I inquired.

"Ah, yeah, Boss, Emily was complaining of hunger pains. So, what's a loving sister to do?" Ashley sympathetically explained.

"I'm not the one who was starving; I have willpower," countered Emily.

"Ladies, frankly, I don't care. When either of you are hungry, get food. Okay, so do you have any news? Emily, any luck in Clarke County?"

"Actually, yes. I spoke with Deputy Feltner, a kind man, but he thinks it's his father you need to speak with, not him. His daddy was in the war and a friend of Joe Brathwaite's. Deputy Feltner said he had to come to Winchester tomorrow on business so he could bring his father with him sometime around 10:00 a.m. He also said his father would require hot coffee when he gets here. I insured him that was not a problem."

"Excellent work, Emily, excellent. Ashley, have you made any progress with the box of letters?"

"Working on it; there's a bunch of stuff in there. I'm almost finished separating everything; I'll get back to it when we finish lunch."

"That's fine, but understand everything in that box is highly confidential. Nothing, and I mean nothing, is to leave this office, physically or orally."

"Hey Boss, there is one name that keeps popping up in the box: a guy named Gunner Tate. I can't determine where he lives or if he made it home. One thing I can tell you is that he and Joe were close."

"That's good, Ashley. Keep digging; find me all you can on this Gunner Tate. I'll be back in just a bit. I'm heading over to see Max; I've got several names to run by him. If Osborne calls, tell him where I am."

I arrived at the old Shell station to find Sam under fire. A constant target, the lad was also dear to the old proprietor's heart. Max would be lost should Sam ever leave; each filled a void for the other.

"Ceasefire! I come in peace!" I said, walking toward the open garage door.

"What's that supposed to mean? You come in peace—ain't nobody yelling at you yet. Give it a minute; you'll say something stupid. Now, Sam, tell Sherlock what you did."

Somewhat embarrassed, the lanky sixteen-year-old searched for words. Nothing appeared broken, and I saw no one injured. What could he have possibly done to warrant this reaction?

"I, ah, I left the back door open on Cedrick Mumford's Dodge, and... and Felix climbed in, curled up on the floorboard, and went to sleep. When Cedrick came and picked up his car, he shut the door without noticing Felix and drove off," Sam explained.

"Oh my, is Felix all right?" I asked.

"Yeah, when Felix woke up halfway across town, he jumped from the back to the front seat, and Cedrick damn near soiled himself. He brought the cat home; nobody hurt, I guess, but there could have been," as Max finished the story.

"Well, I'm glad Felix is okay. Look at it this way: the cat got an unexpected ride through town."

"See, I told you, wait long enough, and you'll always say something stupid. Now, what do you want? You aren't here to talk about cats taking rides.

"You're correct; I didn't come here to speak of cats, although I am glad Felix is okay. Max, you ever heard of a Gunner Tate?"

"Naw, can't say I have—who's he supposed to be?"

"A war buddy of Joe Brathwaite's. You've never heard of him? You know everyone, but you don't know him?"

"Is he from here? I don't know of any Tates living around here. When the war started, they took men from five or six counties to form the 29th Division. If I were a bettin' man, as you know I am, I'd say he was from Clarke or Loudon County. Lots of Tates in both of those counties. Why ya asking? Is he important? Did he have something to do with Jo's murder?"

"I don't know; it's just a name that has come up. How about Jebediah Feltner? Do you know anything about him?" my questions continued.

"Doesn't he have a boy that's a Clarke County deputy? I believe there used to be a Jeb Feltner up around Gore. I can't say I know much of either of them," Max replied as he rubbed his unshaven chin.

"We believe Tate is from Loudon County; that's what Kate Brathwaite told me. I just wondered if you knew anything about him. May I ask you another type of question, a riddle?"

"Sure, I like riddles—fire away, Sherlock."

"How could someone kill a man in plain sight, then, without anyone noticing, place a white feather into his shirt pocket? How could he do that?"

"That's easy; he'd put the feather in the man's pocket before he killed him," explained Max.

"Before he shot him? How could he do that? Wouldn't that draw suspicion from the victim?" as I dug deeper.

"Not if the victim knew him. The real question: how did the shooter know the man was going to be there in the first place at that precise time?" Max asked.

"He was set up!" I shouted—the victim knew and trusted the man who killed him. But how? What am I missing?"

We paused for a moment; then Max presented several unexpected questions. "Don't you have more questions to ask me? How about that odd key he had? I also heard Jo's prints were on the car. Got any answers?"

"How could you possibly know all of this? None of this has been made public information. How do you know about Jo's prints?" I asked in shock.

"You kiddin' me? The Winchester Police Department has more leaks than the Titanic, and you know how that ended. When were you gonna tell me about all the feathers?" as Max's interrogation of me continued.

"Why don't you tell me about all the feathers?" I asked, still in awe of the amount of leaked information.

"Just like the guy in the shed out at Nain and the mob kid in the ditch in Middletown, right?" Max's questions mounting.

"Er, right. How do you know all this?" I asked, still trying to learn Max's sources.

"Are you kiddin' me? Hell, son, everybody knows: there aren't any secrets in this little town. You know the story about the white feathers, right?"

"No, Max, I do not—neither does Osborne. What do the feathers represent?"

"Well, it goes back to the war. It wasn't used with the American troops but was a big deal with the Brits. See, any able-bodied male walking the street of London during the war, not in uniform, was considered a coward. To insult or embarrass the man, an unassuming woman would walk up to them and place a white feather in their pocket, saying they were a chicken, afraid to fight for England. See, they couldn't do that to the American doughboys; they were all in uniform."

"But why is this happening here? The war is over, and according to what you just said, it applied to the British, not the Americans. Why is the killer leaving a sign?" scratching my head as I asked.

"Do I have to do all your work? Figure it out, Sherlock, that's what you get paid to do!"

With my scolding completed, I walked inside the garage office to see for myself that Felix was okay. Unsurprisingly, he was asleep on his rug under Max's desk—all was well in the cat world. I considered asking Max if I might find space in the corner to settle in, to listen and learn. In a matter of seconds, I gained more information than a week of questioning numerous individuals. Again, I was in awe of my elderly mentor: if he could only find a little patience with Sam.

Instead of returning to the office, I detoured to the police station. As expected, the federal agents were combing through the interior of the dubious sedan. To my amazement, a new officer was leading the investigation: a canine named Socks.

"Brody, you've got to see this! This dog, sorry, Agent Socks, has sniffed out eight kilograms of pure heroin. It was in a secret compartment fabricated into the rear floorboard. It was so well hidden that we never suspected it the other day. The dog has been trained to find all kinds of narcotics. Allow me to introduce Sock's handler, Agent Marion Pettigrew," came the words from an excited Lt. Osborne.

"Agent Pettigrew, I've read of such animals. I believe the concept originated in Ghent."

"Yes, Mr. Forde. You are the private investigator, correct? I've heard much about you from some of my fellow agents."

"Please, Sir, don't hold that against me. We got off to a somewhat poor start. So, tell me, when did the federal government begin using such techniques?" hoping to satisfy my growing curiosity.

"We simply expanded the use of bloodhounds—the same principle, just trained the dogs to search for different prey. We are a work in progress; not all departments believe the use of dogs has a future.

I'm convinced the dogs will have a bright future at all levels of law enforcement," explained Pettigrew.

Agent Pettigrew returned to Socks and their work. Osborne and I stood amazed as the black and brown German Shepherd with white feet sniffed every inch of the enigmatical automobile. When the mission had been completed, Socks was rewarded with a gentle pat on the head, followed by several slices of bacon—where had I seen that before?

"So, Wilbur, are you thinking of a possible new partner? Agent Socks is impressive, and he doesn't say much," I commented.

"That's not true. You should have seen him when he discovered the hidden compartment in the floor: he went nuts," Osborne countered.

"So, we now know what the feds were after, now what? How does this all fit together?" I asked.

"I don't know, Brody, but we are closer than we realize. We need a break, something that connects the dots. Something else: I want to apologize for my words earlier today. You're a skilled investigator; I'm just angry. I want all this to stop. Winchester is my home; I love this town and fear what it is becoming. No one is safe when men like Luca Marchetti and Gio Cappelletti walk the streets," confessed Will.

"Who, exactly, is Gio Cappelletti? What do you have on him?" I asked.

"Cappelletti was a *button man* for the Cosa Nostra; he worked for Luca Marchetti," Osborne answered.

"Are you sure?"

"No question about it. Chief Johannsson knew him in another life—when he was a detective in D.C. Agent Colgate also confirmed it when he was partners with the chief."

"Will, are you telling me that Chief Johannsson and Agent Colgate were partners?"

"That's what I'm telling you, although I don't know what happened between them to cause such a rift. They hate each other, but neither is telling why," Osborne replied.

"So, two members of the Cosa Nostra have been murdered, and we have no suspects. Is this killer that bold, that smooth, or are we just unproductive in our jobs? Why can't we figure this out?" I asked.

"There's one more thing about Cappelletti: his body has a slashing cut on his left arm. The Foleys said they saw Lester cut one of the men who tried to grab him just before he was killed. Brody, Cappelletti was one of those men: we have the proof," Osborne said with a measure of satisfaction.

"We need Dr. Stenner to make a comparison of the knife and the wound. Can you see to that, Will?" I requested.

"Already done. He said he would have the results by this afternoon."

The puzzle grew; more pieces added, yet the picture remained hidden. My father used to say, 'The wise man in business can see opportunity around the corner before others realize there is a corner.' Did that logic apply to this investigation? Did we have the corner in sight, or were we aimlessly following the horde?

The remainder of the day faded into the late evening. I drove the girls home, then turned my Chrysler toward Piccadilly Street. Since I had not studied the contents of Joe Brathwaite's war letters, photos, and mementos, I brought them home.

Ashley divided the papers into three-section groups in an orderly manner. First were a few photos, mostly group shots. Some had names printed on the backs. How young and innocent they were. The second group consisted of letters sent by Kate; I hesitated to read them. Perhaps tomorrow, but not tonight. Turning my attention to Joe's letters, I slowly began to know the man I had never met. His simple words expressed his sincere love for his wife and daughter. Much talk centered on expanding the farm and saving enough money to buy a tractor and a few implements.

I continued reading until my eyes surrendered, dropping into a deep sleep. Try as they might, fatigue conquered the demonic invasion. In what seemed like a few minutes, I awakened from my eight-hour slumber. How invigorating I felt.

Chapter Twenty-Three

I enjoyed my morning ritual; some may think of it as being in a rut, but starting each day in a well-planned manner allowed one to begin on a positive step. Unfortunately, the second step often interrupted the positive flow. Curse that second step.

On the windshield of my sedan was an envelope addressed to me. Inside were simple yet daunting words: *I must see you: Winchester National Cemetery, 10:00 a.m., at the Maryland State Memorial. Come alone!*

I'm not sure what to make of this, so I didn't tell the girls. I was not a fool, however. Once I got to the office, I called Lt. Osborne and informed him of my meeting. He would be there by 9:30 a.m. with three officers in plain clothes strategically positioned. Two snipers would also be poised to react should this not go well. Was I about to become the next murder victim?

How quickly the morning had changed.

Before leaving the safety of the office, I told Ashley I needed to see Max and would return shortly. The drive to 401 National Ave. was rather short, taking but seven minutes, but in that time, my heart had gone from a normal beat to a rapid rhythm, increasing by the minute. Sweat dripped from my face, and my hands struggled to grasp the steering wheel. I couldn't remember being this frightened.

I parked the car, trying not to draw attention to myself. Did others see the fear in my eyes? How would I know him? Would he be alone? I walked through the cemetery, not knowing where the Maryland Memorial was. Finally, after ten minutes of searching, I found my destination but saw no one.

I continue standing facing the words chiseled into the granite, honoring the men who gave the ultimate sacrifice, wondering if I was about to join the dead on this hallowed ground.

Suddenly, without warning, a beautiful woman dressed in black, wearing a widow's veil, slid her right arm under my left and softly gripped my hand. My perspiration-soaked hand didn't seem to bother her. My heart rate peaked when my new friend laid her head on my shoulder and whispered into my ear, "Mr. Forde, slowly turn and face me, lift my veil, then kiss me passionately."

"What?"

"You heard me, kiss me with the passion of a lover."

Wondering if I was still asleep, dreaming all of this, I complied. The lady in black then returned the affectionate grasp of my hand. We walked deeper into the cemetery, stopping at times to gaze at the names and dates on various headstones. If I were not so frightened for my life, this would have been a rather enjoyable stroll, although I would have selected a more suitable location. We eventually found a bench on which to sit. Had the mystery reached its climax?

"Mr. Forde, I was a dear friend to Lace; you know her as Jo Brathwaite. We worked at the Ivory Tower, you know, in Martinsburg. I saw you there a few days ago with a cute little blonde and that fellow pretending to be a landscaper, kneeling over by the roses."

"Okay, our cover is blown. How about you? Do you have any friends here I should know about?" I asked, my heart still pounding.

"No, I don't think so. Please trust me, I mean you no harm. I don't see anyone that would harm us, not now anyway."

"Do you have a name? You look familiar. Have we met?"

"I have a name, but I am not ready to give it yet. Yes, we have met indirectly; I was at the funeral, Lace's funeral."

"Why can't you give your name? What shall I call you? Why have you reached out to me?" I asked.

"We don't have time for all these questions right now. I asked you here to tell you, and that copper killing those roses, that your lives are in danger. Serious danger. So is mine if they find out we are talking. Why have I reached out to you? I have nowhere else to go," confided my mystery lady.

"Who should we be afraid of, Emiliano Marchetti?" I asked.

"Yes, he's one, but you have other enemies, several dangerously close to you," she advised.

"Who? Please give me names. Who wants to hurt us?" I pleaded.

"Not now. We don't have time to go into all of this. What I have to tell you will take too long here. We need to have a safe place, somewhere we can talk, and this time, I mean alone," the mysterious woman demanded.

"I need a little time to arrange a place. How can I contact you?" I asked.

"Can you trust that old geezer that has the gas station with that stupid mailbox?"

"Yes, he can be trusted, but I don't wish to involve him. What are you afraid of? Are you being followed? Wait! How do you know about Max?" My curiosity grew.

"I followed you there last Sunday. As for being followed, yes, sometimes, but it's not like you think. You see, I was Luca's favorite dame; Mr. Emil believes I am carrying his future grandson, but I'm not the one that was pregnant, am I?" she said, giving knowledge few possessed.

"You're telling me Jo Brathwaite was carrying Luca's baby?" I asked, trying to piece together the puzzle.

"Mr. Forde, in our line of work, how could you know? Yes, she was three months along. Luca's old man wants a grandson; he heard one of us was pregnant and still thinks it's me. It's a way to stay alive and to be protected in a violent life. The sad thing is Lace really loved Luca, but men like him love many women—for a while anyway. I figure I've got about another month before Mr. Emil will know I am not carrying his heir to the throne," she confessed with fear in her words.

We both sat silently, each pondering our next move. In a matter of minutes, so much had changed, yet, in reality, nothing had changed. Osborne had nervously dug a hole in the flowerbed that could be used for the next burial, wondering if he should do anything. I gave a small nod, indicating all was well.

Not sure what to do next, I offered, "Miss whomever, let's do this. I know you have an automobile; we photographed it, as well as you, at the funeral. Take it to Max's garage and schedule a tune-up and oil change. Ask to use the phone, call my office, allow it to ring twice, and then hang up. Repeat the sequence, then wait for me to arrive. We can talk in the back room of the garage."

"I don't know, that could be dangerous for all of us," she said, nervousness still present.

"If you believe you have been followed, don't make the call. If danger presents itself after the calls have been made, remove the hat you will wear as a signal. Hat on, I come in, hat off, I buy gas, then leave," I advised.

"Could we possibly meet this afternoon? Say, around 2:00 p.m.?" Urgency replaced the nervous tone.

"Absolutely. Now, understand, do not speak, hang up. I don't want either of my associates involved should this thing go sour," I instructed.

The mystery woman reached for my hand again, slowly kissed me, then said goodbye. The encounter ended as she walked away as gently as she had arrived. In seconds, Osborne was on the scene.

"Well, that was certainly interesting. Did you happen to get any information that we might use?" probed the lieutenant.

"Yes, and no. It's complicated. You can call off your boys; all is good for now," I advised.

"How'd we do? Did she suspect she was being watched?" asked Osborne.

"Not at all, my friend. Your cover was perfect. Now, fill up that hole you've dug before you get arrested for desecrating a flowerbed," I chuckled.

Before returning to the office, I gave Osborne the little information I could, which wasn't much. He took notes, then turned the conversation on 'my new friend,' as he put it.

"Is this what big city gumshoes call *deep cover*? You sure looked to be enjoying yourself," my friend jokingly asked.

"All in the line of duty, my friend, all in the line," I said, defending my actions.

Now back at the office, the interrogation continued.

"Whoa, somebody is wearing Chanel N° 5, and is that—is that, yes, it is! Somebody got kissed by a woman wearing blood-red lipstick. Boss, isn't it a little early in the day to be kissed like that?" Ashley quizzed.

"I guess I am... what did you call it the other day? I'm the bee's knees."

"Ah, no! I'm the bee's knees; you're more keen-looking, not bad, but not nearly as gorgeous as someone like me," Ashley countered.

"Honestly, Ashley, how vain can you be? Mr. Forde can be the bee's knees if he likes, right, Sir?" said Emily, defending me.

"Whatever you say, ladies. Now, can we focus on more important issues? When may I expect Mr. Feltner? Any word on the whereabouts of Gunner Tate?" I asked.

"Yes, Mr. Feltner will be here around noon. As for Tate, no word yet. Sheriff Jackson said he would call when he caught up with him. He said it should be sometime later today," replied Emily.

"Excellent. Okay, for now, ladies, I would like you to read every letter in Kate's box again. When I say read, I mean to put yourself into the letters. Imagine you are writing them, then think of yourself as receiving them. We have to find the messages that are between the lines. Do you understand what I am asking?" I instructed my staff.

"No problem, boss. We can do that. If anything is to be found, we'll uncover it. Now, what about that perfume you seem not to want to talk about? Are you hiding a woman in your life?" Ashley continued her own investigation.

"Ah, nothing on the perfume you think you smell. No, and yes to your other questions, in that order," I answered.

"Wait! What order did I ask? Why can't you talk normal like the rest of us?" a confused Ashley fired back.

Our tug-of-war discussion ended when I entered my private office and closed the door behind me. While I appreciated and enjoyed our morning rhetoric, the cemetery encounter had me on edge. The mystery woman seemed trustworthy, but was she really? Could she be setting me up like Gio Cappelletti may have been?

The remainder of my morning was spent reviewing the growing list of unanswered questions. How was the white feather placed into Cappelletti's pocket? How were the kidnapped teens selected? Random or specifically chosen? Where have Johannsson and Billings been in the past two days? The confusing question: what was the connection between the three murdered men? Two appeared obvious, but how did Rolf Schlesinger figure into the equation? Did he see something that forced the end of his life, or was he involved?

The questions, with an additional dozen or more, swirled like the leaves in an autumn breeze, never completely settling. The confusion within my mind stopped as Emily opened the door, announcing the arrival of Mr. Jebediah Feltner.

"Good morning, Sir; please, come in and have a seat. Ashley, would you join us and bring your notepad? Also, Emily, could you kindly bring each of us a cup of coffee? Would you care for cream or sugar, Mr. Feltner?"

"Just dip your little finger in my mug, little lady; that's all the sugar I need. You sure are a pretty thing!"

"Ah, yes, they both are, thanks for noticing, Mr. Feltner. And I want to thank you for coming in on such short notice," I replied, not sure which O'Connell sister he was addressing.

"It ain't no problem, Mr. Forde. My son, Ezekiel, is a deputy, you know; he brought me since he had to come to Winchester, anyway. So, how can I help you?"

"I would like to ask you several questions concerning Joseph Brathwaite and his time in the war. I have been told the two of you were close friends even before the war and served together in the 29th Blue and Gray Division. Can you tell me a little about Joe, his friendship, and maybe the time in France?" I asked, beginning my interrogation.

A deafening silence consumed the room, and the veteran's eyes sent the chilling sounds of artillery and gunfire as his mind returned to the hell of war. The clock's ticking echoed off the walls as Ashley and I waited. What anguish had been revived in the aging veteran by hearing my words? After some deep contemplation, the words came.

"Yeah, Joe and I were friends before we signed up—had to, you know. Joe never knew what hit him. I was there when it happened; his head just flew off his shoulders. That's all there is to tell."

I took a couple of deep breaths, carefully selecting my next words. The demons that haunted my dreams were but fairies compared to what this man, and so many like him, must live with. I couldn't imagine standing next to a man, and then, in a second, his entire head had left his body. And this was just one of hundreds, or even thousands, of men killed in sight of this poor soul. Now, here I was, asking him to relive it. Why was I pausing? There were no careful words to select.

"Mr. Feltner, can you tell me of some of the relationships you and Joe had? For instance, can you tell me of a leave or, if any, good times you may have shared? Who were some of the men Joe was closest to?"

"Well, as hard as it might be to believe, they were some good times. I remember when we all got stuck in this old barn," fighting to hold back the laughter. "I don't know exactly where we were, just somewhere in France. Homer, Joe, Coop, Frosty, and me decided we was goin' get some French wine. Well, we found three bottles of Vinaigre Balsamique in a deserted house. Now, none of us could read French, but Coop, our expert, said it was a French Bordeaux: the best of the best," related the veteran with chuckling sprinkled within his words.

"Wait a minute, you said Vinaigre Balsamique? That's Balsamic Vinegar; that's not wine," I said with a grin on my face.

"Yep, that's what it was, all right. The problem was that none of us would admit we didn't know what it was. We was just too proud. You know how it is when a bunch of guys git together. We just sat there drinking the strongest vinegar you have ever tasted. For the next three days, we all did the Texas two-step. On the good side, we was all cleaned out inside, through and through. It really cleaned out your gizzard!" Laughter erupted from the depths of Feltner's lungs.

After a hearty laugh at our friend's expense, the stories began to flow. The minutes grew to nearly an hour when a valuable piece of information surfaced.

"Yep, Marty and Vern came back claiming they had been in a knife fight with three Huns, but when the truth came out, they had been spurred by an old rooster when they tried to steal some eggs. The boys could really tell the tales. That was the night we made the *Promettre?*"

"You made the Promettre? What did you promise? Whose idea was it to make this pledge?" I asked.

"As I remember, it was Homer Hunt. Yeah, Homer came up with the idea since he feared dying and had a new baby back home. A real shame his wife and baby both died from the Spanish flu just after he got home," Mr. Feltner uttered with sadness in his voice.

"Who all made the Promettre? What was the promise each of you committed to?"

"Well, Homer, of course, me, Joe, Marty, Coop, that's Duke Cooper, Gunner, Vern, and Frosty. We all promised that if any of us didn't make it back home, those who did would take care of the widows and kids," the honorable man said.

"Who is Frosty? I've heard of the others; I'm unfamiliar with Frosty," I inquired.

"Foster Cobb; Mr. Forde, he's crazy, *hill people*, you know!" Feltner advised.

"Yes, I've heard of him and them. I have been told he may be dangerous, but no one says what makes him dangerous. Can you help me? What are his issues?" I asked, still trying to understand *Hill people*.

"Ain't no issues, he's just nuts! Look, we all did what we had to do in the war, me included. But Frosty did it because he loved it. We called him Frosty cause he's got ice running through his veins. He was a cold-blooded killer in the war. Like I said, he loved it. All of it."

"That is interesting. Was he a capable shot? Was he considered a marksman?" I asked.

"I guess you could call him a marksman; he was a decent shot, but that wasn't his favorite weapon. He was just as deadly with a bayonet or a sharp knife. I'm tellin' you, Forde, stay away from that one!"

"He didn't have any family, did he? Why would he have joined in the Promettre?"

"He thought he was our protector. Heck, he was our protector; he saved each of us several times. He might be crazy, but we all owe our lives to Frosty Cobb!"

"How so? Can you give me an example of his heroics?" I'm intrigued.

"He could smell the Huns—he also has the eyes of a hawk. Once, two krauts crawled almost on top of our trench. We were all trying to get a little shut-eye, you know, whenever you could. They would sometimes get close enough to toss a grenade on top of you. Well, Frosty smelled them and crawled out without them hearing or seeing him. He was able to get around, come up behind them, and slit both of their throats. He stole their weapons, boots, and helmets for souvenirs. He may be crazy, but he was the deadliest soldier among us."

"Why didn't he just wake you up? Why would he take such a dangerous risk?" Ashley asked.

"Because if he had awakened us, they would have heard him, and we would all be dead. They had grenades, and it was dark. No, ma'am, Frosty did what had to be done, and he did it well. He wasn't the only single man in the Promettre; Gunner Tate didn't have a family either.

I think they just wanted to be part of something. In war, your buddies are your family—can't put it into words—you're just family."

"This man, Tate, is he a good shot?" I inquired.

"Are you kidding? Gunner couldn't hit water if he fell out of a boat. That's just his name, Gunner. He's a nice guy but couldn't hit the side of a barn. Now, he could scrounge with the best of them."

"Scrounge, boss, what is scrounge?" Ashley asked.

"Steal, he could find things, like food, water, whatever was needed," I answered.

"Steal is such a dirty word, Mr. Forde. We like to think of it as commandeering items necessary for survival. That's what Sarge used to call it. Whatever it was, Gunner was the best at it, but he was better at commandeering and loading the rifles for us than firing them."

Our time had ended. Deputy Feltner returned to retrieve his father and needed to get back to Clarke County. I thanked Jebediah Feltner for his time and the stories. Many held the gruesome truth of war, but some showcased the innocence of youth and the highest level of devotion.

The office was now clear, allowing the three of us to compare notes. Laughter turned to tears, then back to laughter, repeating the old man's stories. We all agreed that Frosty Cobb had to be considered a strong suspect in the killings. He not only had the ability, but he also possessed the mind of a killer, possibly a serial killer. As the clock struck three, the phone rang twice. Could this be the mystery lady calling? Before I could speak, Emily answered, silencing the ring.

Chapter Twenty-Four

"Yes, Lt. Osborne, Mr. Forde is right here. Sir, it's for you," she said, handing me the phone.

"Brody, you're not going to believe this; Detective Billings, under orders, has pinched Robert Poston for the three murders. He's being charged as we speak. Can you come to the station? Johannsson says he's got the goods on Poston. I'm not so sure; I think it's all circumstantial. Can you come now?"

Running the risk of missing my important call, I responded to Osborne's plea. Before leaving, I called Max's station, asking if a woman had stopped in for a tune-up. I was surprised to learn no one, male or female, had been in. I instructed Ashley and Emily to call a cab for their ride home at closing time. With all bases covered, I headed to the station to support my friend.

Inside the courthouse, press members were being physically removed, but surprisingly, I was permitted to stay.

"Brody, glad you made it. Johannsson has Poston in a holding cell downstairs; this is never good," explained the nervous Osborne.

"What happened? What evidence has made Robert Poston a suspect?" I asked.

"Billings found out that Poston had threatened to kill Luca Marchetti outside of the Poston house earlier this month. He has a witness, Dorthea Fleming, who goes by the name of Dot. Brody, you know her; you kissed her this morning. She's your mystery lady," Osborne informed.

"What? No, it can't be!"

"It can, and it is; she is the witness. She swears she saw and heard everything," continued Osborne.

"Did she mention this this morning?" I nervously questioned.

"No, she never said a word, and I strongly suggest we keep that between us for now," Osborne advised.

"But what about the other men you had in the cemetery? Won't they talk?"

"Truthfully, I was alone—there weren't any snipers or anyone else there, just me. I didn't know who I could trust; it was such short notice. The guy you saw with me was my brother-in-law. He's out of work, and I told him you would pay him a *fin*."

"So, we went there this morning with no backup, and now I owe your brother-in-law $5? What would have happened if it had been a setup?" I questioned.

"You would probably be dead, but look on the bright side; you wouldn't owe my wife's brother the fin," explained Osborne.

"That's hardly comforting. So, can we see Robert Poston?"

"We can try. Let me do the talking; it will be better that way," pleaded the lieutenant.

"Maybe we should call for some of your backup. How's that sound?" I joked.

"This is no time to be funny. Just follow me, and please, keep quiet," Osborne said desperately.

We proceeded to the rear staircase leading to the holding cells. The cells, like the stairwell, were dimly lit, with green paint peeling from the walls. On either end of the long corridor, two patrolmen stood guard. The cell door was locked, with the powerful Johannsson standing over the seated Poston. Blood dripped from Robert's lower lip, and one eye was swollen.

"What the hell are you two doing here? I don't need your help interrogating this suspect!" barked the chief.

"Is that what you call it, interrogating? It looks like you're about to beat a confession out of him," I reasoned.

"Naw, that ain't what you see, Forde. He slipped. In fact, he's about to slip a whole lot more. When I'm finished, he'll confess!"

"Ah, Chief, Sir, are you sure you want to do this? I mean, Sir, what has he done that makes you believe he's guilty?" begged Osborne.

"I don't answer to you, Lieutenant! But, if you need to know, this *palooka* has a record. Now get the hell out of here before both of you get some of what he's about to get!" Johannsson threatened.

"Chief, please, what has he done?" Osborne again pleaded.

"I told you to git, now git while you still have a job, and take the gumshoe with you!"

Before either of us could respond, two officers at the end of the hall came to escort us away.

"Robert Poston, I am a lawyer! Would you like me to represent you at this time? A verbal yes, with these witnesses, will suffice. Am I now your legal counsel?" I pleaded.

Still bleeding, the frightened man nodded his head in the affirmative and slowly said, "Yes, Mr. Ah, what's your name? Will you represent me?" the barely conscious Poston asked.

Johannsson's dagger-filled eyes met mine. Grateful for the steel bars separating us, I realized my new client needed the same protection. Any hope of finding a middle ground with *Goliath* was gone. Making matters worse, Johannsson realized he must stop, giving the appearance of backing down in front of his men. Not sure what his next move may be, I brought my tone to a more moderate level, trying to offer my adversary an honorable escape.

"Chief Johannsson, I am asking you, in the presence of all these lawmen, to cease your interrogation and allow me time to meet with my client—in private. Will you agree to this at this time?" I requested in a calm, professional voice.

With his right fist drawn back, the veteran cop paused, then relaxed his arm, staring silently into the face of the accused. After several deep breaths, he turned and asked one of the patrolmen to unlock the cell.

Fear ran through my body as my protective door bore wings and flew open. Johannsson exited the cell, not touching my client but denying me immediate time with Poston.

"All right, Forde, you won this round, but make no mistake, this ain't over. Lieutenant, would you kindly inform this *shyster* of the process he must follow to meet with his punk client? Now, step aside before I forget my manners, Mr. Forde!" threatened the massive man.

I moved to my left, allowing the fuming chief to pass. The two patrolmen followed their boss, resuming their posts at the end of the corridor.

Osborne cited the necessary steps to become Poston's legal representative. First, I had to file my status as a licensed attorney at the Winchester Courthouse. Second, I needed to present signed documentation, making me Robert's attorney with both the city of Winchester and the Frederick County Sheriff's office since several of the crimes Poston was being charged with occurred outside of the city limits. Once all the paperwork was filed, I would have access to all evidence pertaining to the case. What had I done?

Before leaving, I advised Poston to remain silent until I returned tomorrow. Lieutenant Osborne and I stepped outside the station for fresh air and a moment to discuss what had just happened.

"So, Brody, you are now a practicing attorney. Are you nuts?" Osborne said as he evaluated my latest actions.

"I had to do something; Johannsson was going to kill him. I didn't know what else to do under the circumstances. At least Poston's safe for the night, isn't he?" I questioned.

"Yeah, he's safe, for now. I'm not so sure you are, though. Are you okay?" my friend asked.

"Yes, I'm fine. So, can you tell me what evidence the police have on my client?"

"This is what I know, but I think there is more. Dorthea Fleming swears she heard Poston threaten to kill Luca Marchetti while standing on the porch of his mother's boarding house. Brody, I believe her."

"You heard her say that? When, where?"

"Several hours ago, in the real interrogation room upstairs. Johannsson got a tip on her several days ago and had Billings checking her out. They know she works at the Ivory Tower and that she knew Jo Brathwaite."

"But how do they fit all this together? I mean, why do they think Marchetti was there in the first place? And, if Billings has been tailing her, how do they not know about this morning?"

"Billings lost her last night; she drives a Ford roadster and, apparently, handles it well. She shook him until this morning, and, by luck, Billings saw her heading out of town toward Route 50. This time, she wasn't so fortunate; he cut her off, sending her car into a ditch."

"So, where is she now? Is she all right?"

"Johannsson's got her on ice in a private room at the station. Quite frankly, he doesn't know what to do with her, but he will not let her go. Not right now, anyway."

"What do you mean, on ice in a private room?" I asked.

"Look, I know you don't like the chief, but he's not as bad as you think. He's got her safe upstairs in an empty office with a bed and access to a toilet. He's also got a patrolman's wife with her."

"Yeah, you're right; your boss is a real sweetheart. I just volunteered to represent a man to keep your chief from beating him to death!"

"So, you gonna be her lawyer too?"

"Don't tempt me; I just might. It's not the worst idea I've heard today. So, for the record, what is he holding her on?"

"You're going to love this one: reckless driving, resisting arrest, and endangering the life of a lawman."

"I can't take any more of this tonight. Can we meet tomorrow morning at my office? I need time to take all this in," I exclaimed, followed by a much-needed exhale.

We parted, Osborne, going back inside the station while I headed to the comfort of my hotel. As I passed through the lobby, I signaled the hostess to send my meal to my room. I craved privacy, though I doubted the demons would allow it.

My mind raced until well after midnight, but there were no demons. Feeling strange without my usual haunting, I created a reputable replacement: Chief Sonny Johannsson. I struggled to understand him; he was a decent man in one instance, then a barbarian in the next. What drove him? He stood toe to toe with federal agents, defending justice, and then today, he violated a man's civil rights. Was it the power that corrupted, or did one become infected by constant exposure to a violent environment? Whichever it was, Johannsson was contaminated, and he seemed to revel in it.

Chapter Twenty-five

Thursday morning arrived, and I shared the news from the previous evening, including my meeting in the cemetery. Emily didn't seem the least bit phased, but Ashley, well, it was quite different.

"Boss, can I be your second chair in court? I have always wanted to be in court."

"Ashley, there isn't going to be a trial; we will solve this case before it ever gets to the courtroom. I've got all my paperwork in order; I need to go to the courthouse this morning to file everything. I need you to visit the hospital to see how Homer Hunt is doing. Emily, any word on Gunner Tate?"

"No, sir, but I will try to reach Sheriff Jackson today. Do you believe he is part of this?"

"I don't know. Right now, I'm not sure of anything. I need to speak with him."

I headed to the courthouse expecting trouble, but, to my surprise, everything went well. With all the paperwork in order, I asked to speak with Chief Johannsson. In a matter of minutes, I was seated across the beast.

"Billings, Osborne, get in here! I want both of them in this. Do you have any problems with that?" barked Johannsson.

"No, Chief, I am rather pleased they are 'both in this,' as you put it."

Now, strangely, the four of us were seated in the closed office. My heart raced, and perspiration began to surface on my forehead. Johannsson leaned back on his desk chair throne, both hands behind his melon-sized head. My earlier question has been answered: it was the power that had polluted his mind.

"Well, boys, we have a situation, don't we? For better or worse, we're stuck with each other, except I'm the boss, right?"

"You hold the biggest badge in the room, but, sir, you are not my boss, right, *boys*?" I sarcastically countered.

"Yeah, that's right, Mr. Forde, I've got the biggest badge, but you seem to have the most positions: gumshoe and mouthpiece. Hell, you're a jack-of-all-trades, but how does the rest of that go? Ah, yeah, and master of none. Yep, that's you, master of nothing, absolutely nothing."

"I may surprise you, Sir. For starters, if I see even the slightest sign of abuse to my client, I will have you charged. If you think I can't *put the screws on you*, ask your old buddy, Colegate. Ask him how that worked."

"Are you threatening me? You'd better walk softly, boy. I'm not that *weak-sister*, Colegate."

"And you'd better stop calling me boy! What are you so afraid of? You're right; we have a situation, one that we all are in. Why don't we stop fighting each other? There is a firestorm coming, a fire that will consume bodies, innocent bodies. Chief, for better or worse, we need each other; we are the only ones who can save this town. How about it? Can we stop all this infighting now, before it's too late?"

Johannsson and I sat looking eye to eye, neither flinching, while Osborne and Billings sat in disbelief. As our staring match continued, the thickness of the air could be cut with a knife. Finally, the behemoth stood, wiping his brow with his left hand while offering his right to me. I responded to his olive branch, feeling the immense power in his handshake. The firmness of his grip was not intentional; it was expected.

"So, may I ask about Miss Dorthea Fleming? I understand she is in custody. May I speak with her?"

"She ain't actually in custody; I got her upstairs for her own protection. She's one of Marchetti's dames, and they're looking for her. I'm not sure how she fits in all this, but she's involved, and I ain't about to let her slip through," explained Johannsson in a moderate tone.

"She was a close friend to Jo Brathwaite; that's her connection. Why is Robert Poston a suspect?" I asked.

"The Fleming chick heard him threaten Marchetti, something stupid to do," interjected Billings.

"Do you really believe Poston has the nerve to mess with someone like Marchetti? Why would he do that in the first place?" I questioned.

"Because Poston loved your dead girl, Jo Brathwaite, that's why. He didn't know who Marchetti was until it was too late," Johannsson answered.

"But Chief, say you're right on Marchetti; why would he have killed the others? Makes no sense," I continued.

"Who do you think did it, if not Poston?" asked Billings.

"I'm looking into a man named Foster Cobb, who goes by the name Frosty. I've been told by several that he not only has the know-how but also the mental capacity to follow through. Yesterday, I interviewed Jebediah Feltner; he gave an explicit history of Cobb's abilities as a killer."

"But why? What is his connection with Marchetti, Cappelletti, and Rolf Schlesinger? I'm sorry, Brody, that doesn't fit either," reasoned Osborne.

"Lieutenant Osborne, Will, yesterday, Jeb Feltner told of a pledge that eight war buddies made should any of them not make it home. Frosty Cobb was one of those men, and so was Joseph Brathwaite. Now, how all this fits, I don't know, but I'm certain he's in this somehow."

"I know Cobb; he's spent several nights in my house. Yeah, he's capable, all right. There's only one problem: I pinched him the week

Schlesinger was killed. He was cooling his heels in the same cell your new client is in. There ain't no way he killed Schlesinger," Johannsson boasted, derailing my logic.

We spent the next hour comparing notes and trying to fit pieces together, yet nothing matched up. The time together, while often tense, never returned to the opening act. I agreed with Johannsson concerning Miss Fleming's situation; however, while guaranteeing Robert Poston's safety, he would not release him. For my safety, Johannsson felt at least one of the two detectives should always be in attendance when we meet, which will be at 10:00 a.m. on Friday morning. All our meetings will be at the station, leaving Ashley outside this circle. Making her understand that it would not be easy.

Before leaving, I decided to meet with my client. He was just being served his lunch when the cell door opened, allowing access. I convinced him of the need to be patient and that I would get him released as soon as it was safe. Since he had been arrested for murder, his life might be in danger from the Cosa Nostra family. After all, if the local police believed he killed Luca, the mob may believe he had something to do with it. In reality, he was safer in jail than out.

Finally, back at the office, the toughest part of my day began: informing my staff of the new collaboration agreement with the Winchester police. The news hurt Ashley, as I knew it would. Fighting the tears, she asked several emotionally charged questions.

"I thought I was an integral part of this firm? Now it's back to the boy's club, I guess? What have I done wrong except being a woman?" pleaded Ashley.

"You have done nothing wrong; please don't think that. You will be told everything as I know it. I know you're hurt, but we must know what Johannsson knows, which means we have to be honest with him. So, while I work with the police, I need you to head this office. You can begin by finding something, anything, in those letters; I know there is a clue in there. You are our best chance of discovering it. Can you do that for us?"

"Boss, I just wanted to be there when we break this case. I'm okay; I'll find something in that box. I won't let you down."

"I have another assignment for you if you are up to it. Would you call Mrs. Poston? You and she made a nice connection; I believe she could use a friend today. Would you be willing to be that friend?"

"Yes, I would like to help her and be her friend. Do you want me to call her or stop by?"

"For now, how about a call? You never know how people will react when under this type of stress. I think a short phone call will suffice."

That said, I settled at my desk to enjoy a mid-morning cup of coffee and a quick glance at baseball scores in yesterday's *Winchester Star*. My Red Sox team was not doing well, except for Earl Webb; he was the only one who could actually hit the ball. We should have never sold Babe Ruth to those hateful Yankees: New York had stolen enough from my family.

"Mr. Forde, I have Lieutenant Osborne on the phone. He says it is urgent."

"Thanks, Emily, I'll be right there."

Our conservation was short; the only thing I learned was that my presence was necessary and that there had been a development. I decided to bring the key Ashley and I found at the Poston home; wise or not, it was time for full disclosure.

Stepping into the courthouse, I was again met by a large throng of officers from the city and county. Before I could learn the root of the disturbance, I was ushered by Lt. Osborne into the chief's office, where Sheriff Neumann, two of his deputies, Detective Billings, and, of course, the king himself, Chief Johannsson, sat. No one was talking; I was amazed at how the mood of this office had changed in just a few hours. Taking the last chair, I joined the group, waiting for his royal highness to call his subjects into order. I hoped he had brushed his teeth since this morning; he must eat garlic and onions every meal. At last, the lion roared.

"Well, Mr. Forde, you can rule out Frosty Cobb as a possible murder suspect; his body was found early this morning in the exact spot Luca

Marchetti was found. Before you ask, yeah, it's definitely murder. Sheriff Neumann, would you tell this detective what your men found this morning?"

"Cobb was stretched out, just like the other guy, Marchetti, except it was much worse. Cobb had been tortured slowly. Both hands were cut off; there were twenty to twenty-five cuts on his legs, arm, and back to increase the pain. They also cut out both of his eyes and, to finish the job, they used a *Chicago typewriter* on him. They damn near cut him in half."

"A Chicago typewriter? What's a Chicago typewriter?" I asked.

"You mean a city boy like you never heard that? I figured a big city gumshoe like you surely heard of a Chicago typewriter. I guess you ain't got mob killings in Boston, huh?" Johannsson returned, figuratively speaking.

"Yes, Chief, we have mob killings in Boston. And, no, I've never heard that phrase before. Once again, you are educating me. So, what exactly is a Chicago typewriter?"

"Brody, if I may, it's being shot to death with a machine gun, usually a Thompson .45 Caliber. The mob has more machine guns than the Army, very deadly," explained Osborne.

"Thanks, Lt. Osborne. So, where is the body now? In the morgue, I presume?"

"Yes, Dr. Stenner has the body; at first glance, he believes Cobb was tortured for approximately forty-eight hours. How could anyone be part of something this gruesome? How much more can this town take?" pleaded a disheartened Osborne.

"Boys, we know who did this, and we know why. Plain and simple, this is payback, and Osborne, if you think this is bad, you have no idea what Emiliano Marchetti is capable of. He didn't get the name *The Burner* because he teaches Sunday School in Forde's church."

"But why did they pick Cobb? What does the mob know that we don't? We ruled Cobb out; remember, Chief, you had him in jail when Schlesinger was killed," recalled Osborne.

"Cobb knew or saw something; you can bet on that. I've dealt with the Cosa Nostra in D.C., and like I said, you boys have no idea what they're capable of," informed Chief Johannsson.

"Well, since this happened in the county, this mess is all mine. I never thought I would say this: any help you can give the Frederick County Sheriff's Department, well, you'd be welcome," the sheriff requested.

With that plea, the initial meeting ended. The county officers were now gone, so it was time for round two.

"Before we begin, Chief Johannsson, detectives, I have something I need to share with you. This key was discovered in the Poston home, in Jo Brathwaite's room. I did not disclose this earlier because your department had decided Miss Brathwaite's death was a suicide, thus closing the case," I confessed while placing the key on the Chief's desk.

"Let me see it. Don't we have a key like this one? Yeah, that *spaghetti bender* that got himself killed on Main Street had one, didn't he?" recalled Billings.

Johannsson walked to the back room of his office and opened the massive safe, retrieving the key found on Cappelletti. To no one's surprise, they were identical.

"Any of you boys ever see keys like these?" the chief asked.

In unison, the three of us shook our heads no. The keys were longer than usual keys, thicker, and possessed more teeth. Johannsson, again seated on his throne, tossed both pieces of the mysterious metal onto his desk, reared back in this chair, and, as was his custom, returned his hands behind his head, interlocking his thick fingers.

"Well, they're industrial keys, like the kind you might find at a factory or on a ship, something you want to make damn sure ain't nobody going to get past," explained the Chief.

As Johannsson was finishing our locksmith class, his phone rang, bringing wrinkles to his forehead while fiery red dominated his unshaven face. It was somewhat encouraging to see the chief treated in the same manner I frequently received. He cursed continuously into the candlestick phone, making threats of bodily harm and at least once offering his resignation. It wasn't until he hung up that the identity of his wrath was revealed: it was the mayor. Apparently, Sonny Johannsson was an equal-opportunity bully; he didn't spare anyone from experiencing his wrath.

"How the hell did that fool become mayor? He doesn't have a clue of what we're dealing with. With all this going on, he wants me to take my picture with him on the courthouse steps. Can you believe that? He believes that since Cobb was killed, obviously a mob hit, this mess is over. He said peace now reigns supreme. What a *sap!*"

"His uncle is a hot shot over at National Fruit; that's how he won the election. It's about who you know," Billings offered in a surprising manner.

"Chief, before you go, may I speak with Dorthea Fleming? I have several questions I would like to ask concerning Jo Brathwaite. I would also like to have one of my women with me, as well as the woman you have with her. Will that be okay with you, Sir?"

"Yeah, sure, but do me a favor., don't become her lawyer, too. I've had enough trouble today."

"Thank you, Chief. I plan on seeing her within the hour."

The day had gone relatively well, much better than anticipated. Strangely, I wished I could have met Frosty Cobb, although with his reputation, perhaps it was for the best. I was disappointed that I did not meet my first FFV several days ago, and now I missed the hill people experience. My education was lacking.

All that behind me, it was time to focus on Miss Fleming. While waiting for the cab carrying Ashley, I asked Lt. Osborne if he would be available late this afternoon. He agreed that we needed to talk.

As promised, I met my eager protégé on the steps, stressing the need for delicacy. This meeting would be similar to our Poston house visit, so she could listen for information I might miss. Remembering Johannsson's request that I not become her lawyer, well, I didn't answer: we'd have to see how it goes.

I entered the once office, now the makeshift cell of Dorthea Fleming, with Ashley closing in on my heels. Miss Fleming had lost much of her allure since yesterday morning. She was still wearing the black outfit, missing the veil, lipstick removed, and her hair exhibited the signs of a restless night. She maintained her natural beauty, and as our eyes met, a slight smile appeared.

"Mr. Forde, long time no see. They didn't tell me you were coming, or I would have freshened up. Have you come to rescue me? Who is your delightful little friend? Honey, would you happen to have a hairbrush?"

"No, ma'am, they took my handbag before I was allowed to come upstairs," answered Ashley.

"Ma'am? I'll bet I'm younger than you, dear. How old do you think I am?" the captive damsel asked.

"I don't know, I wouldn't want to guess. How old are you?" Asked Ashley.

"I'm twenty-two; I'll turn twenty-three in November. Do you believe that?" acknowledged Miss Fleming.

Ashley stood amazed, as did I. How could someone so young appear to be so much older, so mature? The provocative makeup and clothing played a part, but not all of it. Life choices often accelerate our aging; had I been asked the question Ashley so delicately deflected, I would have said at least thirty. My decision to include my associate had already reaped dividends.

"Miss Fleming, we need your help. Are you willing to answer a few questions concerning Jo Brathwaite and the Ivory Tower? We need to find out who killed Jo, or Lace, as you knew her. Will you help us?" I asked.

"What's in it for me? Can you get me out of here if I help you? I'm in here because I tried to help you so you owe me," explained the former mystery lady.

"I promise I will see what I can do. Fair enough?" I answered.

Miss Fleming abruptly turned to patrolman Kline's wife, asking for a cigarette. Mrs. Kline obliged, lighting the tobacco stick before handing it to her. After several deep drags, the captive woman turned back, offering full attention.

"What can you tell us about Jo Brathwaite? How did she come to work at the Tower?" I began.

"I found her sitting at the drugstore lunch counter in Winchester, drinking a Coke. The Tower was looking for a couple of new, fresh-looking girls; she was perfect. The innocent face and what a body; I was so envious. We started talking; she was looking for work and desperately wanted to get off that farm. So, I introduced her to Luca," answered Fleming, followed by a deep drag of her cigarette.

"How did Luca figure into all of this?" I questioned.

"Are you joking? Luca owned the Tower. He was a powerful man, a very powerful man," bragged Fleming.

"And now he's a powerful dead man, just like Jo. How could you corrupt such a naïve little girl? You're the reason she's dead," Ashley assigned blame.

"Mr. Forde, where did you find this stupid, little child? Why is she here? To insult me? Sweetie, don't pass judgment on things you couldn't possibly understand. Just go back to that little world of yours and count your pennies," Fleming sarcastically lashed out.

"Alright, everyone. Back to your corners. Ashley, please remember why we are here. Miss Fleming, I ask you to respect my associate by not demeaning her. I will not tolerate it. Understand?"

"Agreed, I'll behave myself; it's been a long night, Mr. Forde. By the way, I enjoyed our kiss yesterday. How about you? Was it delightful for you?"

Refusing to be drawn into the spider's web or add to my already fuming assistant's rage, I returned to the interrogation. "So, how did Jo travel back and forth? It's a long way to Martinsburg. She didn't have a car, did she?" I asked, continuing my interrogation.

"She rode with me usually, along with another girl. You won't believe this; her name was Ashley, just like you, sweet pea," Fleming sent a smirk in Ashley's direction.

"You said her name was Ashley; what happened to her? Does she still work at the Tower?" I asked.

"That's another sad story. She stepped off the sidewalk in Martinsburg one night, about a month ago, and was struck by a truck. Nobody saw it happen; it was just an accident," explained Fleming, displaying just a hint of emotion.

"How did the accident affect Jo? How did it affect you?" My questions grew.

"It rattled Lace, me too. I mean, we rode together for nearly a year. You get to know people when you spend that much time in a car together."

"So, what is it that you wanted to tell me yesterday? Who wants to hurt me or us?"

A solemn frown appeared, silencing the woman. Pausing a moment, she turned again to the nicotine provider for a repeat performance. No words were spoken as the cigarette encore proceeded. With fresh smoke in hand, fear replaced the antagonistic attitude, stirring an unexpected eruption. "You got to promise to protect me. Can you do that? Can you help me?" pleaded Miss Fleming.

"How can I promise something I know nothing about? I have given my word; I will do all that I can. I'm assuming you're speaking of the Cosa Nostra family. Is that who you mean? Who else wants to hurt us? Let's start with this: who killed Jo Brathwaite? Give me names!" I demanded.

"You already have their names. So does that idiot son of the boarding house lady," as the woman's sarcasm resurfaced.

"Is Robert Poston one of the killers?" Ashley asked.

"No, he didn't kill her; he loved her. He used to come to the Tower to see her, to be with her, you know," revealed Fleming.

"Did she love him?" asked Ashley.

"No, she hated him. Two reasons: one, he was poor; he thought on a small scale, she wanted more. Second, he kept nagging her; he couldn't take the hint she wanted more than being a poor man's wife. But that wasn't his biggest problem. He saw Lace arguing with the men who killed her, but he only knew one of them."

"Luca Marchetti, right? So, who were the other two? You said we already have their names, but who are they?" I asked.

"Besides Luca, the other two were Gio Cappelletti and Rolf Schlesinger; they killed her."

"But why?" cried Ashley as I passed her my handkerchief.

"I don't know, I mean it—I do not know. Lace and I were supposed to have dinner after the parade, you know, the Apple Blossom thing, but she never showed up. I never saw her again. That's the honest truth!" Tears flowed from her eyes.

We paused for a moment, all drying our eyes and collecting thoughts. Why did they kill her? What did she know that made her a threat?

"Miss Fleming, may I call you Dorthea? You still haven't said who wants to harm us. Can you tell me now?" I asked, returning to my previous question.

"Yes, Brody, if I may, you may call me Dorthea, or better yet, Dot; it's what most men call me. As for your second question, I don't actually have names; I mean, I don't know exactly who. It's just a couple of things I heard, you know, at the Tower."

"What things? Tell me exactly what you heard," I stressed.

"Well, about two weeks ago, I heard Luca really giving it to some man over the phone. He was screaming about some late shipment. Then, a couple of days later, a Spanish-speaking guy, I think from Baltimore, came in the Tower and told Luca that there was a problem, a big problem in Winchester."

"What was the problem? Did they say what kind of problem?" I continued to push.

"Yeah, he said that some *little rich boy* playing private dick was snooping around, and he might need to be *taken for a ride.*"

"What's that mean, Boss? To be taken for a ride?"

"You're so precious—you truly don't know, do you, child? It means that—"

"Ashley, I'll tell you later, I promise. Let's get back to the rest of what you heard. Okay, again, why would they kill Jo? You surely must have some idea. Did she do something? Perhaps she said or saw something? Was it because she was pregnant?"

"I told you, I do not know. Yeah, she was with child, but I don't think that had anything to do with it. Luca's old man wants an heir; if her baby were Luca's, that would have been *Hotsy-Totsy*, especially if it were a boy."

"You still haven't told us anything, nothing we can use. Why is Ada Jo Brathwaite dead? You are begging for my help; tell me something, anything that helps me understand all of this."

"You know, as we talked, I think Lace did have something she wanted to tell me to get it off her mind. She was acting a little stranger than usual. I just thought it was the baby."

"A little stranger, how? What was different?" I persisted.

"I can't put it into words; she was acting differently, that's all."

We exchanged possibilities of Jo's peculiar behavior in her final days, but nothing substantial, at least for now. Sensing we were going in circles; I ended our talk. I left cigarette money with Mrs. Kline and a little additional funding for the necessities of my newest client. Yes, I had Miss Fleming sign a contract, making me her attorney of record. I can hardly wait for Johannsson to learn this.

Chapter Twenty-Six

B efore leaving the station, I left a message at the front desk for Lt. Osborne to contact me as soon as possible. Ashley, still fuming from some of our newest client's comments, and I returned to the office.

"Hello, Emily, any calls?"

"Yes, Sir, the hospital called... Homer Hunt passed away a little while ago. I'm sorry, Sir; I know you were friends."

"Thank you, Emily; yes, I believe we were friends. He was a good man. You know, life's funny in a way. Here was a man I only met twice, and yet, I will miss him. Anything on Gunner Tate?"

"No, sir, nothing. Should I call Sheriff Jackson again?"

"No, let's not continue to bother him. He will contact us when he has something. Can you call the sheriff in Warren County? We are looking for a war veteran named Duke Cooper. He was also a friend of Joseph Brathwaite's. Ask if they can help us in finding Mr. Cooper. He's not a suspect; we just would like to speak with him."

"I'll get right on it, sir."

"That's the strangest thing... Hey, boss, come here. I need you to see this."

I headed into the conference room, where I found Ashley poring over all the letters Kate sent Joe while in Europe. I looked, yet didn't see anything earning my assistant's overflowing excitement.

"Okay, I give. What am I missing?"

"Look at Mrs. Brathwaite's letters, not the ones she received. Look closely at the ones she sent—what do you see that's different?"

"The handwriting is different. I see two, no, three different handwritings. Kate Brathwaite didn't write the most intimate letters to her beloved husband; she is illiterate."

"You got it, boss. But what does it matter? So, she can't read or write. What difference does that make?"

"It means at least three people know what was written and received in this box... not just Kate. Okay, let's say her daughter was one; who might the other two be?"

"Boss, how do we ask Mrs. Brathwaite if she is read? That's a personal thing. I mean, are we going to offend her by knowing or accusing her of being illiterate?"

"When she first came into our office, I left her with you to complete all the paperwork. Did she actually sign the contract? For that matter, did she read or attempt to read the document?"

"Ah, sir, while you two were talking, I pulled the Brathwaite file. I can't tell you if she read anything, but she definitely did not sign her name or initial the three boxes. She also didn't date the document as asked."

"That's why we hired her; my little sister is detail-oriented. I'm more of a roving-minded kind of person."

"You meant to say absent-minded person, didn't you? That's what Daddy calls you."

"Anyway, what does it mean to our case? So, she can't read, so what? Lots of people can't read," reasoned Ashley.

"I don't know, possibly nothing, but it is worth knowing," I answered.

We three realized it was well past noon, and hunger was setting in. I sent Emily downtown to the Five-and-Ten lunch counter, figuring that would be a quick fix for our dietary needs. Meanwhile, Ashley returned to work studying the contents spread on the conference table. So much had transpired in the past three days, yet we seemed to know less. For me, I now had three clients; the firm was growing, but we just didn't seem to make any money. These really were hard times.

Upon her return, Emily brought more than lunch—she had Lt. Osborne in tow.

"Boy, I should have placed my order before coming by... I'm starving."

"Not to worry, my friend. Emily, please show the efficiency of the Forde Detective Agency. We anticipated your arrival, so we bought you lunch. Hope you like ham and potatoes," I exclaimed.

"Indeed, I do. Thank you very much... and, Mr. Forde, you could prove your efficiency if you would just fix your door. Seriously, that missing dot after the 'O' drives me crazy!"

"And, what do I always tell you?" I asked.

"You say, *to get used to it*, you did," countered Osborne.

"Wilbur, my friend, the door is correct. My middle name is 'O'. That is why there is no dot. When I was born, my parents couldn't decide on my middle name. Father wanted to name me Orville, while my mother insisted on Oswald. Mother said Orville sounded like the name of a New England train station. Father said Oswald sounded like the name of a jailbird... like some sociopath. Neither gave in, so my middle name is just O."

"Boss, this is nothing personal, but you've got a strange family. And what's all this mother and father stuff? Why do you call them that?"

"Because, unlike you and Emily, I don't have a *daddy* and a *mommy*; I have a father and a mother. They both love me very much; it's just different. Not bad, just different."

"Yeah, but look on the bright side, boss, you had a maid."

"Brody, you had a maid? How much money do you and your family have?"

"Yes, Will, I had a maid growing up. As for money, we get by."

We all enjoyed a delicious lunch as my three friends speculated on all I must have had growing up. By the top of the hour, it had been determined my family owned the entire state of Massachusetts, most of Manhattan, and the eastern seaboard of Canada. I remained silent. My family owned property in all three areas. Like I said, we get by.

"Will, I don't know if you've heard, Homer Hunt died this morning. I know you believe he knew something he wasn't telling, and I'm sorry I challenged you on that. I have an alternative; how about we question his nephew, Tink?"

"I say it's time we went to the movies. We'll take my car. I can park in front, but you can't," offered Osborne.

"Ladies, hold down the fort, watch out for Indians, and if you see any, call Max... He'll turn them into a mailbox," I joked.

"What's that supposed to mean? Turn them into a what?" questioned Ashley.

"Just drive by Max's, you'll see."

"How can we drive by anywhere? You won't let me drive your car."

With my car keys safely in my pocket, Osborne and I headed to the theatre. We arrived just as the employees began filing in, parking in front of the theatre. Still seated in the patrol car, Osborne spotted Tink Hunt strolling the street. The moment we stepped out of the car and onto the street, Tink Hunt spun and sprinted back the way he had come.

"Stop, police!" Osbourne shouted, kicking himself into gear. He ran after the man, taking Braddock.

I, on the other hand, was slower to respond, and ran down Loudon a few seconds later.

The race continued several blocks; I kept pace with the lanky young man as we dodged pedestrians down South Loudon. Without warning, Tink sprinted diagonally at the four-way intersection of Loudon and Clifford Street, nearly being struck by an oncoming bus. Hunt stretched his lead as he crossed Braddock, nearing Washington Street, as freedom drew nearer.

Suddenly, in a flash, the athletic Osborne appeared from between the buildings and tackled the fleeing nephew, both ending up on the cobblestoned sidewalk. Osborne restrained the suspect and sat him with his back against a dogwood tree.

"Why... why are you guys chasing me? What... what've I done?" asked the out-of-breath suspect.

"Why did you run? I identified myself as police and ordered you to halt, but you chose to run. What are you hiding?" questioned Osborne, catching his breath.

"What would I be hiding? I sell popcorn; you think I'm stealing salt, butter, or something?" Hunt snapped while struggling to free his hands.

"No, you are scared of what we will ask you about Uncle Homer. Was he here the night Gio Cappelletti was killed?" I intervened.

"I don't know nobody named Gio, Cappy, or whatever. No, I ain't seen my uncle in months," he said, the sarcasm increased.

"See, I think you're lying. Now, we can make this easy or hard; it's your call. I'm asking you, was your uncle here the night the man was shot in the street?" Osborne asked, leaning into the young man's face.

A crowd began to gather as Osborne continued his interrogation. Realizing the mood of the forming mob would probably side with the boy; I suggested we move this to my office. Osborne made Tink's choice simple: he could be placed under arrest and spend some time in jail, or he could go to a comfortable office with a cold bottle of Coke and answer our questions. All of our questions. Using sensible discretion, he chose the latter.

Still cuffed, Osborne escorted Tink Hunt into the conference room, removing the cuffs once seated at the far end of the room, away from the door. The sight made quite an impression on Emily; she demonstrated a level of compassion, making sure the Coca-Cola was cold. As for Ashley, she was ready to lynch him.

"Alright, Tink, why did you run? Your uncle was there that night, wasn't he?"

"Yeah, Mr. Forde, he was there. I reckon it doesn't matter much anymore; Uncle Homer died this morning."

"I am sorry for your loss. I had grown very fond of your uncle. Now, we need to know: why was he there? We need to know everything. Why was your uncle there?" I asked.

"He was there to kill the man in the street. He gave me five bucks to help him."

"What did you have to do to earn that much money?" asked Osborne.

"I had nothing to do with the killing... I swear! That was all Uncle Homer."

"Tell us everything, starting with you. What did you do to earn that much money?" I asked.

"Well, first, I helped Uncle Homer to the third-floor balcony. He was weak, you know. He brought an old rifle used in the war. Real heavy, it was. He said that the man was a really bad man and that he had to do this—that he promised it a long time ago."

"Did he say what the bad man had done to deserve to be killed?" I inquired.

"He said he killed a girl, killed her in cold blood for no reason. Unck said he killed a bunch of bad men in the war and that this was just one more he would add to the list. He was just doin' what the army had taught him to do—to kill bad people," Hunt explained.

"Did it ever occur to you that you and your uncle were breaking the law? I mean, that was war; this was murder," surmised Osborne.

"Not the way I saw it. Unck was just doin' what the law can't do. I mean, what is the law doin' about all the people gittin' snatched? Nothin', absolutely, nothin'. Unck was just gittin' justice for the dead girl."

"Tell us more about that night. How did Homer know the man would be there at that time?" I asked.

"Unck told me the man thought he was goin' to be meetin' a guy to get some dough, but we both knew he wasn't goin' be gittin' nothin' but lead. Me and Unck just snuck out on the third floor outside balcony and waited. As the guy passed the theatre, a sharp-dressed *egg* stopped him, just for a second, and, BOOM, Unck put one in his head—best shot I ever seen!"

"You mean to tell us, as sick as your uncle was, he could pull off a shot like that? One perfect kill shot? Is that what you expect us to believe?" Osborne quizzed.

"You don't know Uncle Homer... Anything Uncle Homer drew a bead on was dead; he never missed. You can ask anybody; nobody could shoot like my uncle, nobody."

"So, what happened after your *Unck* made the shot? How did he get out of the theatre without being seen? What did he do with the rifle?" I continued.

"That was the perfect part. He never left the theatre. He was sitting in the audience, waiting for the movie to start. You walked right by him; you never noticed a thing. Unck said the best place to hide a tree was in a forest—he was right. See, Uncle Homer was an expert at camouflage. He said sometimes, during the war, he would cover himself in the mud, and the krauts would walk right by him. Then he would shoot them before they could turn around."

"What about the rifle? I know he didn't hide that in the audience. What happened to it?" continued Osborne.

"That was the best part. The Handley School Band has been practicing here for the Independence Day show, you know, the one on the Fourth of July. They had a bunch of fake wooden rifles in the back that they'd be using in their show; they kept them in a large barrel behind the stage. Unck just slid his rifle into the barrel with the fakes. He even brought a dead fish to put in the bottom of the barrel to hide the smell of fresh gunpowder. A couple of coppers looked, but the lights back there ain't really good, and the fish stunk, so they didn't stay long. They never noticed the real gun. And, to make things even better, the coppers were just plum lazy—as usual!"

"So, how did he get the rifle out of the theatre? Surely someone noticed," continued the decorated detective.

"Y'all think you're so much smarter than us poor hillbillies. That was the other best part! I came to work early Saturday morning, a little after 6:00 a.m., as usual. I've got a key to the place because I got to come in early on Saturdays to clean up the mess to get ready for the matinees.

While you all were lookin' for that all-important West Virginia car... I walked right down the street behind you, Osborne. You two were so worried about the dead man's car, you never saw me; I was behind you all the time. Y'all are some sorry detectives."

We sat stunned, never imagining a story like this. But did this help or hurt our investigation? The lad's confession seemed creditable; Lt. Osborne was left with no other choice.

"What is your given name, and how old are you?" asked Osborne.

"Theobald Wilson Hunt, and I'm twenty-two," Tink Hunt answered.

"Mr. Theobald Wilson Hunt, you're under arrest for conspiracy to commit murder on one Giorgio Cappelletti. Turn around, son; I gotta put the cuffs back on," ordered Osborne.

Hunt offered no resistance and fully cooperated with Lt. Osborne. After the two left, Ashley changed her position regarding our suspect.

"Do you think that was fair? I mean, you and Lt. Osborne asked him many questions, which he freely answered. Then, when he had given everything asked of him, Lieutenant Osborne took him to jail. Don't you see something wrong with what just happened? Boss, do you think—"

"No! Absolutely not! I am not going to represent him. The state of Virginia will appoint a capable attorney to his case."

"So, where does this leave us? How could Mr. Homer have killed the others?"

"Ashley, he didn't kill the others. We have been looking at this wrong from the beginning. We're not looking for one killer; we must look for three. Tink Hunt's confession makes him an accessory, although he will not be standing trial for murder. His statement makes Homer Hunt one killer; again, no trial because of his death. If the boy's story checks out, we have solved the Cappelletti murder. The unanswered question: who are the other two killers?"

Chapter Twenty-Seven

An overcast sky welcomed May's final Saturday morning. Oh, you, Month of May. So much had happened since you began: we'd suffered multiple kidnappings in multiple states. At least a half dozen murders and those were just the ones that we knew occurred during your time. Dear May, you ushered in my private investigation agency's first real client, and somehow, you gave me not one but two clients as an attorney. How smooth you made that happen. Together, we antagonized a city police chief, possibly a county sheriff, and most definitely a senior federal agent. At your beginning, we had one employee, a competent secretary who now operates as a full-time investigator while her younger sister fills her previous role. May, you have but two days left, then you will sleep the sleep of hibernation until next spring. Oh, sweet Month of May, what blooms of excitement will you produce in your final forty-eight hours of 1931?

Neither of the girls will be working today. Ashley begged, but I insisted she take some time for herself. In so many ways, she reminds me of my sister, Lucy. Both were full of energy, innocence, and trust. I miss you, Lucy, so very much. As for today, I will miss you as well, Ashley; I pray you enjoy your weekend.

Lt. Osborne was also off this weekend, spending time with his wife and children. My friend has had a very exhausting week as well, the climax coming with the arrest of the young Tink Hunt. How difficult that was for the dedicated lawman. If Hunt was found guilty, and he most certainly would be, he could spend the next twenty years of his life in the Virginia State Penitentiary. Will did nothing wrong, yet he would emotionally beat himself up because he did the right thing.

I began my Saturday morning at the jail, visiting my two clients. I brought a carton of cigarettes for Miss Fleming and the change of clothing I had Emily purchase yesterday. We talked for about an hour, learning nothing new about the case but quite a bit about her. Life had been challenging, but she had made intelligent choices until she met Luca Marchetti two years ago. The son of a notorious gangster proved to be more than she could resist. He was rich, handsome, and possessed an addictive charm. He swept her off her feet while never touching a broom. Now, none of that charm could do Luca or the broken women left behind any good; just a deadly path of unfilled promises and dreams. Dorthea Fleming was but one of those left behind to pick up the pieces.

Robert Poston's situation was similar, but the pain was probably much deeper. Miss Fleming loved the lifestyle Luca could supply, but she had not sacrificed her heart. Robert not only committed his heart, he unconditionally gave it to Jo Brathwaite, only to have it tossed away. Like Dorthea, Jo was searching for an unattainable life. She yearned for sophistication she believed only wealth could deliver. Born into economic poverty, Jo shielded herself from anyone who could not elevate her from its clutches: Robert Poston never had a chance.

Both clients had an arraignment hearing on Monday morning, although I anticipated Miss Fleming's charges would be dropped. As for Poston, Chief Johannsson seemed to be playing hardball. Though all evidence had been provided, something was not being disclosed.

What could Johannsson be hiding?

The remainder of Saturday was spent considering the ever-growing number of questions. If I was correct about the three killers' theory, how did they all pull it off? How could they coordinate such an elaborate scheme? The methods of death all link to the war: Schlesinger was gassed, Marchetti killed with a bayonet, and

Cappelletti by an expert sniper. But why? Why was Marchetti moved and carefully positioned? And the most troubling question: was Tink Hunt's story credible? Could a very sick Homer Hunt have pulled off that single shot from the outside balcony of the theatre?

The demons raged tonight, setting me up with two hours of rest and then poisoning the early hours of Sunday. Perspiration had again soaked my pillowcase and outer sheet as my nightmare projected a horrid, self-imagined glimpse of Jo's body bobbing in the Shenandoah River. I moved to this once-peaceful small town to flee my demons, yet they followed and bred, growing the demonic family residing in my mind. I prayed to you, my dear God: did you not hear them? Please help me before I, once again, lose my mind.

With little sleep, I arose to face another day. Grabbing a coffee and a Danish in the hotel dining room, I rushed out the door, trying not to be late for Sunday church. Mother, I'd disappointed you by not fulfilling so many promises; attending church would not be added to the list. Tragedy struck us all; Father had moved on, and I was trying to piece together the fragments of my life. If only you could apply your religious logic to yourself as you had to me; I worried about Mother; I prayed you soon get help and find your personal peace.

I was no challenge today, as Max destroyed me in two short matches. My performance was so inadequate Max nearly joined Felix in sleep, nodding off several times.

After dropping the second game in less than twenty minutes, my worthy opponent finally broke the silence. "What's wrong with you? Let's face it: you're not a very good chess player, but today, you're the worst I've ever seen. So, what's on your mind? I know you've got questions; let's hear them."

"Max, this thing just keeps growing. I guess you've heard about Homer Hunt. I only met him twice, yet he left an impression I will never forget. I prayed for his family today."

"You are really hooked on that church stuff, aren't ya? I mean, you really believe all that Bible nonsense?"

"Yes, Max, I do. What do you believe, if I may ask?"

"I used to believe, but when my Mary died so young, well, I just stopped believing anything," my friend confessed.

"I know. It's difficult to keep faith when you lose someone you love. You should come to church with me one Sunday, Max—it might help."

"I ain't looking for help, you are... and, if I were going to go to church, I'd surely pick one with an organ or a piano. What's up with all that? What do you call it, no mechanical music in the worship service?"

"Just following the examples in the New Testament, that's all. Back to the case, what can you tell me about Homer's nephew, Tink?"

"Decent kid, not the sharpest tool in the shed. I hear he's in the *hoosegow*, something about conspiracy to commit murder—that right?" Max asked.

"Yeah, that's about the size of it. Max, you know I can't discuss the details; he has been charged and is awaiting an arraignment, which was in the paper. Is there more about Tink or Homer that I don't know? Things don't add up," I exclaimed.

"What don't add up? Homer was one hell of a shot; ask anyone. The kid said Homer made the shot, then Homer made the shot. You don't think Homer killed the other two, do you?" Max continued.

"No, Max, I do not. Will you answer me this: how skilled is Tink Hunt?"

Max paused, walked to the small office window, stared at the passing traffic, then turned and answered. "Tink Hunt can kill a gnat on a fly's ass at a hundred yards and not hurt the fly."

"He's the shooter on the theatre balcony, not Homer! So that story he told Osborne and me on Friday was just a lie to get us to look the other way," I growled, embarrassed of being gullible.

"Max, I've got to go. Please forgive me; I have got to speak with Lt. Osborne at once!"

I stormed out, abandoning my Sunday refuge, promising to return as soon as possible. It was still somewhat confusing, but the pieces were beginning to come into focus. If we could prove Tink Hunt was the Cappelletti killer, perhaps he could be persuaded to cooperate, especially if his charge was about to be amended to first-degree murder in a death penalty state.

Now, outside the Osborne home, I pounded on the front door like a madman, adrenalin dominating my actions. Finally, the startled lieutenant opened the entrance to the quintessential example of the perfect home.

"Homer Hunt did not kill Cappelletti; Tink Hunt did it. He's our third killer! We need to amend the charges to first-degree murder. We have to make him talk, whatever it takes!"

"Slow down, my friend. Say you are right. Can we prove it?" Will asked.

"Yes, I believe we can. I also believe he can help us determine who the other two killers are and how they were chosen. Once we know the identities of the other two, we can figure out who the mastermind is," I surmised.

"The other two? What other two?"

"Will, we have three victims, with three separate killers. Tink Hunt is killer number three, I'm positive. I believe Foster Cobb killed Luca Marchetti; that's why the Cosa Nostra tortured and finally killed him. What I do not know is who's the first killer. Who murdered Rolf Schlesinger?"

"You mentioned a mastermind. What does that mean?" a confused Osborne asked.

"Someone has to be planning all of this. Think, Will, who knew the three men who ended Jo Brathwaite's life? Someone extremely intelligent put all of this into motion, but who?" I concluded.

Not wishing to take any more time from Will and his family, we agreed to meet early Monday morning to update Johannsson and, with his blessing, make the necessary adjustments concerning Tink Hunt. While not actually working this weekend, the Ambrose O Forde Detective Agency had made progress.

Miss Month of May, I thank you for this day!

Demons gave a repeat performance Sunday night, so Monday would be a struggle.

I sent a cab to gather my staff with a sealed note informing them I would be at the courthouse until late morning. Each had their respective assignments; the office was in capable hands.

Surprisingly, the two arraignments went well, but with a twist. Johannsson had dropped the charges on Robert Poston but decided to prosecute Dorthea Fleming. Apparently, she had several questionable warrants in West Virginia and Maryland. To prevent extradition, the chief decided to keep her in Virginia on the trumped-up charges issued by Detective Billings at the time of her arrest. Fate had a strange way of making bedfellows, and here I was again, agreeing with the pompous chief.

Poston's situation was different; Johannsson, for no apparent reason, dropped all charges. I remembered the warning of '*not knowing what Chief Johannsson is capable of*' from the federal agents: could this be an example? Regardless, Mother Poston would be glad to have her son home. For Miss Fleming, while she would disagree, the decision was in her best interest, possibly saving her life.

In an even greater turn of events, Johannsson agreed with me concerning Tink Hunt. The previous charge had already been changed to first-degree murder, and his arraignment was scheduled for later today. A small smile appeared on the chief's face when he learned I would not be defending the newest murder suspect. With all this behind us, Osborne and I retreated to my office.

"Well, it's about time! Emily and I have been hard at work while you boys have been... What is it exactly you call it, fighting crime?"

"Yes, my dear, that is exactly what we have been doing. Now, if you can pull yourself away from that doughnut, please join us in the conference room. Emily, I need you to remain in the outer office in case someone comes in. Also, where are we in finding Tate?"

"He has been found, but not in Virginia. Not recently, that is. He has been with his boss on a horse-buying trip in Kentucky and Tennessee. They have been out of the state for over a month."

"Well, that's good news, I guess. You did great work, Emily, thank you."

The conference room door was now closed; I brought Ashley up to speed with both the weekend and this morning's events. With her eyes wide open and her mouth gasping for breath, I began by repeating my theory of the three shooters and their military connection. With that completed, I presented the remainder of my hypothesis as both now struggled for air.

"I am certain of the second and third shooters, no question. I believe the initial killer is one of the men who made the *Promettre*, the pledge, in France. We know Hunt, one of them anyway, is a killer, and I firmly believe Foster Cobb killed Marchetti. The retaliation by the Cosa Nostra confirmed that. Gunner Tate can be eliminated, as he has been out of the state for the past two months. I don't suspect Jebediah Fletcher; he's not the type to do this. This leaves us with Duke Cooper, Martin Bagent, and Vernon Lawson."

"I knew Duke the Coop; sadly, he died several months ago, much like Hunt... He brought death home in his lungs. If you're right, either Bagent or Lawson is our man—if you're right. Brody, this is really reaching," warned Osborne.

"I know, the problem is, Will, how do we move forward? We don't have anything remotely linking these two men to this."

"Boss, Emily and I both know Mr. Bagent. I can't even begin to suspect him. He and Daddy sometimes fish together. No, boss, it's not him; it has to be that Lawson fellow," informed Ashley.

"I've got one more thing—Lt. Osborne, you and I have to return to the Ivory Tower," I said, using an affirmative tone.

"Why, tell me why we need to go to a state where my badge means nothing and we cannot trust the local authorities? Johannsson gave strict orders: no Winchester cops were allowed to enter the state of West Virginia. I'm sorry, Brody, I can't follow you on this one."

"I'm ready, boss. When are we going?" exclaimed Ashley.

"You are not going, and that is final!" I ordered, bringing a nasty frown.

"Boss, I can—"

"No, absolutely not! If I find out that you have stepped one foot in the so-called Mountain State, you are fired! Do you understand me? I'm not kidding; I will fire you and your sister if you disobey my direct order! Understand?" I shouted as forcefully as I could.

"Yes, Sir, I, I understand! So, you're just like all the rest; you're treating me like a little girl, a *little lady*, as they usually say. I thought you were different—I was so wrong about you!"

Fighting back tears, Ashley dashed out of the conference room and the outer office, slamming both doors as she exited each. I appreciated her anger and sympathized with the plight of modern-day women. In this instance, I would rather have her be upset now than dead later. I would not change my mind.

"Brody, I admire your protective nature. Your assistant will calm down in a day or two— give her space. She's very loyal to you, give her a little time. So, when are we going to the Ivory Tower?" advised Osborne.

"You changed your mind? What about your job?" I asked, shocked by the change.

"Well, when we break this case, and we are going to break this case, my position will be fine," rationalized the dedicated lawman as sweat began to surface on his forehead.

"Yes, we will break this case. As for the Tower, how about tonight? If my hunch is correct, we are running out of time," I warned.

"Tonight, it is. Let's leave around 6:00 p.m. Before we go, I will issue arrest warrants on both Lawson and Bagent. They'll be picked up as soon as we find them," the Lieutenant guaranteed.

Osborne left, returning to the station, while I explained Ashley's anger to Emily. The two sisters, only a couple of years apart in age, were sometimes miles apart in their thinking. But, make no mistake, a bond existed between them that was not often found in siblings. They sometimes were fierce rivals and antagonists to each other, but they were, most importantly, each's support group and best friend. They were sisters.

Chapter Twenty-Eight

I was shocked to see another man standing with Lt. Osborne as I pulled into the police parking lot. I'd seen the stranger but couldn't place him. He was tall, in his early forties, and appeared nervous, pacing back and forth as I stopped in front of them. I also saw both men sporting nice clothing, highly polished shoes, and fresh haircuts.

"Brody, I don't know if you've met Cletus Davenport. Officer Cletus Davenport? His daughter, Robin, is one of the teenagers who has been abducted."

"Officer Davenport... are you certain you want to do this? We have no authority; this could cost you your position. I'm acting on a very thin hunch; no evidence, just a hunch."

"Mr. Forde, my baby girl is missing. My wife and I are desperate; a hunch is better than nothing. I hear you're a smart man... Yeah, I'm certain," answered Davenport.

"I don't mean this in an insulting way, but Wilbur, that's a stylish suit, and is that a silk tie? I'm traveling with two very dapper gentlemen."

"Well, my attire didn't sit well on our last time there, so I decided to make a better impression. Honestly, though, I borrowed this suit from the undertaker at Jones Funeral Home. He always dresses nice, funerals and all, and we are the same size. On the condition: I gotta have it back by Wednesday, big funeral scheduled."

"This is my Sunday best, Mr. Forde... Only wear it for weddings and burials," replied Davenport.

"Sounds great. Okay, gentlemen, hop in. Let's go to Martinsburg!"

In the early part of the drive, we discussed what we knew to be factual regarding the kidnappings. Davenport was not aware of the Pennsylvania connection or pertinent details related to the West Virginia Buick discovered following the Cappelletti murder. Learning how little this veteran member of Winchester's finest knew was frightening and encouraging. The conversation intensified once we passed through the small community of Inwood, West Virginia.

"So, why are we heading to Martinsburg? The lieutenant didn't tell me much, just that you two were going and if I would like to join you. So, what's in Martinsburg?"

"My investigation is twofold: second are the abductions, but my primary case is still the murder of Ada Jo Brathwaite. I am convinced both cases are connected and that all roads lead to the Ivory Tower," I answered.

"But why? What's in Martinsburg, and what exactly is the Ivory Tower?" the officer continued.

Still driving, I reached into my jacket pocket and pulled out the key found under the rug in Jo's room. I held it up, allowing my new friend seated in the back to get a good look.

"So what? It's a key, odd-looking but just a key. What makes it so important?"

"Cletus, I have one too, exactly like it. We took it off of the dead body of Gio Cappelletti, a known member of the Cosa Nostra crime family. We know that they operate the Ivory Tower as a front. We're just not sure what illegal business they use it for. That's what tonight is all about, right, Brody?"

"Yes, that is why we're heading there. Does anyone want out before it's too late?"

"This is going to get messy, isn't it?" asked the worried officer.

"Yes, Mr. Davenport, this is going to get messy," I answered.

Little else was discussed in the final twelve miles, and we eventually parked just up the street from the Tower, each of us fighting back our rising anxiety. Before leaving the protection of my car, we each checked our weapons, spinning cylinders, or racking loads, depending on personal preference. I was astonished to find how many weapons Osborne and Davenport carried. Each carefully concealed three pistols, whereas I carried but one.

We were stopped at the entrance to pay the required cover fee, which I handled. Once inside, I tipped an additional $5 to be seated near the bandstand directly across from the suspicious padded door. The lively music and crowded dance floor would help, but the distraction had to be perfect.

A familiar face approached our table. "Gentlemen, may I ... Well, hello again; I'm glad to see you," the hostess said, extending her warm welcome to me.

"How could I stay away? What's on the menu tonight? I so enjoyed my lobster and Whiskey Highball," I complemented.

"So, a Highball for you, how about your friends? What would you gentlemen like?"

"I'll have what he's having," said Osborne.

"How about you, sir?"

"I'll have a shot and a beer, as strong as you got, honey," answered Davenport, causing Will and I to stare in amazement.

"Sounds wonderful; I will be back in a moment with your orders. Oh, sir, Jade is not working tonight, but she said to give you this should you return," the hostess whispered softly into my ear while seductively sliding a piece of paper into my left hand. I privately glanced at the note, revealing Jade's name and address; I didn't think our first date went that well.

In a matter of minutes, our drinks arrived and, to my surprise, Davenport consumed his shot and beer is seconds. Osborne and I refrained; our adrenaline rush would not tolerate alcohol at this moment.

The band started playing *Happy Days Are Here Again*, bringing a huge crowd to the dance floor, and everyone joined the singing. It was time we made our move.

"Okay, this is it. I need the two of you to cause a distraction so I can use this key to open that door. If this thing turns ugly, or the key doesn't work, save yourselves, run for the door, and don't look back," I ordered.

"Brody, we are lawmen; we are not going to run and leave you behind. Right, Cletus?"

"Absolutely not. You walk over, or staggering might be better, toward the door. Move slowly, and if the key works, get through it as fast as you can. We'll be right behind you," assured Davenport.

I take a deep breath, slowly rise, and stagger, as suggested, to the padded door. Surprisingly, no one came across as being the least suspicious.

While I was making my way across the room, Davenport stood up and began shouting at a man seated at the adjoining table. "I thought I told you I'd kill you if I ever saw you again. Now, stand up and get ready to take your medicine!"

The startled man leaped from the comfort of his chair, not having a clue what this crazy, unknown man was accusing.

"Who the hell are you? What are you talking about? I've never seen you before in my life!" responded the gentleman.

"you're that coward that's been sneaking around with my wife! Son, get ready—'cause I'm about to beat the ever-loving fire out of you!" Davenport threatened with his right fist drawn, ready to fire.

The commotion brought three of the largest men ever seen out of the back room to handle the situation. Meanwhile, the distraction had worked; I had carefully inserted the key and turned the lock, opening the door that revealed a dark staircase leading downward. The opening of the door alerted another three men with pistols drawn. The commotion caused the band to stop and sent shockwaves throughout the room.

With the door open, I rushed down the narrow corridor into the dimly lit cellar, which contained six large cells filled with prisoners. As I was near the bottom step, I heard, "Stop, stop now, or I'll shoot!"

Osborne threw his body in the path of two, but the third followed me down the rickety staircase. The sound of gunfire—three, maybe four shots—hit the basement floor as I gazed in disbelief: I had found the missing teenagers.

My assailant had reached the bottom step; he was less than thirty feet from me. Not having enough time to retrieve my pistol, I sprinted by the remaining cells, desperately looking for refuge, when I heard, "I told you to stop. Now I'm going to have to kill you!"

The sound of gunfire increased the beating of my heart until my left shoulder burned—I'd been hit!

Several more rounds rang out as I spotted a door; I had to get to that door before it was too late. I heard two more shots and then the sound of someone plummeting—hard.

I reached the door and pushed it open, reaching what I believed would be safety, only to hear even more threats shouted in my direction!

"ON THE GROUND, NOW! FACE DOWN... ON THE GROUND, NOW!"

I instantly do as I am told, too afraid to reach for my pistol. Was this the end? Was I about to join my sister, Lucy? With my shoulder on fire, my left arm is abruptly grabbed, and I am now lying on my back, facing my attacker. My nightmare came to light.

"Well, Mr. Forde, we meet again."

"Agent Colegate? Is that you?" I asked, my speech somewhat distorted.

"Yes, it is. Lay very still; you've been shot. Spivey, get a doctor. The rest of you, secure the scene—all of it, upstairs and down. No one leaves until I say they can leave. Is that understood?" ordered Agent Colegate.

"Osborne and Davenport, they're, they're upstairs. Are, are... are they okay?" I struggled to speak with blood spewing from my mouth.

"They're okay. I need you to lie still; I'm going to prop you up just a bit so you don't choke on the blood. Are you hit anywhere else?" asked the agent.

"I don't,"—I gasped— "I don't believe so." The pain increased.

"Just be as still as you can be. I've got help on the way," explained Colegate.

"How?"—I coughed and gasped— "How did you know?"—I coughed again— "We were here?"

"I received an anonymous, very convincing phone call," explained my once adversary.

Our conversation was interrupted when Officer Davenport joined us. Osborne had suffered a gunshot wound in his right leg during the commotion, but I was assured he would be fine.

Davenport's situation was different; he was openly crying. During the distraction, he received several punches to the face and was even cut with a knife, but the tears running down his cheeks were of joy, not pain. Officer Cletus Davenport tightly held a young woman dressed only in a white gown. It was his daughter, Robin. She had been one of the prisoners in the cells I had run past. Though heavily drugged, she was safe.

"So, what, what happened?" I gasped, blood spewing from the corner of my mouth. "Are all of the... teens here?" I asked, my voice weakening.

"We have all that covered. You need to get to a doctor, so how about we meet when you are better? I promise, Forde, if any of the missing teens are not here, we'll get them before it's too late," Colegate pledged.

The now-freed teenagers were transported to the King's Daughters Hospital in Martinsburg, as were Osborne and I. Within the hour, I had been sedated and drifted into a deep, demon-free sleep.

Several days had passed before I realized the severity of my wounds. I had been transported to Winchester Memorial Hospital, where the bullet was removed. Dr. Stenner, though not my surgeon, acted as my general doctor and informed me the bullet had entered my back three inches from my neck, just missing my spine. It passed through the top of my left lung and lodged behind one of my ribs.

"You are one lucky man, my friend. If that bullet had been an inch to the right, you'd either be dead or wished you were," Dr. Stenner explained.

"Thank you, Doctor. Thank you very much."

"You'd better hold back on trying to talk too much. Use short sentences; you need time to heal," Stenner recommended.

"How are Osborne and Davenport?"

"Davenport is in high heaven; his girl is home, safe and sound, thanks to you," praised my new physician.

"What about Will? Is he okay?"

"He's doing well. He caught one in his right leg; it will keep him off the job for a while, maybe permanently," the doctor informed. "Oh, your secretary, Emily, said to tell you she and Ashley had everything under control at the office. She said you'd understand."

"When can I be released? I need to take care of something," I asked.

"Well, I see no reason I can't do that, on one condition—no driving. Understood?" demanded my doctor.

I agreed to Dr. Stenner's orders. I wasn't sure I could drive anyway. I needed to talk to someone and to get back to work. Who should I call? Max, of course. The phone rang several times before a familiar voice was heard.

"What? Who's this? I'm a busy man. What do you want?" barked my old friend.

"Max, it's me, Brody. I was wondering, can I come by and ask you a couple of questions?"

"Sherlock, that you? I heard you caught a bullet... You able to drive?"

"No, the doctor will not clear me to drive. I don't even know where my car is. Could you come by and pick me up?" I asked.

"No, I ain't got time for all that. Your car is here; Davenport dropped it off a couple of days ago. I'll send Sam over; he ain't safe, but he's better than nothin', I guess," cautioned Max.

"That's fine; I'm still at the hospital. Tell Sam to stop out front; I'll be ready," I said.

Max was right. Sam behind the wheel of my Chrysler, while I wouldn't call him unsafe, was definitely an adventure. We arrived safe and sound, much to the surprise of his employer.

"Should you be out and about so soon? I mean, I heard you lost a lung. Is that true?"

"No, Max, I didn't lose a lung; it was punctured, though. I'm just lucky it didn't hit my spine. Max, can we go inside and talk just a bit? Do you have time?"

"Look, Sherlock, I own this place, not the bank. I can do anything I want when I want... understand? Right now, I need a break, so let's grab a couple of seats in my office. Sam, bring us a couple of Cokes and get one for yourself. You man the front while me and the detective rest for a spell."

While we were getting settled, my mind flooded with the same questions: How did the kidnapping operation work, and how was Jo Brathwaite involved? The Winchester police were about to close this case, but had it really been solved? Unfinished business still existed. We had temporarily halted the operation in Martinsburg, but who was the mastermind behind it all? We were treating the symptoms, but we needed to find the cure.

"Max, I trust your opinion. Do you believe all this is over? If Jo Brathwaite were your daughter, would you be satisfied with the police report?" I asked as the slightest taste of blood formed in my mouth.

"What exactly are they saying? The only thing in the paper was that the kids had been found safe; they had been locked up in West Virginia. Something about being sent to Baltimore... some slave trade thing. I heard of things like this in Cuba during the war, but here, in America? No, if it were my kid or Jo was my daughter, I wouldn't be satisfied," as Max validated my point.

"Neither would I. Max, I will ask several personal questions; if you are uncomfortable answering, tell me. The first question is, can Kate Brathwaite read?"

"Sadly, no, she can't read or write. She has to get someone to read everything to her," Max admitted.

"How about the letters Joe sent from the war? I assume Jo read most of them, but did you ever read to her?"

"Me? No, not war letters. I have read several things to her over the years but never read anything Joe sent. My wife Mary used to read and write letters for Kate all the time. So, what?" Max answered and asked.

"I believe the identity of who's behind Jo's death is hidden in those letters; I just need to find the key linking all of the *avenging angels*."

"What's an avenging angel? Sherlock, you gotta speak sense. What are you talking about?"

"Max, may I use your phone? I think I know who it is. Please, may I?"

"Sure, call whoever you need to. What ya thinkin? Who did it?" The old man's curiosity rose.

"Not now. I have to make sure before falsely accusing someone," I explained.

Wasting no more time, I called Lt. Osborne, who was resting at home, and asked if he could arrange a meeting with us and Chief Johannsson at once. He said he would do so and asked if I could come by and pick him up since he could not drive. Realizing we were both grounded, I asked if I might borrow Sam for the remainder of the day. Sensing my urgency, Max agreed.

My excitement was not containable. I tossed the keys to the youthful driver, and we headed to the Osborne home. I left Max with the promise of telling him everything as soon as I was certain.

I picked up the confused Osborne, who had been placed on temporary leave without pay due to his bullet wound. Since he had gone to West Virginia against direct orders, the mayor had invoked his authority, tying Johannsson's hands in the process. Davenport had not been suspended since he was not aware of the directive, and he had been *falsely persuaded* to accompany a superior officer into the forbidden state. Boston had nothing over this town for playing politics.

Mrs. Osborne protested her husband's decision to attend the late
evening meeting; after all, he'd been given the same orders as I
to rest through the weekend. Following their short discussion, the
dedicated lawman kissed his love goodbye and hobbled to my sedan.
Once inside, we took a short detour to the home of my faithful
assistant, Ashley.

Now parked in front of the quaint little house on Cecil Street, I
was pleased to see the O'Connell sisters sitting on the front porch,
poring over the Sears catalog. I blew the horn, disrupting their study
of the latest fashions. Emily rushed to the car while Ashley chose a
slower, less deliberate walk. With each in hearing range, I asked if
they might join me and the lieutenant back to the office. When I
suggested a break in the case, both sets of eyes opened to their limits,
and within seconds, we were on our way to our second-story office
on the corner of Loudoun and Piccadilly Street.

We stopped in front of the building, and my staff was instructed
to examine everything we had on Jo Brathwaite's case while Osborne
and I met with Chief Johannsson. Sam then drove Osborne and me
to the police station.

With my left arm in a sling and Lt. Osborne hobbling with the aid
of crutches, we finally made it to Chief Johannsson's office. We were
both surprised to find Agent Colegate and a stranger seated, awaiting
our arrival.

"Boys, come on in; good to see you. Mr. Forde, this is Martin
Bagent; he is the man who murdered Rolf Schlesinger. Osborne,
how're you getting along? You look well."

"I'm doing well, Chief. Thanks for asking," answered Lt. Osborne.

"Forde, you look less for wear; how're you doin'?"

"I'm very short of breath, but, all in all, I'm also doing well.
Thanks for asking," I answered, somewhat surprised by the Chief's
sympathetic words.

"I invited Agent Colegate to this bull session so he can get on his
way and this town can return to normal. So, what's on your mind,
Forde? You called this get-together," Johannsson directed.

"Everyone is anxious to close the book on the past month. During that time, there have been five murders and over twenty kidnappings. On the surface, we could say that the circle has been completed, but we all know that is not true. Someone had to be in the center of that circle, calling the shots," I surmised.

"We agree, Mr. Forde. That's why I am here," blurted the again arrogant Agent Colegate.

"Do you believe one man is behind this? If so, I disagree. There were two. First, Luca Marchetti was leading the kidnapping, all from the confines of the Ivory Tower. How, I am not exactly sure, but he was definitely in charge," I boldly stated.

"I can fill you in on that. I agree; Marchetti headed the kidnapping ring—but things got complicated when Jo Brathwaite accidentally discovered the hidden prison in the cellar. She had seen Rolf Schlesinger unlock the door on several occasions. One night, he unknowingly dropped his key, and Brathwaite picked it up, eventually hiding it under the rug in the house on Braddock Street. Unfortunately, one of the other girls witnessed her taking it and told Luca," Colegate explained.

"So, they had to silence Jo. She could not be allowed to live," I stated, with pain in my heart.

"Just so you know, the girl tried to reason with Luca; she thought he loved her... Men like Luca Marchetti are animals. Love is not in their vocabulary; your dead girl is just another tragic story," Colegate continued.

Colegate then laid out the kidnapping process. They were to be between the ages of sixteen and nineteen, attractive and strong, with no physical abnormalities. The targets were often alone for long periods of time, not being immediately missed. The 'hook' was they would be asked for directions in an isolated area by the driver of an out-of-state automobile, like the West Virginia Buick. While they were distracted, two men would jump out of the back, grab them, place a bag over their heads, and then stick a needle in their arm, putting them into a deep sleep.

Once sedated, they were transported to the basement of the Ivory Tower, which I exposed the other night. They were stripped of all clothing, everything, then dressed in a long, white gown and placed in the appropriate cells: boys and girls. They were given sedatives regularly to keep them in a semi-conscious state. They were fed, taken to the bathroom, and bathed; they would be sold later, so appearance was important.

When enough teens had been collected, they would be loaded onto a freight boxcar and shipped to Baltimore, then loaded onto a freighter headed to Cuba. The Cosa Nostra was trading healthy, attractive teenagers for the heroine that would be distributed up and down the eastern seaboard.

"But how did Jo Brathwaite figure into all of this?" I questioned.

"She was never part of the kidnapping... Her curiosity caused her death. When she picked up the key dropped by Schlesinger, she went into the basement and saw the prisoners. What she didn't know was that one of the other girls saw her when she came back upstairs. Brathwaite kept the key and hid it under the rug, where you discovered it," Colegate continued.

"The Ivory Tower, the rear door I escaped from, is less than a hundred yards from the railroad. That's where Jo got the splinter in her hand," I surmised.

"Yes, I suppose you're right, Forde. See, the last day the Brathwaite woman was seen in Winchester she was speaking with three men: Marchetti, Schlesinger, and Cappelletti. They lied to her, saying everything would be fine; she just needed to trust them and come to work that evening—which she did. Once there, it became obvious she had been deceived, so she tried to run using the same basement door you used. She failed to see the train tracks, which caused her to fall, striking her head on the iron rail and collecting the splinter you found in the morgue.

"They carried her back into the cellar, stripped her of all clothes, and put her into a dress of one of the captured girls. The rest, you know;

they stopped on the Shenandoah Bridge, then threw her over the side. Her body came to rest on the bank where the two boys found her."

We all sat silent, personally grieving the loss of life of someone so young. My thoughts returned to the words of Max: '*Forgive the action, forget the intent.*' Some would believe Jo got what she deserved; after all, she had chosen a sinful course, paying the ultimate price. Others would pity her, saying she was trying to find a better life. For me, I had come to love and admire a woman I never met. Beginning with Adam and Eve, we all sought forgiveness for many of our actions. Over time, intentions faded, becoming mere fables distorted from generation to generation until no one remembered or cared.

Less than a minute, which seemed like hours, passed before Lt. Osborne sought more information. "That's all fine, but how were the teens chosen? Was it random, or were they targeted?"

"That's where Schlesinger figured in. He was local and knew almost everybody. He was a *bag man*, trying to move up in the organization. He handled the selection and orchestrated the kidnappings," told Johannsson.

"An ingenious plan, so simple, so effective. What we're not sure of is what you just asked. Who was the mastermind of the torturous killings of Schlesinger, Marchetti, and Cappelletti? How does this *sucker* fit in? He has not said a thing since being picked up by Detective Billings on Wednesday. Who is he, and how does he figure in all of this?" inquired Colegate.

"I can answer that. He's the first *avenging angel*, following the Promettre, made by eight war buddies in a foxhole on the Western Front. They made a pledge: that all survivors would protect and help the families of the ones that weren't so fortunate. Before we move forward, my question is, are you sure you have the right man? It has to be either Mr. Bagent sitting here or it is Vernon Lawson. Are you men sure you have the right man?" I asked, repeating my question.

"Lawson has a solid alibi when Schlesinger was murdered. He was found dead deep in the woods near Gainesboro... He had been

bitten by a rattlesnake. Been dead quite a while, according to Sheriff Neuman," informed Johannsson.

"So, Mr. Bagent, I believe you killed Rolf Schlesinger. We found traces of flour on the right running board of the truck in which Schlesinger was found. Correct me if I am wrong, but you are employed at a flour mill, right? Also, the knot used to hold his head back was a specific type of knot, a technique taught only in the United States Army. But, gentlemen, he is not the man behind all of this. The mastermind is—"

"FORDE, STOP, NO MORE! Osborne, I need you to leave this meeting. Forde, you, me, and Agent Colegate need to talk— ALONE! You, Bagent, you need to stay as well."

"But, Chief, I'm an officer of the law. Why am I the only one being pushed out? I don't understand. What have I done wrong?" pleaded Osborne.

"You and me, we'll talk later. For now, GET OUT!" yelled Johannsson.

Reluctantly, the embarrassed and confused lieutenant followed his order, leaving the room. What was going on? Why was I so rudely interrupted?

"Alright, Forde. Tell us who's behind all of this. You've got the floor," barked the chief.

"Okay, first, I need to ask Mr. Bagent one question. How were you notified, and what were you told about killing Schlesinger? Be honest, you did kill him, didn't you?"

"I got a letter in the mail... from Joe Brathwaite. At least, that's who it said it was in the letter. He knew things nobody else could know. You know, secret stuff between men fighting in a war," answered Bagent, tears streaming down his cheeks.

"What did the letter say? Do you still have it?" I asked.

"No, it said to destroy it once Schlesinger was dead; that's what I did. I burned it. It told me that he had killed Jo and that I had to honor my pledge—to kill him. The letter said he was often seen at the Ivory Tower late every Monday night. I waited for him to come out one night, snuck up behind him, and clubbed him with a hammer. I threw him in the back of a truck I stole and drove him to the abandoned shed out in Nain. You know the rest."

"Why the torture? Why did you gas him slowly? Was that in the letter?" My curiosity got the better of me.

"Yep, I did everything just as Joe had written... But how could Joe have written the letter? I saw him get his head blown off in France... I was there!" related the grieving veteran.

"Mr. Bagent, Joe didn't write the letter. It was written by someone who had full knowledge of everything, someone who read the letters sent by Joe to his loving, trusting wife, Kate. The same man who sent the other two letters to Foster Cobb and Homer Hunt. The only person that could possibly be the mastermind is... Flavius Brathwaite!" I announced.

"That's good enough for me. Mr. Martin Bagent, you are under arrest for the murder of one Rolf Schlesinger. As for Flavius Brathwaite, I need more. What, other than reading some war letters, can you prove he is behind all these mercy killings? I need more, Forde," exclaimed Johannsson.

"Before I give you more, may I ask a question: what does Mr. Flavius Brathwaite do to earn as comfortable living as he appears to have? He dresses in the finest suits and drives a car nicer than mine. I mean, what does he do?" I inquired.

"He's a bootlegger, Mr. Forde... a very successful one. He supplies places like the Ivory Tower, very upscale places, the best of the best. And, before you ask how he gets away with it, he's also a *chief corrupter* for the Cosa Nostra; in other words, he's got major protection," informed Colegate.

"Help me here, what's a *chief corrupter*? I've never heard of this term?" My ignorance, again, showed.

"For an educated man, you sure are stupid. It means he bribes top politicians for the mob," explained the federal agent.

"Well, you can tell the mob they just lost one of their top stooges. Chief, please issue the warrant for conspiracy to commit multiple murders," I said.

Before another word was spoken, Johannsson ordered the officer standing outside the door to escort Mr. Bagent into another room. The first shoe dropped when Osborne was ordered to exit; I now feared I was about to be kicked by the others, all alone with two very vicious, vindictive men.

"Agent Colegate, would you like to inform Mr. Forde why I cannot issue the warrant he desires?" requested the chief.

"Mr. Forde, if I said I was sorry for what I am about to say, well, I'd be lying. I'm actually enjoying every bit of this... almost as much as when I saved your rich, petty little life in Martinsburg. Mr. Forde, there is no Flavius Brathwaite, at least not anymore. I have placed him in protective federal custody. He is now a CW, a *cooperating witness* for the Bureau. He knows names, dates, and everything we need to win the war against organized crime," Colegate explained with a huge smirk on his face.

"NO, NO, YOU CAN'T DO THAT! He's behind the murders of—"

"Who's murder? Three pieces of trash. Look me in the eye and tell me the world isn't better with Luca Marchetti, Rolf Schlesinger, and Gio Cappelletti dead. According to you, which, at best, is very thin, he relieved society of three deadly men. Hell, I think he should receive a medal, don't you, Mr. Forde?" bragged the pompous Colegate.

"What about Foster Cobb? Did he deserve to die by the revengeful hands of the mob?" I said, grasping for straws.

"What about Cobb or whomever? His execution of Luca was as violent as anything I have ever seen. The Cosa Nostra would have probably hired him to work for them if it hadn't been Marchetti's kid. And, here's the best part... Mr. Forde, feel free to call anyone you or your family knows; regardless of the connection, it won't matter. The director himself signed this decision, you know, J. Edgar. Now, if no one has anything else, I would like to bid both of you a fond ado, hoping our paths never cross again!"

Colegate left the room with a sarcastic tip of his hat, riding off into the sunset like a cowboy in a motion picture show. Now alone with Chief Johannsson, I seized the moment. "Chief, you're surely not going to allow this, are you?"

"What would have me to do? That jackass is a G-Man; there is nothing either of us can do. If you're going to make it in this racket, you'd better learn to know when the jig is up—I had to," acknowledged the chief with pain in his eyes.

We both sat quietly for a moment; I was beginning to understand the source of Johannsson's anger. I feared that seed had just been planted in me. "Chief, may I ask another question?"

"Depends on what you ask—sure, fire away."

"I know the why of the three white feathers, but how did the feather get into Cappelletti's pocket? It had to be there before he was shot, so how did it get there?"

"Flavius Brathwaite put it in his pocket to be used as identification. Cappelletti was to present it to a man who he believed was going to give him a bag full of drug money. Cappelletti was a bag man, a courier for the Cosa Nostra, and part of the kidnapping team. He was trying to move up, just like Schlesinger."

"You mean to tell me Flavius was standing beside Cappelletti when he was shot?"

"Yeah, that's kind of dumb, isn't it? That kid made a clean shot, which is impressive if you ask me. By the way, he confessed everything just a little while ago and made a deal with the district attorney. An exceptional deal, actually."

Another question, if I may: why was Luca's body moved, and did Foster Cobb actually do it?"

"Ain't no question, Cobb killed Marchetti. We got the knife, a perfect match, according to Doc. Cobb stalked Marchetti and then, when the time was right, was grabbed just outside of Martinsburg by ole Frosty. That boy was just plumb-crazy. He hunted Marchetti, and when he got him, used all he learned in the war—I mean, he tortured him in ways you can't imagine. The problem was that Cobb thought he was sending a message; instead, he was leaving a calling card leading directly back to him. It didn't take the mob to find ole Frosty Cobb... then returned the favor."

"So, where do we go from here? What can I tell my staff? What will the cover story in the newspaper say?" I inquired.

"We have two solid killers, Cobb and that kid, Hunt. That is all we need. Son, you're new to this game; if you're going to make it in this business, be happy with what you get. All in all, this turned out good, don't you think?" Johannsson leaned back in his chair and placed his massive hands behind his head, interlocking his fingers. The figurative king of the city was at peace.

Pleased with the outcome, Johannsson yelled to the officer to bring Bagent back so he could be charged with first-degree murder, possibly facing the death penalty. How could everything go so wrong in a matter of minutes? Nothing was spoken until the soon-to-be condemned man returned to his chair.

"Mr. Martin Bagent, I charge you with the murder of Rolf Schlesinger. Before you say another word, Mr. Forde, isn't there anything you want to say to my prisoner?"

"Ah, yes... Mr. Bagent, I am an attorney. Would you like me to represent you at this time?"

As I consider closing my agency, not accepting Johannsson's definition of 'turning out good,' this late evening just got crazier. Johannsson interrupted before Mr. Bagent could respond to my offer.

"Don't answer, Bagent. I can't believe this is happening again. What I'm about to say to you two must never leave this room. Do both of you understand? So, help me, God. If a single word leaks, I will personally bury both of you. Each of you will suffer if the other speaks. DO YOU UNDERSTAND?"

Without uttering a single word, Bagent and I nodded in agreement. It was then that I noticed a wink in the barbarian's right eye, now turned pardoner.

"Bagent, I'm dropping all charges against you. Nothing has been or will be recorded concerning your involvement in this mess—it was all just a misunderstanding. Regardless of what most people think, I am a good lawman, but sometimes, the morally innocent get scooped up on the scales of injustice. That ain't going to happen tonight; I cannot, with a clear conscience, charge a decent man while a guilty man walks free because he promised to squeal on criminals higher up the line. It just ain't right! Martin Bagent, you are free to go... but if you so much as spit on a street in my town, I will run you in for being a public nuisance. Understand me, this is over; you are free to go."

Mr. Bagent, with tears in his eyes, stood and shook the chief's hand before quietly leaving the room. I remained seated in shock, trying to figure out the simple yet complicated Johannsson. We were, again, alone. I was confused—should I leave or stay? I hadn't received my orders. Then, at once, they arrived.

"All charges against the Fleming chick have been dropped; she'll be released in the morning. I strongly advised her to leave this area, somewhere far away, and never return. I told her California is beautiful this time of year. She could probably use a few dollars. Do you think you can make that happen, Private Investigator Forde?"

"I think that's possible. Is there anything else?" My head was spinning from the last five minutes.

"Good! Forde, I'm going to make this as clear as I can: I don't like you, and I doubt I ever will. You think you are going to save the world; you're so damn smart—well, you're not. I've been a *copper* all my life; I've had to make deals regular people could never understand, like tonight. Decisions like the one I just made cost me a good job and allowed a jackass to become a special agent with the feds. I made a promise to myself that if another world-saver ever got in my way again, well, they'll never find his body. So, you understand, this is not a threat; it's a promise. Now, I got work to do—git. What're you waiting for? Your friend Osborne needs a ride home. Git, before I change my mind," the Chief ordered, leaning forward with his hands resting on his desk and the slightest grin peeking out the left side of his mouth.

My friend? I had forgotten all about Osborne. Under orders, I could never tell him what happened; the chief was not a man who bluffed. No one must ever know what happened concerning Bagent—but what do I tell Osborne? My father used to say that in business, less is more. Did that philosophy apply in this situation? I hoped so.

Chapter Twenty-Nine

I found Lt. Osborne sitting just outside the station and Sam asleep in the back seat of my car. The suspended lawman displayed a face covered in despair, deeply concerned for his future. When he saw me, he slowly rose from the public bench and took his place in my car. I woke the sleeping Sam, who delivered us to my office and then drove himself back to the garage. Not a word was spoken until Osborne and I passed through the office door.

"Well, ladies, we can close the Brathwaite case. Before anyone asks, there are confidential details; as you will discover, this sometimes happens when a case involves the federal government, like this one. Tomorrow, we will all go to the Brathwaite farm to inform Kate that her daughter died a hero, which is true. For the rest of you, I have a few things I want to say."

We all, including Lt. Osborne, took seats at the conference room table. Emily picked up the papers concerning the Brathwaite case and filed them in the appropriate folder. Ashley had brewed a fresh pot of coffee, which we all took advantage of. I was now ready to make my announcements.

"First, Ashley, I want to apologize for not including you in the Martinsburg raid. I thought there might be violence, and I cannot allow you to be hurt. Do you understand?"

"That's okay, Boss; I know what you decided was best. It's just difficult to be a woman sometimes," confessed Ashley, tears leaking from the corners of her eyes.

"Understood. Now, I have several surprises for each of you. Ashley and Emily, it has become a bit of a problem for me to transport you to and from work. There is one way to correct this dilemma: I have arranged for each of you to purchase a new car. All you have to do is go by the Chevrolet, Dodge, or Ford dealer and choose your new rides. Now, ladies, I want you to get what you want, but nothing nicer than what I drive: no Cadillacs or Lincolns, please."

"Can I get a convertible? Can I, Boss?" yelled the exuberant Ashley.

"Really, Ashley, a convertible in the wintertime? Is that a practicable choice? Mr. Forde, may I select a four-door?" Emily requested, using the voice of an angel.

"Ladies, whatever you decide... you've certainly earned it. Now, Mr. Wilbur Osborne, I have a question: would you be interested in leaving the Winchester Police Department and joining us at the Ambrose O Detective Agency? Moving forward, we could use an experienced man like you. And, before you answer, Ashley, I am promoting you to the position of a full-time investigator. That will give us three investigators. So, what do you think, Will, want to become part of the team?" I asked as Ashley, Emily, and I interlocked our arms, forming a united semi-circle.

"I, I don't know what to say. Honestly, I'm not sure I still have a position with the police, getting wounded and all. I think the chief understood what I did, but the mayor is really upset with me. He said there's no place for a renegade in the ranks; it's somewhat funny, I never considered myself a renegade," Osborne confessed.

"One more thing, Will. If you accept the position, you will also need a new car; I've already made your arrangements as well. I will require you to have a six-cylinder, something with speed—you never know when you may need it."

"Seriously, how can you afford all of this?" the puzzled Osborne asked.

"We have a policy around here, er, Will. We don't ask, and he doesn't tell. Works for us, right Emily? And, also, we eat great food all the time. You gotta join us; we're already a team!"

"It would be nice if you joined us, Mr. Osborne—you would be a very positive addition," Emily added.

"Mr. Will, Emily talks weird sometimes, but she means well... you'll get used to it. I have a couple of questions before we close this case. For instance, who exactly is the killer?"

I paused, trying to select words that would satisfy all in the room, realizing I couldn't divulge much of the truth. As I was about to begin, Osborne intervened.

"Ladies, there were actually two killers, Foster Cobb and Tink Hunt. When Jo Brathwaite found out about the connection between the kidnapping ring and the Ivory Tower, she was killed by the three men Mrs. Poston had seen outside of her boarding house. Cobb and Tink Hunt, who stepped in for his uncle, Homer, got justice for Ada Jo Brathwaite."

Osborne's speech was interrupted when an unknown, slender young man entered the office. His identity was quickly confirmed when his parents came into sight.

"Mr. Forde, I'm searching for a Mr. Forde. Are you him?" asked the lanky lad as he pointed toward me.

"Yes, I'm Forde, please call me Brody... and I'm betting you are Jubal Witten. It is good to finally meet you."

"It's sure good to meet you, Mr. Forde, and you, Miss Ashley, whichever one of you is her."

"I'm Ashley, and you come here; I need a big hug!"

Tears filled all eyes as Mr. and Mrs. Witten thanked all of us for finding their son. Until now, everyone in this case had just been a name on a ledger, a statistic. But now, the name on the paper had a face, a voice, a heartbeat. For the first time since Katherine Brathwaite had entered this office, the walls echoed with laughter—joyful laughter, a sense of accomplishment I had never felt.

"Mr. Forde, ah, Mr. Forde, did you hear me? I was asking you a question."

"I'm sorry, Jubal, please, what were you asking?"

"I was asking that when I was locked up. I don't remember too much, but there was a real pretty lady that said she was goin' get us all out of there. She sure was pretty and had really nice dark hair—that's about all I can remember. Can I meet her? I want to thank her; she gave us all hope."

Ashley quietly retrieved the picture Mrs. Brathwaite had given us of Jo and her at a wedding. She handed it to Jubal and asked, "Is this her? Is this the lady who promised to rescue you?" she said, fighting back her tears.

"Yep, that's her... She sure is a pretty thing. Do any of you know where she lives?"

The celebration halted while we told the Witten family of Ada Jo Brathwaite and her sacrifice in solving this heinous crime. After a few minutes, joy returned as Mrs. Witten said they needed to get home so she could start *puttin' meat back on her boy's bones.* As the family left, we were stunned to see a new visitor: Detective Jason Billings.

"Sorry, I missed you boys at the station. Wilbur, you look worse for wear; Forde, you're one lucky son of a gun, I'll tell you that."

"You are so right, detective; I am a fortunate man, indeed. If that bullet had been an inch farther to the right, I might have never walked again... or even be dead."

"I ain't talking about you being shot. I'm talking about these two women you got working for you. Don't you know what they did?" Billings asked.

"What are you talking about?" my curiosity peaking.

"We'd all be better if we sit; this might take a while," explained Billings.

We moved to the conference room, and everyone took seats except Detective Billings, who preferred to walk and talk. "Well, me and the chief were sitting in his office, hittin' a little of the hooch I recently found, when these two busted through the door—first, Ashley, then, I don't know the brunette's name. Blondy started demanding Johannsson send help for you and Osborne, that you were going to be killed if he didn't send backup. Johannsson said he had no jurisdiction to do that, so Ashley, right?"

"Yes, I am Ashley, and this is my sister, Emily. Haven't you told enough? Let's forget the whole thing—okay?"

"No, now, where was I? Oh, yeah, Ashley pulled out a colt and pointed it right at the chief's head. He said, 'You think I ain't ever had a gun in my face, *little girl*... you'd better put that thing away before you get hurt. It ain't even got a hammer. Who do you think you are scaring, me or you?' Well, about that time—Emily, right? Well, Emily pulled a second gun, walked right up to the chief, placed it against his head, pulled the hammer back, and asked, "Is that better?" Well, they got his attention all right, I'll tell you that. It sure got my mine, I mean, when I heard the clicking of that hammer going back..."

"So, what did Johannsson do? What were you doing, Detective Billings, while all this was happening?" I asked.

"What was I doing? I was about to bust a gut; I wanted to laugh so bad... but I knew if I did, Johannsson would have shot me. What happened was Johannsson called Colegate and told him he had a couple of undercover agents in the Ivory Tower and that the case was about to be busted wide open. He said if the feds wanted to be part of the biggest raid in years, he'd better git to Martinsburg and take as many men as he could. Like I said, Forde, you got two good women working for you—they saved your and Osborne's lives."

"Ladies, is Detective Billings accurate concerning this event? What have you two got to say for yourselves?" I asked as my eyebrows rolled up.

"Boss, can I get a convertible? I always wanted a car with no top... Can I?" a pleading Ashley interrupted, evading my question.

"Well, I think that about settles that. Jason, I want to thank you for not shooting my staff and for relating this story to me. I see that moving forward, we need some training on how to play well with others. Right ladies?"

"No problem, Forde. I would advise you, though, never mention this in front of the chief, and it's a good idea that neither of them be seen in the courthouse anytime soon. With all that said, I gotta go; the wife is expecting me home for dinner. Osborne, take care of that leg; we need you back to work," Billings said as he exited.

The four of us remained in the office, reflecting, as it were, the events of the past month. Will asked if he could think about my offer for a few days; much would depend on the security of the position and his wife's reaction. The meticulous Emily took the lead in planning the remodeling to accommodate additional offices. Ashley was on the phone telling a friend she was getting a new convertible. For me, my emotions bounced back and forth; we had solved two crimes, but so many had died in the process.

I was drawn back into the moment by Lieutenant Osborne. "Brody, did you hear me? Did you hear of the plea deal Tink Hunt managed?" asked Osborne.

"I'm sorry, Will, my mind drifted a moment. What about Tink?"

"Strangest thing, Tink said he would tell everything if provisions were provided for his mother," explained Osborne.

"What provisions did he seek? How many years did he get?" I asked.

"Well, out of nowhere, his mother's house was paid off; the deed will be delivered to her sometime next week. Also, a bank account with $1000 was opened in her name; nobody knows anything about how all this happened. Do you have any ideas?" questioned the confused Osborne.

"Me? No, how would I know anything? I've never met the woman and barely knew Homer or Tink. So, everything worked out?" I countered.

"Yes, Brody, everything worked out, especially for Tink. He killed a man in cold blood, but the plea deal reduced the sentence to voluntary manslaughter. He got five years with the possibility of parole after three with good behavior. And get this, he will serve his time here, in the Winchester Jail—working for the county under the supervision of Sheriff Neumann. I've never seen anything quite like this, have you?"

Pausing a moment, I answered, "Why, no? I'm not from here, remember? How could I know of anything like this? It sounds like a *Southern thing* to me."

Made in the USA
Middletown, DE
04 October 2024